DAUGHTER OF LAZARUS

JUNIPER ARDEN

Flamespringer Press

ISBN 979-8-9872417-1-4 (hc) — ISBN 979-8-9872417-0-7 (pb) — ISBN 979-8-9872417-2-1 (ebook)

Library of Congress Control Number: 2023901458

First Edition: June 2023
Printed in the United States of America
10 9 8 7 6 5 4 3 2 1

For the latest news about the author and upcoming releases, visit www.juniperarden.com.

To those who are brave enough to become the hero of their own story

GODRUS
HOUSE OF PERCEPTION
ALLEY OF THE GODS
MINBORN
FETLAND
NESVLA
ELDIRE
JA
CASTLE TRYFLIN
IRIBUS
THE KINGDOM OF EMPEIRUS

SAVEK COAST
EMPEIRUS
VIR
LARKINGSPORT
SAPPHIRE
GUORDEN'S BEACH
CIRCUS
CALLEEIT

Pronunciation Guide

People

Aimelie: aim-ell-ee
Annora: a-nor-a
Anzac: ann-zak
Belline: bell-een
Calix: kay-lix
Calleeit: ca-lee-it
Dimity: dim-it-ee
Elouthera: el-oo-ther-a
Gissaira: ji-zair-a
Ione: ee-own-ee
Jedda: jed-a
Modgen: maw-jen
Renai: ren-ay

Places

Empeirus: em-pier-us
Godrus: god-rus
Javir: ja-veer
Nesvla: nes-vla
Savek: sa-vek
Tryflin: trif-lin

DAUGHTER
OF
LAZARUS

PROLOGUE

Even Dimity's heart rattles at the fall of her father's heavy fist.

"Enough is enough," Lazarus booms at the others. When he speaks, the fluffy white clouds cradling the Earth stir with uncertainty. His curly white beard is long and full, and a matching shock of ivory sits atop his head. "The beings cannot be allowed to continue with this folly. Wars, murder, thieving; they simply cannot dwell in peace without being guided. Tell me, then, how Earth is to join the Alliance?" He shakes his head. "Something must be done."

"Nothing must be done," Dimity claims, and the clouds begin to resettle around the blue and green globe. "These inhabitants are our godly creations. We cannot abandon them just because they are not yet wise enough to partake in intergalactic conversation."

"So you say, Dimity." Her father strokes his beard lazily. "And what of the rest of my council?"

From across the orb, another goddess tilts her head. The painted teardrops on her cheeks sparkle beneath a set of matching silver eyes. "I see no reason to suspect that the Earthers won't grow mature enough to join the Alliance one day."

The god of all gods chuckles, a deep rumble. "Elouthera; always the optimist. Tell me, is there anyone else who opposes the removal of Earth from our care?"

Dimity fidgets with the cuff of her glittering white sleeve beneath the table, begging for another to take her side on the issue.

The goddess Ione shifts nervously in her seat, her short blonde hair swishing with the movement. "What would happen if the Earth *was* removed?" she asks timidly.

Lazarus opens his mouth to speak, but—

—Ping—

A black coin tumbles through the air, landing in an incessant spiral before it ends with a clap of a hand. All eyes drift to its sultry owner.

"I'll tell you what would happen," the female with hair like fire drawls, her voice smooth like black velvet. "The Earther race will continue down their remarkably disappointing path until they succumb to self-destruction, and all we will be left with is an embarrassing fluke on our part and perhaps a tinge of sadness in our hearts—"

"Your heart is *black*, Jedda," counters Dimity.

"Silence, both of you," Lazarus cuts in before his two daughters start something they would soon regret. The clouds around the globe eddy in response to his voice. "We shall have a vote. The highest count will determine Earth's outcome. All in favor of maintaining reign over Earth, raise your left palm."

One by one, the deities decide whether to lift their hands to uphold the maintenance of the creation they call Earth. When the count is finished, the opposing vote is called.

Lazarus frowns at his wife Valea. "Alas, there is a stalemate."

Uneasiness hums through the electric air of the Council Room. Dimity closes her amber eyes, drawing in a deep breath as a slim, dark figure leans forward at the end of the table; one whose person might have been easily overlooked had he not moved. His tone of voice makes the hair of her arms stand on edge.

"Might I suggest a rather ... *intriguing* way to settle this matter?"

Lazarus waves an impatient hand. "Go on."

The shadowed god continues. "Jedda believes the

Earthers to be innately cruel and worthless, while Dimity sees their potential to be good. Perhaps, however, your daughters could find a way to agree while putting their beliefs to the test."

The two sisters glance reluctantly at one another.

A quiet chuckle. "What if, both of them willing, they would agree to take an Earthly form for a human lifetime, where they would be exposed firsthand to the current conditions of the planet? Upon death, once they've returned to their immortal forms, they can declare whether or not their opinions of Earth have changed." The god's gray eyes twinkle with excitement when he speaks.

The council members still, Dimity and Jedda included.

Lazarus huffs a laugh with the stroke of his fluffy white beard. "And who is to ensure their safety after 'taking an Earthly form,' Anzac?"

Anzac thinks for a moment, then smiles. "Even if one of your daughters was murdered by another Earther, they would still return to their immortal form. But, I do suppose it would be less stressful if two more deities accompanied our fair goddesses around their time of incarnation. Protectors, if you will."

Murmurs of concern and worry rumble across the seated council members. At this, Dimity tries to release some of the tension in her stomach, but even the thought of having a lifelong protector hardly does anything to soothe her growing anxiety.

"And who is to determine who defends our daughters?" Valea asks, placing a gentle hand atop her husband's.

At this, the table's occupants increase their anxious bickering, the clouds nestling the Earth shifting to a mottled gray. Through the bumbling of a hundred mouths, one voice stands out above the rest.

"I, for one, will volunteer."

The table hushes, the immortals turning their heads to face Elouthera, who sits poised as ever. The Goddess of Dreams and Mysteries turns to Dimity. "I will follow you to ensure the justice of our Earth and all its inhabitants," she says with her pebble-smooth voice and silvery hair.

Dimity bows her head in gratitude, though she is quite certain that she and her sister have not formally agreed to this mad idea yet. *And will they even ask us for our opinions?*

But Jedda purrs, "And who would come and see this blue and green sphere with *me*?"

I guess that answers that.

The remaining beings hide their faces in vain. All except one.

"It would be my honor, Jedda," Anzac replies, a dark smile playing about his lips.

Jedda echoes his smile with her own, one that manages to look more like a sneer.

Dimity looks up at her parents, who are exchanging worried glances. She is sure they do not look half so worried as she feels inside.

Lazarus turns to his daughters. "This is no game," he booms, white beard rustling as he speaks. "On this planet, there will be beauty and there will be chaos, but I will not stop you if this is what you agree upon. If you choose to take this path, you must know that after you have incarnated, no deity—not even myself—can interfere with you in human form, save for those protectors who have incarnated with you.

"Once you have experienced a true Earther lifetime, if you *still* cannot reach an agreement, then perhaps I will decide myself. But given how dedicated the both of you are in standing by your decisions, I will permit this alternative measure, as Earther lifetimes are but a fraction of our own." Lazarus leans forward in his marble seat. "What say you, my dears?"

Dimity's stomach roils at the thought. One month for a deity, but an entire *lifetime* for herself? She imagines the thought of a mortal birth, leaving all her immortal life behind. *What will the world look like? How will the Earthers treat me? Will they know that I am not one of them?* Dimity is sure that upon incarnation, her godly powers will be lifted, and she will be able to lead a true, mortal life. But who is to say that she will not run into danger? *Or worse,* Dimity thinks. For as much as she believes Earthers to be generally good-natured, the goddess knows that there are some whose agendas are more aligned with her sister's: torture, starvation, murder.

This is not something to be taken lightly. Still, what other choice does she have to save their precious creation? Some of the immortals may have given up on Earth, but Dimity believes that the good of humanity will prevail if given enough time.

She glances around the white table at the others. Political banter and bribes would be all that she would have to turn the tides in her favor, and against Jedda, such a pursuit would be near pointless. Her sister has always been far more persuasive than herself, a feat that is mainly due to her aggressive tendencies.

As though she heard Dimity's thoughts, Jedda turns her sinister eyes toward her sister's. "You know as well as I do that I can never say no to a challenge."

Yes, and that is why I must take this opportunity, however damning it may turn out to be.

Dimity holds her sister's stare, solemnly lifting her chin as she extends her hand across the white table. "I will do whatever it takes," she says, and as the two sisters grasp hands firmly, the only world they have ever known dissolves into a black abyss.

Part I

Ember

OLIVER

"Sir Hedvick," Oliver calls from his seat at the head of the High Council.

A moment of silence answers, just a moment too long.

"Sir Hedvick?" Oliver asks, this time a bit louder.

A grumble of snorts and murmured apologies is offered by the old, tired knight. His long white beard shakes each time he voices his regrets for having entertained an untimely nap.

"Master McHenry, please excuse my folly. I am not as ... *alert* ... as I once was," Hedvick blubbers.

Oliver's deep green eyes soften with a smirk. "You are forgiven, sir. What news do you bring from the queen regarding her political affairs?"

The old knight's faded brown eyes squint into the

light of the window as if it is there that he can see the past. He shifts in his seat. "Her Majesty has decided that the throne has need of the iron found in the territory of Javir. Too little found here, and we need more for our forges."

"Preparing for war, are we?" the shipmaster japes, his cold blue eyes glinting with amusement.

"More than you know. The queen is seeking to take over Javirian iron production by whatever means necessary. If we cannot win them to our cause, she has ordered us to review arrangements for conducting a siege on Castle Tryflin."

Sounds of distress bloom across the table from end to end.

"Another war within our continent is the last thing we need. And for what? Iron?" Docketry, the Lord of Merchants, frames each question with his wobbling brown mustache. "We have sufficient iron to last us for all of the next fifty years. What could the kingdom possibly need more for?"

Hedvick shrugs his shoulders, still brawny, despite their age. "To further enhance the strength of the Royal Military."

More rumbles of discontent swirl from seat to seat. Oliver runs a hand through his brown hair. *Is there no end to her madness?*

"There must be other options, aside from inciting

war," Lord Docketry assures. "Perhaps the Javirians will decide to share some of their ore for the throne's noble cause."

"Perhaps if we try hard enough, we might catch a flying goat, too," chides the shipmaster.

The Royal Ambassador, Lord Earlmence turns to his colleague. "Lord Docketry, the Javirians do not have a very ... *forthcoming* attitude toward their neighbors. The territory itself is not unfriendly, it's just a bit ... isolated, when it comes to being a part of external issues."

Oliver nods his agreement. While the Throne of Empeirus holds the highest rank of control over the kingdom, each territory has limited freedoms—an allotted amount of power over its own locals, so as not to let the throne abuse its reign. A sliver of a territory squeezed between those of Nesvla and Empeirus, the territory of Javir has a long history of refusing to partake in the contribution of goods that might in any way affiliate themselves with a war. *Surely, they will find some excuse not to donate goods to the queen's absurd cause this time, too,* he thinks. *And I don't blame them.*

Lord Docketry shakes his head with dismay, brown mustache slicing through the air with each turn. "Why can people never seem to get along?"

The oversized mahogany doors open at the end of the Great Hall with a groan. Council members share a confused glance as the Captain of the Royal Guard stalks down the room's airy hall, his silver eyes pinning each member with an unsettling gaze.

"Captain," Oliver says by way of greeting. The rest of the council members bob their heads. "To what do we owe the pleasure?"

The captain stops a few feet away from the master, resting a hand upon the pommel of his golden sword. *A silent threat; a silent promise,* Oliver notes.

"The queen has ordered me to reinforce her stance on the issue of Javirian ore. As you well know, she will only endorse taking the castle by storm," he declares with the arrogance of a snake.

Of course. Luck be damned.

The Lord of Merchants palms his forehead in distress; the shipmaster rolls his icy blue eyes. A chorus of groans fills the cavernous Great Hall.

Master McHenry has used up the last of his patience. "If Her Majesty has the intention of losing half her army to an insignificant territory, then storming Castle Tryflin is a great way to do it. The Javirians are highly skilled at defense. Over the course of their existence, more than ten different armies have tried taking it over with not one of them succeeding in the past seventy years."

"Are you comparing the strength of the Royal Guard to that of the foot soldiers of lesser territories?"

"I am stating historical accuracies, Captain."

The councilmen shift restlessly in their seats. The captain continues to hold the master's stare.

"How do provisions look for the Javirians?" the shipmaster asks. "Would it be so bad to wait them out?"

Sir Hedvick frowns. "The Javirians are well-stocked for at least a year, maybe two. Starving them out would take longer than the queen would want to wait. We all know this. Our own provisions might not last a year, since the island territory of Calleeit broke away from the kingdom a few years ago. Even if we take Castle Tryflin by storm, we'll need additional coin for more."

"And where might this coin come from, good Sir?" asks a red-haired male at the end of the table.

The old knight retorts, a smile hiding beneath his voluminous beard. "Lord Sprightly, I thought that was your forte."

Lord Sprightly laughs. "Perhaps it falls upon me to make money out of thin air as well. It should be of no news to all of you that the Royal Treasury has been scraping the bottom of its coffers for several years now. And for several years, we have been spared war. That being said, the previous War on the Horns nearly broke our economic system altogether with its extensive costs, and we still have not properly recuperated from it. I am no fan of hampering the queen's mood, but there is simply no way we can supply any more coin for provisions."

"And who might you be?" the captain asks drily.

"Lord Sprightly, Royal Treasurer."

"Ah, a penny-pincher. That's why you're against war."

"Ah, a guard. That's why you lack intellect."

"Perhaps we should leave this issue to rest until the morrow," Oliver interrupts, more of a declaration than a suggestion.

"Agreed," says Sir Hedvick. "A good night's rest helps everything."

Oliver rises from his seat, the rest of the council members doing the same. The captain finally tears his silver eyes away from Lord Sprightly's death-stare, and without a word, turns on a heel to exit the Great Hall. The members begin nodding their goodbyes, one-by-one disappearing through the mahogany doors.

Only Master Oliver McHenry is left alone in the Great Hall, running a thumb over the thin, silver band on his pinky finger.

THE WAIF

The wooden door of the Dog's Head Tavern swings shut with its typical thud. From beneath her gray cloak, the Waif counts her coins from today's winnings and frowns. *It's less than I expected. I thought the Dog's Head was the place to go for noblemen?*

"Out of the way! I said out of the way!"

Piper looks up at the sound of wagon wheels making their way around a bend. The horse-drawn cart is stuffed with vegetables and going far too fast, swerving around the corner of a local tailor's building, and nearly toppling over an elderly woman.

Insanity, she thinks. *What good does it do to hurry if it risks hurting innocent people?* She moves closer to the edge of the dirt path, taking in the familiar sounds of the slums. Dogs bark in the nearby houses, joining a chorus of bawdy calls from the courtesans perched atop their shanty balconies. To add to the bustle, a merry singing comes from a dirty man propped against the side of the road, plucking his lute with care.

She digs a hand into her coin purse, nearly scraping the bottom. Removing her second-to-last copper, she tosses it into the poor man's hat as he nods his thanks. *May the gods be with you more than they are with me.*

Piper turns her dark eyes to the north and sighs. Far away in the distance, she can make out the image of a crimson and gold banner, emblazoned with a coiled snake. *A rather aggressive symbol*, the Waif notes. *Then again, I can't think of one more fitting.* A gale of wind off the Falvedrie Sea sneaks beneath her hood and twirls around a lock of her brown hair, sending shivers down her spine. Pulling herself back to the present moment, she returns her hands to the warmth of her pockets and continues traipsing toward her destination.

Along the dirt road, several vendors are lined up at their wooden stands, caterwauling about their goods. Just a few yards away, Piper picks his voice out amongst the cacophony.

"Fresh apples, peaches, pears, you name it! We have plenty of new produce, straight from the farm!" The young man in the rusty-orange clothing yells his day's wares. His copper eyes match his attire perfectly, like two shiny coins pasted to his head.

The Waif winds her way through the herd of people blocking her path amidst the chaos of the street. With her gray hood shading her eyes, she approaches the beckoning salesman.

"Any plums today, Robbin?" she asks with a pleasant smile.

Robbin returns her smile with a wink, leaving his assistant to finish his transaction. "A thousand for you, my lady!"

Piper blushes, her modesty not feigned. "I only need a few. The ladies at the Sapphire were asking about you earlier. I thought I would stop by and check in on you."

"Oh? I've been busy, but no worse for wear. And how fares my mysterious lady?" His face is fair; not markedly handsome, but certainly not unattractive.

She smiles wider at his forward flirtation and shakes her head, shadows dancing across her ivory skin. Piper turns her dark eyes to the vendor and grins. "Time has not changed you one bit, Robbin."

"How could it? I plan on staying true to myself for the girl who holds my heart in her shadowy palms."

This makes the Waif laugh. Robbin grants himself a small chuckle and turns to bag up three ripe plums of the deepest purple. Waiting, Piper props herself up against the wooden crate of apples before her. She leans forward on her elbows, watching the merchant prepare her order before returning with her fresh fruit.

"How much?" she asks.

"One kiss."

A laugh bubbles from her lips. "How about a firm handshake?"

A flicker of contemplation crosses his copper eyes, stopping her heart for one beat, two, *then*—

Sighing, Robbin extends a hand. "Deal—but only for the nonce. Next time, you'll owe me *two* kisses to make up for the one I lost today. And they'd better be good."

Piper grasps the hand of the young merchant and nods deeply. "I can promise you nothing." She smiles, before weaving her way back through the cobblestone roads of the slums. Only then does she pull out the plump, green apple she had hidden in her cloak sleeve and take a satisfying bite.

VEGA

She watches the fine green powder make its way beneath her nails while she works upon her table of oak. The only sounds in the tiny dorm room come from her steady breathing and the crackle of a blazing fire. With deft fingers, she takes another pinch of green powder, dousing the small ruby. The manipulator holds her hands over the gemstone, waiting. After a few seconds, the powder soaks into the stone like water soaks into sand, and the once-red ruby is now undeniably green. A smile spreads across Vega's pointed features, one that recognizes the simplicity of the illusion all too well.

At the House of Perception, such experiments using colored powders are considered basic and are typically reserved for trainees. Powders are used to train the eye to become attuned to the art of manipulating one's physical environment—a feat that is thought of as unnatural for the beginning student. Once the apprentice accepts the idea of altering their reality, they can advance their forms of environmental manipulation—something that Vega has been studying for quite some time now.

Satisfied with her minor accomplishment, the manipulator digs through her desk things and removes a small scrap of blood-red velvet. Closing her eyes, she hovers her steady hands over the fabric without the use of powder; this time only visualizing her desire. Her lime-green eyes open slowly, entranced in concentration as the bright crimson dissolves into a rich hue of emerald green. Vega leans back in her wooden chair. *It shouldn't be this easy.*

Most acolytes spend years of study under a master before they transition from using powders to using only their willpower. In fact, some students never stop using powders. It is said that manipulation is one part study to three parts natural ability. When Vega first enrolled at the House of Perception, she wondered if she could ever live up to the masters, to the history of their incredible creations. But after less than a year of using powders, the newbie-manipulator was quickly advancing to upper-level courses in using sheer will. There was no explanation for it, save for some natural ability that Vega could never understand.

Some families have the fortune of a strong manipulating bloodline, such as the Cregs of the east coast and the Apparons of the north. Oftentimes, marriage contracts would be made to enhance the abilities of a future child. To have one strong bloodline would make the child's abilities robust. To have *two* of these bloodlines would make their gifts legendary.

Vega had neither. Growing up on her wealthy parents' two-hundred-acre estate, the only child had been groomed for court since the day she came into this world. If being locked into courtrooms had taught her one thing, it was that people are seldom ever as they appear—and can be changed if they are. This same thought was the one that had her father sending her to a far-away school to become a master manipulator. Two years and 143 books later, Vega stands as the star pupil of the House of Perception. And while such an honor should be as much a delight to herself as it is to her father, Vega still feels that there is something more, something about the art that perhaps even the masters have not yet explored.

A small, round table mirror reflects her lime-green eyes back to herself, proudly displaying her pointed features. Her black hair, courtesy of her mother, has grown past her chin to meet the center of her moon-pale neck. Vega sighs, daring a glance at the clock on the fireplace mantel. *Eleven o'clock,* she thinks with surprise. There are no windows in her dorm room, but if there were, she would throw open her curtains and gaze upon the starry night sky.

There is nothing that Vega loves more in the world than the night sky in Wembleton. While the mornings and daytime hours bask the city in a pinkish glow, dusk brings relief from the heat and the birth of the stars and the moon. There is hardly ever a cloud in Wembleton, and for that, Vega is grateful. She could watch the stars for hours, memorize every crater in the face of the moon, cling to the hope of witnessing a shooting star for an eternity. And with every thought or sight of the night sky comes a silent tug, pulling Vega deeper into its glittering oblivion.

But tonight, she has chosen to continue her studies, if they could be continued, and Vega winds up catching herself again in her bedroom mirror. Her mother's voice sings to her from long ago.

"Your eyes," her mother would joke with her as a child. *"Like a cat in the dark!"*

She smiles a pretty smile; one full of whispers and mystery. And then it strikes her.

Vega leans closer to the rounded mirror on her desk and focuses on those lime-green eyes. *What if ...* She closes them. She steadies her hands, this time, with her palms before her face, and very slowly opens them. Candlelight dances off the same dazzling green that was there before.

It was a silly idea anyway. Sighing heavily, she turns to a thick burgundy book on her desk and begins to read about the power of will, noting every word in the tome she has read front to back and over once again, until sleep begins to tug on the lids of her eyes. *It must be well past midnight by now.*

Vega stands from her wooden chair, stretching her muscles out from sitting so long in a cramped position. She paces to her armoire and changes into her woolen shift, readying herself for sleep. Crawling onto the bed, Vega cranes her head over to blow out her bedside candle, only to find in the mirror that her eyes have grown a lovely shade of lavender purple.

ANNORA

SIX YEARS EARLIER

The queen sighs quietly from the dais as she watches her court dissipate out of the Throne Room. It had been more than three hours today, full of countless propositions and very few moments of rest. The citizens that had come for titles, land, or money had been listened to justly, and she had granted the requests of those who had truly earned such honors.

Her gold and aquamarine crown presses heavily upon her head from such a long display. *As it should*, Queen Annora thinks. *A queen's duty should never be taken lightly.* When the last of her subjects find their way out of the oversized mahogany doors, Annora rises with as much grace as she can muster. At three-and-thirty years, her body had somehow lost whatever youthful resilience it once had before her reign, and now instead took to cramping after sitting for too long. Her gown of autumn-gold silk pools around her ankles as she turns to one of her council members.

"Any word from my husband?" she asks the gray-haired man.

He retrieves his notebook and quill from the table below the throne. "None as of late, Your Majesty. Last we heard, he was meeting with the Royal Treasurer."

The queen nods. "And my children?"

The man smiles warmly. "Master Tasman sent us a page informing us that the princesses' lesson was very productive today. After their class, he dismissed them to their rooms, but I suspect they have made their ways else-where in the castle by now." The man gives Annora a knowing smirk.

She allows herself a modest chuckle, knowing exactly where she can find her beloved daughters. *Aimelie will be playing near the pond in the White Garden, Adrianna will have found some lord's son to pester, and Annalise ...* Annora's smile grows wider as she pictures her eldest daughter scouring every shelf of the Royal Library, devouring knowledge like she needed it to breathe. *She will make a fine queen someday.*

Queen Annora exits the Throne Room, making her

way through the halls, whose blazing torches cast shades of orange and red against the stone. She is accompanied by two members of her Guard, as well as her handmaid, Belline. As she navigates around the twists and turns of the castle, Annora pauses by a crimson-painted door. *Dria,* she thinks. *Should I check?* She debates opening it but decides not to, preferring not to delay a visit to her husband any longer. *I will intrude later.*

Annora loves her children with all her heart. Each one of her three daughters has such a unique personality, and she can see all of them making strong rulers one day. But Dria had never exactly shown the regard and care that her sisters had. Growing up, Adrianna was prone to intense temper flares when she did not have her way, once even going so far as to slap little Aimelie across her innocent round face. *Poor Melie*, Annora reflects. *She only wanted Dria's doll.*

There is no forward reason as to why Adrianna has always been so temperamental, and it worries Annora beyond compare. The queen and her king take care to make time for raising their beloved children as often as they can, and discipline is as much a part of their parenting as it is for any other parent, but Dria had never shared a stable relationship with her mother or father. Many times, the child would purposely pin blame on others around her or lure them into obscene dares. Occasionally, Annora would find her staring out of her bedroom window, focusing intently on something she could not see. The queen often wonders if Dria might suffer from a touch of madness, but such mental instability had never found its way into either of the royal bloodlines before.

Annora and her crew stop before a thick mahogany door. *The Royal Treasury.* She reaches a steady hand out when it suddenly opens of its own accord—or her husband's, rather. Annora beams at the sight of her King, whose brown eyes and dirty-blond hair had not gotten any less handsome over the almost fifteen years she had known him. He loops his arm through his wife's and dismisses her party, leading her down the corridor toward their private chambers. Once inside, Tiberius takes Annora's hand and presses it to his lips.

"It's been too long since I last saw you," he murmurs in a voice reserved only for her.

Annora sits her exhausted self in a plush, red chair and laughs, the sound sweet like honey. "It's been six hours, love."

"Six hours too long," he counters, pouring them both a glass of deep red wine.

Annora playfully shakes her head, her brown locks loose at last from the absence of her crown. "What news from the Treasury? Good, I hope?"

King Tiberius presses his lips into a thin line as he hands his wife her glass of red. "Not as good as it could be," he declares, taking a seat opposite of Annora's. "Annalise will have her hands full with the Treasury alone once she assumes the throne. I think it's time that we increased her duties."

Annora runs her thumb along the rim of her wine glass, staring into her muddied reflection as if it holds the answer she is looking for. But her intuition reminds her that Anna has been the most prepared of all her heirs from the day she was born. "I know she is coming of age, Tiberius, but ..." Worry ages her comely features as she looks up from her glass.

Tiberius leans forward in his chair to rest a hand upon the queen's face. "She is fourteen, and she is ready. She always has been," he whispers, before kissing the top of Annora's forehead.

A muffled scraping sound comes from behind one of the paintings on the wall. The king and queen halt their movements, and Tiberius presses a finger to his lips while he carefully maneuvers himself in front of the painting. Like a hunter sneaking up on his prey, he whips the painting from the wall in the blink of an eye, but nothing except stone is there to greet him. The royals share an uneasy glance.

"Perhaps it was just mice?"

Tiberius runs a muscled hand over the gray stone.

There are cracks in the mortar between some of the bricks, but it doesn't look like they are large enough to use as peepholes. With a heavy sigh, he replaces the painting with as much ease as he can conjure.

"Let us hope."

NARELLE

The sky-blue lace is tight and thin, leaving almost nothing to the imagination. Her feet are adorned in matching satin slippers, glistening with citrine stones, and swinging nervously while she sits perched on the burgundy bedspread. His face is common and plain, but not much older than she is, which she supposes is a blessing.

He begins by unlacing his breeches and finishes with untying her corset when she begins to visibly tremble. His hands rove all over her tan body while he plants coarse kisses upon her bony shoulders. Fighting all her instincts to run or kick or punch or scream, she lies her rigid back upon the large, cursed bed and—

Narelle gasps, breathing heavily as she takes in the

familiar sight of her moonlit room. Sweat soaks the white fabric of her bed, and she closes her hazel eyes in relief when she realizes that the recurrent nightmare has run its course. The orange comforter is loosely draped over herself, and she kicks it off as she climbs out of bed.

The moon is large and bright, its white light flooding her small abode during such a late hour. A pitcher of water has been left on her desk, and she pours herself a glass to calm her nerves. *It was only a dream*, she tells herself. *But dreams usually foretell desires. They should not sweep you back into time to replay the fears that had once devoured you.*

It has been eight years since she was sold into her current occupation as a courtesan of the Sapphire. That first night on the job had broken something in her, and every year, every *day* since then had fragmented her heart even further. Growing up, there were only two things that Narelle had ever wanted: a happy marriage and a happy family. *Was that too much to ask for?*

Her father thought so, when he deemed those dreams and his only daughter's life less important than the debt he owed to numerous gambling dens. A raging alcoholic, Narelle's father had little time for work and even less time for his family—which her mother soon had trouble forgiving after finding another woman's underthings stuffed beneath the sheets of their bed.

She shakes her head at the poisonous memory, coercing herself back to reality. *I need to get back to sleep,* she thinks, but she is not ready to submit to her nightmares once again. Setting down her glass, Narelle shuffles to a dark wooden chest stowed at the end of her bed. The Sapphire encourages its employees to continue its tradition and opt for white décor, but after the brothel stole the last of her innocence, the least it could do was allow her the freedom to choose her own color scheme. *They cannot take that much from me, at least.*

The chest came with the room. In fact, the only things Narelle had brought with her at sixteen years old were a locket from her mother, a handful of coins she had kept hidden from her father, and a picture of her late grandmother. She keeps most of those precious goods stowed within this chest, along with a few more peculiarities she has accrued over her long years.

Narelle gracefully opens the lid. On top of the stacks of possessions sits a small, white dress, stained by mud and time. *Where is she? She should be back by now.* Her eyes wander to the blanket-strewn window seat and the singular pair of well-worn shoes that sit beneath it. *I should purchase her another pair the next time I'm in town.*

She remembers the rain that day, how it poured over the little girl's cheeks and melded with her tears. She recalls the sound of horses and the grunts of guards. *Too proper to be of common birth; too well-dressed even for a noble.* The doubts began to claw their way in, but when the child paused a moment too long to think about giving her name, Narelle only had one probable reason to propose for the appearance of the so-called urchin. *"Piper,"* the little girl decided. And since then, Narelle had taken her in as her own, never bothering to question—or to remind her—of her much more refined upbringing. *They would never look for her here,* Narelle had told herself, *and she had never asked.*

Running a slender hand over the fabric, she smiles as she closes the chest, shielding the belonging from the unsavory atmosphere of the brothel. A dog barks outside in the dead of night, drunken shouts coming from the tavern next door. Narelle stares out her bedroom window, trying to pinpoint the whereabouts of the nocturnal sounds around her.

A knock at the door tears her away from her thoughts. Shoulders caving with relief, Narelle paces over to the shabby door and opens it.

"I've been worried si—"

But the man at the door is not whom Narelle expects to see. No, Narelle has never expected to see this man ever again.

"I hope you don't mind my coming by at such a late hour," he apologizes, the smell of alcohol on his breath.

Narelle's own breath catches in her throat at the sight of the familiar man's face. He is around her age, perhaps twenty-five or so, and has not changed much at all. Black curls cover his head, and his face remains unremarkable. Beginning to panic, she attempts to close the door, but not before he grips it with an iron fist.

"The lady in the foyer told me you should be up anyway. Don't worry, dearest. I've already made a healthy deposit," he says, cupping the side of her face. His eyes are still the same murky shade of gray, his lips still curl into a predatory smirk that could have sent wolves running.

"That's a lie, sir. The Sapphire isn't open to patrons this late at night."

"Every place is always open for me this late at night," the man drawls, using the back of his heel to close the door.

How did he get in here? Narelle wonders, beginning to tremble imperceptibly. *It could have been any other man ...* Her hazel eyes begin to dart behind him, searching for another employee who might have been roused from sleep, perhaps by their own similar nightmares. *Only their nightmares have died upon waking, and my nightmare has been brought back to life.* But there is nowhere to run, nothing to do, and no one to help. She swallows. *I must do this. I must do this to prove to myself that I can. I will have no more nightmares; I will not let him see me cower once again.*

Narelle places a shaking hand on the man's chest.

"Allow me just one thing before we get started," she half demands, half pleads.

The man's gray eyes narrow.

"I need a drink," she says, before turning to the absinthe on her vanity and draining half the bottle.

OLIVER

There are few places in the slums that Oliver would opt to set foot in, but the Dog's Head Tavern had always been one of them. Its large, oak sign boasts a painted face of a bulldog and its name in plain script; something simple and certain in the kingdom at long last. Oliver's boots carry him farther toward the welcoming sight as he breathes in the familiar scent of ale and cigar smoke. *Who knew that such common scents could be so comforting?*

It has been a week since the first mention of the queen's wishes to impose a siege on Castle Tryflin, and the vote called by the High Council today supported anything but. There were pros and cons pointed out by each side, but Oliver and most of the other council members liked to think that taking stock after the recent and costly War on the Horns should be the kingdom's top priority. Royal funds are short, the soldiers are still regaining their strength and numbers, and the people are wanting for a bit of peace after such a bloody rebellion.

Yet however much logic there was behind vetoing the siege, Oliver knows that the queen will not be happy. *If the council was not here to keep her power in check, the whole kingdom would be under siege.*

It was this thought that had Master McHenry swapping his courtroom attire for the inconspicuous outfit of a working-class man, sneaking from the confines of the castle to decompress at his favorite hideaway.

The alehouse is noisy, crowded, and far from clean. A sheen of dirt rests on almost every table, illuminated by the yellowed tavern lights that are occasionally sent swinging in response to some drunken duel. The smell of sweet smoke drifts on a current of air, so thick it is almost palpable. A gale of sensuous laughter erupts from a table in the corner while Oliver slowly approaches the worn, wooden bar.

"Just a mug of ale, please," Oliver asks the bartender.

The middle-aged man nods, exchanging the subpar drink for double its worth. Oliver turns to step over a puddle of what is hopefully ale on the floor, carefully navigating his way around each table until he reaches the one he is looking for.

Most men don't come to the Dog's Head for its notoriously stale ale and even more notoriously stale courtesans; the local patrons choose to spend their time at the tavern playing *halsen*. A classic card game created by the wealthy, cheaper *halsen* decks have made their way into even the poorest of the kingdom's slums, and it just so happens that such a game is one of Oliver's hidden talents.

The table is large and round, half surrounded by matching wooden chairs and the other half by booth seats covered in olive-green leather. Smoke rises from the men's cigars in upward clouds, twining their way around the wrought iron lantern above the table. The light itself is just bright enough to see one's cards, but certainly not bright enough to make out figures from afar. Oliver waits until the game is won, and an angry player removes himself from the table.

He sits in the empty booth seat and surveys the table, green eyes analyzing his future opponents. Each player hesitantly drops a handful of coins in the center of the table, to be won by the player with the highest score.

This must have been the dealer's seat, he thinks with some satisfaction. Collecting himself, Oliver silently deals each player their cards, fingers sliding over their crimson-inked backs. He finishes setting up the cards into three neat rows, then draws one at random. The game has begun.

The clock chimes ten, and Oliver is already getting

bored. *It's too easy,* he thinks. *If only Harper were here.* Oliver smiles to himself at the memory of his belligerent sister screaming across the dinner table over a game of cards, her coppery hair bouncing in the air. *She was the only one who could out-play me.* Oliver takes a sip of ale, washing away the memories of his old home.

Ten-thirty rolls around, and Oliver ends the first game with a sweeping victory, sending one man away and gaining a pile of coins. The remaining two men take delight in the challenge of good competition, so it seems, and fork over a few more coins to the pool.

"I thought you'd be worse," remarks one of them. "I can't say I've had the pleasure, but there's a *halsen* player who is dreaded by all others. They call her the Waif. I think you might have what it takes to give her a run for her money!"

The drunken man with the ale curses so loudly after losing to Oliver's card that half the alehouse turns to gaze upon the circular *halsen* table. Even the quiet man fidgets with rage after Oliver finishes the match with yet another incredible win.

"Who *are* you?" a man wearing a top hat asks Oliver.

His green eyes sparkle with amusement as he opens his mouth to respond—

"I'll tell you who he is," a cheerful male voice springs from the corner. "He's my next opponent." Lord Sprightly swaggers to the table with a grin.

"Lord Sprightly," Oliver greets the red-haired man as he takes an available seat.

"Master McHenry," Sprightly returns his greeting. "Of all the places," he wonders aloud, shaking his head.

Oliver laughs. "I like to hide in the last place that people would think to look for me. But I suppose I'm not the only one?"

Lord Sprightly smiles, blue eyes shining beneath his reddish locks. "No, you aren't."

Oliver eyes the lord more closely. The Sprightly at a council meeting is certainly not the same as the Sprightly at an alehouse. His rusty-orange hair is still shaggy and mussed, his gait is still lanky and full of splendor, but gone are all the gaudy, court-mandated jackets that befit the position of the Royal Treasurer. Instead, the young man has taken on similar attire as Oliver: a rough-spun tunic and trousers followed by a pair of tattered boots. *Better for anonymity.*

"Up for one more game?"

The tavern door slams open with a thunderous push. Voices drop so lowly, one could hear a pin fall from one of the ramshackle tables, and Oliver and Sprightly soon find out why. Heads turn with awe or fear as the Captain of the Royal Guard stalks his way toward the *halsen* table, where the two men currently sit. *How did he know we were in here?* The feeling does not sit well with Oliver.

"Master. My Lord." The captain's silver eyes glide over

the surrounding atmosphere, obviously much less distinguished than his usual accommodations.

The council members nod. "Can we help you, Captain?" Oliver asks curiously.

The captain only takes another step forward, this time unsteadily and off-kilter. *He's drunk*, Oliver realizes with astonishment.

"The queen requests your presence on an issue of the utmost importance."

Sprightly and Oliver exchange looks. *The queen is requesting a meeting at this hour?*

"Did you leave her in the Great Hall or in her bedchambers?" Sprightly jests impolitely.

The answering scowl is enough to send most men running, but the Lord and the Master know they have naught to fear. *Why would the captain hurt two of the queen's most high-ranking advisors?*

While Sprightly may have shrugged it off, Oliver decides it best for them to check in on the validity of the situation by following the captain out of the tavern door, ignoring blatant stares from its not-so-humble occupants.

The night weighs heavily on the men during their trek back to the castle. Stars of one thousand shapes and sizes glimmer on display for the world to see, while a balmy breeze blows in from the nearby harbor, filling Larkingsport with its warm, salty air. The two council members trail the captain in silence. *What could this possibly be about?* Oliver wonders. *Perhaps there has been a mix-up.*

The men climb the steep, white marble stairs leading to their magnificent castle. Even at night, the colossal creation rests on its hill with formidable characteristics: Its sharp, spiraling turrets claw up into the darkness like a hand from the grave; its expansive round windows watching on every side. The gardens are blooming with flowers the colors of jewels beside its foundation, which stands as pale as the moon on a clear night, save for the enormous red-and-gold standard posted front and center, whipping fiercely in the wind. The captain makes to turn right and move into the gardens, the council members on his heels. *The gardens? Why would she be in—*

Oliver whips his head to the left just in time to see the captain grab Sprightly by his tunic and slam him against the wall of hedging, twigs snapping in the process. A grunt splurges from the lanky lord's mouth, his messy reddish hair snagging on the adjacent thorns.

"What the *hell* is the meaning of this?" Oliver blusters, making to break up the fight until the captain shoves a palm into the center of Oliver's chest, causing him to stumble backward in the process.

"Couldn't just pass the bloody vote, could you?" the captain's silver eyes glare with rage.

Oliver presses a hand to his chest, worrying less about

the pain and a great deal more that his ally is in peril. "You mean the vote on the *siege*?"

Sprightly's blue eyes are finally beginning to come back to consciousness.

"Tryflin ... Too above you to follow the queen's orders," the captain slurs.

Sprightly grits his teeth. "What are you going to do about it?"

It takes a moment for the master to register what is happening. Oliver realizes that right now, this red-haired man is his only ally, and perhaps even his friend. *And if he is, then my friend and I are in danger ... because the queen has sent her captain to win us to her cause using physical means? Is this truly the way of royals?*

The captain yanks his hand back into a fist, ready to lay into Sprightly's glib face. Oliver has two seconds to decide what to do: fight or run. Sprightly prepares for impact until a choking sound emerges from the captain's throat.

Oliver's arms are closed around his neck, bracing him in a headlock. *Run, you fool! I have no idea how long I can hold this for!*

Sprightly nearly collapses onto the ground with relief, dashing from view around the corner of the hedging. Oliver struggles to keep the captain pinned; his arms are fatiguing with every second. An elbow jabs Oliver in his left rib, and it forces him to release his grip, stumbling in agony.

The captain whirls, his eyes the color of steel ready for use, like he lives for the fight. Oliver clenches his jaw. He can feel his stomach dropping. *I'm outmatched*, he thinks. The moon looks upon the men with sorrow, its light shining down on them like the garden is their stage. *Or my deathbed.*

"Is this how the queen wishes to treat with her own council?" Oliver asks, trying to buy himself time.

The captain laughs. "The queen has nothing to do with it. You annoy me, Master McHenry. You and that shit of a Royal Treasurer, too. But *you* especially annoy me."

Oliver's confusion must be obvious.

"I've seen the way she looks at you, and you're a fool if you can't see it, too."

Dear gods, he can't be serious.

The captain spits on the soil, dark as the night sky above it. His black hair glistens with the light of the moon, setting it, too, aglow with silver that could match his eyes. "Tonight, the queen will see just what you and that wretched Treasurer are capable of," he says, gesturing to his already-bruised neck.

"And how can you prove that was from me?"

He smiles a sickening, seething smile. "I am the Captain of the Royal Guard, and lover to the queen. My word against yours, Master."

The captain pulls out a dirk, shining with moonlight, and advances.

The sound of a *clunk* as something hard collides with the captain's temple, sending him collapsing to the black ground.

Oliver releases a breath that he didn't know he was holding, buckling over. He looks up from the ground at the lanky treasurer.

"You saved my life," he says, barely more than a whisper.

"Not yet," says Sprightly. "Let's move, before the fool wakes up from his dreams of rutting the queen."

Oliver steadies himself, following Sprightly out of the cursed garden and back down the white marble steps, away from the castle. *We can't go home*, he realizes with a start. The thought is enough to send his stomach to his throat.

"Where are we going?" Oliver asks with his hand braced on his ribs.

"I know a safe place we can lie low for a few nights, at least."

The master nods before pausing to contemplate why on earth the Royal Treasurer would know of such things.

They break into a run, Oliver tailing Sprightly's bobbing red hair through the black night. The familiar street signs and low lanterns that once greeted them with warmth and hospitality now seem a bit less gracious. A lutist plays a soft tune, the man's fingers strumming with drunken effort; the scent of tavern ale smells a bit staler than it had before. The men's footsteps and panting increase as the edges of the wealthier parts of town begin to deteriorate into the beginnings of the slum district. *Oh gods, why here?*

Stray cats meander through the dark alleys, purring with joy or hunger, Oliver cannot tell. The cobblestones in the road are less even, and several times he almost twists his ankle. Two courtesans in bright-blue robes greet them on their balcony, telling them to run into their brothel anytime. They pass slapdash buildings with boarded-up windows, and urchins sleeping under upcycled produce bags. One such urchin is lying on the counter of a nearby vendor stand.

Oliver's breathing is growing heavy, and his soul is growing tired. *How much farther?* Finally, Sprightly's pace slows when he rounds a corner down a pitch-black alley. Oliver stops, shaking his head. *This is madness. I've seen him at council meetings in the past, but I only truly met him earlier tonight. How can I trust him?*

Sprightly seems to sense this. He sighs. "I know. I'm thinking the same thing. But where else do we have to go?"

He's right, Oliver realizes. There is nowhere and nobody else to turn to. Both men had been groomed for court from a young age. Neither have maintained strong ties with their family, and even if they had, the likelihood of their help at this particular moment would be useless. *I have absolutely no choice.*

Swallowing the last of his fear, Oliver follows Sprightly down the dark, narrow path between two poorly constructed buildings. He stops before a nondescript wooden door, fiddles with a lock, then gives it a light kick. It's too dark to see the interior, but the ramshackle door opens to what smells like ... *bread?* The Lord shuts and locks the door, then stumbles over what sounds like metal, then glass, then metal again, until he finally manages to light a candle without burning out the match.

The tiny room is set alight by Sprightly's burning flame, which sends their shadows dancing across its cramped, yellowed walls. *Traitors' shadows*, Oliver thinks with dread. *What have we done?* A small bed is covered in tattered blue cloths, tucked into one corner. In the other rests a disheveled desk covered in reams of papers and ink and quills. A fraying teal rug lies atop the wooden floorboards, but aside from its age and use, everything seems to have been kept in good condition. Another narrow doorway is set into the buttery walls of the closet-sized bedroom, but it remains closed.

Sprightly catches Oliver eyeing it up. "You can go in if you want. It's been boarded up for years now, so no one's likely to bother us."

Oliver makes the one step it takes to reach the knob and twists. The smell of bread and pastries fills his nose, overwhelmingly pleasant and consoling. Yet that is about the only thing he can consider pleasant. Sprightly holds up his candle to expose a thick coat of dust on the old bakery's counter and glass display case. Cobwebs occupy most of the room's corners, and the chalkboard writing of the delicious menu is smudged from time.

"You took us to an old bakeshop?"

Sprightly smirks, rather less amused than he usually is. "I knew the owner and bought the property once she passed. Thought I might reopen it in her honor one day. If I ever had the time."

Oliver reads his sadness and wishes to press further but thinks better of it. "Partners in crime and I don't even know your first name," he quips, trying to keep their dire situation light. "You can call me Oliver."

The Lord smiles his witty grin this time, shaking Oliver's hand. Blue eyes glittering with ornery delight, he replies, "It's Modgen; Modgen Sprightly."

THE WAIF

The Waif ascends the blue-tiled steps of the Sapphire, the heels of her brown leather boots clicking against its ceramic work. Bordering both the noble district and the slums, the brothel is quainter than most—if a brothel could be considered quaint. The tall, white brick building is shaped like a townhouse, its perimeter lined with emerald-green shrubs. Oval, wrought iron windows peek out from its surface, windows that are usually draped with curtains to hide its unspeakable happenings from the public eye.

She passes through the sapphire-blue door and enters her unfortunate home. *Of all the places to run to, why must I have chosen this one?* Still, it could be much worse. The Sapphire had supplied Piper with food, water, and protection, so long as she shared a cut of her income. And besides, running here had earned the Waif her closest friend.

The courtesan moves with a feline grace from her post in the main room, cobalt robes swinging with each step of her long, tan legs. Her chestnut hair has been pinned up in a messy bun, and a few loose locks draw even more attention to her sultry hazel eyes. "Piper! You didn't say goodbye this morning," Narelle complains, embracing the Waif in a sisterly hug. "You know I worry about you."

"I'm sorry," Piper apologizes, at last removing her hood. "It was early when I left. I thought you were still asleep."

If Narelle could be viewed as blatantly seductive, then Piper could be seen as the epitome of elegance. Dark brown waves frame the young woman's ivory face. Her slender, elegant body looks far too polite to be draped in such a shoddy cloak, but it is her eyes that are far more distracting: deep, intelligent brown eyes, smaller than Narelle's doe-shaped ones but no less potent.

"How was it?" Narelle asks, hazel eyes gleaming. The courtesan is perhaps five years older than the Waif, but her bubbly disposition always makes Piper feel ancient.

"No less eventful than I supposed. Shamile and Torren got away without betting too much, but Elbert lost an arm and a leg. I have the money under here." She pats the side of her stomach where her coin purse rests, recently refilled from her winning game this morning.

Narelle smiles, pride shaping her tan cheeks. "I'll stick it in our bank," she says, before vanishing up the blue velvet stairs to stash the money in their shared room.

Left alone, Piper glances around the brothel's lobby. *None of the others are down here. Perhaps they are busy with clients?* Waiting for Narelle's return, she takes a seat on a nearby blue-cushioned chair. *This is not where I belong*, she thinks with a heavy sigh. Sometimes it comes to her that this was not the beginning, that she should have amounted to more than a simple thief who excels at playing *halsen* and winning gambles. But those are the days that drag her down, and she would not let it be one of those days today.

Narelle's heeled footsteps can be heard traveling back down the steps. Piper is just about to stand when the sapphire-blue door opens with a groan. The young women look up from their positions.

Heavy leather boots clunk against the white floors as three hefty men stroll into the brothel. The Waif eyes each one with curious, dark eyes. The first is smaller, with stubble along his jaw and a tough look about his square face. The second is of average height, thin in comparison to the others, with thinning brown hair. The third, however, seems to be the leader. His gray-blue eyes are hard and determined, with a fixation on accomplishment; that much she can tell right off the bat. His shoulders are large and sculpted, and his rusty-brown hair is shot through with gray. Towering a few inches over the others, it is clear that he has been acquainted with a position of power. And there is something else, something that Piper can't quite place about this man ...

The Waif discreetly pulls up the hood of her gray cloak before they see her, sinking farther into the shadows.

"Can I help you, sirs?" Narelle flashes a lovely smile that would sweep any man off his feet.

The leader returns her smile, however uncomfortably, and shakes his thick head. "No, my lady, but thank you for the offer. We come on a different sort of mission," he tells her in a voice like gravel, *a voice like ...*

Narelle looks at the men, thinking for a moment. "I think Bethanie may be finished with her client, if you prefer redheads?"

The man huffs a laugh. "I think you mistake my meaning, miss. We are here on the basis of an investigation."

The men still have not bothered to look her way, but Piper gets the sneaking suspicion that her time is running out. *If I stand now, do you think they would notice? Surely, they would hear my footsteps.*

Narelle begins playing with the ties on her cobalt-blue robe. "May I ask what this investigation is about?"

The leader of the group makes to pour himself some brandy from a side table. He takes a sip, swallowing as he examines the ornamental gold ceiling. "Ever heard of fate, my lady?"

The courtesan nods her head, wiping sweaty palms on her robes and leaving wet prints on the silk. "What of it, sir?"

The man begins to pace about the floor, turning and taking in the sight. "Some people claim you can change it; others believe it to be unchangeable."

"And what do you believe, sir?"

The man smiles. "I believe that some people's fates are so strong, they can never outrun them." He finishes the glass, placing it back on the side table. "It is a special duty of ours to continue an ongoing search for someone who has been lost to both time and speech. We travel everywhere, all over the kingdom in hopes that our elusive female might soon turn up and lead us home. A few months ago, rumors began circulating that a certain figure has been living in the slums while winning her hand at countless *halsen* matches."

A quick and hesitant glance at the Waif from Narelle.

"Deciding to hunt for our ghost, we heard it from a young merchant that she dwells in a local brothel—this one, in particular."

Bloody hell. I knew better than to trust Robbin.

The leader turns toward Piper, who sits perched on her blue velvet chair. "He also mentioned that she wears a gray cloak. Might I ask you to remove your hood, miss?"

The Waif blushes. "By what logic do you think I should obey orders from a pack of thugs?" She instantly regrets speaking too formally for a female of common birth.

Two of the men glower at her with beady eyes, but the leader says nothing. He only steps toward her a few paces, and from his pocket removes a small strand of beads fit for a young girl's wrist. It is a fine piece of jewelry. *Too fine for men of their status* ...

Piper's breath catches in her porcelain throat. "That has a high price for men of your rank."

Narelle's pretty face twists in confusion. "Those colors ... The lost princess ..." The last words are barely a whisper. Her confusion dissolves into suspicion as she takes in the men again. "Whom do you work for?" she asks with more confidence this time.

"Not the snake that currently sits on the throne."

Narelle's gaping mouth is her only reply.

Piper clenches her jaw; processing, thinking. She tries to steady her breathing while keeping her dark eyes on the leader's own. *He speaks treason openly for a common thug. He is too disciplined, too familiar* ...

Her stomach turns as she peers closer at the bracelet. Emeralds and onyx. The green and black stones glitter in the brothel's low, amber light as Piper slowly leans in closer to get a better view of the item. *A piece of the past, lost to time* ...

The man's hand pulls back just before she gets too close. "To hold it, you must show us your face."

If I do so, I will jeopardize everything that I have worked so hard to maintain. What will Narelle think of me once she knows? How do I even know if this is real? It could just be some elaborate hoax, set up by the Crown to see my head on a pike.

Piper steals glances at the other men. Haggard, hard, worn like old leather. *Why would they still be searching if they work for the queen?* The queen had called off the search for her sister years ago, only months after her initial disappearance. *It was her honor to sweep away any trace of the girl she fought to be rid of.*

"How would you know if you found your ghost?" she questions quietly.

The leader squares his muscled shoulders. "I remember, and I will never forget."

I still may have time to run, Piper thinks. *And if I did?* That would mean leaving Narelle and her shelter and protection. And for what? *I would have the same problem in a different place.* Her entire body trembles at the thought of undoing all her work, at erasing the persona she had tried so carefully to maintain. But she can feel the familiarity pulsing with each breath she takes, and the bracelet has her reaching for her gray hood once again.

Amber light bathes Piper's ivory skin and earthy features as she shows the men her true face. Unshaded, uncovered, her high cheekbones and soft chin speak of nobility, certainly not of a life growing up in the slums. Her perfectly shaped lips form a thin line as the men stare in shock.

Hood removed, the Waif has a much better view of the leader's face: The curve of his thick jaw, his slightly pushed-in nose, just an ounce of stubble coating his ruddy skin. *It is him*, she thinks with some dismay and some relief.

She extends her palm, awaiting her long-lost bracelet. The leader drops it into her hand without hesitation, shaking his meaty head with disbelief, attempting and failing to hide his speechlessness.

Narelle moves to stand by her, placing a tan hand on her shoulder as she takes a closer look at the fine piece of jewelry.

Piper runs a thin finger over the beads, tears beginning to prick the backs of her brown eyes. *Not here. I can't cry right here.* Instead, she blinks back the tears and looks upon the leader's face, now softened with relief, joy, and the beginnings of confusion.

"Captain Ivo," she finally greets him.

"Annalise Larking." The former Captain of the Royal Guard names her at last.

SVEN

The walk back to the harbor should be a short one, or so Sven thinks. It has only been an hour since he and Tym left that shanty inn to follow their captain back to the marsh. Ivo told them there would be no problem with leaving the lost princess behind to sort out her personal issues. *Unless she becomes lost again*, Sven worries. He rubs a palm over his square jaw and continues to troll behind Ivo and Tym, watching the passing slum views finally dwindle from sight.

The town has returned to its typical hustle and bustle this morning, the gulls that chirp overhead adding to the crescendo of bickering merchants, hammering from the forges, and the sound of wheels rolling over the uneven cobblestone road. One such cobblestone nearly wrenches

Tym's left foot out of place, but the skeletal man returns to his balance like a cat.

Just a few more minutes, thinks Sven, trying to calm his nerves. *Then it will be on to the boat, and just across the inlet.* At least that is what Ivo told them, after going through a complete rundown of today's plans last night—which was necessary, given the sensitivity of their current situation.

"You seem to have a very unhealthy attachment to my deceased sister, Captain. You can take your ilk and go sob somewhere else. I don't have time to waste on past troubles. Oh, and don't bother stepping foot anywhere near my castle again, or you may well end up 'the lost guards.'"

Sven shivers at remembering the queen's rage during their dismissal from the Royal Guard years ago. Ivo and his men have steered clear of the capital for as long as they could, until they had hope enough that outweighed their wills to live. *It would be a small sacrifice for seeing the true heir on the throne.* Their current residence is hidden just across an inlet from the Falvedrie Sea, through a dense, white fog that crawls over a marshland. And amidst that thick fog juts an old watchtower, tall as a giant with views of land and sea.

The pale castle comes into view, its oversized red and gold standard a stain on its brick even from a distance. Sven's meaty palms begin to sweat. *We are undercover; no one will recognize us.* Except for their old friends from the Guard, and the ones who were more so their enemies.

Ivo's thick shoulders press on through the crowd, shouldering his way between the pedestrians. The harbor is only twenty-or-so yards away now, and Sven can see their dinghy afloat by the nearest dock, its plain blue sail beating in the wicked winds of the Falvedrie Sea. Dallis waves a hand as the men approach, jumping off to start untying the ropes.

Tym turns to Sven. "I hope you're not sick this time," he jokes.

Sven rolls his beady eyes. "Hope not too. That's why I didn't eat this morning," he grumbles, and so does his large stomach.

Ivo exchanges greetings with Dallis, then steps into the dinghy with him to finish loosening the rest of the ropes. A rogue wind blows its way down Sven's shirt collar, sending the fabric fluttering like the sail he is watching. Tym's eyes narrow at him. *No, not at me,* behind *me,* Sven realizes with a start. He whips his head back to catch two royal guards making their way to the dock for their morning rounds. *Gods,* he swears. *And not just any guards. One of them is Captain Desmond Jrehart.*

Dallis and Ivo drop their ropes, ready to depart when Desmond, the new Captain of the Royal Guard and one of his minions move close enough to recognize the men and their tattered reputations.

Ivo grabs a paddle and looks to Sven and Tym.

"Get in," he orders, but before they can make a move, iron hands clamp around their biceps.

"Look what the tide brought in," Desmond drawls, one of his silver eyes swollen and his right temple marred with a gash.

Sven opens his mouth to speak, but no words come out. *There is only one thing we can do now.*

"*Row!*" Sven screams, before springing into a hundred maneuvers that he and Tym had gone over so long ago; punching and twisting and blocking punches, but it is all for naught. Desmond and his rats are simply younger and more fit. Sven can hear a grunt that surely comes from Tym, but he keeps struggling against his captain's replacement.

He misses an opportunity to block, and a fist collides with Sven's square jaw. Desmond yanks him into his own chest, locking Sven's thick wrists into irons, the latter witnessing the sound of his freedom being put to death. Seconds later, a matching groan sounds from Tym's pair.

"The queen will never be more pleased," the new Captain gloats.

Huffing with exhaustion and contempt, the only satisfaction Sven can find is in watching his friends bob across the Falvedrie Sea, shrinking from view like the last shred of hope he had been carrying in his broad chest.

ADRIANNA

The queen lounges atop her throne of gold, swirls of antique metals adorning the top of her seat. Her long, honey-blonde hair is tied neatly in a braid that drips down the length of her back. Watching as they approach one-by-one, her icy blue eyes pick apart their every need and want. The peasants could have waited until tomorrow to voice their petty concerns, but Queen Adrianna Larking would not have it said that the throne did not often hold court. *Then again, maybe I don't really care what those scoundrels have to say about my rein.*

Already, there have been two deaths in the past week. No one of import, of course, only two very zealous farmers in support of the "true heir." *A constant battle*, she concedes. In truth, Adrianna knows many would be smiling to see herself drawn and quartered, but these rebels are the least of her worries. At least they hold their secret meetings in the darkness of cellars and candlelight, unlike her own trusted advisors, whose betrayal they make known in plain sight.

It has only been one night since her beloved Captain entered her bedchambers with a face half bloodied from the wretched hands of her Master of the High Council and Royal Treasurer. *Two men that I trusted*, she seethes. *I shall have their lying tongues. Snakes hide everywhere in my kingdom; it is simply part of a queen's duty to find them and cut off their heads.*

For the nonce, however, Adrianna must deal with the mob of plebeians dirtying her polished floors. The noise is enough to make her sick. The constant chatter of a thousand witless mouths, gossiping together about their useless lives. One such life drags his soiled cloth shoes to the front of her dais, resting his knees on the marble floor. For once, the chorus of voices slows to a halt.

"My queen, I have so humbly come to you for your acclaimed generosity," the man states in a poor man's version of the southern dialect. His hair is a dark brown, but overgrown and shaggy, and his clothes are stained from the gods know what.

Adrianna rests her head on an upraised hand and lets out another shallow sigh. The hundred rubies set into her crown glimmer in the buttery afternoon light. "And for what do you seek my 'acclaimed generosity?'" the queen asks, sounding about as interested as she looks.

The man bows his unkempt head toward her white marble floor, keeping his eyes low. "My case is not as rare as one might hope. Most of us, actually, are having some difficulties leading our farmers' lives. Money's hard to come by, Majesty—"

"*Your* Majesty," a guard to the queen's left corrects.

"Your Majesty, beg pardon." The middle-aged man lifts his eyes up to the queen's. They are a cloudy brown, and weary, betraying just a hint of repulsion. "You see, things just haven't been the same for us farming folk since ..." He pauses hesitantly. "... the old regime."

Whispers blossom in the crowd.

At this, Adrianna removes her chin from the top of her hand and straightens her posture. Her jaw is set, and wanted or not, the scum has her full attention now.

"We were just wondering ... if you might consider ... changing the food tax back to the way it was before?" The farmer's swallow is audible.

Before my parents died, you mean? Adrianna smirks. "If you mean to tell me that you are poorer than dirt because of my food tax, I suggest you find a better occupation than sweating your brains out in a field all day. My food tax is going to help restrengthen this kingdom's economy." Adrianna suddenly remembers something her father once told her, something about kindness keeping peace.

She leans forward, her light blue eyes peering down at the man's grimy face. "I do, however, thank you for bringing this to my attention. I shall look into modifying the tax to make it more feasible for your situation."

The man nods his thanks. She expects one of his companions to take the stage next, but upon his return to the crowd, her Captain and one of his men come bursting through the grand mahogany doors at the end of the Throne Room. The court gasps, people stumbling out of the aisle to make way for her infamous soldiers. Each guard is escorting a man in irons, which Adrianna finds to be curious, until she peers closer at their faces. *Gods, they actually came back, the fools!* A twisted sense of cruel delight slithers down her spine, and she tightens her grip on the throne's arms to reign in her excitement.

Captain Desmond Jrehart comes forward first, devastatingly handsome despite having suffered injuries to his face. The queen remembers the men's names like she dismissed them from their line of duty yesterday: *The one with the blocky head; that's Sven. And the tall and thin one there; yes, that would be Tym.* She grins when the exiles approach the dais, her guards jerking each man to his knees. Again, the vermin that is her court remain hushed.

"Your Majesty," Desmond says, his silver eyes meeting her blue ones. "We found these outlaws making for a boat on the harbor. Thought we should teach them a lesson about disobeying the queen's commands."

Adrianna laughs. "You thought right, Captain." She turns her attention to Tym and Sven, who look as defeated as they do angry. "Anything you have to say for yourselves?"

Sven turns his small eyes to the white marble floor, but Tym turns his directly toward the queen. *How dare he?* Adrianna thinks, appalled by his defiance.

"We all know why you sent us away. You didn't want us to find out the truth," Tym declares.

The queen grits her teeth, feeling her stomach tighten. "And what truth is that, Tym?"

The wisp of a man shakes his head. "You know what I mean. We questioned the maids from that morning, the ones that had been cleaning her room for years. That jewelry box hadn't made its way into her room until later that night, and we know for a fact that Princess Annalise was with Tasman all day in the library. There was no time for her to sneak away before supper, which is when she would've needed to give the poison to kill them in their sleep. But you knew that already, didn't you?"

Sven dares a nervous look at her, and the court's tittering whispers make her face flush almost to the point of matching the shimmering rubies upon her head. *You will burn for that*, she almost says, but burning would require time, and that is a precious commodity to a queen.

"'*Exiles*,' is that what you call yourselves?" Adrianna asks, voice like velvet. "Is the word 'traitor' too bold for you? Maybe after hiding for so long in your underground holes, you have actually convinced yourselves that your ideas have merit. Maybe it is even your life's work to try to convince the rest of the world of your wrongness. But not anymore." Adrianna gives a curt nod to Desmond, who pushes Tym to his knees. Sven begins to squirm and yell in the hands of the other guard, and the court begins to shift restlessly yet again.

"Take his head!" the queen declares.

Gasps and cries and squeals shoot out from across the court as Desmond pushes Tym forward, coercing his back parallel to the cloudy white ground. The captain draws and raises his golden sword into the air, ready to make a swift blow to the neck. The gleaming metal prepares to bite into his flesh when a word pours from his mouth.

"*Anna!*" Tym belts, just before Desmond's sword cuts straight through his thin neck.

The head lands in a bloody heap and rolls its way to the bottom of the dais.

"*By the gods!*" an old woman in the crowd gasps, clutching her fragile heart. Another citizen looks as pale as the colors of the Throne Room. The remaining exile turns away from his headless friend, looking even more hopeless than he did a few moments ago. Adrianna looks at the head, its eyes meeting hers in silent conversation, and then turns back to face her court.

"Let this be a lesson. Take it with you today, and on

the morrow, and every day after that. My reign is not to be trifled with. And I will not accept treason. You are dismissed."

The oversized mahogany doors open just in time for a flood of pedestrians to flee outside and into the main corridor. *Imbeciles.*

"My Queen?" a strong, male voice asks.

"Captain."

"What of his accomplice?" Desmond glances toward Sven, who is hunched over and sulking.

Adrianna ponders a moment. "Teach him how to use his tongue for good. See what you can pry from his rotten mouth."

The captain and his guard nod, dragging Sven's blocky figure off to the dungeons without a struggle.

While the thought of torture gives Adrianna some satisfaction, she knows deep down what this means for her reign. *Traitors in my own court, then the return of my exiles. How can I be safe if they have already figured out ways to claw their way in? They know more than they think.* Only a handful of guards and her lady-in-waiting, Renai, remain by her side. She dismisses them all with a flick of her wrist, even Renai, who had been a friend of hers since the very beginning.

Adrianna stares at the lifeless body lying on the floor and wonders about the last word her victim had chosen to scream. *He could have chosen to use his last breath on any word*, she thinks, *but* ... 'Anna.' The queen shivers. *Could it really be* ... Unwillingly, she lets her mind drift back to the past. Citrine eyes, a black bottle, deep red wine. She shakes the memories from her head and draws herself back to reality.

The only person waiting for her is headless, pooling red blood upon her white marble floors.

AIMELIE

Aimelie pushes around a piece of caramelized onion on her golden platter. Her small chin is propped up by a hand while she sits at the grand dining table, listening to the complaints of her elder sister Dria as she rages about her eventful afternoon at court. Beside her sit a select few members of the Queen's Council and a handful of noblemen. Next to Adrianna, perched haughtily in her chair, is her lady-in-waiting, Renai.

"You should have seen the head; such a ghastly thing it was," Adrianna proclaims. "One can only hope that the servants were diligent enough to scrub the red out of my pristine floors."

Aimelie's stomach, once grumbling for food, now roils

at the gruesome thought. Her soul was not made for such dour company. Once, the royal dining hall would have been filled with her mother's bubbly laugher echoing across the dinner plates, her father's glorious tales of staving off enemies at the Battle of Elshwer, the kindness and wise words of her eldest sister ...

Annalise, where are you? Even after six years, Aimelie does not, *cannot* believe her beloved sister to be dead. The guards might whisper of dark tales, and the city folk might gossip in their cups about a ghost in the castle, but Aimelie knows that Annalise was smarter than to just disappear into the oblivion called death. *She was always so strong, so full of grace and knowledge beyond her years.*

A gale of laughter accompanied by the clinking of wine glasses pulls Aimelie away from her melancholy thoughts. If anything was left of her appetite, it is now entirely gone. Aimelie closes her blue doe eyes, so similar to her remaining sister's and yet so different. She catches the tail end of a petty nobleman's joke.

"And when the farmer's wife opened her eyes, she asked what it was. I said, it's called a bank!" The room explodes into a symphony of conceited laughter, the nobleman's wine beginning to run out of his crooked nose.

Aimelie turns to Dria, who is seated at the head of the table, to her left. "May I be excused?" she asks in her honey-soft voice.

Adrianna rolls her eyes. "Is my company not good enough to please you, sister?"

Melie swallows. "My stomach ... I'm not feeling up to eating at the moment."

The queen twirls a finger around a blonde curl while she uses her free hand to swig from her cup of wine. "Then leave. Go back to sulking in your room for the rest of the night. You're good at it."

Aimelie stands, smoothing out her blush-pink dress, and slips off into the hallway. The guards give her modest nods in their red and gold armor. Step-by-step, she takes the corner staircase, making her way to the fourth story of the castle. Upon reaching the top, Melie turns left, padding down the oxblood carpeting and stopping before an ash door. She grabs hold of its ornate golden handle.

The bedroom has been converted into an office area, mostly filled with books and parchment, but Aimelie still likes to sit in it from time to time. The emerald curtains are drawn, letting fingers of golden sunlight bask the furniture and tomes in shrouds of lemon yellow. A fine mahogany desk stands watch amidst the chaos of cluttered bookshelves and ink pots. The fireplace, once bursting with a powerful, fiery glow sits cold and empty, without a trace of soot. Aimelie takes a seat in a deep-green armchair beside the fireplace. It sits opposite of the black one, which faces her own.

This was always her chair. Growing up, Aimelie

suffered from recurring nightmares—cruel and twisted things, waking her from a dead sleep with gasps for breath and chilling sensations. Being the youngest of her siblings, Aimelie's royal parents were not hesitant to give attention to their baby, but they had shared a room around the corner of their daughters' corridor and the guards had strict orders to keep the girls inside their rooms come nighttime. To Melie's delight, she discovered a hidden passageway that connected all three of the sisters' rooms. Adrianna was of little help; she was too concerned with her beauty sleep. But Annalise could be woken with a whisper and a tear, and soon enough the two sisters would chase away Aimelie's faulty fears with a delicious story.

She can still remember her voice: soft, but strong; hushed in the way that a wind warns of a coming storm. There was a certain grace to her sister that Aimelie had always admired. *And to think that people believe her to have poisoned my parents.* The stories had grown wide and varied, even as time continued to pass years after the death of Queen Annora and King Tiberius. But she remembers the look on Anna's innocent face, the way the world seemed to collapse around her as Dria shot out her accusatory finger. There was nothing to do but run. *I don't blame her; I might have done the same had they threatened me to time in the dungeons before a trial with little in my favor.*

The clock strikes seven o'clock, startling Aimelie out of her dazed state. She glances toward the oval mirror hanging on the emerald walls and takes in her appearance. Her blonde locks and sky-blue eyes are a reflection of Adrianna's visage, but Aimelie has her mother's rounded features, more doe-like than wolfish. Dark circles line her large eyes, and her full lips are curved in a timeless frown. *What happened to me?* But she knows all too well the devastating effects of loneliness; Anna's disappearance leaves her hollow even years later.

A soft knock on the ash door makes her jump, but she grants permission for the visitor to enter the small office. Expecting Adrianna and preparing to be scolded for some thing or another, Aimelie's expression of shock must be evident on her pretty face.

"Sorry to interrupt, my lady." The well-groomed man is no older than Mel, clad in gray slacks and a teal tunic emblazoned with the Larking crest. "The queen wished for me to introduce myself to you."

It is not the boy's soft brown eyes or hair that Aimelie is interested in, but rather the colors of his noble attire. Each of the three sisters were assigned a set of royal colors, which one day might befall them to raise as their standard. Adrianna's colors are already in use, the red and gold hues staining every wall of the castle. Annalise's would have been emerald and black, in honor of her paternal grandfather. If the reign would fall to Aimelie, hers would be a flag of teal and silver. Since childhood, each of the sisters' advisors, rooms, and personal objects had corresponded to their unique colors.

Taking the silence as a cue to speak, the boy persists. "Her Majesty has suggested that you be schooled in diplomatic affairs, after a few recent ... *unfortunate* events."

"She wants me to deal with the lower-class squabbles because she'd rather not," Aimelie replies with the politest form of disappointment.

The boy smirks, avoiding agreement with such a damning remark. He pauses. "I am to be your mentor for this endeavor." He looks a bit uncomfortable, shifting his weight to the other foot.

Aimelie's queen sister might not be one to cater to others, but Melie herself gains fulfillment from helping people. She gestures to the chair. "Please, sit."

The boy nods and moves to rest upon the arm of the black chair. He eyes the office warily, with interest.

Aimelie likes to think she knows how to read people well, and when she finds kindness in others, it fills her with a glorious sense of hope. She feels just a little more whole, like her sister's absence is overshadowed just a bit. "What can I call you?"

The boy smiles shyly. "They call me Linden, but you can call me anything you'd like."

Aimelie gives what might have been a hum of laughter, glancing back to that mounted mirror to find that her lips have curved upward into a beautiful arc. It has felt like years since she has shown the world her magnificent smile.

"Well then, Linden. When shall we begin?"

VEGA

Vega smooths her royal purple tunic over black trousers, adjusting the top button so the shirt exposes just a bit of her pale neck. She straightens the stack of parchment on her desk, stealing a glance in the mirror at her familiar lime-green eyes and short inky hair.

It has been three weeks since she figured out how to manipulate her own physical characteristics, and Vega believes that she finally has it under control. *Well,* almost *under control.* The only thing she can't seem to determine is how long the manipulations last. Her first try resulted in lavender eyes that remained for only a few minutes, but upon changing her hair color, Vega stayed a platinum blonde for the entire day—and had to stay locked inside her dorm room lest anyone think that she dyed her jet-black locks.

A light knock sounds at the door. Vega takes a shallow breath and grabs the knob. *Here goes nothing.*

"Good morning!" Christa greets her friend cheerfully, chestnut ringlets bobbing in the dimness of the doorway.

Vega smiles, making room for her friend to stroll into what little living space she has. "Morning. How was class?"

Christa props herself up on Vega's lumpy bed. "Rough, as always. I'm glad I'm out." She looks around the closet-sized dorm room. "So, what is it you wanted to tell me?"

Suddenly, Vega isn't so sure that she wishes to spill her secrets of manipulation to her best friend. *What if it's too much, too serious, too ... unethical?* She has never read about the extent of manipulation on oneself in the House of Perception's Code of Ethics, but perhaps there was some clause that she missed, some phrase that she had misinterpreted. Vega fiddles with the top button she had left open only minutes before, shifting in the silence.

"Vega?" Christa giggles, waiting for an answer.

Vega sighs. "I suppose there's no better time for this." She pauses, bracing herself for her colleague's reaction. "I ... I made a discovery."

Christa's blue eyes squint in the candlelight of the

room as Vega lifts her hands to her face, passing over her entire head. *Focus, focus …* She lowers her pale hands, exposing her face. Christa tilts her head, and for a moment Vega wonders if she has been mistaken of her gifts this whole time. *Could I have been wrong?*

"Veg, I don't think—"

A warmness, a tingling sensation spreads in a blossom from the crown of her head down to her neck.

"Oh, my *gods!*" Christa clamps a hand over her mouth, then frantically points with the other at the table mirror.

Vega snatches the mirror off her desk. *It worked!* She smiles, admiring her colorless, gray eyes. Her ink-flooded hair has retracted into an inch-long crop of golden curls, showing off her high cheekbones and narrow features. *Lazarus almighty, it actually worked!*

"*Vega!* This is insane! This shouldn't even be possible! Where did you learn how to do that?"

Vega shakes her head, placing the small mirror back on her desk, the flame of the candle flickering with the movement. "I didn't. I just … came up with it." She blushes.

Her friend jumps into a standing position. "We need to tell the masters!"

"*No!* Christa, we can't. Not yet, anyway." Vega's palms begin to sweat. *That could be the death of me, or at least result in my expulsion from the university!*

"You'll be head of the Perception Board if we just show them what you can do!"

Vega's faded gray eyes return to her natural lime-green ones. "Christa, this is my discovery; it should be my choice."

But Christa moves the two strides it takes to get to the door.

"*Stop! I'm not ready, I—*" Vega shoots out a hand, heat sparking through her fingertips.

Christa halts dead in her tracks. Her chestnut ringlets swing as she whips her head around to face Vega. "Why are you standing like that?" her friend asks, blue eyes clear and innocent.

Vega's face twists in confusion. She reigns in her pale hand, finding with a peek at the mirror that her blonde hair has also shifted back to normal. "I was just stretching my arm out," she lies, hoping it doesn't sound as ridiculous as it does to her.

Christa chuckles, tilting her round face back to the ceiling. "Well, I guess I should be on my way, then."

Vega opens her mouth, then closes it. "I guess so."

"See you in a bit, love!" Christa sings as she and her bouncy curls vanish outside into the hallway.

Oh, now I've really done it. Not only has Vega taken advantage of basic manipulation skills, but she has just conjured something new altogether. *There is nothing normal about altering a person's* mind, *let alone it being considered* ethical. *I'm going to burn in Anzac's shadowy palms.*

Immediately, she grabs her bag and heads out the door, willing her petite frame down the countless twists and turns of the stairways in her dormitory. Acolytes stare while she paces across the black-and-white checkered tiles of the lobby, making her way to the enormous oak doors and their elaborate golden handles. One thorough push sets the large door wailing, beams of creamy morning light sneaking into the lowly lit interior.

Once out of the House of Perception, Vega's shoulders loosen ever-so-slightly. Along the narrow road she walks stand dozens of traditional Wembleton houses in black, white, tan, and ivory. She heads east, traveling around the large black clock in the center of the path. *Almost ten*, she notes.

Other scholars in outfits of deep purple and black pass her by, and Vega can swear that they are staring at her. She has always lacked close friendships. It isn't that she doesn't have *any* friends—she and Christa are well-acquainted—but the heart of the matter is that Vega never truly feels like she can open up to any of them. Being vulnerable is one of the scariest things that Vega can imagine doing, but that same fear is what keeps her feeling rather unsatisfied.

Vega's tiny feet carry her down the Alley of the Gods, only two blocks from the House of Perception. She doesn't usually find herself attending ceremony to worship for the reason that she already feels undeniably connected to the gods, but today's new revelation has her feeling like she needs some bastion of comfort that only the temples can give.

Hands in her purple pockets, she eyes the Alley in as much awe as it gave her when she first witnessed its beauty. Temple after temple lines the road of smooth pebbles, waxing and waning as she passes them by on quiet toes. Each temple is unique: some large, some small; some are plain or bold, while others are delicate or complex. Countless temples rise from the pebbles, many towering at least ten yards into the morning mist, and a few are so sacred that they have domed ceilings to allow the most pious of worshippers to make their visits even during a storm.

Most temples at the beginning of the Alley are dedicated to the lesser gods, but as the pebbled path rises gently to the crest of a hill, such altars are reserved for the most powerful deities. It is up this slope that Vega begins to walk, passing the minuscule but ornate white Temple of Ione, the Goddess of Purity, Kindness, and Charity. Next in line stands the Temple of Anzac, whose crooked black columns spiral from the ground like dead branches. And across from it, Vega finds the altar that has been tugging her along all this time: the Temple of Elouthera.

The domed temple has been constructed of creamy

white granite with flecks of black and gray, its columns twisting gracefully into an upward surge. The black cement floor has been adorned before it dried with a trove of fine silver and gold jewelry, allowing for something like walking over a river of the night sky. Its granite walls open to a room with a white reflecting pool in the center. At the front of the room, embossed into the granite wall, are shapes of stars in twenty different sizes.

It is cold and quiet, the smoke of a musky incense filling the air of the temple. The only sound that can be heard is the muffled sweeping of a hunched-over elderly woman and her broom, dusting away stray leaves that blew in from last night's storm. Vega kneels beside the reflecting pool, releasing a heavy sigh that sways a chunk of her inky black hair.

There is something wrong with me, she thinks. It is this exact thought she has been hiding from herself for months now, trying to tuck it away in the far corners of her mind. But how could she not think it? No girl with strong manipulatory bloodlines has had abilities like hers or come even close. *I'm even better than the people who are supposed to be teaching me*, she concedes. After morphing her own physical characteristics and the fiasco with Christa earlier ... *Can I actually alter not just a person's physical traits, but their minds, too?* Vega doesn't need to check the books to find out whether this one is permitted or not, and the fact that she has already done it makes her so sick, she could throw up in the reflecting pool before her.

She cups her face with pale hands, trying to think of something, *anything* that could possibly help her cause. *Maybe I could withdraw from school? Then I would never have to manipulate again, and I could avoid any more incidents. But then ... what would I do instead? Run away? Start anew?*

This thought does not sit well with Vega. At fourteen, her mother decided that she wanted a life of freedom, and traded Vega and her father for the opportunity to join a group of traveling oracles. The Nevs, they're called. Vega's fists curl.

As if in response, the water in the reflecting pool trembles ever so slightly. Putting those unhealed wounds aside, she continues to ruminate. *Perhaps I could take on a normal job, like sewing or working with clay? A normal day, a normal life ...* But the idea of having to shed her dreams and spend her life as a commoner sends a crack down Vega's fragile heart.

She tilts her head down to gaze into the pool, and it is only then that she realizes she is crying. Her thin shoulders tremble as she brings her palms to cover her face once more. The weight of her troubles is like lead in her stomach, pushing her down further and further into nothingness.

All her life, there had never been anyone to truly look up to, no one to support her. It had always fallen on Vega to pick herself up, to choose to be a better person, instead of being like her parents, or her many rude professors, or those other scholars who were so jealous of her abilities that insults were their only defense. *Do they know that I envy them? For their simple lives and how they don't have to worry so much about sealing the truth from their lips every waking moment of the day? Or the fact that they fit? They fit together, and they fit into society, and they don't have to be an outcast? Do they, too, wonder what it is that they came here to do, to contribute to this world?*

A flash of burning heat pulses through her whole body, and she wonders for a moment why she is feeling rage. *Why can't it just be easy? Why can't I just fit into this world?*

The sound of wood clanking on the ground has Vega lifting her face from her hands. Her immediate thought is, *Why is it so bright in here?* Her second is, *Why is that old lady gaping at me?*

The old woman has dropped her broom and stands as if she is seeing a ghost, eyes wide in terror and mouth ajar. Vega turns behind her, but she is the only other person in the temple, which is now oddly bright, especially around where she is sitting.

She looks down at glowing hands to find them stained with what looks to be tears of liquid silver. Leaning forward in a glittering champagne dress, Vega gazes upon the reflecting pool to find a headpiece proudly displayed upon long silver hair, and a face that is no longer her own. Her pointed, elven-like visage is gone, only to be replaced by silver eyes and a set of matching painted teardrops on her cheeks. *Lazarus almighty ... am I ... am I ....?*

The old woman lets out a bone-chilling scream.

Part II

Smoke

Adrianna

Adrianna snorts into her wine cup like an amused hog. The shipmaster's joke was too funny not to laugh at, and it has been too long since she last shared this sort of entertaining company. Alongside the shipmaster sits the Royal Ambassador and a figure who she believes to be the Lord of Merchants—though their names are all a blur. *This wine is getting to my head,* the queen acknowledges. To her right rests her lady-in-waiting, Renai, whose dirty-blonde curls sway with the shake of her head. A small voice in the faraway edges of her mind warns her to stop intoxicating herself, to pull herself together and act like the queen she is supposed to be, but Adrianna hasn't had time to pamper herself for what seems like days. *And besides, they're loving it!*

The sound of jokes and laughter ring through the

Great Hall, rattling off its pale stone walls. The nobles and the few members of her council—those whom she deemed worthy enough to trust—are thoroughly relishing their after-dinner apéritifs. The Royal Ambassador, Lord Earlmence, is stealing the attention at the moment.

"In all fairness, though, the men must have some bit of wits if we haven't found them yet."

Dria rolls her baby blue eyes and takes another drink of wine.

The shipmaster responds in his smooth, icy voice. "It can't be too much longer. Unless they plan on leaving the kingdom and forging new lives, we're bound to find them here."

The Lord of Merchants nods. "I wouldn't worry. I'm sure they're hiding in some lesser building that we just haven't checked yet."

"They're young and small. They've probably traded their council attire for old produce bags to pose as urchins," the shipmaster jibes.

The queen bursts into laughter, throwing her arms up to clap her hands together, but ends up knocking her wine glass off the mahogany table.

"Damn it," she curses, laughter turning to rage. *Where is the bloody maid? The maid should be over here by now!*

A few moments too late for Adrianna's liking, a young girl comes frisking over with a pan and broom. Her small brown eyes flicker nervously from the edge of the mahogany table to the broken shards that have splattered all over the floor. She begins to kneel—

"*Where have you been*?" the queen demands, fury sharpening her wolfish features as the silence of her colleagues begins to eat away at her nerves.

The petite maid's dark eyes are shock-full of fear. *Too much like Anna's.* Her tiny hands hover over the puddle of wine and glass like a statue, frozen in time. Dria can no longer contain her disgust. "Well, what are you waiting for? Get with it, you *dimwit*," she spews before back-handing her across her motionless face.

Gasps break out amongst the guests at the long table, the girl fighting tears as she hurriedly scrapes up the mess. *Oh, I probably shouldn't have done that*, Adrianna admits to herself. Before she can say another word, Renai rises from the table.

"My queen, I have a matter of the utmost importance to discuss with you in private, if you would?" Her amber eyes are silently pleading.

Adrianna forces a nod, ignoring the spinning stares of shock from the other nobles at the table. She stands, almost losing her balance, but Renai grabs hold of her arm to steady her. The queen turns to face her guests, smoothing the imaginary wrinkles from her golden silk gown.

"You will forgive me for my early departure," she

mutters, before leaving the dining hall with her best friend.

Renai walks the queen back to her royal chambers in silence. The only sounds come from their footsteps, muffled over the crimson carpet, and they are almost to Adrianna's chambers when she feels her insides take a turn for the worst. *I'm going to lose my dinner in a moment, here.* Renai opens the door just in time for Dria to dash to her golden chamber pot before emptying her stomach. Her lady-in-waiting sighs, shutting the door and shaking her head. She moves to hover over the queen, gently patting her on the shoulder.

Adrianna spits in the pot and covers it with the golden lid. *How ladylike,* she thinks casually. She gathers up her golden skirts and stands with the help of Renai.

"Oh, Dria," Renai fusses. "Come and sit. You need to rest."

The queen plops beside her friend, nearly toppling over as the world continues to spin. She sighs in despair. *In front of my own council members, too.* Renai runs her hands through the queen's honey-colored hair, working it into a loose braid.

"It's my fault," Dria slurs, which Renai muffles a laugh at, because it obviously wasn't anyone else's. "I shouldn't have drunk so much before dinner. I just felt ..."

"How did you feel?" Renai asks gently.

Dria shakes her head, her friend slapping her shoulder

for moving while she was working on her braid. "You know what I mean. It's ... hard. So much to look after, so much to remember. I never feel like I have time for myself anymore, I never feel ... good enough," she admits.

Renai says nothing, just persists in her attempt to finish the queen's favored hairstyle.

Adrianna continues. "Even when I was little, it was like I was just *born* to be misunderstood. Had everything I could ever want, but ... it was my *parents*."

"Your parents?" Renai questions with curious amber eyes.

"It was always *Aimelie*, always ..." The queen grits her teeth. "*Annalise*. They bestowed showers of attention upon them, hardly gave any to me." Dria's cheeks begin to blush, but Renai cannot see from her angle. "All I really wanted was to be special in their eyes," she finishes, feeling smaller than ever. *Why am I telling her all this?*

Her best friend completes her braid, the twisted blonde locks lying heavily down Dria's spine.

"Well, you'll always be special to me," Renai rests a hand on Dria's shoulder.

A slow knock at her heavy mahogany door tears her attention away from her friend. *Only one person knocks like that*, Dria knows. *My other half.*

The door opens, and with all the prowess of a jaguar, Captain Desmond Jrehart saunters into the queen's crimson and gold bedroom. He stops before the women, who are lounging atop one of the red sofas.

"Lady Renai." He greets the queen's lady-in-waiting.

"Captain." Renai inclines her pretty head.

The captain observes Adrianna with mischief dancing in his silver eyes, and a flutter of adrenaline dances down her spine. He turns to Renai, one of his eyes still bruised and a scab covering what is most likely going to be a long scar on his right temple.

"I can take it from here," he dares to say for the queen, and Renai bobs her dirty-blonde curls as she stands to depart. She stops just before Dria, taking her hand.

"If you need me, you know where to find me. I live to serve." Renai smiles, and Dria gives her hand a gentle squeeze.

"Thank you, Renai," she attempts, but fails, to say without slurring.

The door shuts, and Desmond drops himself next to Adrianna. She has gathered her wits enough to avoid toppling over if forced to stand, but her vision is still waving like the Falvedrie Sea on a stormy evening.

"I came as soon as I heard." Desmond takes the queen's hand. "You need to be more careful, Dria. There are eyes everywhere."

The queen sighs, leaning herself into his broad, muscled chest. "I know," is all she says, because as much as she loves Desmond, she doesn't feel the need to wallow in her self-pity again. *That was stupid of me. I shouldn't have let myself be that sentimental, even with Renai.* She steals her drunken self for a moment, silently picking at a fraying thread that has worked free of her gown's beading.

"Are you angry with me?" she asks in a whisper.

Desmond lets out a breezy laugh into her blonde hair, tickling the back of her neck. "How could I be, when I might very well have done the same thing?"

Adrianna lifts her head to peer into the captain's quicksilver eyes. "You know, sometimes I wonder if we were destined to be together," she divulges in a small voice, tracing a finger along the bruise of his temple, then along the collar of his black shirt.

The captain's answering smile is full of secrets and shadows. "You already know the answer to that," he whispers back, pressing kisses to the crook of her slender neck.

Dria runs her hand from his collar to the top button of his shirt and attempts to undo it, but her current state is just enough to prevent her fingers from being successful. *Damn it,* she curses in her ever-boggling mind. *I must look pathetic.* Desmond seems to sense this, and spins her around in his lap, unlacing the back of her golden gown. By the time she wriggles it off, the heavy gold silk collapsing on the ground, the captain is already undressed.

She stands there for a moment, surveying her paramour. He was kissed by the gods; every muscle perfect, every rise and fall of his arms and legs ... *And his chest...* She watches each of those muscles shift as her lover, her captain, her soulmate, moves to scoop her up.

Adrianna can hardly contain herself before Desmond takes her on the enormous feather bed. No doubt the occupants on the other side of the wall can hear, but Dria doesn't care. Right now, she owns the world, and only she and Desmond are inside of it. She rakes her fingers through his charcoal-black hair, nails clawing at his wide shoulders as she searches for something to keep her tethered to the physical realm. It might just be her drunken stupor, but Adrianna swears that her bedside wine looks to be boiling.

She loses herself in the moment, the world around her dissolving into nothingness. She is burning and she is freezing; she is water and she is air; she is fire and she is earth. And above the ragged, rise and fall of her chest is the night; her mysterious paramour and the other half to her broken, black heart. She clenches handfuls of the comforter as she stifles a cry.

The queen climaxes, and the sound of shattering glass breaks the cacophony. She screams as she watches the wine decanter, the glass of her dressing mirror, and the crystal of her bedroom chandelier burst into a million pieces, showering the space around the bed with shards. *What the bloody hell?* Her braid undone, golden locks fall tangled and loose around her wide blue eyes as she tugs Desmond flush against her.

The only sounds are her uneven breathing and the rumbling of the captain's sultry laugh muffled against her bare shoulder. *What is he laughing at?* the queen wonders with puzzlement.

"This is no laughing matter, Des! What the *hell* just happened?" She frets, failing to catch her breath from both pleasure and fear.

The captain looks up as he continues his mysterious laugh.

"*Finally,*" he grins like a wolf, and she swears that shadows dance behind him.

His sensuous laughter fills every corner of her room, every crack in the walls, every nook and cranny of her body. And when he finishes, the sound of his ragged breath is more appealing to Dria than ever before.

NARELLE

"I'm not mad at you," Narelle tells Annalise Larking in her sapphire-blue robes. "I'm just …"

Annalise stares at her with unflinching dark eyes. "Upset? Unhappy?"

"Disappointed," Narelle finishes. She shakes her chestnut hair, which she wears long and loose after a long day's work. "But I told you before, I understand why you are going. Gods, I would do the same in your shoes."

It has been only two days since the arrival of the former Captain of the Royal Guard and his men, as well as the revelation that 'the Waif,' or 'Piper,' is actually the lost princess. *Two days since my life was turned upside down,* Narelle thinks. It is not that she didn't take the news well —after all, she had been keeping the secret for years, now —but that she wasn't quite ready for her almost-child to leave the nest she had so carefully built for her. *She is choosing this of her own accord, and it is indeed a hard truth to face.* But the courtesan could never be contemptuous toward Annalise, toward the only member of her family that she has left. *Besides, this is her destiny, and you can't outrun fate.*

Annalise lets out a sigh, bouncing her weight from heel to heel. Narelle senses her discomfort, even if the young woman doesn't say anything.

"Come sit down," she commands, taking Annalise's hand and leading her to the window seat that has so long served as the princess's bed. Narelle's hazel eyes focus on something far away. "Before my father sold me here, I had dreams." She bites her lip. "I wanted to marry for love, to start a family, settle down on a farm somewhere and live a life that was simple, but happy."

Annalise frowns, resting her palm atop Narelle's tan hand.

"When the debt started growing, and there were no more coins left, and my father sold me to the Sapphire, I —" Tears prickle at the backs of her eyes, but now is not the time. She swallows. "I never thought that I would ever be able to live that dream, or anything close to it. But then you came along."

The princess huffs an embarrassed laugh.

"Do you remember the day you found me?" Narelle asks.

Annalise nods. "Bits and pieces. I remember the feelings, mostly. Fear, dread, and something like hope."

The courtesan turns her hazel eyes to her feet. "I had just finished with a client. I bathed and changed and was brushing my hair when I heard a knock at my door. When Gissaira told me to come downstairs, I thought it might have been my father. Still, I followed her to the lobby, and ... and then I saw you." Narelle pushes to her feet and kneels to open the cedar chest at the foot of her bed. Gently, she pulls out a muddied nightdress that used to be white, along with an emerald silk slipper.

Annalise's jaw drops.

"You were so afraid, soaked and wet from head to toe despite there being no rain that night, and you were missing a shoe. At first, I thought you may have been an urchin—and I guess, in a way, you were—but then I looked closer. Your posture was too straight, your face was too beautiful, and your demeanor ... Even though you were scared, you looked strong."

A silent tear drips down one of the princess's cheeks. She looks determined to keep the rest in.

"You said you were seeking shelter, that you were on the run because your older brother abused you and he had taken over the family estate. When I saw you were shaking—from fear or cold, I couldn't tell—I couldn't resist any longer. I pulled you inside and told the madam that I would take care of you. She just shrugged and said that as long as I paid for your food, it wouldn't be an issue. So, I took you up on this very window seat and began to brush out your hair. I learned that you were five years younger than I was, and that you liked dogs. You wouldn't tell me what noble family you came from, even though I had some ideas. Anyway, you got your shelter, and I finally got my dream."

Annalise wipes the tears from her deep brown eyes and sniffs. "You kept them all this time?"

Narelle smiles and nods. "They're adorable. Just look at how little you were!"

The princess laughs, a perfect image of fair beauty.

Narelle folds up the dress and sets the slipper on top of it, closing the lid of the chest. Standing with a groan, she moves to pour two glasses of merlot, handing one to Annalise as she sits beside her again on the window seat. "They knew you on sight," she notes.

The princess takes a sip. "I know. They knew me well."

Narelle swirls the wine in her glass, watching the tiny hurricane spin rapidly. *Just like my head when I think about what this will mean for us.* "What will the people do when they learn that their lost princess is lost no more?"

Annalise remains quiet for a few moments, staring into the bloody depths of her own drink. Finally, she answers. "Rebel."

The sheer weight of the word is enough to set Narelle to downing the rest of her wine. She empties her glass, wiping her mouth with the back of a tan hand. "Where will you go?"

The princess taps her thumb on the cushion of the window seat. "Ivo gave me the location of a hidden tower that has been abandoned for some time. He told me to meet him there when I'm ready."

"You're not ready yet?" Narelle figures.

"I'll never be ready. I'm just going to have to do it."

The courtesan smiles. Annalise always finds the strength to face her fears, although this kind of challenge seems to be incomparable. If Annalise can't win over her people, she will never get the throne. If she can't find political alliances, she will never keep her crown. People still might believe the false accusation that she murdered her own parents. And equally unnerving is the fact that this entire plot is treasonous, which is something that could put Annalise—and Narelle—in grave danger. *Gods, shine your luck down upon us. We're going to need it.*

TIBERIUS

SIX YEARS EARLIER

Tiberius sits at the dinner table in his private chambers, scrutinizing a map of the kingdom, *his* kingdom, which gives him no satisfaction given its current state of affairs. *The Eldrics of Nesvla unhappy with the trade agreement; Minoretts from Fetland rallying for the redrawing of borders to return to them the land their ancestors grew up on ...*

The king drinks deeply from his golden chalice, but even the wine does naught to soothe his tightening stomach. In fact, it seems to upset it more. He runs a strong hand through his goldenrod curls.

"Breathe, Tiberius," Annora instructs her husband gently. She had always been his better half; kind, caring, and full of radiance, balancing out his stress with her carefree laughter.

It is to his better half that he looks now, pushing the yellowed map aside. "Breathing is a bit difficult when half the world is leaning into our walls, Nora."

"And yet, there is nothing more that we can do but breathe and try."

The king smiles this time. His wife's nonchalance about even the most pertinent of issues has always been enviable, and it makes his brown eyes twinkle with pride to know that she has chosen to be his queen.

A cheerful knock on the door has them both turning to find their youngest princess waltzing across the burgundy carpets.

Eleven-year-old Aimelie is clad in a tiny gown of teal and silver, her big blue doe eyes half hidden behind an unruly mop of curls that bounce with every exuberant step.

"Where are your sisters, Melie?" the queen asks her daughter as she pushes a stray curl from her youthful face, so much lighter than her own dark waves.

Aimelie tugs on the bottom of her teal sleeve. "Dria told me this morning that she wasn't feeling well, but Anna should be coming soon. I saw her in the hall on my way here!"

Tiberius takes another sip of his wine. It bothers him that it is yet another day that Dria has found some excuse to avoid being around her own family. "Hopefully Anna is indeed on her way," he replies, trying to ease the worry blooming across his wife's face; worry that sets his heart to aching.

In perfect timing, another knock sounds on the door; this one quieter and more reserved.

"Come in," Tiberius calls.

Dressed in fine emerald silk, Annalise slips through the mahogany doors. At just fourteen years of age, the heir to the Empeirian throne already carries herself with poise and grace. Tiberius finds himself studying his eldest daughter's character, regaining some of his ease and confidence. *She is ready*, he reminds himself, and this time he does not need convincing.

"Anna! Come join us, sweetheart. Pull over a chair," her mother encourages.

Anna obeys with a shy smile and sets up a chair between her parents and sister. "Did Aimelie tell you about Belline's son?"

Annora regards the daughter now sitting on her lap. "What about him, Melie?"

The two sisters share a brief gale of laughter, and Anna explains. "Modgen thought it would be a good idea to flirt with the baker's daughter, but it didn't exactly go as planned ..."

Aimelie cannot contain herself: "Clarice pushed him into the White Pond!"

Tiberius tips his head back and echoes his wife's hearty laughter. He imagines what the scene must have looked like: Modgen's rusty orange hair bobbing with every flowery compliment, Clarice's face twisting in repulsion, the red-haired boy flying face-first into the clear waters of the White Pond.

Modgen has been Annalise's best friend since they were old enough to talk. The extroverted son of Annora's lady-in-waiting was born as witty as they come, and his showmanship would have been highly amusing to watch. Still, the king is leery of his eldest daughter learning some of his less polished habits. "Modgen should take care to guard his tongue," Tiberius warns. "It may cost him worse than wet clothes someday."

Annalise shrugs in her chair, brown eyes still glimmering with amusement. "If there's anyone who can talk their way out of a pinch, it'd be Modge."

MODGEN

On the third bite of apple, he chucks it against the wall, watching it explode with a *thud*. As the juices drip silently down the yellow walls, Modgen can hardly remain sane. *We've got to get out of here*, he acknowledges, left foot twitching as he sits at the end of his mother's former bed.

Oliver peers up from his seat on the rug, his forest-green eyes twinkling with humor.

"We're two traitorous men wanted by the Queen of Empeirus, hiding in the slum district lest they take our heads, and you think this is funny?" Modgen asks, reddish curls shifting in the candlelight.

Oliver shakes his head with a faint smile. "You're right."

The lanky boy leans the back of his head against the

buttery bedroom wall. *If it could be called a bedroom*, he thinks. He remembers his mother's kind smile, how she always smelled of flour and something sweet, going to pray with her at the Royal Temple.

His mother was the late Queen Annora's right-hand woman, a lady-in-waiting tending to all her needs and, growing up, her best friend. She passed on her bright blue eyes to her only child, but such was the only trait she shared. Lord Sprightly lets out a heavy sigh. *This place is making me as sentimental as a maid.*

Oliver stands with a groan. "We need to have a meeting," he says, opening the bakery door.

"A meeting?" Modgen snickers. "Bit of a small council, don't you think, ex-Master McHenry?" He follows him into the other room that was the bakeshop. The shop remains quaint and fragrant, the scent of pastries and fresh bread still clinging to the air.

During their time seeking refuge here, the boys had rid the space of its cobwebs, straightened up the tables, even went so far as to clear the coat of dust off the once-shiny surfaces. They had to find something to keep themselves busy. *Life sucks living as wanted men*, Modgen realized days before.

Oliver maneuvers his way behind the bakery's old display case and sales counter, taking up a random piece of chalk and wiping away the old blackboard's writing with the bottom of his sleeve.

Modgen lights a candle on one of the two wooden tables, seating himself backward in a chair and wrapping his lean arms around its rounded back.

Oliver leans his elbows on the counter. "It's been two days."

"Two days too long," Modgen murmurs, cautiously eyeing the boarded-up door. "We need to leave soon. Too long in one place, and they're bound to find us."

"Precisely. But where are two wanted men to go?"

The Lord twiddles his thumbs, then lets out a laugh, shaking his rusty orange locks. "Nowhere in Empeirus," he realizes. "The queen will have her men scouring every corner of her domain, and you and I both know the snake will stop at nothing."

The former master nods, brown hair catching a glint of candlelight. "So, you're suggesting that we leave the territory?"

Modgen sighs. "I feel like becoming an exile in a foreign territory is better than spending our outnumbered days here like cowards."

The men are silent for a few long seconds, processing the heavy truth about their lives. *One night, one man, one mistake* ... The memory flashes through Modgen's mind: the glow of the moon; Oliver's face—brave, but fearful; the weight of a jagged rock in his right hand. *One hit to the bastard's face, and I doomed us both.* He swallows. *But what else was I supposed to do? Let him murder Oliver in his drunken madness?*

Oliver rouses Modgen from his thoughts. "Then we'll need to pick a territory." Master McHenry begins jotting down the names of the continental territories on the old board. He stands back, rubbing the back of his neck. "Godrus?" he asks, awaiting Modgen's judgement.

"Too cold, and too far north. Fetland?"

"Not much to do there aside from taking up a life in agriculture."

Modgen snorts. "Let's not be farmers."

Oliver agrees. "I've always had a desire to visit the Nesvlan mountains?"

The Lord thinks for a moment. Spiraling towers of gold, orange fields of wild poppies, magnificently rugged mountains with peaks shrouded in mist, world-acclaimed tea leaves ... "Definitely a possibility. Keep that one."

The next name on the list incites a laugh from Oliver. "Do I even need to ask about this one?" he wonders aloud as he crosses Javir off the list.

Modgen chuckles. "And Calleeit? I don't think they'd take well to Empeirian immigrants either."

Oliver shakes his head in agreement, drawing a solid white line through the penultimate territory on the list. There is no need to ask about Wembleton, as their current criminal state brooks no time for traveling that far across the continent. "That leaves ..."

"The Savek Coast? That wouldn't be bad. We could be fishermen, take up a little cottage in a fishing village, spend our days sailing on the Sea." Modgen looks up to find Oliver quiet, turning over the piece of chalk in his hand. "That's where you're from, isn't it?"

His green eyes glance up from the chalk. He opens his mouth but can't seem to find the words to respond.

Modgen waves a hand at his friend. "Forget it. I like Nesvla better," he adds with a dashing grin.

Oliver flashes him a smile of gratitude and scratches out the last territory on their list of potential escape routes. "Nesvla it is," he declares.

"Great! This is exciting. I can see it now. From noble-born Royal Treasurer to Nesvlan tea merchant: The incredible journey of Sprightly's success as an Empeirian exile."

At this, Oliver cannot help but laugh. The sound echoes off the darkened walls, filling the gloom with a beacon of hope. Sure, their situation is not pleasant—no, not in any way one might twist it. But without making light of it, Modgen knows that things could quickly turn from bad to worse.

Two desperate, deprived men coming to terms with just how seriously they have destroyed the nearly limit-less possibilities of their lives ... Modgen gains confidence from the lightheartedness of Oliver's character, and he is sure that Oliver does the same. "Well then, that means there is only one thing left to do."

Oliver looks at him with perplexed evergreen eyes. "Nesvla is two territories west of Empeirus. We could travel by horse and avoid the main roads; there would be no need to book passage on a ship. We know most of the routes the Royal Guard takes, anyway."

"Agreed, but that wasn't what I was going to say. We need our money," Modgen points out, rubbing his thumb and index finger together.

A few quiet seconds float by. Those forest-green eyes grow wider than saucers at Modgen's implication. "You don't really mean ..." He trails off as he reads the sincerity in Sprightly's sparkling blue eyes and swallows. "No. There is no way we are setting foot anywhere *near* that castle again. Do you have a death wish?" Oliver stares in disbelief.

Modgen throws his hands up in a gesture of surrender. "You're right. Let's just steal our horses and live like paupers on the streets, and when we happen to stumble upon an abandoned house in the Nesvlan mountains that isn't overrun by wild animals—"

"Okay, I get it; we need coin. But we can't just waltz back into the castle with the queen having a warrant out for our heads!"

Modgen pauses. "Or can we?" His smirk broadens into a devilish grin. "They talk about people hiding in plain sight. What better way to do it than right beneath their petty little noses? Name the one kind of people that royals and nobles alike never bother to acknowledge."

The former master thinks for a moment and grimaces. "Servants?"

"*Exactly.*"

An exasperated chuckle. "So, let me get this straight. You want us to pose as servants to break into our old chambers, swipe our bags of coin, then still manage to break out without any trouble so that we can take up lives as Nesvlan tea merchants?" Oliver crosses his arms, leaning his back against the blackboard to keep from falling over.

Sprightly mulls over what his friend has just said. It's not the best plan; in fact, it seems to be quite terrible. *What are the odds that they haven't changed the locks? Or worse, that they haven't thrown everything of ours out? What if they catch us on our way in or out of the castle? Will the servants realize that two of their coworkers do not belong?* But it is this or nothing. A shot at freedom or staying locked up in his late mother's bakery for the gods know how much longer.

"Yes. Yes I do," the Lord replies nonchalantly. "Or we could just stay here in the dark, stealing food from the produce stand down the street until the guards turn up one night to break down our quarter-inch thick door?"

Oliver palms his green eyes, running his hands over

rich brown hair. "All right," he says on an exhale. He turns to erase the existing chalk on the board. "I suppose we should focus on the major plan, now."

Modgen sniggers. "If only because if this one fails, the Nesvlan mountains will be awaiting our arrival for the rest of time."

ANNALISE

Annalise Larking huddles beside the front door of the Dog's Head, pulling out a scrap of yellowed paper. The map shows the town and all its landmarks, the Dog's Head included. *An accurately drawn picture of the castle, the harbor, the sea ...* And just beyond the mainland circled in bright red ink is a marsh, dotted with speckles of land. *He said they've been hiding there*, she recalls. *What better choice do I have?* Besides, the worst that could happen would be a wasted trip, and right now, Anna has all the time in the world.

She begins folding up the makeshift map that Ivo gave her when the tavern door is thrown open.

"... absolutely insane. Heard about it yesterday. The head of her council and that treasurer of hers," a heavyset man blubbers.

His colleague shakes his stubbled jaw. "Can't believe that. Right beneath her nose." The conversation begins to trail off with the growing distance.

The lost princess pushes off from the tavern wall and tries her best to keep them in earshot. She usually isn't one to pry, but in times like these, she needs all the information she can get.

"... fired them. She says when she finds them again, she'll have both their heads."

A piece of parchment on a wooden post flickers in the breeze. Annalise walks over to it, skimming the information. *It's a decree for the heads of those men*, she realizes. *Twenty-five thousand golden suns for their safe return!* Her eyebrows shoot upward. *They must have been very important to my sister. I wonder what they did to make her so angry.*

The men she had previously been trailing fall into another crowd of pedestrians, and Annalise deems it time to head to the harbor. If all goes well, Ivo and his men will be waiting for her with their boat. Anna passes some more quaint shops, a blacksmith, an art boutique, even a psychic's tent set up on the side of the road, but she cannot stop anywhere today. *As much as I'd like to delay this meeting, I must be on my way. It is my duty*, she decides, and with that, she approaches the edge of the Royal Harbor.

Boats come into view, like a thousand tiny speckles of color blotting the Falvedrie Sea. Wooden docks jut out from the shore like fingers splayed across a sheet of blue-green cloth. A feeling of unease sparks in her belly, one reminiscent of choking on tears and seawater from so many years ago.

In the corner of her left eye, an enormous pale figure looms above white marble steps, its red and gold banner eyeing her with disgust. *Why does it seem that all roads lead me to the past?* Anna tugs her gray hood lower, searching for Ivo and his men in the web of ships and their travelers.

A man with a burly orange mustache and a pair of golden hoop earrings screams at his shipmates in a foreign tongue. A set of twins in lavender dresses prowl their way down the boarding plank of their ship, hips swaying with conceit. To her right, Annalise can hear an accent from the Savek Coast ordering workers to be more careful with the lobster when they unload it.

A blue sail. He said to look for a blue sail. There are purples, oranges, greens, reds, and yellows, but Anna cannot find one single blue sail. She begins to crack her knuckles, a nervous habit she picked up during her teen years. *Ivo, where are you?* Defeated, she takes a seat on an empty cargo box and continues to stare out into the horizon. The familiar waves loom before her like a waking nightmare, taunting her with every breath she takes. A memory surfaces, and her stomach begins to turn sour.

Anna has never much liked the sea, the smell of the salty air or the sound of each wave crashing against the sand. The thunderous power of the ocean was something that she found both inspiring and terrifying, and the thought of being sucked under was, and still is, one of her worst fears.

Perhaps that is why she has such horrifying nightmares of her past experiences with it, plummeting to what she thought was going to be her death, and then being tossed ashore by a rogue wave was worse than her wildest fantasies. Watching those same waves now, thinking about having to sail across the deep waters ... Acid stings the back of her throat.

She jumps off the empty cargo box and empties her breakfast over the edge of the dock, shaking in a cold sweat. The lost princess takes a deep breath, calming herself and spitting one last time before she hears the sound of armor approaching. *Ivo?* But it is not her late father's Captain of the Royal Guard. This guard is clad in golden armor from head to toe, and he stops behind her as she finds the strength to stand again. *One of my sister's men.* Anna swallows.

His golden helm muffles his voice. "My lady, I'm sure you've heard by now, but I'm making certain to ask every person I can. Have you seen any suspicious activity of late, particularly involving a tall, red-headed male or a brown-haired man with green eyes?"

Annalise shakes her head. "I haven't, sir. But if I do, I would report it to Her Majesty immediately."

The guard huffs a laugh. "Loyal as Ione. May the gods be with you," he blesses her as he turns on an armored heel.

Anna releases her breath and turns back to face the docks. *I have to get out of here now*, she realizes, for as fearful as she is of the sea, she is even more fearful of the devil that sits the throne and the power she currently wields. More ships are arriving, but there is still not a blue sail to be seen. *He told me to be here just after dawn. It's been half an hour since the sun has risen.* Behind her, more clanging sounds. Anna turns to discover a fresh group of guards making their rounds. *If Ivo won't come to me, then maybe I'll just have to go to him.*

A two-passenger boat is tied to the dock in front of her, silently awaiting its owners, who are hopefully nowhere to be seen. The cluster of guards is approaching rather slowly, and Annalise judges that she likely has just enough time to slip away undetected. Her worn leather boots clunk against the wood before she kneels to untie its ropes.

"We're looking for a comely man of about three-and-twenty. Have you seen him?" Anna hears a guard ask. She can't hear the mousy man's reply, but she's sure that the footsteps grow nearer.

She hurries unraveling the last of the ropes and, with a silent prayer to the gods, steps into the two-seater. She grabs hold of the oars, but just before rowing off into the choppy blue abyss, Annalise slides a silver moon next to the cleats where the boat's ropes were tied only moments before. *Hopefully that's enough for them to purchase a new one.*

The powerful blue waters lap eagerly against the sides of Anna's stolen boat, and she needs to use all her strength to push against the current. *Gods, protect me and grant me the strength and courage ...* It is a game of forward, back, then forward and back again, but little by little Anna moves farther out to sea, until she is floating atop calmer waters. *Where to now?* she worries, pulling out Ivo's poorly drawn map again. *Let's see ... If the harbor is here, and I row out just a little more, there should be an inlet to my right—*

"There it is! My boat!" A frantic man's voice carries across the water from the docks, where he stands beside an armed guard.

Oh gods, Anna swears. *Lazarus have mercy.*

"Cretch, Miles, get in the *Wanderer*!" the guard orders. "We have a boat to catch!"

Only one word comes to mind as Annalise Larking drops the map in her lap and reaches for the oars: *Row.* Her arms pump through the waves like there is no tomorrow, oars propelling her out to sea one yard at a time. In the distance, she can see the guards bolting for a small dinghy, beginning their chase. Far to her left, a boom of thunder rolls through the darkening clouds. *A storm at sea, and I'm on it. Perfect*, she thinks as her heart hammers in her chest and the oars become slippery in her palms.

The guards' boat cuts quickly through the choppy waves, much faster than the princess's boat is capable of. *If only there were two of me, then maybe I could out-row them.* The guards are gaining one row at a time, but Annalise cannot give up. *How much farther?* Like a blessing from Lazarus, a narrow section of murky water veers off to her right between two small islands.

Anna doesn't think twice before she turns her boat, rowing for her life. Adrenaline runs through her veins, keeping her arms thrashing like a rabid animal. *Just a little bit more*, she promises herself, though she has no idea how much longer it will be. The paddle in her right hand nearly frees itself with a strong wave, and Anna digs her nails into the wood to keep her luck alive.

She makes it into the inlet, losing sight of the guards by grace of the tall grove of trees that have flourished on the marshy land. Anna isn't sure which side of the marshes the tower is on, but she doesn't have time to pull out the map to find out. With a grunt, she rams her little boat into a shore of sandy mud and jumps out, ditching the oars and all.

The guards' screams are getting closer, and Annalise makes to enter the forest before her.

A puddle of sandy mud sucks at her left foot. She tries pulling, but it won't budge. *Why? Why can't things ever just go as planned?* Anna reaches down to her ankle and shifts all her weight to her right foot, until her left boot finally pops free, sending the lost princess tumbling sideways and tripping over a decaying log. Her palms hit the surface of the smelly mud with a smack, and though she feels disoriented from the fall, it sounds like the guards have found the docked boat.

Stumbling to her feet, another rattle of thunder shakes the morning air. *I need to look at the map.* She runs into the forest a little more, then turns to take solace behind a thick oak tree. Pulling free her map, she listens to the guards, who are now most definitely ashore.

"Well how far could she be? Go get her, Miles!" the guard in charge yells.

Okay, it should be somewhere east of here. Footsteps sound from behind, and Anna tenses as the man who is presumably Miles jogs nearer. *I need to move; I need to hide somewhere else. But I don't have enough time, and if I move, he'll hear me. He's too close.*

Miles slows to a halt, then moves forward a few paces. His breathing is ragged, and Anna can hear that he is on the other side of the oak that she is standing behind. Heart in her throat and hands beginning to tremble, she closes her brown eyes, trying to keep her breathing quiet. She searches inside herself for something calming, something to cling to, but Miles moves forward another step. He is directly to her right now, and if he turns his head just a smidge to his left, she will be entirely exposed.

A feeling of warmth spreads within Annalise's chest. For a split second, she feels serene and still. The world grows quieter; the bugs stop their humming, the sound of the forceful waves is dampened, and for a moment, she feels … different. *Stronger. Powerful, even.* She squeezes her shaking hands into fists, and when she opens her eyes, she finds a thick, white fog creeping over the muddy bogs.

Miles swallows. "Um …" He withdraws a step.

The white fog seeps across the ground, the gap between it and the guard growing ever smaller. Anna is frozen like a statue, lost in awe and fear. But still, she finds herself thinking the same recurrent thoughts: *Leave. Get rid of him.*

Miles yells back to his fellow guards, "Um … sir? I don't know about this." He takes another step back, then another.

The fog spreads around his sides now, making to encircle Miles in the middle of a mysterious swamp, and such a thought is what sends him running back to his friends at the shore, mud sucking at the heels of his golden boots with every retreating step. A chorus of arguments and rebuttals floods the air around the shoreline, but after the fog continues to creep toward them and the sound of distant thunder draws nearer, the guards decide to retreat to the water and call off the search.

Anna's fists slowly unclench, and she releases the tension in her neck as she lets out a long sigh. Just as gradually, the dense white fog recedes from the shoreline, then past her, until it finally dissolves into thin air as if it had never existed. *What in the name of Lazarus?* The warm sensation is gone now, uncannily correlated to the timing of the fog. She shivers.

I need to find Ivo.

Annalise

The map still in her hand, Annalise treks through the rest of the woods, making sure not to trip over any more logs or fallen branches. She watches a gull cry overhead, sending a shiver down her spine. *Where am I?* she wonders. A swamp spider dips itself from a nearby tree branch, most of Anna's courage sinking with it.

Leaving the Sapphire wasn't just scary; it was dangerous. Spending the last six years of her life in a safe place with Narelle, there wasn't much reason to leave. *Until now.* It suddenly strikes her after stepping over a mossy rock just how serious her situation is. *Being all alone out in the open, trusting old allies and new ones ... Ivo and his men could have merely been great actors still indebted to my sister's cause. What if, gods forbid, this is all a trap that I am walking straight into?*

But despite these worries, Annalise reassures herself of the duty and honor that her father surrounded himself with in choosing his men. *And besides, other than Narelle, I really have nothing to lose.*

At last, the world opens up to dry, sandy ground bordered by a strip of blue-green water on its right from an inlet. *This must be where I would have ended up had I kept paddling.*

The lost princess looks up. Built on the sand, the old watchtower stands tall and proud beneath a thundering sky. Its gray stone walls are covered in patches of moss, and vines of ivy ascend its height, which reaches high into the morning mist. It is much larger than most watchtowers, its width almost six yards across, and how many levels it holds Anna cannot say. Scattered windows have been built into the stone, but a low fog clouds around the top of the tower, hiding the rest from sight.

Anna approaches the tower's wooden door, the sounds of insects and bog animals singing back to life. *Here goes nothing*, she thinks. With a dainty hand, she taps on the door.

No answer.

She looks to her left and right, unnerved to be so exposed, out in the open. She waits a few more moments before knocking a bit harder this time.

Not a sound, aside from the nature around her. Another rumble of thunder crackles and raindrops begin to drop from the heavens, dampening the gray fabric of her cloak. *I need to get inside*, she frets, but suddenly the wooden door opens with a moan, and without a word, strong hands pull her inside.

Ivo slams shut the door, locking several locks, and turning to face Annalise Larking in the entrance. At ground level, a small kitchen with a wooden table and chairs sit vacant with a candle burning where food should be. The princess takes in the damp scent of rain mixed with bread and stew, rather earthy but not uninviting.

"I thought you would be Dallis," he grumbles.

"I thought you were supposed to find me at the harbor," she responds, confused as can be. "And who is Dallis?"

The former Captain sighs. "I sent Dallis into town to warn you not to attempt getting here anytime soon. We ran into trouble at the harbor a few days ago and have been avoiding it ever since—well, those of us that got away, anyway. Desmond and one of his men took Sven and Tym. The gods only know what the queen's doing to them now ..." his voice trails off.

Anna's heart sinks to her stomach. *I know what she will be doing to them*, she thinks with disgust. *She will be using every torture device imaginable to pry information from their mouths, and when they break ...* Annalise cannot let herself think that far ahead; about what it might mean for her own safety, about the safety of Ivo and Dallis and Narelle. *No, I can't let that happen.*

"I don't know where Dallis is at the moment, but we can't leave this tower at the nonce." Ivo clenches his jaw. "In the meantime, perhaps we should get you acquainted with our humble hideout."

The short trek up the first flight of steps has Anna and Ivo emerging into the second level, which seems to be ... *A war room?* the princess wonders. A long table occupies the center of the small area, which is bordered by bookshelves and trunks overflowing with blankets and parchment. Chairs surround the nearest side of the table, while the other has none. A large, detailed map is spread over its cedar surface, weighed down by various carved figures in different shapes, sizes, and colors. Annalise slips over the two steps it takes to get to the table.

A brown wooden horse head sits atop the drawing of the watchtower on its marshy lands. To the island's west is a depiction of the harbor, and to the west of that are drawings of every location in town. South of the main town, Anna finds the slums. The Sapphire is painted in shades of white and cobalt, and she can make out the market stands farther down the street. Much to her interest, however, are the red Xs etched over different places all across the map. She casts a look at Ivo.

He crosses his thick, muscled arms. "Those were the

places where we searched for you. Crossed them off after no success."

Her eyes stop at a red X scribbled over a drawing of the Dog's Head. "You should have tried that tavern more than once. That's where I make my income."

Ivo's gray-blue eyes widen. "Doing *what*, exactly?"

Anna smiles. "Playing *halsen*."

A lighthearted chuckle is heard from someplace Annalise cannot sense. Light footsteps sound from the level above, along with the intermittent sound of metal on stone.

Anna tenses, looking up only to find an old man hobbling down the steps, her heart stopping in disbelief. His dusty green cape is closed by links of silver, lying heavily across his frail chest. Wrinkled hands curl over a dark metal cane, its handle shaped like a curved black feather. Her mouth begins to twitch when she takes in the sight of the man's familiar blue eyes and oversized mustache, now white with age. His brown hair is gone, but his kind smile maintains the precious ability to warm her heart.

"You've hardly changed a bit," Master Tasman notes in his gentle voice.

Annalise wipes a tear from her brown eyes, choking back a sob at the sight of her former tutor. *Six years*, she thinks. *Six years, and a lifetime ago. A different world ago.* She remembers scouring over ancient books, learning to write—first in print and then in cursive, mastering arithmetic and then algebra, listening to enlightening lectures on the histories of the kingdom and its territories.

"You've grown bald," she quips with a light smile, and at this he laughs again.

The lost princess strides toward her old master and embraces him with her cloaked arms. *He still smells the same*, she takes comfort in knowing. *Like fire smoke and fresh parchment.* Master Tasman carefully pulls away to get a better look at Annalise.

She knows what he will see: an understated twenty-year-old woman wearing a gray cloak, whose pants are tucked into shabby leather boots with mud stains from the marshes. No makeup, no fancy hairstyle, not a trace of perfume. Just a face that could easily be missed, especially in large crowds. She awaits judgement, but it never comes.

"Hiding at the Sapphire, was it?" He shakes his head, bushy white mustache cutting through the air with each turn. "Six years, you've been right under our noses, and we still couldn't find you. Well, here you are, and now we haven't the slightest idea of what to do with you." He chuckles.

Ivo clears his throat. "Actually, there is one thing we can do," he corrects, shoulders proud and tall. "I served for your father as I intend to serve for you. As the Captain of your Royal Guard, it is my duty to brief you on the current state of the kingdom."

Anna's eyes widen, but a smile blooms across her lovely face. *With what luck have I managed to obtain all of this?* She walks with Master Tasman back to the map table and seats herself in a chair across from Ivo, who leans forward with his hands splayed on the map before them.

"We've assigned the most pertinent locations with a carved piece of wood, courtesy of Tasman. Since the map is only of Empeirus, there are no pieces for surrounding territories, like Nesvla or Javir. A blue gem for the Sapphire, a green ship for the harbor, a red apple for the markets in the slums—"

At this, Anna smirks, reflecting on Robbin and the fruit she had a habit of pilfering. Her eyes travel upward to where Ivo now points, and the smile instantly curdles.

"And of course, we can't forget about our primary conflict," he notes gloomily, tapping the top of a red snake which sits coiled above the castle.

Anna's stomach twists. "My sister. Why were her guards after you?" It seems a bit presumptuous, but she thinks that was the case.

Ivo glances to Tasman, shoulders caving ever so slightly. "The day you disappeared into the Falvedrie Sea, Adrianna assumed the crown under the growing belief that you had drowned. Your body had never been found, and after a month, the new queen officially called off the search. Most everyone worked through their grief in private, but some of us felt compelled to keep looking, and there were mentions of a nameless ghost who moved from tavern to tavern. It got me and my men wondering.

"After a year of her reign, a handful of men realized how unfit Adrianna really was. She was cold and callous; so at odds with the way you and Aimelie and your parents were." He shrugs his huge shoulders. "It wasn't that we were disobeying the queen's orders, per se. She had called off the search for you, but she never explicitly stated that it was a punishable offense if people did.

"One night, it was just me, Sven, Dallis, and Tym, and we were out enjoying our night off. I don't know what nudged me to go in, but for some reason I felt drawn to the Dog's Head, so we went inside. I bought each of the men an ale and had to open my mouth. I asked the bartender if he'd seen the gray ghost, and when he shook his head and asked me why, I said that we hadn't given up our search for the lost princess." Ivo shakes his thick neck.

"Little did we know, Desmond, *Captain Jrehart*, frequented the tavern often, and overheard our revelation. He told Adrianna that we could be inciting a treasonous act to see her off the throne, and that was the end of that. Luckily, she was merciful that day and left us with our heads, but she threatened our lives if we were ever seen lurking around the castle anytime thereafter."

Anna takes a deep breath. *So much to learn, so much to consider.* "And when you were caught in the harbor ..."

Ivo nods. "Too close for her liking, I guess. Every time we make a trip to town, it must be done carefully. From now on, we are going to dock our boat down here." He taps on a beach south of the harbor. "This way, we can avoid dealing with that issue."

Master Tasman huffs a laugh. "Guorden's Beach, yes. If there isn't now a surplus of guards walking about the city under heightened security."

Annalise's eyes light up in recognition. "Which there definitely are, but not for your heads."

The men exchange looks.

"It seems my sister has been betrayed by the Master of her High Council and her Royal Treasurer. There are wanted posters everywhere throughout town. I would suggest lying low for a little while."

"And I might suggest the same for you, Princess," Ivo declares. "Your safety is paramount, and if the queen learns you are still alive ..."

Annalise nods. "I know, I know. I've been doing it for years now." She gives a sorrowful smile, an expression much too old for her age. A moment of silence passes between them, and Anna finds herself toying with her fingers.

Master Tasman stands, pushing to his feet with the help of his black cane. "Gone are the days when a poor man can work his way up to riches. Taxes are outrageously high, the divide between social classes has never been so wide, and crime is more popular than ever. The Royal Guard has become as lenient as its queen, turning a blind eye to imposing threats, and sometimes even joining them. And at the top of this rusting chain sits our monarch, stuffing her contemptuous face with iced pastries and sneering at the common folk like they are roaches beneath her silk-slippered feet. The people are angry," he finishes.

Ivo looks to the lost princess. "Not everyone is afraid to make a stand, Princess. There are supporters hidden amidst the rubble of the fallen kingdom, and many more folks who can be turned, given the current state of our affairs."

Annalise turns her dark eyes to the map and its markers. "I need allies. But how?"

Tasman nods. "You will need to make use of your connections, Annalise. I'm sure you already are familiar with a few safe bets, ones who will make excellent contacts throughout town."

Anna's brown eyes sharpen. "You mean spies?"

"Trusted links to the city that will serve a few main purposes: to gain information, to recruit new contacts, and to spread rumors."

The princess swallows. This is much more serious than she thought. It is not just executing a plan; it is treason. *But it must be done.* "I was taken in by a courtesan who is five years older than me. Her name is Narelle, and she works at the Sapphire. She would be perfect."

Ivo picks up the cobalt gem that sits above the sketch of the brothel, casually tossing it in his meaty hand. "Any others?"

She drums her fingers along the cedar tabletop as she thinks. "I know a merchant in the market near the Sapphire. He goes by Robbin, though I'm not sure how genuine his loyalty would be ..." *And considering that he is the very merchant that sold me out to Ivo and his men only days past, I doubt that he would be a wise option.*

Ivo places the carved gemstone back on the map. "You'll need to make a trip back to town, but we can't risk doing such until this fervor dies down a little. In the meantime, you should continue your studies with Tasman. There is still a lot you need to know."

Annalise beams at her old master, attempting to hide the anxiety that is gnawing at her like a dog with a bone. *So much to process, so much to do, so many things that could go wrong.*

"Oh, I almost forgot," Ivo rumbles in his gravelly voice. "You need your own symbol," he tells Anna, tapping on the map.

The princess snickers. She stares at the red snake, poised and ready to strike. *Should I choose something strong, like a lion or a bear? What about something venomous, to match the snake's bite? A scorpion from the southern lands or a deadly spider could do.* Annalise broods for a moment. *It's just not my way.* And then it comes to her.

"Make me a black crow," she decides.

Ivo looks puzzled, but underneath his large white mustache, Tasman chuckles with glee.

"You want to be a common bird?" Ivo asks her in disbelief. No doubt he would have chosen a stallion or a tiger.

Annalise laughs, the sound sweet like honey. Tasman takes a few aimless steps around the tiny room. "A bear might be strong, a snake may be poisonous, but there are many attributes of the crow that others tend to overlook."

"Like?" Ivo urges for an explanation from the old man.

"Like trickery, deceit, and most importantly, wisdom. Strength is one thing, but to outsmart an opponent is quite another." The old master turns to Annalise. "Well chosen, my dear."

Aimelie

The tufted teal ottoman groans quietly as Aimelie Larking leans forward to add more blue to the canvas. *Just a little more in the center*, she critiques. The painting is an amalgam of purples, yellows, oranges, blues, and greens; more abstract than realistic. It isn't something that Melie usually aims for, but today, she needs a painting that encompasses the full range of her emotions.

The guilt gnaws at her sensitive heart, chewing up her happiness and spitting it out. *I didn't mean to do it*, she cries to herself, but little can soothe the growing tension in her stomach, the worry snowballing bigger and bigger with every day the sun rises and falls with still no word.

Melie floods the tip of her paintbrush in red. She globs

the bright paint right next to the blue, overlapping them slightly to form a ruddy shade of purple. Her curly, golden hair shines healthily in the sunlight, and she wears a teal and silver gown that has already been stained at least three different colors in the past few minutes.

I shouldn't have done it, she chastises herself. *I knew the risks.* Working another spot of orange into the piece, she drowns her feelings with the familiar scent of fresh paint, and the smoothness of a brush handle. Melie is so absorbed by her painting, that a knock on the door jerks her right hand, sweeping a smudge of green into yellow.

"You may enter," she calls, washing her paintbrush in a small jar of water and setting it upright to dry.

Linden enters, wearing his usual teal tunic and gray pants. His soft brown eyes and hair are more uplifting than Aimelie would have expected them to be, and she wonders if perhaps she has gotten so used to his presence that she felt rather lonely the past three days when he left for a family wedding in Fetland.

"Princess Aimelie," he greets her with a bow, and Melie just laughs.

"Sit down, please; you're making me feel absurd," she smiles in her stained painting dress.

Linden grins, moving into the matching seat beside her. With the silver curtains drawn, the sunlight beaming in through the large windows, and the sound of laughter,

Aimelie's room almost seems pleasant again. *Like a memory of cheerfulness brought back to life.* Linden eyes her canvas, eyebrows upraised at the utter gracelessness of the work.

"It's not supposed to be anything," she explains rather embarrassed. "It's just a way for me to express my emotions."

Linden gives her a warm smile. "You must have a lot of very complex emotions," he chides, which earns him a merry laugh from the princess.

"I find it easier to express myself through art than to put my feelings into words. Anyway," she says as she screws the lids back on her paints. "Enough about me. What's in the folder?"

Her mentor pulls out a stack of papers—all written in different hands, all signed with different names—and each one addressed to the Queen of Empeirus, Adrianna Larking.

"The queen has bestowed upon me a list of complaints from the farming district that are to be remedied the best they can at court come Thursday," Linden informs her. "She believes it's time for you to hold the session."

Aimelie's already-hollow insides wither with dread. "I don't mind helping my sister, or helping the farmers and their families, but isn't it a queen's duty to be part of her court?"

Linden's brown eyes twinkle with amusement as he tries to fight a smile. "It is not my place to speak," he admits, yet his eyes betray his opinion on the matter. Instead, he hands her the documents, watching her curiously while she browses through them.

The princess begins filing through the letters. *So many; there have to be at least seventy*, she thinks with both shock and dismay. Ever since her wicked sister's imposition of the food tax, people everywhere are struggling to feed their families. *The worst part is that the food isn't even being imported.* A vision of a poor man laboring over the growth of his crops comes to Melie's mind. Her hands nearly wrinkle the seventy-something forms as she envisions him having to pay an arm and a leg for his own handiwork, just so that he can keep himself and his family alive to do it all over again.

She brings her attention to the letter she happened to flip to, and skims through its contents.

"Your Majesty,

I have only one acre of land to farm, but it is simply not ~~enuff~~ *enough. I need more land, at least three acres worth, to provide enough food to feed our family and our lord."*

Melie saddens at the hopelessness of the farmer's words. But the feeling is nothing compared to the disgust she experiences upon reading her sister's response, scrawled carelessly across the bottom of the page.

"One-and-a-half more acres. No more, no less."

Aimelie looks to Linden, blue eyes furious. "What is *this* supposed to be?"

Linden bows his head. "Your sister has written what she would bestow upon each patron if she were at court. Given that you will be the one holding court on Thursday, it will be up to you to deliver each of her wishes to all the patrons that attend."

Just for a second, rage exceeds her guilt, and Aimelie has a sudden urge to dump her paint all over her sister's handwritten orders. Her manicured nails hold the papers tighter, leaving crescent-shaped imprints on the parchment.

Linden looks up at her with caramel brown eyes. "I wish I could tell you otherwise, but I don't make the decisions. I only give them to people," he says quietly.

Melie releases a heavy sigh, full of burdens and guilt and heartache that has been festering for far too long. Yet when she meets Linden's eyes, she gives him a smile.

"Enough work for today. Paint with me," she orders, waiting for an excuse to rise from his handsome lips.

Instead, Linden barks a laugh. "You want me to call off the rest of our itinerary to *paint*?"

"With me, yes." Melie's blue eyes twinkle with delight. She shoves her abstract piece aside and moves the easel between the two of them, replacing the old canvas with a fresh ivory one. After handing him a brush, she nudges her teal ottoman closer to his own and retrieves her own paintbrush.

He dips his brush in a tin of bright yellow paint, then pauses before turning to Melie. "What are we painting?" Linden's brown eyes glitter with humor.

Melie shrugs her slender shoulders. "Anything you want."

Her mentor pauses to ponder for a moment, and then lifts his brush to the canvas, creating a ring of long, full ovals. Linden cleans his brush before dousing it with a chocolate brown, then begins filling in the center of the ring with brown dots.

"Ah," Aimelie sounds her recognition of the chosen object. While Linden is filling in the sunflower, she uses a deep green and sets to work on the stem and its leaves. They work this way for some unknown length of time, painting in a comfortable silence until Linden begins to chuckle. Melie sets down her brush.

"What's so funny?" she asks him with a smirk.

Linden shakes his short brown hair. "All the orders, all the details, all the 'do this' and 'do that' from your sister, and here I am disregarding everything she's told me to paint with you." He continues to laugh.

Melie mirrors his amusement, brushing back a stray strand of her golden hair. "And what's wrong with that?"

He stops his laughter to examine the subtle seriousness of Aimelie's charming face. "Since the dawn of time, we were told to follow certain guidelines. A servant isn't supposed to dine with his master. A farmer is a laborer, not a friend to nobles." Linden pauses, eyeing the mediocre sunflower. "A mentor should be only a mentor and shouldn't stray from the order of their position."

Aimelie leans forward ever so slightly. "I'll tell you a secret," she whispers, those big eyes glowing. "I don't care about those kinds of rules," she divulges, and then returns to a healthy distance away from her mentor.

Linden's caramel eyes widen and a handsome smile blooms across his face. "You are nothing like your sister," he tells her, and she feels like she had needed to hear it spoken aloud to give her that shred of relief which she has so long been searching for.

She makes a pointed glance at the stack of documents and shoots Linden a smile. "You could say that again," she quips. Melie picks her paintbrush back up and begins painting a sky-blue background. "The way I see things, we have a limited amount of time here on this earth." A memory of Annalise's untimely departure flutters in the depths of her mind: The feeling of her holding Melie so tightly the night their parents passed, the sensation of a black hole forming in the pit of her stomach upon learning of her eldest sister's disappearance.

She pushes the thoughts away, continuing with her explanation. "When we meet the gods after surviving a lifetime of hurdles, we are judged by our deeds and personalities. Were we vain and cruel, caring little about other people and their struggles? Or did we live with kindness and compassion, trying hard to help uplift those who have fallen before us?"

Aimelie has Linden's full attention.

She looks once more at the folder of papers. "I believe in attempting to make the world a kinder place, and following Dria's orders would do anything but that. I choose to serve the people, the realm, regardless of how full their coffers are, or what gods they pray to, or what their favorite color is," she says with a smile, her blue eyes shining. "Because in the end, changing the world for the better doesn't come from how much money we make or how expensive our clothing is. It comes from who we are as people, and how we opt to treat others."

Melie finds Linden staring at her intently, keenly observing her doe-eyed face. "You would make a fine queen," he whispers sincerely.

That could be considered treason, Melie thinks with a sort of rebellious pleasure that she rarely embraces. She blushes, shaking her honey-blonde curls. "That should have been my other sister. Annalise would have made the world a better place." Melie stops herself before tears can threaten her composure.

Linden nods softly, then looks to their completed painting. The sunflower is bright and cheerful, with all the tenor of a summer afternoon.

"It's not half bad," he remarks, slouching back in his chair.

Melie giggles, rubbing the last of the wet paint onto her ruined teal and silver dress. "I rather like it," she agrees.

An awkward silence falls between them, one of not knowing how to move on from their previous conversation. Melie turns to say something to Linden but finds him studying her once more in silent admiration. He quickly redirects his eyes to the folder of documents and makes to hoist them onto his lap.

"Tomorrow at noon, then?" he asks her. "I will have to push our time up so that we can fulfill everything we didn't go over today." He grins.

Aimelie chuckles as she nods. They stand, and Linden bows to the princess. "Enjoy the rest of your evening." He bids her farewell as he slips out of the silver door, caramel eyes vanishing with a kind smile.

He is such a pleasant person to be around, she finds herself thinking as she cleans up the painting supplies. Yet, as much as the thought is comforting, her intuition warns her of something she would rather ignore. *He may also be dangerous.*

The sheer weight of the idea is enough to sit her down once again, this time on her bed. She brings a hand to her stomach, trying and failing to calm herself with deep, steady breaths. The afternoon sunlight is glowing orange now, signaling to Melie that dusk is falling fast. *So might I be, if I don't tread lightly*, she reminds herself. But the sunflower stands proudly, yellow petals almost brilliant enough to send Aimelie's worries and guilty conscience to bed.

Almost.

ANNALISE

Annalise massages her temples with long fingers. She rereads the handwritten sentence once again: *"The Queen's High Council: Royal Ambassador, Lord Earlmence; Lord of Merchants, Lord Docketry; Master of the High Council, Oliver McHenry..."*

How do I even know if this is all still accurate? she wonders. Her old master had given her the book just yesterday, and she has been browsing through it ever since, with hardly any breaks. It is brimming with descriptions of newly appointed individuals and their notable actions of recent times. *Well, as recently as five years ago, before Tasman and Ivo and his men were dismissed from Adrianna's inner circle.*

Such is the reasoning for Anna's worries about its accuracy. *Times change, and people change with them.* Based on street knowledge from her previous life in the slums, she is sure that Desmond Jrehart is still her sister's Captain of the Royal Guard, and Aimelie is still in line for the throne, but ...

Aimelie, Anna sighs. *I would do anything to see my little sister again.* She closes the book, which is giving her a pulsing headache, and stands to stretch out her legs.

It has been a few days since she last was outside of the tower walls, and Anna is already getting restless. Ivo and Tasman tell her that with precautions, traveling to town should be feasible by now, but Anna fears that more guards might recognize her from the harbor incident. And with those two wanted councilmen roaming the streets, the influx of guards makes that possibility a lot more likely.

Annalise rolls her neck, stretching out the last of its built-up tension. She pads over to the wooden bookshelf, which is stuffed full of all sorts of ancient tomes, their spines worn from time and use. Master Tasman brought some of them with him after being dismissed from the castle five years ago, and more have been arriving ever since. *How does he get so many expensive books?*

The shelves are so overcrowded, that the old master has taken to cramming them in every free space and existing cranny of the little library room. *Granted, there isn't much to do when you're stuck in a watchtower that sits on an island,* Anna permits. She allows herself a thought she has been avoiding for some time: *Whatever did Tasman, of all people, do to spike the queen's rage?* Perhaps the lost princess will never know, for she doesn't believe that he would willingly tell her, and she doesn't feel it is her place to ask. *Still, one has to wonder …*

Her brown eyes raking over the titles, she stops on one that was written by the Master of the High Council during the reign of her late royal grandfather, after whom she had received her royal colors. "*Notes on the Progression of a Royal*," the gold-embossed letters read against its olive-green cover. Annalise recognizes the book at once. She used to see her master reference it during a few of their lessons.

"*The character of one of the Royal Family must reflect that which the title denotes: poise, class, and grace*," Anna reads. "*The child will, one day, have the potential to lead our great kingdom to success. How the kingdom's people view their monarch can determine the difference between a nation's peace and civil unrest.*"

Her dark eyes flick to the next paragraph.

"*A female royal should be reserved, especially around men. Should the time come that she is to be courted or wed, the woman should never ask for the favor of a man. Instead, she should continue to be sociable and courteous, but await the man's advancement.*"

The lost princess makes a sound of disgust. *'Sociable and courteous,' and nothing more than something pretty to look at.* There are few things in the world that bother Annalise Larking more than a lack of being genuine. *This book would have been training me to become a liar not only to myself, but to the entire world. What could be worse than living your life as an imposter in an attempt to please others?*

Anna skims through the rest of the chapter, then reads the next heading:

"The Importance of Dance:

As vital as any art, both males and females born of the royal bloodline should be particularly familiar with dance. Such arts must be learned to obtain the highest form of regard from other nobles, including those who may be arranged to form advantageous marriages in the future."

Anna skips down to the bottom of the yellowing page.

"For females:

A woman of royalty should most definitely be accustomed to the following courtroom dances ..."

The book goes into detail on many dances, none of which Annalise is familiar with: the Queen's Dance, the Lily Waltz, the Godrian Two-step, the Dance of the Falvedrie. She glances at the gap in the stone floor where the flight of stairs descends to the next level. Not a peep to be heard, not a flicker of light to be seen. *Ivo and Tasman must be in the kitchen,* she thinks. With that, she flips back to the page on the Queen's Dance.

A poorly drawn diagram helps Anna decipher the steps as she manages to follow the dance. She begins slowly, going over the steps drawn in the book and making sure she doesn't miss anything. She moves left, then right, and then sweeps her right foot over the floor; taps the toes of her left foot and then twirls in a complete circle. The candle flame flickers on her desk, sending her thin shadow dancing with her along the gray walls.

Anna realizes how silly she must look, dancing alone in a tunic and pants with her worn leather boots. *The Queen's Dance is supposed to be performed by a lady in heels wearing a bejeweled gown with a partner.* A small laugh escapes her lips as she moves faster now, becoming more fluent in her movements.

Anna imagines how the dance must look when properly done—the sound of heels clicking on the white marble of the Throne Room, the stares from the audience as they look on with lustful eyes, the lady's dance partner in his finery—and her stomach quivers. Her royal parents had no doubt one day hoped to marry her to some high-up nobleman, but the princess herself had never wanted that. *I would marry the poorest boy in the land if I loved him so*, she remembers thinking.

She envisions herself dancing the Queen's Dance as a soon-to-be queen, taking a nobleman's hand, and exchanging steps. *An emerald dress with black heels, and the man is wearing navy ...* The dance moves more gracefully now, and much faster than before. Closing her eyes, Annalise scuffs the heel of a boot over the floor's stone, then pivots. The light of the candle continues to flicker, her shadow swaying and mirroring her movements all over the walls. She spins and twirls, losing herself in a rhythm only she can hear; the swell of silent music growing louder, she throws her slender arm out upon the completion of a spin—

The sound of shattering glass makes her gasp, covering her mouth with both hands to stifle a scream. A picture frame rocks slowly on the wall where it barely hangs, its glass interior demolished from the explosion. Annalise gathers her breath, preparing an excuse as to why she has destroyed a picture on the wall. Seconds pass, but Ivo and Tasman must not have heard. Closing and then reopening her brown eyes, she moves to examine it more closely.

There aren't any stray objects that could have cracked the panel of glass, and if there were, she was right in front of it when it happened. *Right in front of it* ... The picture frame is hanging directly across from where she threw out her hand at the end of her dance. She dares a glance from the frame to her hand. *That would be absurd.*

An unwarranted memory surfaces in Anna's mind, one of a white fog that came and ebbed based on the opening and closing of her hands. The way it trilled across the marsh upon her will to be concealed, then faded when she was safe. The memory morphs into another, one much more dangerous to remember: A child running for her life, a darkened tunnel with no end—*No, the end was only boarded-up. And yet I shouldn't have been strong enough to break down nailed-up boards with my tiny hands.*

A chill breeze slithers against the back of her neck. *No—that's preposterous. It can't be. Only gods have those sorts of powers.* She laughs to herself, bending down to carefully salvage the pieces of glass that now mottle the floor.

Once the glass has been disposed of, the princess drifts once again back to the library desk. She sits herself in the chair, frowning at the discomfort the wooden seat has to offer. Pushing away her books, Annalise blindly moves to grab her cup of tea. It has grown cold, she soon finds after taking a sip, but she is too lazy to make the trek all the way down to the first floor just to heat it up again. She sets it down in front of her, staring at her glossy reflection on its surface.

Paranoia grabs hold of her once again, and she finds herself stealing another glance at the stone steps. Not a soul to be seen nor heard, but Anna must be sure, for what she is about to try could very well be labeled as insanity. She takes in a deep breath, preparing herself to look like a complete and utter fool. *Just for fun*, she tells herself. Holding a graceful hand over the top of the teacup, Anna visualizes, prays that it will not work, and waits.

One second passes.

Two.

Three.

And then something entirely impossible happens.

A small droplet of tea emerges from the surface of the liquid, hovering in the electric air just beneath her palm. Anna practically convulses with bewilderment and shock as the bead of tea falls with a *plop* back into the cup. *It doesn't make sense*, she thinks frantically. She knows it shouldn't make sense, and this is what scares her the most.

I've gone mad. I am seeing things that aren't real, but I understand that they can't be. Perhaps Adrianna was right to see me off the throne. Who should be ruled by a mad queen? Annalise presses a hand to her mouth, trying to keep back tears. *I have been a waif, a thief, a gambler, and now I am mad.*

Immediately, she turns to the old bookshelf, teeming with tomes. *There has to be something in here.* What she is searching for, she has no idea. *Something on the gods, a book on strange accounts of supernatural ability?* Panicked fingers slip over their hardback covers, shoving them back into their places one by one. *A World in Orange; Apothecary for the Experienced Master; The History of Empeirus Circa 1510 to 1630.* No books on the deities or metaphysics.

Breathing ragged, she thinks about any other possible places to search for information. *I've been to the bookshop in town, but it's mostly filled with fiction and history.* The lost princess is sure there are others, but none so close as that one. She hangs her head in defeat. *This library doesn't have what I'm looking for...* An exasperated breath passes through her perfect lips. *... But the Royal Library would.*

Her hands begin to tremble, and she closes them over top of her beautiful face. *Then I would be undeniably mad,* she knows. The Royal Library is located inside of the castle, where her sister, Adrianna, likely spends her time eating grapes on the throne rather than ruling her kingdom. To sneak her way into the white-walled abode would be crazy.

Of course, most of the kingdom believes Annalise to be dead, which would make slipping in anonymously much more doable, but ... Anna envisions the red and gold banner of her sister's sigil waving ominously in the harbor wind. *Like a warning.* But she knows what she saw, and she knows that she needs more information. *Where else am I supposed to find answers? It's not like I can just tell Tas that I have supernatural powers! How quickly he and Ivo would revoke their plans for seeing me on the throne.*

Anna sighs. *If I am going to even consider this—which is insane—I need to make one hundred percent certain that something crazy is truly going on.*

She paces a few steps until she is halfway across the little library that is her bedroom. Straightening her shoulders and swallowing her fear, she holds out her delicate fingers. The teacup does nothing. She exhales, thanking the gods for preventing another inexplicable episode.

And then it begins to rattle. It is faint at first, but then it gradually builds up its momentum and launches into the air, sailing directly for Annalise's awe-stricken face. She nearly trips backward to stop the cup, but the flying mug halts once between her hands, spilling tea onto the stone floors just before her well-worn boots. Mouth agape, fear choking off any words she could possibly form, Annalise removes her hands from the air around the teacup and slowly paces to her left while she concentrates.

The cup hovers in the air—a bit unsteadily, but still it floats—like it is suspended from some imaginary string. She continues to walk around it, watching curiously as her focus on the object becomes more sharpened and pointed, until she can levitate it so well that it looks to be sitting on an invisible table. She stops her pacing, folding her arms and squinting her deep-brown eyes in fascination.

Her head snaps to the right at a voice, her concentration breaking with it.

"Dinner is ready!" Tasman bellows up from the first floor, and the white teacup plummets to the ground, bathing the stone in a puddle of cold, Earl Grey tea.

VEGA

It has been years since Vega has celebrated Glory of the Gods Day with her family, but she remembers what it is like. Blue and gold streamers, flags, and decorations; the whistling tunes of flutes and the guttural harping of lutes; and most vividly, the enormous blue fires around which celebrators dance to revere the gods and goddesses. While Vega's father was not necessarily the type of man to dance around a fire with strangers, her mother embraced the holiday's wildness. Vega can still recall her mother's citrine eyes dazzling with joy as she partook in the day's extravagant affairs.

She would love this dress, the manipulator notes ruefully as she slips the silk over her petite form. The long, lime-green dress brings out the color of her feline eyes, its thin straps exposing most of her shoulders. *She was always so full of life and zest before she left. Perhaps that was what she was searching for.* Her reminiscing comes to an end when she finds herself staring at her reflection in the mirror, so different from the reflection she saw in the temple a few days ago.

Vega shivers at the oddness of the previous day. Her emotional state must have triggered her manipulation abilities, and for some reason she had channeled Elouthera. *But crying* actual *silver tears?* Vega decides not to ponder too much on that part. She is only grateful that the men who showed up after that old lady screamed never had a chance to see Vega in her altered form. *They probably thought that poor woman mad.*

Satisfied with her change of attire, Vega heads for the lobby, ignoring stares of men and women alike, and at last finds Christa near the large mahogany doors. The small heels of her silver flats click against the black and white tiles of the foyer as she ambles over to her friend.

"Wow, look at you!" Christa beams beside their colleagues in a flowing dress of lilac chiffon. Its cut is much more revealing than Vega's, but Christa doesn't seem to be fazed.

The manipulator blushes, shyly pushing a chunk of jet-black hair behind her ear. "Thanks. You look amazing too," she smiles.

Christa dramatically places a hand on her heart in

gratitude, then takes Vega by the arm. "You've met Trina and Gesset before, right?"

She eyes the long-faced girl and the boy with navy eyes, then nods her head. "I think I met them at your get-together a few months ago?"

Trina and Gesset smile at Vega, exchanging greetings with her as any polite soul normally would. They seem nice enough; Trina is a bit of a talker with a knack for picking out people's flaws, and Gesset cares more about himself than anything else in the world, but both are cordial beings that Vega could stand to be around for the remainder of the day.

The afternoon Wembleton sky is dotted with fluffy pink clouds as Vega and her companions set foot in Darrion's Square. Just two blocks south of the House of Perception, the Square is rarely bustling with life—which is why it looks so outrageously abnormal today, with its hordes of attendees crowding every vendor stand, show, and food cart in sight.

While the houses that line the Square are of typical Wembleton fashion—neutral black, white, gray, and beige—the trees that surround the grassy area have been adorned with gold and blue streamers and ornaments, their branches swaying from the excess weight that has been added in celebration of the gods. Some patrons in the neighborhood have even gone so far as to set out a few Glory of the Gods Day decorations on their front porches: a white statue of Ione sits in front of one house, while Vega spots another bust of Valea, Lazarus's wife, posing matronly upon the steps of a black brick abode.

"Have you ever seen anything so amazing?" Christa exclaims.

Indeed, Vega has not. Wafts of spicy nutmeg and earthy carob float on a rogue breeze from the nearest food cart, the smells comforting enough to make Vega's toes curl. A closer inspection reveals a generous cart full of spiced muffins, the tops of the pastries bubbling over their blue and gold liners. Beside the muffin vendor, wheels of fine cheeses form a backdrop for an elaborate display of sliced peaches, pears, and red and green apples, swirling their way across the wooden cart's counter. The rich scent of freshly baked brie on Wembleton's classic cinnamon-raisin toast adds even more allure to the cheese cart, and Christa lets out a squeal.

They pass a few more carts that are just as enticing. One with a dozen different types of smoked meats and fish, their kabobs seasoned with local herbs; another whose garlicky, mashed lentils are enough to make Vega's mouth water; and the drink cart, kindly offering up free samples of their homemade mead. Figuring that it is too early in the day for alcohol, Vega swipes a cup of their coconut green tea, breathing in the steam that dances on the early autumn air.

Beyond the many food carts are merchants selling a

variety of godly goods, their stands overflowing with decorative masks, capes, statues, and figurines. Their large velvet hats give off the pizazz that the holiday is so well known for.

One well-hatted young man calls out to Vega, "Over here, love! I have a mask that will bring out those incredible green eyes of yours!"

Vega gives the boy a reserved smirk and hides her face with a hand.

"Come on, Veg! He's only flirting with you." Christa jokes with her.

She mirrors Christa's amusement to mask her embarrassment. *Why can't I be more like Christa?* Maybe it is just her discomfort, but Vega swears that the temperature is rising as they walk closer to the heart of the Square's grassy field.

A flutist plays a gorgeous melody honoring Dimity, the Goddess of Wisdom and Justice; soft and flowing but also full of a solid sort of power. In another corner, a middle-aged man picks the strings of his lute in discord, a song for the God of Darkness and Decay, Anzac. Vega shivers, despite the heat. She can't imagine praying to any gods or goddesses who come from the darker side of their religion.

A tap on the shoulder from Gesset catches her by surprise as he points to a ring of small golden fires burning steadily around the main attraction: the blue bonfire. *So that's why I was getting so hot.* Christa leads the way toward the plethora of people singing and dancing around the smaller fires, waiting their turn to twirl to the rhythm of a hymn around the enormous blue fire.

Gods, it's huge, thinks Vega in awe. Its blue flames shoot up at least seven feet high, gray smoke billowing from its flickering flames. The pyre underneath must be five feet in length, the fire's cobalt center burning brightly around the pyramid of wooden logs.

"Now there's a fire," Gesset drawls, a self-absorbed grin staining his otherwise handsome face.

Trina snickers, shoving her purse into Gesset's free arms. "Hold this," she commands him, before storming off into the crowds to find a spot to dance.

The song of Lazarus fills the bright autumn day, its thundering, authoritarian beat so at odds with the sun peeking out from behind the pink clouds. Trina is swallowed by the crowd, her yellow dress nowhere to be seen.

"What am I supposed to do with her bloody purse?" Gesset asks disgustedly. "I want to dance too, you know!"

Christa rolls her blue eyes. "Relax, Gess. You know she'll be back soon," she assures him while grabbing hold of Vega's arm.

"What are you doing?" Vega's lime eyes widen with fear.

"It's a party, Vega. I'm doing you a favor."

She shakes her short black hair. "No, you know I—"

"I do know, which is why I'm not giving you the option of sitting there looking awkward on a bench."

She knows me too well, Vega realizes, and feels a pang of guilt for having accidentally altered her mind a few days ago. Though she doesn't want to, and thinks that dancing in a mob of people is one of the worst things on this planet, Vega knows that trying to stop her friend again might result in ... even worse problems. *Like morphing into a copy of some goddess, or for all I know, turning Christa's head into a watermelon. At this point, I wouldn't be surprised.*

The mammoth, blue bonfire looks even more magnificent as it looms closer into view. Christa parts the crowd to make a gap just large enough for the two of them, chestnut ringlets bouncing overtop of her lilac cap sleeves. Once through the herd, she pulls Vega to the very edge of the pyre, so close to the blue flames that Vega thinks her porcelain skin might melt off her bones.

"You did it!" her friend cheers, blue eyes glistening with pride.

Vega looks warily around the area. To the left of her stands a young couple, whispering amorously in each other's ears, while to her immediate right stands Christa in her flowing chiffon dress. *It could be worse*, she tells herself, nodding at Christa's encouragement.

Lazarus's song ends with a booming clap of symbols and a new one picks up, abounding with slow, rather lustful verses. *Darrion, God of Love and Romance.* Christa begins to move her hips back and forth, rocking gently to the music. She turns to Vega, who stands like a stone.

"Like this, Veg." Christa shows her as she begins to move Vega's arms like a puppet master.

This might be worse than actually dancing, she thinks, watching others' amused glances in her direction. Sighing, Vega shifts her weight from one silver ballet flat to the other, lime-green dress skimming the blades of grass.

"That's it!" Christa cheers, as she breaks into a much more erotic version of the dance that only she could pull off.

Vega shields her eyes with a palm, laughing at the obscenity of the movements. She looks to the happy couple on her left, glad to see that they have chosen a much more modest approach toward displaying their affections in public.

The heat from the blue fire is beginning to press in on Vega, and she wonders if it is time to take a break when the song of Darrion reaches its methodical end. She makes to ask Christa if she, too, needs a rest when a new song starts up—and the world suddenly stops.

Something in this one speaks to Vega like no other has before. She halts her dancing, turning her lime-green eyes to observe the dancers around her as the soft tune rolls on. It is calm and serene, but deep and mysterious. The violin and cello strum long, harmonious notes of what could be considered either intriguing or sorrowful, while the flute and clarinet sound tranquil vibrations.

The couple before her moves like water, graceful and steady, but the man occasionally twirls his lover with a spark of passion. *It is like the night sky, black but for its billions of stars*, thinks Vega, though it comes to her that this is a strange thought to think.

The music becomes a bit louder now, and though she does not know whose song this is, Vega feels ... *It almost feels like they are honoring me*, she thinks foolishly. *I truly should go see a doctor.* Unsettled, the hymn still swelling with orphic dimensions, Vega decides to focus on the swarming flames before her.

The flames dance just as wildly as the people around it, soaking up the energy of the atmosphere, gluing Vega's cat-like eyes to shades of sky and navy and cobalt. She tries to pull away, to take her eyes off the blazing blue hues, but the fire keeps sucking her in, entrancing her with its powerful flames.

All around her the voices of neighboring dancers fade to dust, the lilting sounds of the song carrying her deeper into the flames until the only thing she can see is the playful inferno; its shades of blue melting all other signs of life before she passes out.

ANNALISE

The bright cobalt door of the Sapphire has never been as welcoming as it is now. Annalise reaches for its silver handle, trying her hardest to make the movement full of its usual ease. The boat ride over the Falvedrie Sea had not been forgiving on her arms, and rowing with all the fury of a madwoman had made them even more fatigued by the time she found a spot on Guorden's Beach. *Ivo said it was far enough away from the harbor. I just hope he's right.* She knew that the guards would likely not be searching for her after four days, but Anna was not about to take any chances.

She removes her gray cloak upon entering Narelle's room—*My old room*, she notes—and embraces her closest family figure in a comforting hug.

"I've missed you so much," Narelle tells her as she

squeezes Anna even harder. "It's been so lonely here with no one to talk to."

Annalise inhales her friend's familiar lilac and lily scent and pulls away to examine her hazel eyes. "I'm sorry. I would have come sooner, but ..." she trails off, not wanting to make mention that she might be wanted for stealing a boat. "I missed you too," Anna confesses with a generous smile.

Narelle waves a tan hand, patting the top of the window seat cushion. "Enough sentiment," she laughs. "You're here now. I'm assuming you didn't just come to chat, as much as I'd love it." She stops to tilt her head, chestnut waves falling to one side of her cobalt-covered shoulder as she examines the princess more closely. "Something is the matter," Narelle notices.

Yes, lots of things are the matter. Annalise opens her mouth but isn't about to go into length about her uncanny supernatural abilities. *Not right now. Right now, I need to tell her only what she needs to know.* "I have something very big to ask of you," she admits.

Her almost-sister squints in suspicion, biting a full, ruby lip.

Annalise sighs. "My councilors have advised me to set up a network of trusted sources in town."

Narelle blinks her hazel eyes. "You want me to be your spy."

She smiles at Narelle's forwardness, thankful that she

does not have to say outright just what a paramount job she is asking her to do. "It would only be a matter of relaying information that you overhear about the queen's current affairs, how people are reacting to her reign, and maybe, when the time is right ... help me to plant some seeds throughout town," she whispers, the words almost soundless.

Leaning her head back against the wall of the window seat, Narelle whistles, low and clear. "That's a steep price for raising you fresh off the streets, girl."

Annalise laughs, playfully rolling her deep brown eyes. "So, is that a 'yes,' then?"

The courtesan's hazel eyes meet Anna's own, and she gives her a nod. "You know I would do anything for you," she smiles.

It is Anna's turn to let out an exasperated gasp of air, and she gives her closest friend another hug. "Thank you," she says into her blue silk sleeve. "I owe you for this."

She sits back and begins rummaging through her bag, pulling out a custom stamp, courtesy of Tasman's craftsmanship. The ornate wood is glossy, the intricate seal far more elegant than her sister Adrianna's. Annalise drops it into Narelle's palm.

"If you ever need to write to me, put the letters in the giant oak tree by the Guorden's Beach sign just south of the Royal Harbor. There is a hole in it. Ivo makes a stop every two days to pick up food and check in on town happenings, so he will peek in each time he visits. Just make sure that you stamp the outside of the envelope and its contents with this leaf emblem." *This way, we know that one of our spies has left us mail, and not just a lonely thug.*

The courtesan stands to place the stamp in her vanity drawer, and Anna rises with her.

"Narelle," Annalise finds herself warning. "Please promise me you will be careful."

Narelle paces over to the lost princess and scoops her up once more. "I promise. But you're the one who needs to be extra careful," she points out, releasing her from her grip. "The queen would go mad if she found out you were still alive."

As if she isn't mad already. She dons her cape once more. "I will. I'll be back soon, I promise."

"I know you will," Narelle chuckles quietly, cobalt silk slipping over the wooden floorboards.

Anna turns to part from her newest recruit, the familiar, rickety door slamming shut behind her.

The vendors stand where they usually do, about half a mile down the road from the Sapphire. But while their typical location remains the same, the hustle and bustle they tend to attract is nowhere to be seen. Annalise doesn't even have to wait in line at Robbin's stand, her mysterious form slinking right up to the crates of fresh produce. The copper-clad boy turns to find Anna with her gray hood up, awaiting service.

"The gods are kind today," he announces, placing a hand upon his chest in dramatic fashion. "It's been too long, love!"

The princess laughs. "I know. How are you, Robbin?" she asks him cordially, though inside, she knows his true nature. It was Robbin who had given Ivo and his exiles information about the mysterious Waif and her whereabouts. *Without him, I would still be under the cover of the Sapphire. But without him, I would not be rebuilding my chance at redemption.* Either way she twists it, Annalise cannot trust Robbin nearly as much as she had before.

The merchant leans against the wooden beam of his fruit stand. "*I* am fantastic. Business? Eh, not so much."

Anna's brown eyes narrow. "There are hardly any customers here. Why the sudden decrease in trade?"

Robbin turns his head to the left and then the right, copper eyes carefully scanning the crowds of plebeians passing them by. He moves closer, to a closeness more accustomed to sharing secrets than business theories. "It's the queen," he murmurs. "Her food tax is driving up the cost of all the market goods, and the kingdom's aggravation with it. People can't afford to pay what she is asking—the tax makes it almost double what they used to pay for each ware. What am I supposed to tell them? *'Come, get one for the price of two!'*?" Robbin shakes his brassy waves.

A certain rage rises from the pit of Anna's stomach, one that she knows better than to let free. *Dria always was a demon in the flesh, but this is a whole other level of cruelty. She probably means to starve most of the lower class off and inherit their meager wealth for the throne's personal use.* Her fists ball up under her cloak, and she unwittingly grits her teeth together. *There must be a better way …*

A plum rises mid-air, snapping Anna out of her trance and forcing a gasp from her perfect lips. She drops the purple fruit back into its crate, sending it falling with a soft *plop* just before Robbin whips his head in that direction. *Oh no. There is definitely something wrong with me. Maybe I am just hallucinating? Gods, is that worse than if it were actually happening?*

"What?" he asks, copper eyes wide with concern.

Annalise struggles for an excuse. "I … There was a strange bug that just flew by. It's nothing," she swears, long fingers fidgeting with her pant fabric as she awaits his response.

To her vast relief, Robbin chuckles. "Who knows where those things come from. My money is on the queen —she's probably up in her chambers spawning more fiends like herself."

Annalise gawks, brown eyes as round as the plum she

just levitated and tries hard not to smile for fear that a supporter overheard such an offensive remark about their monarch. "As much as I would love to agree with you, I think you should take more care with your mouth." She smiles. *He reminds me of someone that I used to know.*

"Perhaps you could teach me how to properly use it?"

Anna takes a casual step backward, offering a nervous giggle. "I think you can manage to figure that one out on your own."

"I don't think that's how it works, Piper," he grins, brassy eyes sparkling.

Her former name takes her aback. *Piper*, she remembers. *He still thinks I am Piper and nothing more than a street rat!* Anna's smile widens. "I need to check back on Narelle. She's probably worried sick about me."

The vendor gives her a suspicious glance. "Mm-hmm I'm sure." But he smirks, and the princess knows that he is satisfied with simple bantering. *It must be a game to him, to see how many women he can convince to waltz right into his bed.*

Anna prepares to delve back into the masses but slows her pace. *Ivo and Tas told me to come back as soon as I was finished speaking to Narelle, but I can't stay cooped up in that stone tower for much longer.* She rubs the side of her pretty face in uncertainty, going over the plum incident that just occurred. *None of the books at the tower have any information on supernatural powers, and I am never going to get an answer if I don't look somewhere else.* Her heart sinks. *And the only other place ...*

Her dark-brown eyes stare into the horizon. Far in the distance sits a pale white castle above marble steps, its spires clawing up into the sky. *Perhaps I can go back to being Piper for a day ... or ...*

Annalise stops in her tracks, turning back to Robbin. She swallows, feeling a bit awkward about what she is going to say next. "Could I ask you for a favor?"

Robbin's eyebrows raise with delight. "Anything," he replies in his usual flirtatious manner.

"Good. I need to borrow some of your clothes."

VEGA

The table is cold beneath her pale hands, but that doesn't keep her from portraying the elegance that she is known for. Some might balk at superficial things, but Elouthera is disciplined at maintaining an image of grace and poise—which is exactly what she should exude, given the current state of affairs at council today.

Lazarus sits in his usual marble chair, overseeing the entire long table with his wife, Valea. His white beard helps to conceal his glower, but nothing could have hidden the wrath in his booming voice when he asked whether or not the earth should continue to be a potential candidate of the Alliance. As each planet that the gods and goddesses build grows mature enough to maintain itself, it is introduced as part of the Alliance, a network of their prosperous creations whose people can interact with one another in peace—which is the exact reason why Earth is having difficulty being considered. But aside from its occasional cases of problematic behavior, Elouthera firmly believes that the Earth will be ready in a few more centuries, as she has just told Lazarus.

The air quakes around Jedda's fiery locks while she makes her case against her sister, Dimity. *They always did find a way to oppose one another*, thinks Elouthera, tilting her silver headpiece to one side. Her folded hands tighten imperceptibly as she eyes Jedda, careful to display nothing but disinterest on her lovely face. Yet no matter how hard she tries, she can feel Anzac's dark stare slithering over her silver dress, like the snake she never knew he was.

Dimity counters, calling Jedda out on how cruel she truly is, the Goddess of Wisdom and Justice letting shine a bit of fury through her amber eyes. *They even look like opposites: Dimity with her amber eyes and charcoal hair, and Jedda with her eyes of coal and burning red locks.* And then Elouthera hears him speak.

Anzac sits at the end of the table, his carefree, lanky form swarming with shadows as elusive as his kindness. *Would that I had known better*, she criticizes herself. But she knows that she couldn't have known, and that it wasn't her fault. She listens carefully as he elaborates on some abstract idea about the sisters incarnating on Earth to test their theories on the planet: each would experience the goodness and the hardships that the race has to offer. Only after living out their lives and returning to their goddess forms will they reconvene to see if their first-hand experiences have altered their view on the Earth-Alliance matter.

That sounds dreadfully scary, Elouthera worries, for she is close friends with Dimity and fears for her safety. Anzac goes on to make mention of 'protectors' who will incarnate with them, but who is to say that they will all be together after birth? *The gods cannot control every minute detail of Earther lives. Their parents will never agree*, she hopes.

But Lazarus and Valea reluctantly leave the decision up to their only children, Valea only asking who would risk their lives for their daughters. The table explodes in murmurs of shock and reservations about the idea, Elouthera herself being taken aback. But one look at Anzac's gray and orange eyes tells her enough: That he is planning on going on this trip, and someone needs to be a strong enough match for the combined strength of Jedda and himself, or Dimity could face worse than simply returning with a lost cause. Elouthera knows the malice of Jedda, and that with Anzac on her side, Dimity will need someone who knows his mind, his mischievousness.

Nobody wants to do it, and why would they? It sounds horrifying, dangerous, and painful—especially if they are playing on Dimity's side—but they are all lesser gods anyway. Elouthera closes her eyes, silver lashes curling overtop of her painted silver teardrops, and realizes what she must do. For her friend, for her creation, and for herself. When her quicksilver eyes open, she parts her elegant lips.

"I, for one, will volunteer."

Vega gasps, clutching her racing heart as she wakes up dazed upon a white linen bedsheet. She looks around at the infirmary, watching as nurses scurry to-and-fro to tend to the other patients.

"Oh good, you're up." A kind woman appears to her left. "Do you remember what happened?"

A wave of shock and confusion washes over her, but she blinks her fears away. *I remember,* is all Vega can think as she slowly regroups herself. *Yes, I remember.*

She feels a sense of closure that gives her more comfort than she ever thought imaginable. Despite her situation, the tension loosens in Vega's stomach, and she sighs in relief. "The last thing I remember is dancing in front of the blue bonfire at Darrion's Square."

The nurse nods. "The heat must have overwhelmed you. Your friend Christa and a few others brought you here after you fainted. How are you feeling now?"

It all makes sense. My strange connection to Elouthera, my impossible skills in manipulation, my affinity with the night sky ... I am Elouthera. She bites her lip to quell a laugh, trying to contain her happiness. *Of course, I am. How silly I was to have forgotten it!*

"I feel fine," she answers in the calmest way she can. "Maybe just a bit thirsty."

A thought springs to her mind as the nurse runs to fetch her a drink. *We must have been born without memory ... But will the others experience the same thing? And how will I find out?*

The nurse returns with a glass of water. "Here you are, love. Make sure you drink all of this. I can go inform someone to tell Christa that you are well."

"Thank you." Vega takes a sip of water while she watches the nurse turn away. "Oh, one more thing. Would you tell her that if she needs me, I will be at the Alley of the Gods?"

She nods, leaving Vega to finish her glass of water before she departs her school's infirmary. *Christa won't mind. I'm sure of it.*

She sighs with relief once her small feet hit the cobblestone streets of Wembleton. She feels lighter, freer, like something inside of her has just clicked into place. Something *different.* A bond of some sort, like an invisible wire connecting herself to Dimity. Vega finds it comforting, like finding an old friend by surprise. The happiness leaves her beaming as she ascends the Alley of the Gods, lime dress swishing over the smooth pebbles.

But for all of her newly discovered joy, she realizes that there are a few major drawbacks to Anzac's plan. *For one, where is Dimity?* She could be anywhere in the world. Vega supposes it would make sense for them to have incarnated close together, though there has been no news of a girl with goddess-like powers in the twenty years Vega has been on this planet. *What if she doesn't know yet, that she is Dimity? I wonder what she will look like, what her name is …*

Vega keeps herself from going down another rabbit hole. Instead, she takes a breath and looks inwardly at the connection between herself and her ally. The bond travels a great distance. The other end is quiet, like she is stuck in some slumber of unknown duration, and Vega knows that Dimity is not awake—and certainly not in Vega's general vicinity.

Her feet slow on the pebble pathway as she glances up the hill at the temple of Dimity, flooded with visitors today. The domed rooftop of the temple is so tall, it looks like it could reach the sky, and Vega smiles at the statue of her colleague looking stoically at all her patrons. She turns her head to the left, a laugh bubbling from her lips when the temple of Elouthera comes into view. A mob of civilians has come to place tokens of appreciation near her reflecting pool, lifting her already-high spirits even more.

I suppose there is nothing that I can do right now but wait and play the game, she thinks, and for the first time in a long time, she feels ready, strong, *powerful*, even. Vega turns on a silver heel and begins her descent down the Alley's hill, when a cold front slithers over her exposed shoulder. She stops dead in her tracks. The cold front is not a front at all, but rather a mist of shadow, slipping down her arm and floating across the pathway toward the temple of Anzac.

Vega swallows, citrus-green eyes narrowing with caution. The surrounding temples are teeming with admirers supporting nearly every god and goddess in swelling numbers—all except for Anzac's, whose temple sits empty in its darkness. *I will not be afraid of him*, she tells herself, pushing her petite shoulders back.

It is nearly pitch black, only the faint glow of a few candles giving off just enough light to see by once her eyes adjust. The marble floors, the matching walls, even the small domed ceiling are all black, and Vega swears that she can smell smoke. *Though that might be from standing in front of a giant fire.*

The shadow twines around an onyx column, disappearing into the black air. In the center of the temple where a reflecting pool should be lies a hole in the floor, its center so dark that one cannot tell where it leads. Vega shivers slightly.

"Do I scare you that much?" a male voice enters her head sounding faint and distant, but nevertheless cruel.

Vega freezes. "Don't flatter yourself. You keep your temples cold."

A chilling laughter, muffled by the distance. "I'm glad you're up. It's been boring the past few months."

Her lime-colored eyes sharpen. *He has been up, but has Jedda awoken yet?*

"And it will continue to be boring, because I am done talking with you." He sends her another gale of chuckling, the sound raising the hair on Vega's arms.

"Elouthera, I never knew you could be so harsh," he banters. "But if that's how you feel, then you should know that if you're ever feeling lonely, you can always contact me in one of my many temples."

Vega rolls her eyes. "And if you ever need to contact me, you can talk to the stars."

This time, Anzac's laughter is loud and clear. "You aren't leaving me, are you?"

Elouthera smiles now, and feels a black coin in her purse. "What? The way you left me?" She presses a kiss to it with her pretty lips and chucks the coin into the dark hole in the floor. "For old time's sake," she adds, before stalking out into the afternoon sun, not caring enough to wait for an answer.

ANNALISE

She walks with a purposeful gait, Robbin's loose-fitting breeches stuffed into her own dusty boots. Leaving her gray cloak at the Sapphire for safe-keeping, Annalise hopes that the linen shirt and navy doublet are enough to conceal her bust. Her dark-brown waves have been pinned up into a navy flat cap adorned with a large feather, her earthy eyes stealing wary glances from beneath its brim.

The white steps of the castle grow closer before her. Annalise is not ready, will never be ready, to face the breeding ground of her past terrors. *But I must. It is this or spend the rest of my time wondering myself sick in that damned tower. And however mad this is, it is surely better than descending into madness itself—unless I already have ...*

All she needs is a book, some sort of tome on superhuman powers or godly abilities so she can figure out what the hell is going on with her. *Nothing else*, she tells herself. *Just in and out, and it will all be done.* Lucky for Anna, the Royal Library is separated by walls from the actual castle, and even has its own entrance. The builders wanted the Royal Family to be as safe and secure as possible while allowing for public access to the most elite information.

While it proved to be a helpful source for many, traveling so near the very place that doomed her to a life in the slums hasn't exactly made accessing information easy for Annalise. Which is why she is clad in Robbin's attire, strolling through the crowds dressed like a man. *I am a ghost*, she reminds herself. *And now I am a man, too.* She allows herself a tiny chuckle. *I can't believe I am actually doing this.*

The masses of people start filtering out at the intersection of roads beneath the castle steps. Anna takes them one at a time, bracing herself for the worst. *The last time I walked these steps was over six years ago. That was when my mother and father had a parade through the streets, taking us with them to hand out food to the hungry.* She ponders on the thought for a moment, thinking back to the generosity of her late parents. *That was probably the last time that the poor had been part of a parade as well.*

Guards cloaked in red and gold uniforms stand watch along the perimeter of the white castle, faces masked by golden helmets. Adrianna's colors whip violently in the sea breeze, a fair and final warning against Annalise's plan. An unbidden memory claws its way to the surface of her mind: *"Seize her, the traitor!"* Cold stone walls, incessant darkness, ragged breathing from behind ... the princess jumps at a low, gravelly voice:

"This way for the Royal Library. Nobody is to enter through the castle doors without express permission from Her Majesty, Queen Adrianna. Court is to be held again on Thursday at noon." It takes Anna a moment to process that the guard is addressing a group of civilians, which she happens to be part of. The group of a dozen or so people begins to shift, heading up the last of the white marble stairs to a set of gargantuan crimson doors. *They used to be navy*, she notes. The doors are opened by two visibly unhappy guards, which soon reveal the key to Annalise's heart.

Troves of books sit high and low on red maple shelves, the ballroom-sized library filled with row after row of bookcases—not only on the first floor, but on the second and third as well. Tall, spiraling staircases have been built for access to each level, though most everything that one should need is available on the ground.

Little has changed since Anna was last here. The burgundy carpet is still the same from her childhood, the chandeliers still drop from the high ceiling in their gold, circular forms, and the redwood tables and chairs have not been moved an inch from the positions where she last saw them. *Even the smell is still the same, like worn leather and yellowed pages.*

Her hands begin to tremble a bit, but she manages to steady them with a deep breath. *I shouldn't be here.* Her cover begins to dissipate when the surrounding persons make off toward their genres of choice, leaving Annalise and her masculine clothing left to find someplace else to look less conspicuous. She begins walking down the main aisle of bookshelves, turning her feathered hat to-and-fro to catch the writing on each sign.

Classic Literature, Romance, World Languages … *No, no, no.* Anna stops when she sees it. The sign is all the way on the third floor, but she can read it clear enough: Paranormal. *Oh, gods. I'm not going to be drawing attention to myself at all*, she thinks sarcastically. But everyone seems to be more concerned about their own texts than the other patrons, and the librarians are continuing to write at their large, maple desks, so Annalise clenches her jaw as she ascends the spiraling staircase to the top floor.

There aren't any people up here, only the smell of ancient parchment and untapped wisdom, just waiting to be found. The library had always been Annalise's favorite place, somewhere she could lose herself in an entirely different world, forgetting for a little while that she was one day to assume the responsibilities of the throne. She remembers meeting Master Tasman here quite often, his kind blue eyes brightening at the opportunity to teach his pupil of the world's varied disciplines. But they had never been up here, not on the third floor.

The princess turns down a narrow alcove, drifting by a thousand books coated in dust. *I don't think anyone has picked these up in years.* She rounds the corner to make the next right into the Paranormal section and runs into a chain. Anna squints. *What in the world ...* Heading back the way she came, she reaches the other end of the aisle—the one she could see from ground level—and finds this entrance to be closed off as well. She grits her teeth, sighing in frustration. *I asked Robbin for his clothes so I could risk my wellbeing for a book I can't even get to?* Ivo and Tasman will be furious with her, she knows. But not so furious as the tone of voice from the guard stationed below.

"*Halt, sir! The third floor is off limits. Didn't you read the sign?*"

What sign—Oh, gods have mercy. The wooden sign hangs from the side of the stairwell railing, forewarning visitors at the bottom of the steps. *Forget the aisle way, they should have put a chain across the stairs!*

She looks back to where the guard was standing but finds only an empty space. As it happens, the guard is quick and nimble, and in the second it takes Annalise to register what is happening, he makes it to the mouth of the stairwell. *He is coming for me!* She begins to panic.

There is nowhere for her to run, save for jumping over the railing and falling from the third floor. *How ironic would that be, to actually fall to my death, only six years later?* The guard has reached the third floor and is now brimming with fury.

Anna throws up her hands. "I'm terribly sorry, sir. I didn't see the sign—"

"Give me your hands." He forces her wrists into a rope, tying it securely with sharp, brusque movements.

Her throat begins to tighten. "I beg you to let me out, please. I have a family," she lies in her best impression of a man's voice, but he mercilessly tugs her toward the stairs. Tears threaten the backs of her dark-brown eyes, but she forces her body to keep them in. "Where are you taking me, sir?" she asks, unnaturally deep voice becoming harder to maintain by the second.

The guard doesn't bother to turn around; he only offers a huff of stale laughter when he makes his reply.

"To the queen, you fool."

OLIVER

Oliver messes with the collar of his doublet and pulls his cloak hood down to hide his evergreen eyes. *This is quite possibly the worst plan I've ever been part of—and I helped write it,* he thinks regretfully.

Modgen's own eyes are draped in a hood of sage green, his temperament upbeat as usual. *Is he nervous too? How can he hide it so well?* All around them, the world carries on with its typical daily duties: men hauling sacks of grain, street-side artists selling their creations, women cradling baskets of flowers for sale.

One such woman bumps into one of Oliver's sculpted shoulders.

"Oof," the lady bursts, the basket almost tumbling from her husky arms.

Oliver catches the woman mid-fall, righting her in the timeframe of a few seconds. "I'm so sorry, miss!"

She gathers herself. "Not to worry, sir," she replies, carrying on with her business.

Oliver McHenry sighs his relief, exchanging a worried glance with Modgen, the no-longer-Treasurer Sprightly. They say nothing, for it is too dangerous to speak in public. *It's bad enough that we left our bakery hideout for the unprotected area of town. At least the servants' entrance is on the side of the castle, and not through the main gates.*

The men continue forward, morphing into the passersby like two more peasant boys on their way to work. The moon-white cobblestones open to another intersection: left for heading back to the main town, straight for the rolling hills just west of the city, and right toward the side entrance to the castle. Oliver takes a deep breath before he and Modgen follow the path to the servants' entrance.

Three guards have been posted to the gate: two beside the door, and one making his rounds around the area. *Just as we suspected*, the former master thinks, giving Modgen a discreet nod. The doors are looming ever closer, and he knows that it is time. His hands are damp with sweat as he reaches into his pant pocket and silently drops the ball onto the ground, arms hidden the entire time under the black of his cloak fabric. Modgen does the same with his own, and the world stands still for a moment.

Gods, I beg you—

Somebody's foot breaks one of the spheres, and thick gray smoke begins pluming up into the air. Screams break out within the herd of people, some panicking so much that they drop their goods and bolt toward some alternate destination. It isn't long before the other smoke bomb ignites, and the guards are forced to be relieved of their posts, jarring their gold-armored shoulders through the chaotic crowd.

"What in the name of Lazarus?" one of the burly guards curses, searching through the civilians with wide eyes.

Modgen and Oliver waste no time sneaking through the now-open tunnel, taking the first left and entering a servant's empty sleeping quarters. Modgen shuts and locks the door, pressing his back against the flimsy piece of wood.

"Well done," he praises, a devious grin across his face.

Oliver pulls two crimson doublets out of the servant's closet—much less costly than his own—and throws one to his red-haired friend. "I might say the same to you if we weren't wanted criminals gallivanting our way into the castle." Oliver pauses, thinking about the smoke bomb he had just deployed. "Where did you even get those things?"

Sprightly removes his own doublet with a smirk, leaving his white linen undershirt exposed. "It's never a bad thing to keep people guessing."

"Gods help us," Oliver sighs, placing a pillbox cap atop his thick brown hair. It isn't ideal for covering his face—certainly not like the cape was—but this is the typical attire for a servant of the castle. He throws a matching crimson half-cloak over his muscled shoulders, straightening out the golden broach to make clear that he is indeed an employed servant of the castle. *There, I'd say I could pass as a servant.*

Modgen has dressed in the same outfit, though his tunic is a bit more ill-fitting due to his tall, reedy build. He adjusts the pillbox hat over his reddish waves. "Ready?" he asks, blue eyes glimmering.

We just stormed into the castle with smoke bombs, then disguised ourselves in servants' attire so we can take back our belongings illegally. How can I be ready? Oliver shakes his head, then shrugs. "After all this, how can I *not* be ready?"

"That's the spirit!" Sprightly opens the rickety door and peeks out, motioning for Oliver to follow once there seems to be a gap in passersby.

The hallway snaking its way through the servants' section is tight and stuffy, the brick pathway built solely for functionality, as it is certainly not showy like the rest of the castle. The men had no idea where the tunnels lead to when planning their infiltration, so they decided to go off of general direction—a choice that leaves Oliver even more on edge. *What if we get lost, and need to ask for help? Will they recognize us behind our golden pins? What if we make it to our rooms, and then get lost on the way back? What if—*

Footsteps emerge from their left, and two young servant boys carrying golden trays of fruit turn the corner to pass them by. The boy in the front gives them a casual smile.

"Those look tasty," Modgen remarks, pointing to the intricately carved cantaloupe wedges.

Oliver cringes.

"Fresh from the kitchens. Princess Aimelie's favorite." The boy smiles again, leaving them to their orchestrated madness.

Oliver spins on Modgen. "What happened to, 'no words in public settings'?"

He gives Oliver a patronizing look. "Now we know not to go that way. Unless you want a fresh loaf of bread to calm your nerves?"

The former master clamps his mouth shut before facing the next intersection of tunnels before them, annoyed to death with Modgen's insolence. *This is all just a game to him, a game of dress-up and capture the flag.*

Modgen ignores his obvious irritation. "Third on the right," he reminds him, and together they round the corner. The tunnel ascends into a rather narrow flight of stairs that emerge through a small doorway, the freedom of the wide, open air allowing Oliver to breathe slightly more comfortably as the men take in the destination of their chosen route.

The corridor is bright with the fresh light of the sunny morning, filling the hall with a façade of ease. The doorways lining the hall are trimmed in gold leafing, and elaborate ironwork arches around every windowpane. *These chambers look far too expensive to be for a member of the Queen's Council. No, these doors are fit for the queen's most elite pawns.*

Oliver's fingers casually curl into fists to keep himself from his nervous fidgeting.

"I've never been on this end of the wing."

"I have. Boredom gets the best of me at times," Modgen admits. "Those are the chambers of the queen's lady-in-waiting, Renai, and those ones belong to our old friend, the captain."

Oliver steals one last look at the door, his pine-green eyes memorizing the location. "Not today," he whispers mostly to himself, but Modgen chortles nonetheless.

He leads Oliver down the hall and around a corner until at last, familiar blood-red carpets greet their senses. Modgen fiddles with the ring of servant's keys until he finds a match for his door's lock.

The slab of oak opens with an almost imperceivable squeal, Oliver preparing himself for what might have happened to their rooms after their dismissals from the High Council. *Please be untouched.* Oliver closes his eyes and says a silent prayer to the gods. Modgen finds a tallow candle and brings it to life. The small room is illuminated, revealing what Oliver assumes are possessions Modgen left in their exact same places. Shutting the door, he can hear a small sigh escape the former Royal Treasurer's lips.

"Thank the gods," Mogden hails, setting the candle on his unruly desk to search for his money. He sifts through a few wooden desk drawers, shuffling through files and documents before closing those drawers and opening the ones in his bedside table.

Oliver clears his throat, crossing his arms.

Modgen turns his bright-blue eyes up from his work. "What? I'm trying to rush, here!" he whispers frantically. It takes him two more minutes, but he finally pulls up with a large coin purse in hand and a grin across his face.

Oliver reaches for the door handle, but Modgen stops him.

"Wait, one more thing," he says rather distractedly, his eyes locked onto something near his bed. Modgen kneels on the floor to wriggle something out from beneath his messy bed. The small wooden box is covered in dust, which he blows off, opening it with a ginger care that Oliver has never seen him exhibit before. He can't make out what the object is, but Oliver swears that he sees a chain of silver and the glint of blue before it disappears into Modgen's coin purse.

"There," he says, lazily kicking the wooden case back under his bed and blowing out the candle.

Oliver carefully shuts the door once they exit, Modgen locking it up as if neither one of them was ever there. *One more stop, then this nonsense will be over.* A shadow flickers along a crimson wall behind them, and Oliver's breath catches in his throat. He looks to Modgen, eyes wide, but the former lord just shrugs. His nonchalance is enough to reassure Oliver that he can do this; he can be just as careless as Sprightly, if only to work his way loose of this disastrous plan.

The footsteps are quiet, but they are getting louder than before. Modgen speeds up his gait, and Oliver matches it, hopefully not bringing any unwanted attention to themselves. Oliver's door is just up on the left, but the shadow is nearing their heels now. In an attempt to look inconspicuous, Oliver grabs his own ring of servant's keys and stops at the door just before his own, taking his time before finding the right one, and allowing the person to pass them.

Her blonde hair is long and curly, but Oliver knows it isn't the queen. Not with the lavender ballgown she wears, or the sweet, floral scent of her perfume. The men can only see the back of her, but Oliver knows that dressed in that finery, it can only be Princess Aimelie Larking. She carries on, footsteps soft and light, almost in a hurry to wherever it is that her duties need her to be.

Oliver watches her disappear down the hallway, then moves to his own door, hands shaking just enough to make it embarrassingly difficult to unlock his old bedroom.

Modgen leans toward him as he fiddles with the key. "Hope she likes the cantaloupe."

Oliver offers him a thin smile, but before he can respond, the door pops open. His bedroom is exactly as Modgen's was. Undisturbed, not a thing moved out of place since the time was he was here last. *Praise Lazarus.* But unlike Modgen's chambers, everything is neat and tidy and has its own place. He moves quickly across the floor, opening the bottom nightstand drawer and pocketing a similar-looking coin purse. Modgen stares, his bright blue eyes wide.

"Just like that?" he asks in amazement.

"Just like that," Oliver replies, but the smile fades when they open the door and find another servant stalking down the halls. Oliver swallows hard. *We need to hurry.*

Modgen begins to lose his mask of calm as the heavy-set man moseys his way down the corridor, round stomach stretching the red velvet of his tunic. "How do servants even get that fat?" he asks as Oliver struggles to find the correct room key.

The former master doesn't have time to think, only to concentrate on finding the damn match so that they can book out of this castle with their heads still intact. He spares only a second of time to glance up at the portly man before answering Modgen's question with dread. "Because that isn't just a servant. That's the *Head* of Servants."

Modgen's pale face falls a shade paler. "Let's hurry it up, McHenry. Lord Walrus isn't going away any time soon."

Oliver bites his lip. *Not a match, not this one, not that one ... There!* He plunges the key into the knob and turns the lock with a flick of his wrist, turning around just in time to find the Head of Servants mere feet away.

The man slows his sluggish pace even further. He runs his thick fingers along his dark, bristly mustache while eyeing the boys suspiciously. "I thought I told you two to work on Lord Docketry's room?"

Oliver begins to open his mouth, but Modgen beats him to it. "The Lord was in his chambers at the moment, sir. We didn't wish to disturb him."

The man grunts, his round face jiggling with the sound. "Thought he was supposed to be in his meeting by now," he ponders, more to himself than the men.

"Perhaps he forgot something?" Oliver offers.

"Perhaps," the stout man continues to stroke his bushy mustache. "See that you stop at Lady Elmington's chambers, then."

The boys nod, waiting for his leave, but the man

doesn't budge. *He's waiting for us to move toward Lady Elmington's room*, Oliver realizes. *Who the hell is Lady Elmington?* Modgen turns his back on the man, Oliver following suit. They make it all of two steps before the Head of Servants halts them with his rumbling voice.

"Lady Elmington's chambers are *that* way, you fools! Have you forgotten?" He shakes his head, pointing a meaty finger back toward the captain's hallway.

Dear gods. The boys smile, Modgen smacking his forehead with feigned amusement, and they move around the man quickly and quietly. Oliver and Modgen walk side by side, casually hiding their money bags as they retreat the way they came. *This shouldn't be so bad. We can retrace our steps and leave out the servants' gate again.*

"Styven ... I thought you had brown eyes," the man calls from the other end of the hallway.

The boys stop and hesitantly turn around once more. It is too far away to tell which man he is addressing, and neither Oliver nor Modgen know who Styven looks more like. The boys look at each other, exchanging frozen looks as they awkwardly hide a hand behind their backs. *We're doomed*, Oliver thinks before watching the Head of Servants bring a silver whistle to his lips, the sharp sound piercing through every crevice of the surrounding corridors.

ANNALISE

Every footstep feels like an eternity, the soles of her boots weighing her down like blocks of lead. A trickle of sweat slips down her lower back, her whole body trembling with overwhelming trepidation as she is dragged toward what she knows to be the Throne Room. *And the death of me.*

Passing servants and nobles cast curious looks her way, but Annalise knows what they see: a thin man with a feathered hat, being tugged along by an irritated castle guard. The guard pulls her faster, making her wrists chafe even more from the rough rope knotted around them.

They approach the giant mahogany doors, which two pages open without so much as a glance. *Does this kind of thing happen all the time?* she wonders, before gracelessly stumbling across the white marble floors. Her brown boots scuffle as the guard yanks her forward again, and the entire Throne Room comes into view from beneath her navy-blue cap, the courtiers falling silent from her entry.

The room hasn't changed much since she was here last, and yet there is a world of difference as compared to when her royal parents held it. The room is entirely white; marble floors and painted walls with lofty white columns lining the walkway that has been formed by the onlooking court members, their gawking faces powdered or painted. *Just one of their dresses could feed an entire family for week*s, Annalise thinks with disgust, trying to distract herself from her fleeting thoughts of worry.

Gone are her late parents' colors of burgundy and orange, replaced by the crimson and gold of her middle sister. And while this seems to be the only physical change, the atmosphere is crackling with energy, choking off her air by the second. She swears that the courtiers shift with nervousness, hiding their reservations about the state of the kingdom behind their fine suits and gowns. *That makes more than one of us hiding behind our clothes.*

The marble clicks beneath her dirty boots, sounds echoing across the long hall. Annalise follows the noise with her dark-brown eyes, from the white floor in front of her to the female of her nightmares, and she can feel her horror threatening the back of her throat, begging to let out a scream.

She sits sprawled in a gown of blood-red crimson, its ornate golden detail climbing up the sides of her bodice. The queen is not as Anna had remembered her. The honey-blonde hair and icy blue eyes are the same, yes, but her face looks older, and her body shapelier. *And she looks colder, if such a thing could ever be possible.* She drapes her thin arms lazily over the golden arms of the enormous throne, the picture of annoyance, save for the rigidity of her back so as to balance the golden, ruby-adorned crown upon her head. Adrianna Larking eyes the guard before her with little interest, and just a dab of distaste.

"We were just finishing up, anyway," the queen announces, haughty voice piercing the silence.

Annalise flinches in Robbin's oversized breeches, lowering her dark eyes and praying to the gods that the queen will pay as little attention to her as she does to her castle guards.

"Honestly, Mig, are the ropes really necessary? The boy is so thin he couldn't harm a rat," Adrianna remarks, blue eyes rolling with irritability at her guard. "What did this one do?"

The mahogany doors open from behind them, and another guard, this one without a captor, bursts through with heaving breaths. "Your Grace ... ran to tell you ...

trouble at the servants' gate. Some sort of smoke bombs set off—"

The queen holds up a hand. "Not right now," she dismisses him, and just like that, the guard turns and walks away, doors sealing shut like he was never there.

That would have been a welcome distraction, Annalise thinks glumly. Her captor stops a healthy distance away from the dais, then turns to untie the knotted rope around her wrists. "Caught 'im up on the third floor of the library. Went straight past the sign; didn't even hesitate to hide himself while he was up there wanderin' around," Mig replies, tucking the rope back into his pocket. *So much more comfortable*, she thinks uselessly, for as comfortable as it feels not having her hands bound, the urgency of her situation smothers the welcome feeling into embers.

Mig walks round her back, then gives her a hard push forward. "*Kneel*, you worm."

Yes. Make me kneel to the girl who pinned my parents' deaths on me and forced me into hiding for years. The guard kicks her in the back of her knee.

Annalise Larking falls, knees cracking against the white marble as she catches herself with her now-free hands, just in time to watch Robbin's feathered hat topple from her head across the floor before her, dark brown locks spilling down the sides of her pretty face.

All hope is gone, she realizes when the entire court gasps, and Adrianna begins to chuckle. Heart thundering in her chest, Anna keeps her eyes on the marble, not daring to let the queen see more than she must.

"A *woman?*" the queen laughs, the rest of her court hesitantly joining in. "A woman in men's attire, risking her well-being for a *book*," she muses, bringing a hand to her heavily exposed chest.

Annalise feels heat rising to her cheeks. No matter how dire her situation is, the sheer number of faces laughing at the miserable failure of her disguise makes her sick to her stomach, even more so than she already is. *Just behead me already*. But the queen and her court continue to have a good long laugh, the sounds reverberating through both the Throne Room and Anna's fragile heart.

A brusque movement catches her eye, a blur of lilac fabric and swatting hands. Annalise discreetly lifts her head to the left to find a young woman elbowing her way through the crowd of courtiers. Her long, curled hair is a perfect match to Adrianna's, except her blue doe eyes peer at her in awe, like some unknown creature has just fallen from the heavens. Her full lips are slightly open, and Anna notices that she is breathing heavily, as though something is weighing on her chest.

It takes her three heartbeats to realize that Aimelie Larking stands a mere seven yards away, mouth open in a silent prayer, tears beginning to mottle her big blue eyes. *Lazarus almighty*, Annalise curses, a sob caught in her throat. *She's so grown up, my little sister!* But the sentiment is interrupted when Dria stops her laughing, her icy eyes finding Aimelie gaping from the side of her court. The courtiers quiet down, hundreds of eyes turning to their queen's own to wait for direction.

Anna reluctantly tears her eyes away from Aimelie, and at last meets Dria's cool blue gaze. *There may be no more hope, but I have to try. If not for myself, then for Aimelie, for my would-be kingdom ... for my parents.* The queen's crimson fabric shifts on the throne seat to get a better view, eyes sharpening with a visible internal dilemma.

Something crackles in the air between them—the time and space between not knowing, then realization, and then the blossoming of misunderstanding. Annalise holds her sister's death-stare like no one else is watching, like she isn't on her knees dressed like a man in front of her only remaining family and a menagerie of pawns.

The floor melts away, their breathing heightens, and though it is only a few heated seconds that Annalise and the queen share their moment of silent conversation, she knows that by the end of her sister's realizing who she truly is, she will need to act fast.

And so she does.

Adrianna Larking opens her sharp mouth to speak, and Annalise makes her move.

Leaping up into a standing position, Anna spins and drives the palm of her hand into Mig's droopy nose, dashing for the doors. The queen's court screams with surprise, backing away from the wanted woman. *No, not the doors—those are always guarded.* Her brown eyes dart around the long white room. *Don't panic, Anna. You know this castle better than anyone here. You lived here, damn it!*

"What are you waiting for, you bloody fools? *Seize her!*" Adrianna belts across the Throne Room for the second time in her life, and Annalise imagines her wolfish face turning as red as her crimson gown.

A table catches Anna's eye, pushed up against a wall beneath an open window. *Likely to let in the fall breeze, as the Throne Room does get rather stuffy sometimes.* Guards pour in through the mahogany doors in sets of four, then six. Annalise realizes that this is her only chance. She bolts for the table, leaping onto a nearby chair and hopping onto its top, jumping as high as she can to reach the window.

Pain jolts through her thin fingers as her nails dig into the white brick of the windowpane, arms straining with immense stress, but Anna uses her legs to haul herself up over the square opening of the windowsill. She spares herself one quick glance back to find the mass of guards running to join her, which leaves her no choice.

Anna grabs hold of the glass window that has been pushed over to one side and locates a thick, wrought iron lantern rung just a few feet below her. *If I make this jump, I might be more cat than human,* she thinks, but she can hear the guards bickering about who should go first and knows to take her chance now.

Releasing the top edge of the glass, her brown boots land with a *thud* against the iron rung, arms flailing ridiculously for balance. It isn't until she leans against the castle's brick wall that she can remain stationary for a few seconds before determining her next step. *Where am I to go?* she frets. *Down for ground level, which will no doubt be plagued with guards; left for the front of the castle.* Anna spots a flat level of brick almost directly in front of her, probably some outcropping for a window seat along the castle wall.

She tosses herself on top of it, breath gushing from her lungs as she lands. Adrenaline courses through her veins, like streams running downhill through a forest. *I can do this*, she reminds herself again. *I just have to get to— well, there is one place they would never think to look for me around here.*

Annalise listens to the guards' voices from above as they attempt to climb down from the window using grappling ropes. She takes the next leap, another rung similar to the one before, but her momentum sends her falling forward much too fast to plan her next course. Withholding a scream and dropping three feet through the air, she throws out her arms and miraculously catches a lantern light hanging from a long chain.

The light launches her forward, swinging her around

the corner of the castle, revealing nothing but white brick. The only thing waiting for her is the cool blue of the castle's moat as her hands lose their grip on the lantern, sending her falling once again into water.

The water is freezing cold, much colder than the Falvedrie Sea, and Annalise emerges with gasps, deciding that she bloody hates water more than anything else in this world. The voices of Adrianna's guards are far away now, high above and somewhere around the corner. She claws her way to the shoreline farthest from the castle, and races across the hillside. *If I run into town, guards will be everywhere. It's best to lay low for some time.*

The smell of horses and fresh leather fills her nose as she reaches the Royal Stables. Horses whinny and neigh, some kicking their stalls fervently as Annalise opts for the back entrance to her old hideout. *At least they are happy to see me.*

As it happened, Annalise and her early friends found the stable's hayloft to be a fantastic hiding place and playroom when they found royal life to be a bit too overwhelming. Being located all the way in the back of the castle, such a place would be the last area the guards would search for a random female on the run.

She hauls herself up to the rooftop, using stray wooden crates to gain elevation. When she is at last standing on the roof, she dusts off her hands on her soaked gray breeches and lowers herself near the ledge.

Hopefully no one notices the water droplets on the crates. Anna drops down so that her hands find purchase on the roofing, footing her way down the outside wall and then swinging her legs through the stable window.

She lands, exhaling a small *oomph* sound when she soars into something large and solid.

MODGEN

Modgen Sprightly doesn't know how to feel. He's exhausted from running so far, scared for his life, and mostly, he's agitated that their plan was so close to being perfectly executed until that cow of a man had to blow his bloody whistle. The whole thing happened so fast, leaving Modgen only enough time to whisper to Oliver, *"Follow me!"*

Not that Modgen has any idea of where they should go. Leaving the castle would be too dangerous, as an influx of guards will surely be scouring the city for them. So that means that they will have to find somewhere in the castle, somewhere safe in this velvet-sheathed jail. *Jail ... Maybe the dungeon? No, no that would be terrible*, he thinks, rolling his cobalt eyes while he and Oliver round a corner, nearly toppling into a pink-clad lady.

Jail. This place used to feel like a jail to me, when I was younger and couldn't get out much. A vision of a younger version of himself flashes through his racing mind, one of a pretty girl pushing him into the White Pond. *Or when I couldn't get dates.*

A group of courtiers comes rounding the corner while a man emerges from his chambers, carrying a golden platter of tea. There is no room, no time to stop as Oliver ducks and jars the tray out of his way, the teacups shattering against the crimson-stained walls. Cries fill the hallway from the already startled courtiers, and the men push themselves harder when the clomping of guards' footsteps becomes louder.

"Nicely done," Modgen chides between gasps of air, even as the world goes to hell around them. *A jail, a jail … That's it. At least, that will have to be it.*

The men are nearing the back of the castle now, and Modgen knows that to get to their destination, they will need to drop down to the lower level. He spies the nearest stairwell, warning McHenry before he crosses his path to lead the way down the white marble steps. A sharp turn to their right points them down a hall on the first floor of the castle, and Modgen's heart skips a beat. *I don't know how much longer I can take this*, he complains, but he knows that if he stops, he would likely soon be dead.

The two skid to a halt when a mob of guards comes barreling into the far end of the hallway, all in crimson and gold and with no idea of mercy in mind. *We're going to die here, in this pathetic crimson corridor?* Modgen sighs, hands on his knees while Oliver tips his head back against the wall, both defeated and awaiting punishment. There are no words to express their shock when the guards completely ignore them, storming by without a glance.

The men look to one another, eyes wide with amazement, but there is little time for celebration. Whatever luck the gods had just given them, it would not last long. *The next guards might not be so oblivious.* Modgen launches himself into another sprint, sparing a glance to make sure that Oliver is still beside him, and assuring himself that they are almost there.

The sound of clanging metal can be heard ringing about the hall, and Modgen can feel the heat pluming from the armory as they storm by the half-open steel doors. *Almost there ...* They veer around another corner on their right, then continue running straight through the stable's broad, wooden doors. *They are open. Another blessing from the gods.* His nose fills with the pungent smell of horses and dust, ignoring befuddled looks from the few stable hands that are on duty at the moment.

The familiar wooden ladder still rests in the same place as it had years before, and Modgen knows the feel of its smooth, whorled grain like the back of his hand. *I don't know how many times I used to hide here as a kid,* he reflects, hoisting himself onto the large hayloft. Oliver trails just behind him, the stable hands below sending up a few bellows.

He doesn't know why, but Modgen keeps running until he reaches the open window on the far side of the loft. He looks back to make sure his comrade is in tow when something sizeable slams into his body, sending both Modgen and Oliver tumbling backward into the hay.

OLIVER

Oliver lets out a groan as he rubs the soon-to-be bruise on his forehead. *Good gods*, he swears, slowly blinking his eyes. "What was that?" he asks Sprightly, whose red-orange hair is now strewn with hay. When he doesn't answer, Oliver moves to stand himself up and get a better view.

He freezes.

The woman stands soaking wet in men's breeches and a doublet, but that is not the first thing that Oliver notices about her. That would have to be her face, fresh with an air of elegance and refinement. Her sultry eyes are dark as earth, with thick brown hair to match, dripping with water. She could not be much younger than Oliver himself, perhaps early twenties, and though she is clad in men's attire, there is no mistaking that she is breathtaking.

She gives him a quick glance, but her attention seems to be stuck on Sprightly's awe-stricken face.

"Tell me, Oliver, do you see her too, or have I gone mad?" Modgen asks, swallowing.

Oliver nods. "I see her too."

The woman lets out an exasperated sound, then falls to her knees, tears welling in her dark eyes. *"It can't be,"* she whispers, the sound barely audible. She bites a lip as Sprightly sits up.

"What do you mean 'it can't be?' I *can* be, and *should* be, but you ... you're *dead*," he whispers hysterically, pinching the bridge of his nose as though it will tether him to sanity. "You're *dead!*"

She laughs, the sound bubbling and marvelous even as a tear makes its way down one of her pale cheeks. "You should be smarter than to think I would die that easily, Modge," she chuckles through hushed sobs.

Sprightly's face breaks, and he scoops her up into a great hug, attempting to fight back tears of his own. "What are the odds?" he asks. "What are the bloody odds?"

Oliver doesn't know what to do. *Who is she? How does she know Modgen? And why is she soaking wet wearing men's clothes?* But despite his concerns, he feels it necessary to allow them this moment, however short-lived it may be.

The grumbling sound of a guard's voice breaks the silence. "Close and lock the doors. We have a traitor loose somewhere in the kingdom, and I'll not have her skulking about the castle right beneath our noses."

Oliver and Modgen turn back to the woman, who swallows her tears. She meets each of their gazes with poised brown eyes. "I made a small mistake."

Oliver huffs a laugh. "Then you're in good company."

ANNALISE

When the fuming castle guard came busting into the stable, Annalise knew things were likely to go to hell much sooner than she had expected. She stands in her breeches, trying and failing to brush off the few pieces of hay that have been sticking to her dampened clothes, and turns back to the square window.

The fall isn't that steep; they would surely manage without any broken bones. *Only one way to find out*, Anna decides, then turns back to her long-lost friend and his handsome accomplice. *Modgen*, she muses. *After all these years, all this time ...* She begins to wonder what he has been doing for the past six years, what problems and messes he has gotten himself into, but she crams those thoughts in the back of her mind. *Now is not the time or place for chatting.*

"There's a grate in the grass outside of this building," she says softly, listening to the nearing footsteps of the stable hands. From the sound of their dusty boots, she knows that they are on their way to the ladder which leads to the hayloft.

Modgen and the green-eyed man spare no time readying themselves by the window as they, too, hear the approaching hands, the sound of the wooden ladder groaning quietly. Anna slides her bottom onto the edge of the window and pushes herself with her arms, landing on both feet in the grass.

She breathes a quick sigh of relief, then rushes out of the way for Modgen and his ally to do the same—or try to do the same, as Modgen collapses onto his backside after his feet could not stick the landing. His friend has no time for a chortle when the stable hands reach the loft. Anna can hear one of their voices from above.

"Hey, why—"

Modgen's friend leaps from the window, losing his flat cap when he lands perfectly atop the green grass. The stable hands let out a bark of panic, the man stealing back his cap as the three criminals launch themselves into a full run toward the left side of the stable.

Anna stops in the grass, falling to her hands and knees, searching for the passage entrance like a blind man looking for fallen coin. Nothing but blades of grass graze the palms of her sweaty hands, the sound of bellowing growing nearer as the stable hands use the exterior door of the building to track down the infiltrators. *Come on, come on ... I know you're here somewhere.*

A rough scrape of weathered metal has Annalise crawling to the grate, digging her nails into the crevices until she triggers the minute latch hidden around the edge of the circle. The grate pops ajar slightly, Anna throwing it all the way open with all her strength as she shifts to dangle her legs through the hole, slipping inside the darkness and landing with a soft *thump*. She looks up from above, Modgen making his way through without a word, dropping beside her with heavy breaths—from fear or from running, she cannot tell.

"Try to close the grate on your way down if you can," Anna calls up quietly to Modgen's accomplice while he laces his legs through the entrance.

He grabs the handle on the interior side of the grate and hauls it up and over his head as he falls beside them, encasing them in complete and utter darkness. *Good gods,* Annalise swears. *The last time I was in here was ...* She swallows. *Father showed us these tunnels for escape, only to be used by the Royal Family in case of emergency.* She tries bringing up a picture in her mind of how the tunnels look, but navigating them blindly would pose as an impossible challenge. *We would likely be stuck down here and die of starvation.*

The torch. Anna remembers her father telling her that beneath every grate lies a torch and the tools needed to light it. She takes a step forward, hands extended toward the wall closest to the grate. Her palms bump into the cool, flat surface, and she knocks her right knuckles against a rod of wood, which she yanks off the wall.

Anna runs her hand over the stick until she finds the cloth end of the torch. *There has to be a jar of fuel here somewhere,* she thinks, bending down on the tunnel's ground until she locates an oddly-shaped container with a lid. The intoxicating scent that plumes out of it validates that she has indeed found the fuel.

Modgen coughs, his friend following suit. "How long has that stuff been down here?" he asks, choking back another cough.

"Longer than we've been alive, most likely," she responds, dunking the cloth into the fuel.

"Have you found flint anywhere?" the green-eyed man asks.

Annalise lets the unlit torch rest in the pool of fuel. "Not yet," she says, hands roving for the box that should hold those things. Nothing in between the jar of fuel and where the torch was hanging on the wall, nothing on either side of them, either.

Fear begins to swallow the lost princess whole, its

claws digging into her stomach. *No flint, no fire steel, no lit torch.* She can hear the men shifting restlessly on their feet in the eternal darkness, and knows that without them, they are as good as dead.

I will not panic, I will not cry, Annalise tells herself. She goes over the area once more with her palms, double-checking that she hasn't missed the box. Nothing. She even goes so far as to cross over to the opposing wall and check its crevices, but still turns up empty-handed. Annalise takes a deep breath. *Gods, hear us now. I beg you to help our mortal souls, to light our way in this time of tribulation*, Anna prays, but a small voice in the back of her mind whispers in response: *You are no mortal.*

Her brown eyes widen in the blackness at the sudden remark, clear as can be. Any other day, Annalise might have laughed, might have rolled her dark eyes, and flung the thought aside with the bat of an eye—but not today. No, today she needs a miracle. She and *her friends* need a miracle.

Burning up her doubts until they crumble like ashes, she retrieves the unlit torch from the fuel, attempting to ignore the hideous odor as she brings it to her fingertips. *I am no mortal*, she tells herself, and as stupid and silly and foolish as it sounds, Anna has no choice but to believe it—for Modgen; for his friend; for *Aimelie*, her beloved sister whom she thought she'd never get a chance to see again; and for the miraculous opportunity to restore justice and order to the kingdom that is rightfully hers. *Besides, I already have some sort of supernatural powers, as evidenced by my previous incidents.*

Heat swells down her left arm, a bit uncomfortable, especially as the feeling escalates to something like hot water rushing through her veins. Her wrist twitches, then her fingers do the same. She can sense the warmth reaching the air around her fingertips, heating up with molten energy. But it is not long. The sensation is dwindling, and Anna's concentration is breaking with it. *Don't panic*, she reminds herself again. She gasps for a breath.

"Everything all right?" Modgen questions, worry lacing each word.

The warmth is retracting back up her arm. "Just fine." She closes her eyes in the darkness. *I am no mortal. I can conjure any element easily, for I house the power of a goddess.* She doesn't know why she thinks that. It sounds strange in her mind, but in that moment, the heat shoots down her pale arm and through her fingers, tiny flames igniting the tips of her fingertips and catching the torch on fire in the blink of an eye.

Annalise makes a contained gawking sound, the flames on her hand disappearing as quickly as they came. The heat vanishes, replaced by a cool feeling, relieving the warmth of her magic. She looks to the torch, brown eyes reflecting the flickering orange light.

"You did it!" Modgen exclaims, giving her a hearty clap on the shoulder.

"I did," Anna replies, eyes locked on the dancing flames. *Yes, I did it—not using fire steel or a piece of flint. First levitation, now fire.*

"I take it you know where to go?" Modgen's friend asks. Annalise turns from the torch, which now illuminates every inch of the passageway. His green eyes are basked in the glow of the flames, patiently awaiting her answer. *Dark green eyes*, Anna notices foolishly. *Like the color of pine needles.*

She tears her eyes from his gaze, tossing a glance in each direction of the tunnel. Anna extends the torch to him. "Can you hold this for a moment?" When he nods, she flattens her palm, tracing invisible lines all over it with her free index finger. Her eyes drift shut, and her mental map comes to life. *Right would be north, then left would be south ...* They flick back open, and she retrieves the torch.

"This way," she announces, and the three imposters begin their trek through the underground tunnels, the leading female clad in oversized men's breeches and a navy doublet.

ADRIANNA

Adrianna's fingers brush over the navy-blue velvet, turning the feathered cap in her hands once more. She flips the hat over, rereading the name that has been inked on its interior tag for the seventieth time. *Robbin Flangham*, she reads, gritting her teeth.

The queen has been kept waiting for an hour too long in her own solar, leaving her little to do but bask in her fury until the page announces his arrival. And even more irritating is that her back aches from sitting so long in her tufted crimson chair.

"A princess must never slouch," Dria can remember her late mother saying, but Adrianna is a *queen* now, and queens can do whatever the hell they want. She falls into the cushioned back of the red velvet chair, smiling to

herself at the familiar comfort of disobedience. *Whoever came up with such petty rules anyway?*

Every moment too soon, a knock on the door sounds, the entrance of a page setting her spine back to its typical rigidity.

"Your Majesty, your—"

"Send him in," she barks, not caring to wait for her page's formalities.

He is dressed in his usual merchant's attire, copper from head to toe that matches his beckoning eyes and hair. Greeting Dria with a flirtatious grin, he takes a seat in the crimson chair opposite of her own. She waits for him to get comfortable, then tosses the blue cap into his lap.

He nearly jumps when it lands on him, surprise and confusion written all over his attractive face. "My hat," Robbin states, looking to Dria for an explanation.

"Yes; *your hat.*" The queen mocks him, blue eyes narrowing with distrust. "Do you know where your hat came from, Robbin?"

Robbin's swallow is audible. "I have an idea."

Adrianna chuckles, pushing herself up from the red chair and slowly beginning circle his own seat. "You have many ideas. This was not your brightest."

He turns to face her, copper eyes shining as he pleads his case. "She only asked me for a set of my clothes. I had no knowledge whatsoever of what she was going to do with them."

"What did you think she was going to do in men's clothes? Go to tea with her friends?" Dria shakes her head in disgust, rage boiling in the pit of her stomach, but she savors it, lets it warm her like she needs it to live.

Robbin opens his mouth to speak but says nothing. As one of her many spies in the city, the merchant has been under her jurisdiction from the time she caught him stealing her jewelry as a castle servant.

"*A waste of a pretty face, though,*" Dria remembers saying as the guards had him pinned on the ground, ready for beheading. "*You could win many a heart, I'm sure of it.*" And that is when it came to her. *Why not use him as a town spy? He would be indebted to me, keep a bit of freedom, and bring me the names of those who are plotting against me— especially women, who he seems to be highly fond of.*

The queen continues to lurk in endless turns around Robbin's chair. "Do you have any idea who she was?" she asks, bile eating away at her insides.

His copper eyes dart back and forth as she stalks behind him. "Of course. Her name is Piper. She lives at the Sapphire with her step-mother ... or basically sister, since they are so similar in age. She's been visiting the fruit stand since you've posted me there."

"What else?" The queen demands, wringing her fingers.

He makes a small gawking sound. "What do you mean, 'What else?' She never really opened up to me much. I tried luring her into treasonous statements, but she never fell for it. No backstory, wears a gray cloak rain or shine, pretty sure she's good at *halsen* ..." Robbin nervously toys with his feathered hat, melting from the pressure.

It is becoming harder and harder to fight her wrath now, but Dria convinces herself that the time is almost near to put that to an end. "Do you know what she did while wearing your precious hat?" she asks quietly.

He waits a moment. "No. I had presumed that was why you called for me."

At this, Adrianna cannot help but giggle. It is a hideous sound, more devilish than jovial, and when she smiles, the afternoon light reflects off her perfectly straight teeth. She stops mid-pace directly behind him. "This friend of yours took a walk into the off-limits section of the Royal Library. And when my pathetic guard Mig walked her up to my dais, I got a nice view of who she truly is."

Robbin spins around in his seat. "You know her?" he asks, copper eyes wide.

Dria smirks. "Yes. Yes, I do. In fact, I knew her *very* well, about six years ago when she lived under this very roof of mine." She stops in front of him now, savoring the utter shock and internal battle cloaking his lovely face. "I know her, because she is my sister."

Robbin is exasperated, shocked at the odds, angry with himself for not putting the pieces together sooner and horrified at the cost of such carelessness. "Your Majesty, she's been dead for—"

"*She's not dead!*" Adrianna screams, breathing heavily to try reigning in her indescribable frustration. She takes a deep breath, closing her cool blue eyes for a split second. "The Sapphire." She collects herself, hands clasped in front of her like the perfect portrait of a ruler. "That's a brothel just on the border between the main town and the slums, is it not?"

"That is correct, Your Majesty." Robbin doesn't dare break eye contact, as such would be insulting to his queen. *And his salvation*, Dria reminds herself. *He needs my being content in order to live.*

She slips over to a drink table, golden skirts sweeping across the wooden floorboards. After pouring two glasses of fruity wine, the queen returns to her debtor's seat. "Luring in traitors so that you can turn them in for treason is over. The plan was a failure, most exceptionally in this regard. I have a new mission for you," Adrianna drawls, moving aimlessly about her solar as she takes a sip of wine. "Somewhere in this gods-forsaken kingdom, my lost sister will be planning her retribution, to take back what she believes to be rightfully hers."

The queen's icy eyes rove over a vast piece of artwork suspended on one of her walls, her body simmering with vitriol. "When I sent my guards after her, I expected to see her head off later that same afternoon. Now, after scampering away like some mouse, she hides in plain sight—just as she has for years." Dria returns her attention to Robbin, still listening attentively with his navy-blue cap.

"I want her back," she whispers, hardly audible yet full of vigor. She prowls toward him, wine in hand, squeezing the glass so hard, it is amazing that it does not shatter in her palm. "And you are going to find her for me."

The merchant's mouth parts, his eyes searching for a response that could decline the order without costing him his head. "Yes, my queen," is all he can manage as he tips his rusty hair downward.

The queen makes no answer as she draws another heavy swig from the wine, draining the last drops from the cup. She swallows hard, then turns her sharp eyes to her spy once more. "And Robbin," she calls him. "You do remember what you are to me, don't you?"

Robbin Flangham says nothing, copper features too still to indicate anything but fraying nerves.

"First and foremost, you are *disposable*," Adrianna spits, flinging the empty wine glass into her bedroom wall, every piece of her spy's self-assurance shattering with it. Her heart is so full of vile, it is all she can do to contain her temper to dismiss him as soon as she possibly can. "Get out," she commands, and she need say no more. Robbin scurries away into the corridor, leaving Dria with her seething thoughts.

She sits back down in her crimson velvet chair, placing her hands on its arms as she begins to shake, first slowly, then a bit more violently. It happens to her, sometimes. It has been happening to her much more frequently as well, from bursts of angst that she just can't contain, or from the over-stimulation that comes from her aggressive tendencies. *Is this normal?* She often wonders, and today it seems worse than ever before. The only thing that stops the trembling is to let out her emotions—but such would likely result in the mass destruction of the castle.

Instead, Dria closes her icy blue eyes, replaying the scene over and over in her mind: Mig's entrance, the sound of her witless court gasping at the sight, dark tresses, darker eyes ... *Eyes that stare back in defiance* ... Sweat trickles down the sides of her face, and she bites her lip so hard that she tastes blood. The tremors are so violent, even her feet quake beneath her golden silk skirts. A ragged exhale slowly escapes her mouth, like steam from a kettle. For a moment, all she can smell is smoke, and something burning with her ire.

Desmond, I need Des, she thinks, but she hasn't told anyone about her seizures, even her lover. *Besides, how could I call for him in this state?* She imagines his silver eyes, the way his charcoal hair feels between her fingers, the feeling of comfort when he wraps her in his powerful arms ... and something eases inside of her blackened heart, a sense of home and belonging that she has trouble finding elsewhere. *Most people fan my flames, but Desmond smothers them*, Dria realizes, and a burst of hope emerges from the storms wildly brewing inside of her.

She continues her deep breathing, picturing Desmond in all his forms, taking stock in his imaginary presence. The trembling begins to subside, and Dria stills herself while a droplet of blood makes its way down her chin and onto the gold silk of her gown. Her sweat begins to dry, save for the dampness about her lower back, and she opens her eyes.

Red beads dot the fabric of her dress, and the smell of burnt fabric is suffocating. *Good gods!* Panic seizes the queen when she finds gray smoke spiraling upward around her white-knuckled hands. Biting back a scream, she leaps from the chair, collapsing onto the ground with the movement. Her blue eyes latch onto the crimson chair, but there is no fire. Only two charred handprints remain, smoke furling as the fabric fibers continue to smolder.

Adrianna's bloodshot eyes blink away their haze. Her reddened fingers dig into the wooden floorboards, scrounging for balance as the room sways from her fall.

Not possible, she thinks, she hopes. Dria shudders, eyeing the black handprints once more, their smoke dissipating into the air of the solar in silent opposition.

And the queen begins to laugh, tears streaming down her flushed cheeks. She laughs, through the swollen lip and the smoke, through the pain and the fear, until her vision fades to black and her blonde curls tumble to the floor with an involuntary dip of the forehead.

Part III

Heat

ANNORA

SIX YEARS EARLIER

Annora gives Melie and Anna each a kiss before sending them off to bed. "A princess needs her sleep," she tells them, even though they roll their eyes at the overused phrase. She watches them disappear down the hallway, heart lifting in delight, and drains the last of her wine. *I hope he never chooses this vintage again*, she thinks. *It does something to my nerves.*

The clock strikes nine-thirty, and the king and queen decide to slip off into bed. *A queen needs her sleep, too.* Annora smiles to herself. She removes her various rings of gold and silver, sapphire and ruby, opal and diamond. Now ensconced in a nightdress of ivory, the queen curls up beside her husband on their magnificent bed.

Tiberius sighs as he brushes back her brown waves, listening to the steady rhythm of her breathing. "You never asked where I was this morning," he whispers in the dark.

Annora looks up from his chest. "I thought you went to meet with the shipmaster again?"

Tiberius gently shakes his head. "I went to speak with the jeweler."

Her eyes grow in understanding before Annora gasps in the night. "You went to see about a crown for Annalise." A smile is audible through her speech.

"I thought silver with emeralds and jet would suit her well."

"She would love that," Annora answers, a yawn creeping into the last few syllables.

Tiberius laughs at his wife, pulling her closer under the thick burgundy comforter. "Get some rest, my love. You need it."

The queen huffs a laugh. "Perhaps you should take your own advice, dear," she replies, already half asleep.

The garden's colors are washed out from the blinding sun, but the flowers are unmistakable. Jutting up from the damp, brown soil are three sturdy sunflowers; sunflowers that Annora somehow feels she has planted. The air is thick with humidity, birds sounding calls in their own unique languages. The queen takes a few steps toward the garden, sunlight glinting off her chocolate-brown hair.

The first flower she notices is short and stout, its yellow petals large and grand, black seeds readily showing the world its splendor. The sunflower looks a bit young, perhaps due to its size. Annora smiles at its radiance, at its bravery and willingness to be itself.

To the right of the short flower stands a tall, formidable one. Like a soldier, this sunflower reaches up a foot higher than Annora is tall. Its leaves are broad and strong, and though the sun has given the world a white-washed quality, its colors seem to be more saturated forms of emerald and yellow.

Annora makes to move closer to these flowers, but the third one catches her eye. Just as tall as the strong plant to its left, this sunflower has a rigid stem. But upon closer inspection, the queen finds that its leaves are withering, their customary green color having faded to an ashy brown. Dark spots plague its stem, and when she cups the flower with her hand, she finds it on the verge of decay.

A sharp pain lances through her abdomen. Annora's heart skips three beats as she lets out a scream and collapses on the grassy field before the garden. She lifts a shaking hand from her stomach but finds no wound. *Help, I need help*, she thinks. She frantically looks around for someone, *anyone* to find her medical attention. There is no one in sight for what must be miles; only the whistling breeze offers its condolences.

"Help!" the queen yells, then gathering her breath again, she calls out once more. "Help me, please!"

A sound like rumbling thunder answers somewhere to her west. And to her unparalleled surprise, a flower—the third sunflower, full of death and decay—bends its stem over her pained body, its rotting petals staring into her frantic blue eyes. *What in the name of the almighty gods—*

Gasping with panic, she finds the motivation to try hoisting herself off the ground, but her strength is beginning to fade. *What is happening to me? This must be a dream, a nightmare. Flowers don't move as humans do. Yes, this is just a dream, a fever dream.*

Queen Annora lets out a hopeless laugh, as she tries and fails once more to right herself. Somehow, she wonders if this horror might be linked to the rotting sunflower, still gazing at her struggles with something like unflinching fascination. A small stone lies to the right of her outstretched hand, just a few inches away. She scrounges up the little rock and hurls it at the blackening flower with all her might—only to miss by two feet. *Mad. I'm going mad now, throwing stones at a flower!*

The pain in her stomach is worsening, and her vision is starting to sway. A tear rolls down Annora's cheek, slipping onto a blade of grass and glistening like morning dew. *How can a dream be so vivid? Dreams don't usually last this long, even nightmares.* A tremor passes through her legs, shaking her entire body with the movement. She tries looking up at the other sunflowers, but they are hundreds of yards away now. It is just her and the dark one.

Despite herself, anger boils alongside the slicing pain in her abdomen. *What will come of my children? My husband? My kingdom?* She grits her teeth while she returns the sunflower's dark stare. "Who ... *what* are you?" she forces herself to whisper.

As if in response, the flower's crumbling brown leaves turn to ice. Snowflakes begin to cloud the green scenery behind it, and a single wilted petal sails to the ground before her. The sheer unrealities are enough to confirm Annora's prior suspicions. *This is just a dream, and no one can dream of death. If you do, that's how you know it's real.*

But even as fire begins to dance in a circle around the stem of the heinous sunflower, even as the sky begins to turn a deep purple hue and the snowflakes turn to falling bits of noise like screams, the queen cannot shake the feeling that this is not merely a dream. And if it isn't, she is at least sure of one thing.

Annora blinks back pooling tears, closing her blue eyes. "She is ready," she whispers, before a dagger of pain slices through her gentle heart.

ROBBIN

The madam of the Sapphire has large green eyes, which she pins on Robbin as she finishes counting his money. Ladorra always was a cautious woman, counting patrons' change, then recounting it again, guarding her heart more closely than any one of her ladies. *Perhaps that could be changed*, Robbin Flangham thinks, as he flashes her a beckoning half-smile.

The attempt falls short. *A thousand leagues short.*

"You're sure you don't want Gissaira like you normally do?" Ladorra asks, long reddish curls spilling down the sides of a healthy bust.

Robbin diverts his eyes back up to her own. "I'm sure of it. As long as you aren't an option, of course ..." His grin grows wider at the blush blooming in those snow-white cheeks.

"Right this way," the madam murmurs, turning from the desk to lead him up a set of sapphire-blue stairs. Amidst the long white corridor, she stops before a thin oak door, giving the worn wood a few knocks. It opens under the third one.

Narelle's hazel eyes narrow in confusion at the sight of the fruit merchant.

"He has opted for you tonight," Ladorra informs her, leaving them both with a gentle nod.

Robbin greets the familiar courtesan with a smile, slinking into the room and closing the door behind him.

"I thought Gissaira was more your type," Narelle states suspiciously, eyes studying Robbin's person as he tosses his cape onto the window seat. Her chestnut-brown locks are twisted into a high bouffant, the look adding a bit more formality to the long silk robes that are traditionally worn by women of her occupation.

Robbin huffs a laugh. *Am I that readable?* "No, not tonight. I thought I'd give you a visit," he replies, and at this, her hazel eyes widen with a slight amount of alarm. "No, no—not for *that*," Robbin corrects, waving a dismissive hand at the bed. "In truth, I stopped by for my clothes."

The courtesan musters a smile, then moves to pour them both a glass of brandy. "Then you've stopped too late, I'm afraid. Piper left here as soon as she changed and hasn't been back since." Her hazel eyes betray a bit of apprehension.

And where did she go, after she escaped from Adrianna's grasp? "That beauty has one of my best shirts! Any idea of where I might find her?"

"None at all, but I wish I did." The woman's eyes are as solid and steady as ever. *Perhaps she is being honest? But it won't do for the queen.*

Robbin takes a swig of his brandy, copper hair catching the candlelight. He sighs after swallowing. "Was she always such a free spirit?"

"As long as I've known her," Narelle smiles. "Always so independent, choosing to chase her own dreams. I remember her heading to the library when she was younger; sometimes she'd be there for an entire day before coming home."

His copper eyes are watchful as she stares into the depths of her brandy, no doubt reminiscing about their past. "How long have you known her?"

The courtesan sighs heavily, turning her sultry eyes to the ceiling. "Since she was a young girl." She shrugs. "We found her at the brothel's doorstep one day, all alone and sobbing. She said she was on the run because she was being abused, and I offered to take her in as my own and pay for all her belongings. She is the closest thing I've had to family, probably the closest thing I'll ever have to it."

Interesting, Robbin reflects, hoping everything she said was true. *I wonder if she knows what the princess did after leaving the Sapphire* ... "And she just left, into the daylight, wearing my clothes?"

"If all you care about is your lost clothes, I'd be more than happy to purchase new ones for you," Narelle snaps, annoyance brimming in her seductive features.

Funny, I never had her pegged as being so temperamental. Robbin holds his hands up in submission, one hand still wrapped around the brandy. "It's no trouble, really, Narelle. I just thought I'd drop in to see if she came by." He stands, finishing the glass and placing it back on her side table.

Narelle does not stir. She simply continues to gaze into the amber surface of her brandy, brooding about her lost child. *Or perchance she is brooding about something else. How am I to know?* He imagines what the queen would do to glean more information from her, imagines the lengths that she would go to achieve any bit of wisdom more than he already had. He retrieves his cape, fastening it about his shoulders as he throws a quick glance back at the cobalt-clad courtesan.

"I'm sure she'll turn up, Narelle. You're her only family, too, right?"

She attempts a smile, weak with worry.

"Will you let me know when she comes back?" he asks her, copper eyes full of concern and kindness.

Narelle nods, a stray curl atop her bouffant bouncing with the movement. "Of course. Good night, Robbin," she bids him quietly.

"Good night, Narelle." Robbin bows deeply before retreating from her bedroom, scuffling through the white-washed walls of the brothel and out into the darkness of the night. *She showed up on the Sapphire's doorstep ... has no family left ... likes the library ...*

Nothing. That is what he truly has to offer his queen. No solid information about this shadowy girl, no leads to go off. He imagines the rage that will be strewn across her face when he feeds her mere breadcrumbs, thinking back to his last visit and the word that she had used, the one word that had left his head whirring for hours.

"First and foremost, you are disposable."

The sound of crashing glass replays in his ears, setting him even more on edge than he already is.

A plume of cigar smoke and the scent of ale sends him scuttling to the nearest tavern, dying to drench his misfortune with another drink. *Might as well make it a few. I'm going to need it.*

ANNALISE

Gray, murky waters chop restlessly at the sides of her small fishing boat, reflecting the dusk sky above. Annalise grips its sides forcefully, nails scraping into the wood with every rock and sway.

"... imity," a soothing voice calls from beyond the misty forest.

Back and forth, then back and forth again, she rocks in her wooden boat, like a toy ship in a child's bath. She looks down, and suddenly she is holding a fishing pole, its line reaching far into the distance. The thin string continues to float toward the shore, its bobber dancing atop the unsettling gray waters.

Again, the voice calls out. This time, she can make out a full sentence. "Where are you?"

It sounds far away, so distant that it is almost too

hard to decipher, but Annalise swears that she can make out the shadow of a female turning over stones on the shoreline.

Her breathing begins to heighten when she feels the waves begin to escalate their playful, mocking waltz, her pole nearly ripping free from her clammy hands.

"Di ..."

Anna squirms.

"... im ..."

The voice will not stop. She moves to tear her hands from the fishing pole so that she can cover her ears, but her line latches onto something at last.

"... ty—" the voice cuts out again, still offering snippets of a word that Anna cannot piece together.

Dark clouds begin rolling overhead. The waters grow more fervent, every rock of the boat nearly tossing her overboard. It is taking all her effort to remain in the vessel, but she cannot bring herself to let go of the fishing rod ...

"Reme ... remember!" the female shouts. "Wake up, *wake up!*"

Annalise freezes, hands still on the pole. She is in the middle of the stormy lake now, much closer to shore than before. The tree line is clearly visible, but she no longer sees the female figure. Only, something moves in the brush. She cranes her head, trying to gain a level line of sight despite the bouncing waters.

A dark shadow flickers behind a towering pine, disappearing behind the branches and bows—but this shadow is not the same as before. Something cold and wet begins to plummet from the sky, and Annalise looks up into the purplish clouds. It is raining, but when she looks down at her hands, the raindrops run over her veins like liquid silver.

Her brown eyes dart back to the forest shore, and she finds nothing but trees. Nothing at all, until an army of shadowy men emerges from the evergreens one step at a time, staggering in their attempts to stand as if they are made of true flesh and blood. Only then do the words ring loud and clear.

"Dimity, *wake up!*"

Her dark eyes flash open with a coinciding gasp. Annalise wakes with her sheets balled into her fists, deep-brown locks matted both to the front and back of her head. *Air ... not ... enough ... air*, she thinks as she swallows as much of the stale tower air as she can possibly suck down.

Through the small hole in the brick beside her bed, a sliver of washed-out morning light sneaks into the room, the only bit of serenity Anna has to cling to as she attempts to calm herself down. But the dream, the nightmare, *the name*, she remembers. *Dimity ... Why was she calling for the Goddess of Wisdom and Justice?* The princess palms a side of her sweaty face. *Perhaps she was praying for her aid ... but then why was she telling her to wake up? And better yet, why would I be hearing someone else's prayers?*

Annalise stands herself up from her bed on the stone floor of the library. She paces in her bare feet to the cedar chest filled with her last remaining clothes. She smirks sleepily. *And Robbin's. But I can't give those back.*

After an entire slew of loud-mouthed courtiers had seen Annalise Larking dashing around the castle grounds in his attire, it would be that image of a runaway woman that Adrianna and her men would be looking for. *That is, as long as Dria didn't know that it was me who had been dragged before her dais, though I'm quite sure she did.* This admission alone makes Anna's foul morning even fouler. She peers down at Robbin's clothes, which have been folded up neatly inside the chest. *Best just to burn them to hide the evidence. I will repay him for his gratitude.*

Anna peels her sweat-slicked nightdress from her back, exchanging it for a pair of olive-green pants and a white linen shirt. She would wash her face, but every blink of her eyes draws up a recreation of the sinister shadows clawing their way out of some forest, their faces nonexistent like black phantoms.

The jovial sound of male laughter tugs her back to reality. Annalise smiles, gleeful and strong. *Modgen's laugh,* she chuckles. *How could I forget?* The blissful sound draws her back to yesterday evening, when the mouthy lad was dashing around in a servant's uniform. The dampness of the dark castle tunnels, her grimy nails clawing at the underside of the sewer drain, the constant cramping of her leg muscles as she and the boys dashed across Guorden's Beach to reach her abandoned boat. Her legs still ache from running so much.

And then the sea. Gods, why does every path seem to lead me back to the sea? Anna could not stop paddling her arms across the gods-damned Falvedrie Sea, didn't stop from the beginning of their journey all the way until their blessed arrival at the marshes. And by the time Ivo opened the watchtower door ... *I'm glad he loves me,* Anna chides, remembering how wide his gray-blue eyes were.

Another gale of laughter dances its way up the tower stairs, this one different, less familiar. Annalise doesn't know what to think about Modgen's comrade just yet; doesn't even know if it would be wise to trust her own dear old friend, for that matter. After six years of their separation and a healthy dose of Adrianna's wrath, Annalise knows just what fear can do to even the most loyal of allies—which is why she isn't about to let that slip her mind.

Their speedy arrival left Anna and the boys utterly exhausted, so Ivo and Tasman granted them the mercy of postponing their interrogation until this morning. But relaying all of yesterday's humiliation is the least of Anna's worries.

Adrianna ... she knows. And Melie ... Both of her sisters are now aware of her existence, that Annalise has been alive and hiding in the shadows for all the six years after her presumed death. *How am I supposed to live like this? How will my sisters deal with this reality?* And there are always her more immediate troubles, like the guards who will be on the search for Annalise and her two newly acquired comrades who are *also* wanted criminals, and of course, her superhuman powers that spontaneously take precedence over her body ... *Bloody hell*, Anna curses. *I should have just remained the Waif.*

A pang of hunger has the lost princess tugging on her pair of shabby brown boots and clomping her way down the stone tower steps until she reaches the bottom floor. The men sit side by side at the little table in the kitchen. Across from them sits Ivo, hungrily shoving spoonfuls of food into his ever-dissatisfied mouth.

Tasman is perched at one end of the table and is the first to speak upon her entrance. "Good morning, my lady," he greets Annalise through his white beard.

Anna smiles, first at a cordial Tasman, then at a narrow-eyed Ivo. *This should be fun.* "Good morning."

Modgen offers a wide, easygoing grin that is typical of his manner. She returns his smile, all the while assessing the criminals. They have stripped their red servants' uniforms to expose the everyday garb they had worn underneath. Both men sit in a comfortable silence as they scrape their spoons across the bottoms of wooden bowls.

Modgen's companion looks up from his breakfast, his pine-green gaze finding Annalise's own. He gives her a kind smile, which makes her absurdly uncomfortable. *Gods, I hope I'm not blushing!* She means to turn away, but she stands her ground and approaches his side of the table. "I'm sorry, sir, but I don't think I caught your name yesterday."

Modgen snickers. "You mean yesterday while we were out running for our lives through underground tunnels? Ann, I don't think we had time for names."

She can feel Ivo tense, pinning his iron-clad death stare on the lanky redhead. Master Tasman holds up a frail hand. "Save it for the questioning," he advises.

The gentleman stands from his seat to extend a hand. "I'm Oliver," he informs her as he grasps her own. "Oliver McHenry. And you are?"

Anna freezes mid-shake. *McHenry ... McHenry ... the Master of the High Council?* She hesitantly looks to the others for advice. Modgen presses his lips together, Ivo flat-out ignores them both entirely, and Tasman only lifts his eyebrows as if to suggest that such a decision is up to her. Her eyes return to Oliver's, and she releases his hand.

"Perhaps we might first begin with what you know about me, if that would be all right?" Anna seats herself across from him to get a better view of the former council-man's face.

"Well," Oliver begins once seated, with a pointed look at Modgen's ever-widening blue eyes. "Last night our mutual friend told me that you were the daughter of a wealthy nobleman, belonging to some lesser house. When I asked why you were dressed as a man being chased through the castle—"

Ivo chokes on his porridge. "You were *what?*" His gray-blue eyes stare into the depths of Anna's soul. Even Tasman regards her with a baffled form of reproach. Before she can open her mouth to defend herself, Oliver continues.

"He told me that you tired of not being able to wear such fineries as belonged to the wealthier houses and soon developed a taste for the queen's finest jewels. You'd been devising plans to pilfer what gems and rarities the queen had stowed away until some richer gentleman could buy you all the sapphires you could possibly want." He glances sidelong at Modgen. "Did I miss anything?"

Annalise turns to face Modgen, choking back a laugh. "A gem thief? That's a clever one, Modge."

Modgen leans back in his chair. "I thought it'd be a good backstory, should you ever need to fall on it."

"I'll keep that in mind." Anna returns to Oliver. *Trustworthy, or not to be trusted. Honesty, half-truth, or lie?* Annalise does not like to play politics; she hates worse the act of lying to an innocent. *But what if he is not an innocent? What if Adrianna placed him in my path as soon as she figured out it was me in her Throne Room, then sent a simple pawn to see if he could get any leads?*

But even Anna, who tries to give people the benefit of the doubt, must be honest with herself. *Dria is typically quite rash, but rarely is she cunning. That was always Desmond's forté. And there is no way that she would have had enough time to devise a plan with her captain by the time I ran into the boys in the hayloft. No, their supposed escape was happening at the same exact time as my own.*

She studies his face quickly, disregarding the other members of the table. *Kind eyes, trustworthy eyes. They have solidity, something more than just a mask.*

"I am not a gem thief from a lesser house. In fact, I am not accustomed to wearing gems at all." She shoots an amused smile at Modgen. "My name is Annalise Larking, eldest daughter of the Royal Family and rightful heir to the Empeirian throne."

Oliver huffs a laugh. Then he looks at the others, searching for some bastion of reassurance that he will never find. "This isn't a joke," he says, more of a statement to himself than a question to the others.

"No, son. This is not a joke," Tasman replies calmly.

"I suppose that might be why two former members of the court are here," Oliver reasons. "But how do you know Modgen? He has been part of the council for years?"

Modgen grins. "The princess and I go way back. Our mothers were best friends, so we grew up together. My mother was godmother to the three princesses. So, I guess that would kind of make us like brother and sister?"

"Pretty much," she responds, rather impressed with how Oliver was able to piece everything together so rapidly.

Modgen's smile grows wider. "Yes, and—"

"*Enough.* McHenry knows who she is. Need we put off their questioning any further?" Ivo interrupts, not stopping to wait for Tasman to answer. He turns his attention back to the men. "Let's get to the heart of the matter. Who are you, why do you have the queen's men hunting for your heads, and what makes you think that we should trust you?"

Modgen's mouth closes. Oliver clears his throat.

"You might already know that Modgen Sprightly was Royal Treasurer to the queen."

Annalise stares blankly. *No, I did not know that. I must have stopped reading Tasman's book just before I read that bit.*

"As for myself, I was Master of her High Council, holding meetings to review courses of action for each division of the queen's court." Oliver shifts in his seat. "Modgen and I were opposed to one of the queen's ideas —more specifically, against potentially going to war over control of the ore supply in Javir."

Anna's eyes narrow. *Why the hell would she want ore? The throne already has enough to last it for decades.*

"The current Captain of the Royal Guard, Desmond Jrehart, had a … difficult time … coming to terms with the fact that some of his queen's council members might oppose her idea. After a meeting last week, Modgen and I played a few rounds of *halsen* one night at the Dog's Head in town. Desmond came in, told us the queen had an urgent need to speak with us and led us into the Royal Gardens. Next thing I knew, he freed his dagger from its sheath—"

Modgen interjects. "And I cracked him in the temple with a rock."

Anna gawks. "Did you … is he still alive?"

Sprightly laughs. "Oh, yes. Of course he is still alive. I just knocked him out of his drunken stupor, and I probably left him with an angry scar on the side of his forehead."

Oliver rubs his own temples with a thumb and forefinger, from embarrassment or guilt by association, Anna cannot tell. But she knows what this means.

"My sister will see you dead if it's the last thing she does."

Oliver nods sternly. He remains introspective for a few lingering moments. "And what about you, my lady?"

"Yeah," Modgen chimes in. "What *did* you do, Anna?"

The lost princess turns her eyes low, counting every

grain in the wooden tabletop. *They will laugh*, she knows. *It was such a stupid, simple thing. Anyone could have done it without being caught. Anyone, except for myself.* A tremor jerks her right index finger beneath the table. Anna's stomach turns. *No, not right now …*

All eyes are still on her.

"There was a book I wanted that I couldn't find here, nor in town. I decided to check the Royal Library when I was caught unawares in an off-limits section." She braces herself for the scornful remarks that never come. "A guard found me perusing the books and took me to the Throne Room. I escaped," she says with a shrug.

The table is silent. Tasman's lips press together, Ivo fumes in silence. The men continue to stare at her face blandly. Until Modgen breaks into a cacophony of hearty laughter, his pale face turning red.

"Only you, Anna." Another gale of laughter. "Only you would get in trouble for doing something that *detestable*." Modgen wipes a tear from one of his bright blue eyes.

Annalise can feel the blush transforming her own pale cheeks to a shade of rose, turning almost so red as Ivo's fury-filled visage. *Judging from his grimace, I probably shouldn't say much now.* She feels a gaze settle on her and turns to face the former Master of the High Council.

"What was the book?" he wonders.

She cannot help but smirk.

"Something that is obviously not as paramount as the

rest of the story," the old captain spits. "How many times have you been warned to stay away from the castle? Hell, it should be common sense. Your queen-sister tried having your head once before. What makes you think that she will do nothing to retrieve it yet again? Forgive me, my lady, but this was a rash decision you have made, and one that will be imposing consequences for the rest of your sister's reign, if not, your entire existence—which may have just gotten a great deal shorter if Adrianna recognized who you truly were."

And she did, Annalise knows. *Gods, she must be thrashing in her sleep over such an idea.* Tasman draws her attention away. "How many faces saw you in the courtroom?"

The princess huffs a laugh. "Hundreds, at least. Most were faces I didn't recognize; all were too oblivious to know who I was." She meets Tasman's kind gaze. "And Aimelie ... I saw Melie," she adds, clenching her jaw to stifle the beginning of a sob.

Tasman's faded eyes widen. "And she saw you, too?"

She smiles as she gives him a single nod.

Ivo snickers. "Might you also have had the royal page announce your coming?" He turns his angry gray-blue eyes to Tasman's. "There is no turning back now. We have to prepare for the worst."

"And what would that be?" Modgen asks from across the table.

The former captain meets his curious stare. "That Adrianna is already preparing for Annalise's capture. That nowhere here is safe for her, or *you*, for that matter. And that we need to act much more quickly than we had anticipated."

AIMELIE

Queen Adrianna throws the crumpled-up letter atop Aimelie's coffee table, scowling with disgrace as usual. *What is it this time?* Melie wonders, bending gracefully from her chair to unravel the ball of parchment.

The letter has been written in childish script and is brimming with grammatical errors, but she can read the message clear enough. *It is a letter from a certain farmer and his family that needed more land, the one that I granted an acre more to, despite Adrianna's orders.* Melie's blue doe eyes peek up from the paper.

"Enough," Dria spits, her long, braided hair swaying slightly.

"What's enough?"

"Don't play the fool with *me*, Aimelie. You know

precisely what that is. How sweet for the poor farmer to write you a thank-you letter for disobeying my command and bestowing upon him the *'finest gift of his life.'*" The queen scowls. "No doubt one that he will use as an excuse to make more pathetic serfs just so that he can beg for another acre."

Melie's spine straightens. *She thinks herself so much higher above everyone else.* The observation makes her sick. *Even a poor beggar in town is as much a human as my sister.* But as much as Aimelie wants to believe this, she knows the truth. According to law, Dria really is higher than anyone else. *She is the queen, for the gods' sakes.* Regardless, her large eyes narrow ever so slightly.

"He and his family asked for *one* more acre, so they would have enough crops to supply for the kingdom and feed their family. Why is that so burdensome to *you*, who has everything she could possibly want?"

She can see the wrath before she hears it.

"Everything I could possibly want, is that right? Do you honestly think that I have *everything* that I could *possibly* want? Hmm? I want a good night's rest, I want to be able to go prance about in the ballroom whenever I feel like it, I want to be able to feel what it's like to be peaceful and energetic and happy all the time, but do I get *any* of those things? No, I don't." The queen's eyes are burning with fury, her hands rather shaky. She places her right hand across the bottom of her cloth-of-gold bodice, and

Melie begins to worry that something more serious might be going on.

Neither of the two sisters has talked about Annalise's untimely entrance, and the tension has been driving Melie mad for the days since it happened. She can only imagine what it is doing to Adrianna's nerves. If Anna is still alive, she could pose a threat to the crown—and that is something her sister would never take lightly. *In fact, she'd probably try to kill her rather than decide to live with that threat.*

"Dria? Are you all right?" Melie questions, leaning forward with concern.

"Do you *ever* shut up?" the queen sneers, but Melie can sense that her trembling is getting worse, and her eyes look as though she is straining to uphold her regality.

And is that a cut there, on her lip? Melie wonders. Before she can open her mouth to say more, Dria cuts her off.

"You are no longer sitting in for me at court. Instead, you shall continue your education with Linden, and begin each morning with the task of handing out gifts to the poor after church." She gives the princess a half-smile. "Since you like giving things away to those who need them most."

The queen turns on a golden heel and leaves her sister's chambers without a goodbye. Concern eats away at Melie, an unsettling companion to the guilt that has been ravaging her body for days. *It was me, it was all my fault.* The clock in the far corner of her teal and silver room chimes three, and Melie knows what she must do to at least lessen this guilt once and for all. *You're not the only one who hasn't been getting fair sleep, Dria.*

She stands, smiling at the letter before tossing it into the fire, then pulls on a silver-threaded cloak. With its hood up, she leaves her teal chambers, making the lengthy voyage down to the castle dungeons. Every twist, turn, bend, and door leaves her feeling smaller and smaller, her confidence decaying like whatever else has made its way down here.

The black rails of the dungeon entrance are rusted with age, and the smell of rotting flesh and uncleanliness permeates through them, a fitting greeting for her already sour stomach. The few guards posted outside the door let her pass without question, one trailing behind her for security measures. *One never knows when the gods may grant a criminal enough luck to make a final assassination attempt.* Even so, the cell doors are heavily fortified, solid steel cubes with a small, barred window just large enough to make out a few quite unsavory faces.

Who does she keep down here? Melie dares to question, her big blue eyes averting every gaze with something like embarrassment. She thinks back to a time when a similar question had been posed by a member of the Queen's Council, and recalls Dria's only reply: *"There's an old saying I like to live by: keep your friends close, and your enemies closer."* The way her sister said it, with that serpentine smile, still manages to send shivers down Aimelie's pin-straight spine.

Her stomach sinks with each click of her silk slippers, her blush-pink gown rustling under the silver fabric of her cloak. Even with her hood up, she can feel their stares —vicious, angry, some filled with decades of honed vile. A scream bellows through the dungeon air, stopping Melie in her tracks. *That was him, I know it.*

"My lady, such conditions are not suitable for a woman of your high status. Please, allow me to accompany you ba—"

"No. I'm sorry, sir, but I need to speak to the traitor that my sister encountered at court two weeks ago. Sven, I believe. He was a previous member of the Royal Guard. If you would, I should be grateful if you showed me the way to his cell," the princess finishes, sounding much more authoritative than she had anticipated.

The guard hesitates, his plain features twisting into a visible dilemma. *He dare not defy the queen's sister, though,* Melie assures herself. Indeed, he gives in, though it is plain to see that he wishes it wasn't so.

"Follow me, my lady," he says as he leads the way to Sven's cell.

Following his lead turns out not to be necessary, given that the screeches grow louder and more consistent, a pulsing beacon that could be heard from miles away.

What is happening to him? Aimelie frets, her heart racing ever faster before they reach the door.

I was young, I was naïve; I only wanted to find her.

The guard casts her a final look of warning before unlocking the heavy iron door.

The first thing she notices is the stench, something like old sweat, overflowing chamber pots, and the coppery tang of blood. Her stomach lurches, and for a moment she finds herself forgetting all about her guilt and focusing entirely on how to keep her lunch down.

The cell is dark, the only light sources being a few stray tallow candles burning on the ground in each corner, but it is still enough to see by if she lets her blue eyes adjust, and when she does, there is naught to do but wince with terror.

His gray eyes are virtually swollen shut, red and puffy, and one of them even looks to be leaking blood. His blocky face is marred with bruises and wounds, more round than square at this point, and his pushed-in nose is crooked. *Broken*, Melie thinks sadly. His breathing is labored, which she soon finds is from a certain torture device. His lungs are suppressed by a heavy weight, something that Melie believes to be a block of iron, which must be crushing his ribs. On top of the block are smaller ones, probably adding more weight each time that he didn't give the gaoler an answer that he liked.

And above all the dirt and grime and blood is the

curdling emotion of sheer guilt, the dead weight within herself of complete and utter shame that *she* has done this, that *she* had sent Sven and Ivo and Tym and Dallis to continue their search for her lost sister against Dria's explicit commands to drop the search for Annalise. *I should have never opened my stupid mouth. And what had it cost them? Their jobs, their happiness, and ultimately ... their lives.* At least, Tym's life, when he was beheaded at court. *And soon Sven's life, too.*

"Leave us," the princess orders the guards, watching them file out and close the thick metal door behind them. She turns her blue eyes to Sven, whose own eyes are almost swollen closed as he lies on the table.

"My lady?" he asks in a hushed tone, so broken and small, painful even to listen to.

"Sven," she replies, moving a bit closer for a better look at his face. *He looks even worse than from far away, which I didn't think could be possible.* "I cannot begin to describe to you how sorry I am."

"It was our mistake, Princess. Ivo did his best to keep us away from the castle, but we got caught on our way back to the tower when we were at the harbor ... not your fault," Sven retorts hoarsely.

Melie chokes back a sob, her eyes welling with tears. "I ... I was the one who asked you to defy her orders, to keep looking for her. I was the one who caused you all to lose your places in the Guard, all for the dream of finding my sister again."

Sven gives what could have been a chuckle, then winces in pain. "You've overlooked one very important word, my Princess: *asked*. You never ordered us, like your sister would have. You gave us a choice. And ... my lady ... you've given us a gift."

Her blue eyes narrow in puzzlement, a tear slipping from her left eye.

"Without you, the search for Annalise would never have been successful," he ends, eyes drifting off somewhere in the distance.

Melie lets out a breath of air. "You ... you *found* her? I mean, you *definitely* found her?" She takes another step closer in anticipation.

"Never ... never told them. Even through all this." His drowsy eyes gaze pointedly at the contraption he is strapped into, at the blocks pressing down upon his ribs. "They don't know ... can't know." Sven's gray eyes begin to roll into the back of his head. "Tell her ... she ... was worth it," he manages, struggling to find breath.

"Sven. *Sven.* Stay with me." Melie moves to shake him awake, placing her slender hands on his thick, blood-stained shoulders, but he is strapped into the device and there is not much wiggle room to move his body beneath all the weights and straps. *I cannot help him now,* she cries from within. There is no way that she is strong enough to move any one of the weights.

His weary eyes give one last flutter. "For a ... better ... world," he ends, the last word merely formed by the force of his final breath.

"*Sven!* Look at me, Sven!" She knows it is pointless, that she should be trying to be quiet so as not to draw attention to herself, knows still that all roads lead back to her. If it weren't for the deep, scathing longing for her lost sister, her insolent dream of time turned back, Sven would not be lying dead before her. Tym would still have his head, all of the four guards and Master Tasman would still have their jobs and a safe home to come back to.

But amidst her wavering hold on hysteria, she remembers Sven's words: "... *the search for Annalise would never have been successful.*" Bitter tears turn sweet at the final confirmation of Aimelie's wildest fantasies: *Annalise is alive.*

Her heart thumps in uneven beats, unsure of whether to cry or laugh or fall to her knees in prayer over one or the other. The world is glowing and tilting and burning all at once, Melie's head swimming with a thousand different tunes. *It really* was *her in the Throne Room. Annalise saw me, she knew me, I could feel it!*

She tries calming herself, lengthening her breaths to keep from shattering or dancing in the damp darkness of the dungeons, Sven's blood still all too fresh. *She is alive.*

But where can I find her? Melie runs her slender hands through her honey-gold locks, blue doe eyes searching for an answer in the candlelit cell. Sven's corpse is the only offering.

Sven. The tower. Did they get her to move to the seclusion of the tower? And if she did take up residence there, would she really run back after being caught red-handed by the queen? Aimelie recalls finding the old watchtower as a haven for the men she had unintentionally dismissed, bestowing it upon them both for their valor and as a meager reconciliatory gift for their sacrifices. *The marshes were always overlooked, ever since the tower had been abandoned in favor of a new one built on the mainland, just north of the Royal Harbor.* Her nose wrinkles in thought. *Dria has her rats sweeping every corner of the city, but Anna still hasn't been found. Perhaps she has been hiding out in the tower all this time.*

"Princess Aimelie?" a guard calls from behind the steel door.

Melie lowers herself to her knees before Sven's still body, sending up a quick, silent prayer to the gods who sent his soul to help her find her sister. *You are blessed, Sven. May you rest in eternal peace, knowing the insurmountable kindness which you have done for myself and many others. May the gods bless your soul.*

Guilt begins to eat away at her insides again, and she casts one more look at Sven's swollen face. "... *a choice,*" she remembers him saying. *Sven would want me to keep going. To continue their efforts, to make sure that their choice was indeed a good one.* Giving his corpse a silent nod of respect, Melie stands, exiting the cell, turning to the guards with puffy eyes hidden beneath her silver cloak.

"This man has passed. See to it that you burn him properly, and when you do, I want his ashes placed in the finest urn you can find. You will inform me when this is done. Is this understood?" Melie awaits their response.

The guards exchange looks of confusion, obviously unsure as to why they should treat a traitor with such respect, but the gaoler nods.

"Yes, m'lady," he replies, and both men bow their recognition before Aimelie sweeps her pink skirts behind her, turning her back on the past and choosing to chase a bigger, brighter dream.

ANNALISE

Two hours. They have been talking about her mistakes and their consequences for *two hours* at the kitchen table, planning and conjecturing and coming up with ways to undo some of the damage that she has done. And when she realizes that this is completely her fault, Annalise Larking cannot take it anymore.

"We need to stay discreet for at least a week's time, but I'm just not sure this watchtower can pose as a reasonable hideout anymore," Tasman explains. "Truly, what are the odds that you weren't followed?"

All my fault. Terror seizes Annalise's stomach, throwing her internal state of balance way off-kilter. She tries reigning in a shallow breath, but it is too late. Her brown eyes lock onto the orange in the center of the table as she watches it lose a bit of its vibrancy. *Calm down. Everything will be okay. Just relax, just ...* Small crystals begin to form over its surface, first one, then two, spreading like a patch of snowflakes growing atop its orange skin. *Stop! Stop it!*

But no one seems to notice, no one except—

Oliver squints at the freezing surface of the summer fruit, his green eyes analyzing, deciphering ... He scans the others for signs of reciprocating confusion but finds that nobody else notices during their heated conversation—until he reaches Anna's face. He begins to open his mouth ever so slightly, but Anna's stomach thrashes. *I am going to be sick.*

She stands immediately. "Pardon me. I'm not feeling well."

With that, and without waiting for their approval, she makes quick work of taking the steps up to the next level, pressing a hand to her lips while overhearing bits of their private conversation.

"... just embarrassed ..." says Ivo.

"Adrianna's name is enough to make anybody sick," the former Master of the High Council adds.

She might have been grateful, might have smiled at someone coming to her defense if she hadn't nearly tripped up the stairs due to a sharp pain in her left forearm. Anna bites back a scream. *Like a knife*, she thinks. *No, like ice.* Her stomach pains lessen for the time being, and she uses the opportunity to take the steps two at a time until she practically stumbles into her library-bedroom.

The tremors grow more rapid now, her thin body gently quaking in the dampness of the watchtower. *Too cold in here*, she realizes. In fact, she is shaking so much that her teeth begin to chatter. *What the bloody hell?* Her knees give out and she collapses to the floor. *Almighty gods, please hear me now!*

She claws her way to one of the few blankets she'd strewn on the floor as a makeshift bed and is mortified when a gust of wind bursts from her left hand, sending the cloth fluttering across the stone floor. *No!* Defeated, Annalise curls herself up into a ball, attempting to comfort herself during such a nightmare.

And then darkness descends all around her, cloaking the entire room in a black shroud. A different kind of breeze sweeps by, one that makes the princess lift her tear-stained eyes from the floor. Anna squints, making out a shadow slithering across the wall, near to where the shattered picture frame from her first supernatural encounter still hangs.

"Hello th ... imity," the shadow greets her, its voice faint and far away.

The darkening room begins to tilt and swirl in her vision, turning her stomach further. Her brown eyes narrow on the shadow, which grows into a man-like form. *Gods, no—it's just like my dream. I must be mad!*

"Do you know who I am?" the shadowy male asks, his grimy tone now sounding clear.

Annalise blinks away a tear, shaking from cold and fear. "Do you know ... who *I* am?" she asks between quakes.

A dark laugh. "Still not awake yet, are you? You know, your friend is desperate to see you up. She will need your help if you are to work as a team."

This is a fever dream. "What the hell ... are you talking about?" Anna forces herself to ask, a heavy weight seeming to press upon her shoulders.

The shadow male gives a sorrowful sigh. He picks an imaginary piece of dust off what would have undoubtedly been his doublet. "I really did wish that you would be better competition, my lady. Although, your sister hasn't woken up yet either, so ..."

A memory flashes through her fraying mind: fiery red hair, eyes like blocks of charcoal, a blood-curdling smile. *"... come and see this blue and green sphere with me?"*

Heat like fire blossoms through her veins, melting off any remaining ice.

Jed ....Jedda? Her brown eyes narrow in confusion.

Darkening clouds, darker shadows. A burst of silver rain.

Cold air rushes and swirls all around her skin, damp with sweat; the hushed, female voice from her dream replaying in her mind. *"Remember."*

A deep, lascivious woman's cackle that permeates through the air at a long, white table.

No human has eyes like that. And no human should ever be given that name ... Anna recalls the great domed temples that have been constructed all throughout Empeirus and around the world. *Because ... because Jedda is a goddess.*

"Remember," the female voice beckons.

Another snippet of the lurid goddess and her coal eyes. A feeling like simmering rage as she looks onto Jedda's twisted, carnal features. *It's not right*, she thinks in the memory. *"Your heart is black, Jedda."*

The string of a fishing pole pulling taught, the wet feeling of silver droplets falling from the bruised heavens. A hundred dark soldiers faltering from a line of pines.

"Remember."

Annalise trembles violently, teeth clacking in the chaos of the wind and the heat and the electricity of memories too grandiose to conjure.

The slithering voice of a shadow in her bedroom; the curiously familiar way he speaks and moves.

"Remember."

The thunderous boom of a father figure. A glass orb being cradled by fluffy, white clouds. The *ping* of a tossed coin, whirring on a tabletop.

"Remember."

The fishing line catching on something she cannot

see. An invisible hand reaching from so far away, an invitation to unite.

"Remember!"

And then she is sitting at a white table, with hair black like jet and eyes like hot embers. She recalls her devious sister's plot to destroy their creation—the Earth, she realizes—and how stubborn each of them was in their ideas of what to do with it. She remembers the agreement; her father, Lazarus; Ione's short blonde hair; the way Elouthera's silver earrings dangled like two teardrops of quicksilver that matched her luminously pale face; the formidable handshake with her sister that left them both drowning in an inky abyss.

Because ... because ... I am Dimity, Goddess of Wisdom and Justice, daughter of Lazarus and Valea ... and sister to the Dark Goddess, Jedda.

Anna's heart stops for one beat. Two. Then a third.

And if I am Dimity—

"Well? Can you at least tell me how much longer I will have to wait?" the shadow man asks, with none of the patience that the Master of the High Council had offered her earlier. Another sigh, this one chock-full of derision. "That's too bad. I would have liked to have seen you try."

—then this must be Anzac.

He moves quick as an asp that has been poised to strike, throwing out a hand and sending a shadow pointed like a spear hurtling toward her head. Anna throws herself onto her side, rolling onto her knees and hoisting her less-shaky body into a defensive stance. The shadow bolt she has dodged disappears, seeming to dissolve into the stone wall behind her. All at once, she throws her hands out at her sister's accomplice and forces the remainder of her energy into her hands.

A strong wind begins to twine through the dark room, coursing thickly around her palms. Anzac is still in shadow form. *He must only be able to show himself in this form. Perhaps because of the long distance, or not enough power?*

A low rumbling sound, like groaning roots, comes from the ground behind Anzac. And just when the shadow god throws out his black hands for another shot, Anna launches her own up into the air, sending a circle of green stems lurching up from the stone floor and arcing around the man.

"What the—"

The stems bow into a sphere above his head, almost like a cage, but Anna isn't done. Her dark eyes flash as she crushes her hands into fists, and the stems and flowers constrict, squeezing around each of Anzac's limbs until he can no longer move.

The shadow man grunts, shifting and struggling to snap free of her grip. His breathing grows ragged, and at last, he relents. "Where are you?" he asks, and Anna knows why he wants such information. *He will want to tell Jedda when she wakes, too.*

"I need to know where ... you ... are," he manages before slipping a hand free.

Annalise gives him a bit of wiggle room, and just as she suspects, he takes advantage of it to shoot out a tiny bolt of a shadow. Not wasting any more time, she sends the roots into Anzac's mouth and up through his phantom nose, traversing the stems through the orifices that he would have had in a normal body. Muffles are his only response, the cries getting quieter and quieter, until finally, Anzac disappears, the shadows and the darkness dissolving with him.

The world returns to its normalcy, although now, it is anything but. While their battle must not have fully affected the physical realm, some powers made their way past the mirage. Her winds must have blown every book off the old shelf, many of which have flipped open to random pages. The blankets of her makeshift bed are now scattered about the stone floor, though her old teacup and saucer have managed to stay on the desk. *I'll fix it tomorrow.*

And aside from the physical massacre, Annalise is now plagued by a series of impalpable realizations. *I am Dimity. I am a goddess. And my sister... my sister, Jedda, is somewhere on this planet in a mortal form, just like myself.* Anna cannot dwell too much on it all, she knows. Besides, a growing swell of sheer exhaustion is making its way over her entirety. *My bed, I need to lie down.*

Though the pains and shaking have subsided, Anna has never felt so tired, so empty. *Anzac ... in my room ...* But he must not have realized where she was if he had asked her. *And where is he? He could be anywhere on the Earth, just like Jedda.* Annalise realizes that in this form, she also has a given name. *They will not have the same names, either. How did he track me down in the first place?*

The weight of exhaustion presses further into her bones, and Annalise can form no more coherent thoughts. The last thing she can do is collapse, fully clothed, onto the heavy blanket she calls her mattress before being slammed into an ever-looming oblivion.

AIMELIE

She can hear the pleasant, bubbling sound of water when she exits the castle door, tamping down the grass with every one of her light footsteps. The White Garden has always been Aimelie's favorite place within the castle grounds, the perfect place to brood and reflect without being trapped in the cramped quarters of her chambers.

A white stone pathway runs in intersecting circles around various parts of the garden, each loop connecting in the center of the space to make a flower shape, of sorts. Every loop is different; some with clusters of white trees for escaping the heat, others with soft grasses perfect for picnicking in, others still with floral archways, stems and white petals intricately woven through the openings of the white-gold metalwork. While Melie loves all the loops, her favorite is the most secluded: the White Pond Loop.

The White Pond has its name for its crystal-clear water, tinted white by the floor of pure white pebbles along its bed. The pond is deep and wide, and should perhaps be called a *lake*, but the sight is breathtaking, nonetheless. The entrance to the White Pond Loop is formed by a canopy of white Ione Trees, named after the Goddess of Purity, Kindness, and Charity for their stunning, silver leaves and bark. The canopy leads to a silver, grassy plain bedecked with miniature gardens of white rose bushes, lily of the valley, and white groundcover. The silver blades of grass dance in the gentle gusts blown off the White Pond, shimmering around the scattered ivory benches that have been placed around its perimeter.

As Melie emerges from the Ione Trees, it is only a matter of seconds before she finds herself inwardly squealing with delight, despite having dealt with such unsettling matters earlier. *Sven.* Her heart sinks. But she would not let herself retreat to those days when self-pity was her only means of existing, would not let herself be sucked into the endless and unfulfilling black hole that got her nowhere in the past. *No. Sven served a great purpose in this world, and countless lives have been blessed because of his sacrifice. Without Sven ... we may never have found Annalise!*

The sunlight beams down on her cheerful face, and

she realizes—with no small amount of amazement—that she is *happy*, that she is excited for life and teeming with hope. She moves her blue doe eyes in both directions to ensure that nobody is around, and allows herself a sporadic hop of joy, a giggle burbling from her pretty pink lips.

She is alive! Annalise, my sister, is alive!

Suddenly, she cannot contain her elation any longer. A short pier juts out into the gentle waters of the pond, its silvery wood beckoning in the fall sunlight. *Alive, she's alive!* Melie prances over to the edge of the pier and slips off both of her slippers. Hiking up her blush skirts just to the knee, she extends a foot and kicks the crystal-clear waves, toes playfully skimming the surface. She chuckles to herself, tilting her forehead up to the clear blue sky until something catches her eye in the reflection of a ripple.

"Careful, I don't think the queen allows for princesses to have fun," Linden quips, and before Aimelie can think better of it, she grabs hold of his hand.

"I don't think she could stop me if she tried." Melie smiles, then launches into a sprint, dragging Linden along with her as they plunge into the cool, clear waters of the White Pond.

Her golden locks emerge from the chill waters, her blue eyes wide with an electric sort of energy. It takes her a bit of effort to keep afloat from all her heavy dress fabric, but her ecstasy seems to add a whole new layer of strength to her character. Linden's head pops up only seconds later, gasping for the early autumn air. His caramel eyes lock onto Melie's, both of them all too caught up in the moment. With a single stroke and without a word, Linden takes Melie's head in his gentle hands and presses a kiss to her lips ... only to pull away a moment too soon.

"I ..." Linden frantically looks around the White Pond, and Melie understands why. If the boy had been caught touching a female of the royal bloodline, he might very well have lost his head for it. "I shouldn't have done that."

But Aimelie would not have it. She would not have any more of Adrianna's cruel, vain plans. And Linden has just admitted to wanting the same damn thing that Melie has been wanting ever since the day she first met him.

"Yes, you should have. Because that is what I've been waiting for." Aimelie pushes herself forward, closing the small gap between them and kissing him back, pure of heart and full of pride.

He returns her kiss, which sends Melie's toes curling in the clear water, and then slowly pulls away. Linden's caramel eyes stare into her blue ones.

I have to tell him. Her heart begins to race harder.

"If I tell you something vital, will you keep it a secret for as long as you live?" She knows just how dangerous such a move is. *If he is playing games with me, if he is playing with my heart* ... But Aimelie knows that he is genuine, and she can tell when a person is trustworthy.

Linden laughs under his breath, brushing away a matted lock of hair on the side of her face. "You mean just as secret as this is going to be?"

"Precisely."

He meets her eyes once again. "Most definitely."

"Good," Aimelie replies full of glee and ornery play. "Because I'm going to need your help."

VEGA

wake, Vega repeats in her mind, clinging to the word like it is the very core of her existence, her salvation. *Dimity is awake!* It was this thought that had Vega leaping out of bed this morning, tittering with maniacal happiness that echoed off the walls of her stuffy dorm room.

For the past seven nights, she had been hopelessly yanking on that invisible connection, shaking it with all of her might just to induce even the *slightest* bit of reci-procity on the other end, but Vega ... *Elouthera* had no such luck.

Until this morning. Until she had felt the rousing and steady thrum of Dimity's power, using their bond to 'feel' out where her lost friend is. It hadn't been easy, figuring out where she was. And, in fact, Vega isn't even quite sure that she is correct. *But it has to be close*, she reassures herself. *She has to be somewhere near the capital.*

It is this bit of confidence that Vega has been turning over in her mind as she approaches the Wembleton ship harbor, brimming with hordes of seafarers short and tall, thin and stout. The cry of a gray gull pierces the sounds of harbor life; the lapping of cloudy waters against the hulls of ships, the flapping of sails in the salty winds, a hundred voices of passersby and captains giving orders to their crews and the calls of deckhands and would-be passengers. The vessels bob steadily, stoically, their flags flitting in the wind like a flickering rainbow of blues, emeralds, blacks, and oranges. Her lime-green eyes dart left to right, then left again, until she focuses her gaze on one vessel in particular: *Her Lady's Crown.*

The galley is one of the largest in the harbor, hardly swaying in the wild Orlian Sea; its rich brown hull contrasting sharply with the bright gold Empeirian flag secured atop its crow's nest. *She's beautiful*, Vega thinks, and for a moment it all feels like a dream.

Vega has never been to the mainland before, has never felt a particular longing to go there, in fact. She and her family had always stayed on their chilly island just off the west coast of Nesvla, residing on the family estate with little else to concern themselves with. *A simple, petty life full of simple, petty things.* There was little to do but play court by her father's orders, waiting for a suitor that never seemed to come. "*The Kutchrik Estate needs to have a solidified future,*" her father would always croon. But time continued to pass, slow and uneventful. Vega grew bored, restless. *Everything was so predictable.*

Until the day that Vega's mother up and left them both behind for a life on the road with the Nevs. Her mother's untimely departure was not only a blow to her heart, but also to her confidence. *Was it something I did? Had I disappointed her?* While Vega and her mother were never truly close, they were not detached either. She could not recall any time when her mother was unhappy with any of her actions, no matter how displeased her father was with Vega's nonexistent romantic or social life. *And why the Nevs?* The orphic cult had fascinated Vega's mother for as long as she could remember, and her mother was indeed a free spirit, but ...

Her heart had shattered, her family had fallen apart, and her life was entirely altered. While Cyndeya Kutchrik had left without a personal goodbye, she at least had the decency to leave Vega with a small consolation gift. Her father found the pouch of money with its attached note on the kitchen table the next morning, storming away as if it was left to spite him. But Vega had mustered enough of her courage to open the parchment, reading its contents with as much sympathy as she could.

My dearest Vega,

You are still too young yet to understand why I had to

leave so abruptly, and perhaps you may never be able to, but you must know that I love you with all my heart. I have left for you half of my life's savings (your father is a greedy man), so that you can follow your talents at the House of Perception. I know you will do very well there, my dear.

If you ever wish to find me, look for me in the Nevs' traveling caravans. I will never be too far away.

Love always,

Mama

Vega had never looked, had never *wanted* to look for those cursed nomads' wagons. But while her mother's untimely absence had given her years of unresolved pain, a few of those heartbreaking, damned coins have made their way into Vega's left palm, jangling slightly as she approaches *Her Lady's Crown*.

"G'day to ya," one of the deckhands rings in a Fetlandish accent, stooping on a knee to unload some cargo.

"How do you do, sir?" Vega asks politely.

The sailor chuckles. "Wind's low, and the sea's a bit too smooth for m'liking, but all in all, not so bad. How can I help ya, m'lady?"

"Where is she headed?" she pries, taking a look at the galley's gargantuan masts and sails.

The deckhand places a heavy crate on the ground with a grunt. "Why, Empeirus, of course!" He shoots her a friendly smile. "She'll be makin' port at the Royal Harbor right near Larkingsport."

The capital—the stars are aligned! Vega nods with glee. "Any room aboard?"

He hands her a smaller wooden box to hold while he passes on a much heavier chest to one of the sailors. "Hardly," he laughs. "Might be some room on the floor, unless you can rig yourself up a cot or somethin'." He retrieves the crate from Vega's small hands, then sets it aside. "We leave tomorrow at dawn. I can go get the captain for ya if ya plan on payin' upfront. Probably be about six hundred."

She stifles a choke. "*Six* hundred?" Her feline eyes grow as wide as they can. "Are you open to negotiations?"

The sailor cackles, faded eyes turning up to the pink sky in amusement. "I doubt it, m'lady. This here is a one-month voyage, and food is scarce on the water. Trees don't grow very well in the sea, if ya know what I mean. *Her Lady* is a trading vessel, and we need all the space we got. Room's hard to come by—even more so for a lady like yourself that won't be much help on deck." He pauses uncertainly. "Still interested?"

Perhaps it is the strong, formidable scent of the Orlian Sea, or the lingering resentment from her mother's years-old spite, or that she has recently been taking stock in the fact that she is Elouthera, and that Dimity needs her help halfway across the world somewhere.

Vega nods. "I'd like to speak to the captain, please."

The clanging of forks and spoons punctuates the chatter of a hundred mouths in the House of Perception's dining hall. Christa and Vega sit at their typical two-top table in the corner, propped up against a wall that is close enough to see out of a purple stained-glass window.

"You seem different, Veg," Christa states between stuffing her mouth with a spoonful of turmeric-and-red-pepper rice. "Like you seem … *healthier*, or something."

Vega laughs, lime eyes twinkling. *Can she really tell?* "Honestly, I don't think I've ever felt this good. I mean, I just feel more … awake?" She smiles at the double-meaning of her word choice, watching as Christa pauses her chewing to consider it.

"All right," she says casually, chestnut ringlets springing as she moves her head from one side to another, continuing to weigh Vega's response.

Vega would miss Christa's nonchalant grace. Would miss spending time laughing with her best friend, would miss even the not-so-great food in the dining hall, and the way the black and white tiles click under her boots before the enormous doors of the House of Perception. *And here I am, preparing to do the same exact thing that my mother had done to myself so long ago.*

Christa would hate her for it, would never forgive her should she return. But if she told her, Vega knows, Christa might propose maintaining contact via letter, and Vega cannot decide which would be harder: living with the unhappiness of dropping one of her most joyful friendships forever, or settling for a paper-friendship, starving for a companionship and connection that would never compare to what their friendship had been in person.

"Veg? You all right?" Christa's blue eyes are wide with concern.

"What? Oh, I'm fine," she shakes her short hair. "I just ... I need to show you something." She bends from her waist to seek out the form that the captain of *Her Lady's Crown* had granted her earlier this morning. *Granted me for five hundred coin*, Vega notes. *At least I haggled him down a bit.* She rests the sturdy parchment on the table between them.

"A piece of parchment?" Christa asks disappointedly.

Vega sighs. *This will be harder than I thought.* "No. It's a form of passage for a ship, *Her Lady's Crown*. Christa ... I'm leaving Wembleton."

A spoon clatters to the table. "You're *what?!*"

Several looks of concern turn to face the two of them, but Vega remains calm. *I am a goddess. I can do anything.*

"You're leaving school? You're leaving your life's work, your potential job offers, you're leaving *me!*" Christa cries hysterically. She folds her arms. "You can't. I won't let you."

Vega chortles. "I have to."

"You have to? What could possibly be more important than school, than your best friend, than your future? Well?"

At last, Vega opens her mouth to speak. "I want to travel the world. I want to see how others live." A gentle laugh under her breath. "I've been stuck here, trapped in a place where I just don't belong. My grades ... I've surpassed even the abilities of most professors. If I stay here, I will waste time getting a degree for a job that I honestly wouldn't want. And if I leave, while I won't get the degree, at least I will feel like I followed my heart. At least I wouldn't be living someone else's dream."

She pauses, preparing her emotions, trying to keep them on a tight leash.

"I love you like a sister, Christa. You're like the family I never had, but sometimes we need to make some hard choices. And sometimes that means taking a different path than the one our family walks." She swallows her tears, mostly to remain composed, but also to refrain from accidentally weeping silver teardrops all over the dining hall table.

Her best friend's blue eyes fill with tears that tip over their edges, sliding down her ruddy cheeks. It is all she can do to nod, chestnut curls rebounding with the movement. "Where will you go?" she asks quietly.

Vega bites her lip. *I don't know. Somewhere in Empeirus, hopefully.* "Empeirus, to start."

Christa makes no comment at this. "And will you return? You know, to come visit me?"

Vega reaches across the table to place a small hand atop her friend's. "I will visit at least once a year," she promises, but even Vega cannot believe her own lie. *If I have enough money. If I have enough time. If, if, if…*

Christa snorts, brushing away her remaining tears. "You'd better. I deserve your utmost regard," she laughs, Vega admiring her friend's rebound of confidence. *I know I would likely melt onto the floor in a puddle of sorrow.* "When does the boat leave?"

Vega braces herself. "Tomorrow at dawn."

Her big blue eyes grow wide with disbelief. Christa opens her mouth, and for a split second, Vega swears that she is ready to throttle her once again. But her full lips close, and she steadies herself with a breath.

"Well then, what are we waiting for? Daylight's burning!"

OLIVER

Oliver McHenry is lost in thoughts and words. He pushes the last of his porridge around in its bowl, silently waiting for Modgen to return from upstairs. *To return from waking the princess*, he reflects.

It has been a day, an entire day since they had last seen Annalise Larking after her untimely leave during yesterday morning's interrogation. *What could she possibly be doing up there? She never came down for lunch, or dinner, for that matter.* Ivo had offered to bring food up to her so-called bedroom, but Tasman declined. "Let her be," he said. "The girl needs her solitude like the moon needs her stars."

But such questions aren't the only things sending his mind reeling. Oliver replays the situation with the orange from the night prior, the ice forming over top of its bright skin, the way that Annalise looked at him like she had just accidentally shared with him some forbidden secret. *Oranges just don't freeze at room temperature,* he broods.

"Stuck, are you?" the former captain asks Oliver, who pauses mid-bite.

"On what, sir?"

"You know what. I can see it in your face, master. You look at her, and you won't let yourself believe it. Goes against all your senses, like you're lying to yourself by accepting the truth. I know it because I've been there. We've all been there," he says as he gestures to Modgen, Tasman, and himself.

Yesterday's interrogation had gone rather fairly, and Oliver had pleased the captain and the master with his answers. But excelling at an interview and gratifying on the job are two very different things, as Oliver is finding out. *He will always see us as the enemy. And why shouldn't he? We've been working for the false queen for our entire careers.* The only thing Oliver can do is to help their cause in every way he can, and to gain familiarity with his new allies, which is easier said than done. *And trust is a two-way street, Captain. What makes you think that I would entrust my own life to all of yours?*

The captain continues, his stubbly, thick jaw jarring with each of his words. "Open those eyes of yours, lad. Stop lying to yourself. If this were a game, we wouldn't be playing anymore. If this were a game," he laughs, "you'd be dead by now."

Tasman offers only silence, stroking his white beard solemnly, though Oliver swears he can sense a bit of fear behind it, too. *Fear for the princess, perhaps? They seem to be close*.

The sound of heavy boots clunking against the stone steps sends each of their heads turning, forgetting all about the graveness of their current affairs. Lord Sprightly saunters over to his chair, slouching back and crossing his long arms. "Woke her up from a dead sleep," the redhead says with a dazed look on his face. "How could she be sleeping for twenty-four hours straight? Not to mention that she had every book in the room thrown open."

Tasman's kind eyes search hungrily in the distance, clawing for an answer. Ivo shakes his meaty head. *Twenty-four hours ...*

The female toes her way down the watchtower steps, just as she had the morning prior. *The princess ... the lost princess ...* Oliver watches Annalise Larking move with cautious curiosity. Her earthy brown locks rock and sway just as gracefully as her regal gait, and it is impossible to believe that such a female could be tucked away for so long in the slums. *Hard to believe that she had survived it*, he thinks.

The table is silent as Annalise makes landfall, the

Master Tasman tapping his black cane restlessly on the floor. Oliver watches warily as the princess pads over to the kitchen, dark eyes locked on a freshly-warmed pot of porridge. Without a word, she intently scoops out a large portion and slides it onto the rickety wooden table, shoving spoonfuls into her mouth immediately upon sitting.

They wait, none brave enough to interrupt Her Highness. Oliver cannot help his inadvertent stare while she scrapes the bottom of the bowl with her spoon, scooping up every last oat with the ferocity of a knight in battle. He has never seen a lady eat like this before. Not once in his entire career at the Larking Castle has he ever caught a fawning noblewoman shoveling food into her mouth without a hint of guilt, much less so in front of other nobles. *Well, except for Harper*, Oliver smirks. *But my sister has certainly not been accustomed to lace gowns and courtrooms.*

Ivo clears his throat.

And Oliver finds his gray-blue eyes set on him. He freezes. *Oh gods*, he swears. Ivo's jaw grinds as he sends Oliver an unmistakable message: *Stay away from her or suffer my wrath.* Oliver swallows. *I didn't mean anything, I was just—*

Annalise wipes her lovely mouth with the back of a wrist and places her spoon in the bowl. The table says nothing. Until Modgen opens his mouth.

"How?" he asks her, running a hand through his rusty orange curls.

Annalise smiles, and in that moment, he realizes that there is something different about her today. Perhaps it was all that sleep, all the rest, but she looks healthy, full of life, radiant. *And beautiful*, Oliver notes, though such thoughts would not serve him at the nonce. *Or anytime in the future, for that matter.*

The princess opens her mouth to speak, but Ivo beats her to it.

"Never mind how or why, we have more important matters to contend with." The former captain nods to Tasman, who searches the sage green fabric of his cloak with a wrinkled hand.

The elderly man withdraws a letter, smudged with dirt, and warped by what looks to be watermarks. "Our newest recruit left us a message the last time I stopped by the mainland."

"Narelle," the princess speaks, and Oliver can tell that her excitement is not feigned.

The old master nods, but his soft blue eyes are wary. "She writes that Robbin came by for a visit asking about your whereabouts."

Robbin? Who is Robbin? Oliver wonders, his green eyes traveling to meet Annalise's own. The table is silent, everyone waiting for an explanation as to who this unknown person is.

"Robbin was the fruit merchant who gave Ivo information about me in the first place. And he was also the man that gave me his clothes so that I could infiltrate the Royal Library." She narrows her eyes and turns them down to the wooden table before her. "He was always a friend, but he never once paid a visit to the Sapphire to check up on me."

Tasman waits, reading her expression. "And?"

Annalise meets his gaze. "And ... something doesn't sit well with me about this," she finishes.

"Something doesn't sit well with me, either," Modgen chimes in as he retreats from his chair. "We have servants' garb and the clothing of a wanted woman collecting dust in this damned tower, and the whole of Adrianna's guard is on our asses. Don't you suppose that we at least get rid of the evidence?"

Modgen, never one to waste words, Oliver chuckles to himself. *I think it bothers him when he's in a confined area for too long.*

Annalise nods. "Burn them. The mists around the tower are thick enough to hide the marshes for at least two miles in any direction." She stands from her own seat at the head, then pauses. "I want to make a visit to Narelle to discuss this issue in person. It's been a while since I've seen her, anyway."

Ivo's teeth clench even tighter than normal, and Tasman shifts uncomfortably in his seat, but Modgen stretches out his long, lanky arms above his head with an enviable ease.

"I'll go with her," he decides.

"Perfect idea," Ivo adds, though his demeanor says anything but.

Modgen clunks his seat back down on all four of its legs. "What? If I'm captured, you've no loss there. But Anna needs you and Tas. The two of you are her strongest allies."

"And you are also a wanted criminal by the Crown," the burly former captain finishes. "Might as well throw McHenry in the mix too, so they'll have all three bounties in one place."

"That's not a bad idea."

I'm sorry? Oliver raises his eyebrows.

A groan from Ivo has the table shifting. "What makes you think this is a good idea in the least bit of sense?"

The princess pushes in her rickety chair and lifts her chin. "I'll take my chances. Lord Sprightly is right. He and I have known the roads of the kingdom like the backs of our hands since we were children and traveling with two men offers more protection than one. If something should go wrong, then that's a risk I'm going to have to take. I can't stay in this gods-damned tower anymore. I need to make a move. And as much as you want to deny it, Ivo, I can very well take care of myself. I've been doing it for most of my life."

Annalise Larking turns her dark brown eyes north-ward, searching for the reassurance of her master.

Tasman just barely dips his white beard in the form of a nod, giving his most hesitant approval.

The former captain clamps his jaw shut for one second, two. "Very well. I cannot make your decisions for you, I can only advise you on which decisions are best to make." His gray-blue eyes turn to Oliver and Modgen. "Consider this your test of allegiance, because if either of you fails to protect the princess in any regard, I will personally see to it that both your heads be put on a pike —and the Crimson Queen won't be there to stop me."

VEGA

The lights of the shops in Wembleton's capital are twinkling in a bright array of colors, a final charge against the ever-threatening night. A bakery locks up shop, while in the same moment, a local pub owner props his doors open farther.

Vega and Christa walk arm in arm, enjoying their last stroll together as they take in the early fall atmosphere of rust brown and bright orange and crimson red. Christa stops at the entrance to a milliner's shop, swiping a lime-green tea hat with a terribly wide brim and setting it atop Vega's head, cackling at the sight.

"At least it brings out your eyes," she jokes, while Vega quickly places the garish hat back on the rack to avoid any more stares of amusement.

"*Ooh!*" Christa coos, reaching for a bottle of deep-red

merlot on a vendor's cart. "Veg, do you think that between the two of us, we could finish this before you leave in the morning?"

"Definitely not," Vega says as she takes the bottle out of Christa's hands. *I'm going to miss this*, she thinks sullenly. *I'm leaving all of this behind—my studies, Wembleton, my best friend ...*

The neon bulbs swing on their lines from tree to tree, clinking gracefully on a crisp breeze. The scents of jasmine and lemon balm fill their noses, sending them tottering with linked arms to the nearby perfumery, where they try out a plethora of exotic scents that leave them each with a slight headache.

A few more stops—at a candle shop, a quaint boutique, and a rather lengthy stay at an adorable bookstore—eat up whatever precious time they have left to share, and soon Vega dolefully announces that she needs to return to her dorm to finish packing. The girls continue to make their way down the street in silence, neither caring to elaborate on the dour topic of Vega's impending departure.

Christa breaks the growing tension when they near the end of the road, the 'Alley of the Gods' street sign rising out of the darkness like a faraway beacon. "We need to stop," she presses, pointing to the sign. "Vega, we have to pray to each and every god out there for your safety. I won't let us go home without knowing that I've done everything I could to help you."

Vega rolls her citrus-green eyes, smiling at her friend's kindness all the while. *Would that include praying to myself?* "If it will ease your nerves," she replies, knowing that it would at least ease her own. *Maybe it will earn me some luck from the others.*

The journey will be long and torturous, Vega knows, but there is no other way to get to the capital from Wembleton than by ship. And Elouthera would do anything to find Dimity—not just for her friend's sake, but also for her own sanity. It is like she has been avoiding a mission for as long as she has known about her awakening.

The stars give Vega their blessing from the clear night sky above. Both girls make the long journey from the top of the alley to the bottom, seeking guidance in each and every temple, just as Christa had stated; starting with Lazarus and Valea, stopping at Ione's and Darrion's temples, paying respects to Harshla the Goddess of Weather and Phaytos the God of Land and Mountains. They even stop in Elouthera's own temple, which feels to Vega a lot like talking to herself, but she is flattered by the kind words that her friend sends up for her.

By the time they reach the end of the road, Vega's knees are red and sore from so much praying, and her voice is raw from overuse. Christa had dragged her into every temple. *Well, all except for one.*

"Where are you going?" her friend asks, big blue eyes peaked with curiosity.

Vega shakes her inky black hair. "No. I'm not going in there."

Christa narrows her eyes. "You agreed to pray to *every* god and goddess, Veg. That would include Anzac. What's the problem? Have you gotten on his bad side?" she chuckles, sending her ringlets bobbing.

Vega swallows tightly. "I hope not. Christa, I don't want to go in there. It's … unsettling, to say the least. Have you ever been in Anzac's Temple?"

Christa gives her a look. "Veg, he is still a god. Don't you want to make sure you ask for his blessing, too? In case of emergency, or too much darkness, or feeling claustrophobic, or—"

"*Okay*, fine. We can go in. But let's make this quick, I have to finish my packing."

The black stone pathway leading to Anzac's temple is darker than the night around them. Stealing a breath, Vega closes her eyes as she passes through the familiar black granite doorway. *Dark as night, dark as death.* Only three lit candles offer enough light to see by, once her eyes adjust. Christa stops before the black hole in the center of the floor, situating herself on her knees and extending a hand to her friend.

"Come on," Christa goads. Vega slips her palm into her friend's, lowering herself into a prayer position.

And Christa immediately clenches her thin forearm, fingers locked like steel.

"What the—" Vega starts, before she hears the voice from far away. *His voice.* She shivers.

"Back so soon, Elouthera?" he quips, shadows seeming to slither over the black granite with the sound of his malicious tone. Only this time, it seems to be audible in the temple itself, not just inside of Vega's head.

She ignores him, turning back to Christa, whose jaw is set, and expression is emotionless. "Christa, let go!"

"She won't listen to you, love. She's under my express command," Anzac drawls.

Vega's feline eyes narrow in confusion. *What? That's impossible ...*

"You always did have a way of seeing the best in people, Elouthera. Funny thing though, that she is not a person at all."

Her eyes grow in hysterical disgust as she watches Christa's blue eyes and bouncy chestnut ringlets morph into the form of a shadow—a black, translucent phantom; a shroud of mist with a head and limbs; a coal-colored mockery of a human being. *Christa, my friend; Christa, my family; Christa, my ally and confidante.*

Anzac sniggers, low and serpentine. "Foolish girl," he admonishes. "It was only a matter of time before one of my pawns could find you. A fascinating girl with an uncanny ability to manipulate? Perhaps you could have found a less conspicuous life story, darling. And all it took was a bit of patience, the right amount of time until you could make a move that would have my pawn recognizing your awakening. *Christa?*" he snorts. "Well played, wasn't it? Like black magic," Anzac laughs vainly.

But ... Vega thinks back to her friendship, from Christa's nondescript backstory to her obsessive interest in Vega's manipulatory abilities. Her teeth begin to chatter from cold or fear or something else altogether. Vega's lithe body begins to shake, and she searches inside herself for something, anything to do. *If I scream, someone will surely hear me, right?*

But she knows that no one is around at this time of night, and she isn't about to make a fool out of herself. *My powers*, she recalls, *Yes, of course, my powers!* The goddess points her lime-green eyes at the shadow that was once Christa, focusing on her mind. *I manipulated your mind once before. I can surely do it again ...*

A few seconds pass, and Vega can begin to feel the threads of Christa's mind weaving slowly together like some incomplete tapestry. But in the midst of her efforts, the shadow strikes before Vega completes the manipulation. It shoves Vega to the floor, yanking her hands behind her back.

"Stop! Get off of me!" Vega screams, hoping, praying, dying for somebody to overhear her.

Anzac's self-absorbed chuckle is the only aid offered to her. "I don't know where our precious Dimity is yet, but one surely will lead to the other, right? So long as I have you ..."

"You *bastard!*" she spits, full of bile and rage as Anzac's shadow pawn binds her hands with some sort of rough material. A thousand thoughts plague her racing mind—a *million* thoughts—but there is one that she must ask, must voice for the sake of having tried.

"Where are you taking me?" Vega snaps, struggling in her ropes as she bashes the shadow's face with the back of her inky hair.

The God of Darkness and Decay laughs, knowing that he has just won the fight. A hint of a smile leeches its way into his midnight-smooth voice.

"Why, to me, of course."

ADRIANNA

"That's all?" Queen Adrianna asks, vitriol straining her voice.

Robbin nods curtly, keeping his copper eyes on the solar floor.

It has been days since she had last sent her merchant spy to gather intel on Annalise's whereabouts, specifically at the brothel in the slums where she was last seen. *Well, last seen in the public's eye. I last saw her dodging guards in my own courtroom, scrambling out of a window to remain just out of my grasp.*

Dria clenches her golden chalice, wishing its red wine were her sister's blood. Her lip has scabbed over, and the tremors have lessened over the past few days, but the queen still feels uneasy and on edge when she is upset. *And when am I not upset anymore?*

Dria props herself on the foot of her enormous bed, its fine golden blankets shimmering in the sunlight. "Of course, she liked libraries; she risked her life to set foot in my own," she chuckles seductively. Taking a deep drink from her chalice, she holds the wine in her mouth to taste it for a moment before swallowing. "Tell me, Robbin," Adrianna begins, "what use are you to me if you cannot do your job? Hmm? Why should I keep you if you are wasting both my time and my patience?"

His tan skin fades to white when he meets the queen's icy eyes and swallows. "I am trying with all my might, Your Majesty," Robbin attempts. "I know that I have failed you this time, but I promise not to do it again."

The fear in his brassy features is enough for Dria to carry on. *Let's see how much you mean it, boy.* "What kind of people do you think I expect to work for me? I need loyal ones, yes, but also people who I can trust to do their job and to do it well. If I was desperate for information and needed it to save my life, who could I count on to aid the throne?"

Robbin speaks up. "I, for one, would volunteer."

The world stops. Adrianna freezes as she is sucked back into time and space to a familiar white table, full of faces that she knows by both morning mass and memory. Somewhere in the distance, she knows that she has dropped her wine chalice, but the boom and rattle of her father's voice dominates all.

Lazarus addresses the gods and goddesses with a fervor that she has seen many times before. *Always loud, always authoritative.* Jedda had never liked her parents, but they did take a lot of work off her back when it came to managing the council of gods, even if that work would be split between herself and—

Dimity's long black hair and amber eyes make Jedda cringe. *So graceful, so poised, so wise.* Everything that Jedda has trouble finding in herself. But at times like these, when she is feeling bad about herself, she turns to her other half, her counterpart.

Anzac's gray eyes sparkle with their flecks of red, like embers in a fire, and Jedda's heart latches onto the only soul in the universe that she can relate to. His solution to their Earth dilemma seems to be an interesting one, and Jedda is never one to say no to a challenge, but her body recoils at the thought of separation from her lover. When he opens his mouth to agree to be her protector, her black heart sings with joy. Until it is Dimity's turn to find a partner.

Every god and goddess is silent, all except for one who speaks up with her silver eyes and confident chin.

"I, for one, will volunteer."

"*... my queen?* My queen?"

Adrianna Larking snaps out of her daze, cool blue eyes locking onto the hands that are wrapped frantically around her biceps. *What in the name of Laz—*

The queen shoves Robbin away from her, disgusted by his close proximity.

"My apologies, Your Majesty! You weren't responsive for almost an entire minute; I didn't know what to do," Robbin tries, plucking the chalice from the wine puddle on the floor.

Your Majesty. Oh, yes, Your Majesty. I am the queen ... and I am ... She takes a ragged breath, steadying her attention onto something harmless, like the wine puddle. "You are no longer of use to me, Robbin. I was planning on letting you go as a beggar, but after this ..." She motions to her arms, fighting her anger and shock and fear so that she can form coherent words, "I'm not so sure I want you gallivanting about my kingdom."

Robbin palms the sides of his copper brows, whimpering as he falls to his knees.

The incessant pleading has Dria's temper soaring again, and the wine on the floorboards begins to simmer, steam rising in front of Robbin's horrified face. *I gave him another chance, and he failed me. I trusted him to be alone with me in my solar, and he laid his hands on me.*

"Guards!" Adrianna calls, remembering her life as a queen.

Two men dressed in shiny gold armor enter the room, prepared to do whatever is necessary for her safety. "See to it that he spends some quality time in the dungeon," the queen orders, trying to tune out Robbin's screams and pleas. "Let him learn what it is like to be of no use to the throne."

The guards haul the fruit merchant up off the floor, one on each side, ignoring the steaming puddle of wine between the man and the queen.

"I tried so hard with you!" Robbin cries on his way out. "There is no pleasing a *snake* like you!"

The queen snickers as the heavy mahogany doors shut, pushing her honey blonde braid over a shoulder. *And for that, he will rot for eternity.*

A bubbling sound catches Adrianna's attention on the ground. The wine is beginning to cool down, as is her temper, and the realization of the past five minutes hits her like a slap in her wolfish face. *Jedda ... Yes, of course! How could I have forgotten? All the tremors, all the pain ... They were my powers acting up, trying to wake me up! And—*

Anzac, the God of Darkness and Decay; her protector, her lover. *He could have incarnated anywhere on this gods-forsaken planet. I need to find him.* But a nagging feeling in the pit of her stomach tells her that she already knows where he is, and even his name.

DESMOND

He feels it before he understands it. The locking, the clicking, the snapping into place. His dark heart shakes at the feeling, and he presses a silver-gloved hand to his chest. "You must excuse me," Desmond tells his new recruits. "Continue practicing, and make sure to eye up the sights while you aim. I want to hear some good news when I return." The Captain of the Royal Guard turns on a heel.

Where is she? I can feel her, but I can't find her.

A heavy-set cook nearly topples over backward when Desmond rounds the corner. His gait is tight and focused, and he has to, *needs* to find her. He takes the crimson steps by threes, even with all his weapons, because no matter the weight, it is nothing compared to the heaviness of his heart when he cannot be with her. *Her golden hair, her pale blue eyes, her tireless, impassioned energy ...*

"Pardon me, sir—"

"Not now, Jax," the captain bellows. *There will be time later for those matters. Right now, I need one person, and one person only. I have waited* years *for her to remember herself again.* He turns down the corridor at the top of the stairs and begins looking within himself for any signs of her presence, any invisible strings that might lead him her way. By the time he reaches the second flight of stairs, his heart is pounding, his hands are shaking, and he needs her.

"*You,*" she beckons, her blonde braid swaying against her hips as she stalks down the hallway. Her ivory dress is accented with golden thread, but it is not her usual choice of attire. This one is fitted at the top and loose at the bottom, flowing over her gorgeous curves and leaving little to the imagination.

It takes Desmond all of two seconds to reach her before she grabs the collar of his crimson shirt and locks his lips with her own. He doesn't care if there are servants around or if his fellow guards might see, only that he is with her and that he has found her and that she is safe in his arms.

Adrianna lures him back inside her chambers, and in the time it takes for her to shut and lock the door, he is on her, all over her, and she cannot stop touching him.

"*Anzac*," she whispers into his ear before using her leg to nudge him closer, pressing messy kisses to the side of his neck.

"*Jedda*," he whispers back fervently, like a prayer. *A prayer only to her.* He places a palm on both sides of her face, running his fingers through her honey-blonde hair and undoing her braid with his mouth on her own.

Jedda pulls away to examine his silver eyes. "Why didn't you tell me?"

He huffs a laugh. "You have no idea how many times I wish I could have. I didn't want to jeopardize your experience of life from a human's point of view. Things change when you remember that you are a god." A scene of a bed and shattering glass slips into his racing mind, of how desperately he wanted to tell her everything at the first hint of her powers. "But we're here now, and we're not alone anymore." He smiles, pulling her off the door to undo the laces of her scandalous ivory dress.

The gauzy fabric slips to the floor, and it is Jedda's turn to pull off his shirt and unlace his breeches, kissing his bare skin everywhere above and below his waistline. He pulls her into his arms, retreating to the bed, and lifts the heavy golden covers. Anzac pulls his goddess close, her blonde hair spilling onto a pillow. She uses a delicate hand to lift his chin, forcing him to meet her icy blue gaze.

"We don't know where Dimity is," his lover states angrily. "We don't know what her name is, or what she looks like, or where she will turn up on a map. How are we supposed to fight an evil that has no face?"

He runs his thumb along the scab on her lower lip and thinks for a moment. *Dimity will likely be wondering the same thing.* "You're right that we will have to fight her. We both know Dimity is still going to want Earth to be in the Alliance, and she will do anything to protect that." Anzac pauses, meeting her pale blue eyes. "What is the most powerful way to control the world?"

Jedda remains quiet for a moment while Anzac brushes back one of her stray curls. "Power," she replies. "The throne."

He nods. "I believe that when Dimity wakes, she will do anything to compete for a shot at the throne. She will want to help guide Earth's inhabitants to be better so she can turn the tides in her favor."

"And you think she will need the throne for that?"

Anzac kisses her cheek. "It's hard to make a difference in the world when you aren't in a position that other people fear or admire. A simple civilian's word is nothing against that of a nobleman, and the word of a nobleman is naught against that of a royal. You see, it's not so obsolete, the way all this just so happened to play out. The deity who holds the throne, holds the power to control the world."

Jedda nods her agreement. "We need to eliminate all threats. Enemies on every front, and any one of them could be my sister Dimity. I will do everything in my power to secure the throne—starting with sending my best to succeed where Robbin so blatantly failed." She leans forward to plant a kiss on Anzac's muscled chest.

He lifts her pointed chin with a finger and returns her kiss, then pulls her on top of him, her blonde locks forming a veil of privacy around their faces, meant only for them.

"The others," Jedda stops, her chest against his own while he tugs the covers over her pale shoulders. "How will we know if they're awake, too?"

Anzac smiles, wicked and mischievous. "Well, I've found one already."

VEGA

She can feel its rock and sway before she opens her citrus-green eyes, her sight mottled and fuzzy from the aftermath of what she believes to be poison. A sharp *creak* and a quiet *groan* have Vega's feline eyes fully awake, squinting into the dimness of the dank cabin. She makes to move on her cot, but her body is still under paralysis. *Lazarus almighty.* A slight turn of her head allows Vega to catch a glimpse of the cramped world around her.

"G'morning to ya," a shipmate calls to her from across the wooden floorboards. His face is dirty and unshaven, and he sports a red bandana across his oily forehead. His comrade lazily holds up a *halsen* card by way of greeting before removing his cigar to blow out a ring of sweet smoke.

Vega attempts to move her jaw, but it is tender and clamped shut. *Like my hope*, she thinks drearily.

"Yer friend went to fetch ya some porridge from the kitchen. She'll be back in a few minutes, I'd reckon."

The feeling of a rogue wave has Vega reeling to the left, and she braces herself to roll off the makeshift cot she rests upon, but there is nothing to collide with save for the side of a wooden hull. *I'm on a ship. I'm on a ship, and I have no idea where I'm going.* She recalls the last few bits of memory she has from what seems like so long ago. *The temple of Anzac, the shadow pawn, Christa ...*

Christa. The realization that her best friend for years had been nothing more than a mere illusion conjured up by one of her godly opponents is ... unnerving, to say the least. *And to think that I haven't had a human friend in years.*

Her heart jumps back to the night before, Anzac's shadow pawn shoving her to the cold black granite of his temple. *Are my hands still bound?* she wonders, but with the drug in effect, she doubts that ropes would be needed. *The drug. I've been poisoned.* Vega cannot stop the growing trepidation within her, cannot prevent it from spreading from her mind to her heart to her now-quaking limbs.

She has heard of it before, *Egvivius fasayra*. A lethal drug, even if taken in a moderate dose, and one that will cause physical symptoms that mirror sleep. *Only on the inside; a drop in heart rate, decreased blood pressure and brain activity, and total paralysis.* Used by criminals and kings alike, *fasayra* is a powerful drug used for carrying out powerful acts. *And I have been its most recent victim.*

Somewhere in the shrinking distance lies her body, its strings of control just on the other side of the gap between her mind and the physical realm. *Christa, I need to speak to her.* But then Vega realizes that she has no one, nobody to turn to. *But perhaps all my hope is not lost … I have Dimity.*

Dimity, her ally and accomplice in the preservation and protection of this world. *Dimity, who is thousands of miles away from me and might not ever be able to reach me.* Even though she could feel her friend's presence and awakening, Elouthera knows that she is still far too distant to be of much help right now. *There is nothing I can do but wait and prepare.*

"Hungry?" a familiar voice questions from her feet. Christa, her false friend, stands with a bowl of steaming hot breakfast at the end of her cot.

Vega slowly opens her jaw, releasing a soft groan.

"I'll take that as a yes," she responds with a smile blossoming beneath her big blue eyes. "I'll set it on the floor for you to eat whenever you're ready."

Vega can almost reach the cords that are connected to the rest of her body, can almost feel them in her grasp—

"Remind me again of how much longer we will be on the Sea?" Christa asks the sailors playing *halsen.*

The dirty man with the bandana laughs cheerfully.

"M'dear, we've only just begun! Day one of at least twenty, maybe thirty, depending on the weather," he remarks in his Fetlandish accent.

Twenty days, maybe more? And where? Where are they taking me? The obsessive thoughts are sending Vega into a fitful rage strong enough for her fists to curl. But by some strange grace or another, the dirty man's friend removes his cigar once more to unintentionally answer Vega's question-

"Wembleton to Empeirus is not a one-week feat, miss," the man adds.

Elouthera's heart stops. *Empeirus?* Vega laughs inwardly. *What are the odds?* The fact that Anzac has no idea that he is taking Vega precisely where she needs to go tells her two things: First, that Anzac has no idea where Dimity is, and second, that Anzac is somewhere in Empeirus as well. *Which means that by going there, I can essentially kill two birds with one stone!* Vega stretches her cramped legs and feet. *Both Dimity* and *Anzac somewhere in Empeirus?* She huffs a laugh that catches the attention of Christa and the others.

"That porridge won't stay hot all day, you know," her former friend chides.

"The porridge can wait." Vega sits up slowly, casually turning her jet-black hair toward the sailors. "Will we make landfall at some point to restock or are we sailing the whole way?"

Before Christa can interrupt, the dirty man replies, "*Our Lady's Crown* has a large 'nough hull to provide rations fer two months. We'll be just fine on the water until we reach Larkingsport."

Vega whips her head toward Christa. *Our Lady's Crown. The ship that I was supposed to board in the first place?*

Christa laughs, a fake, disturbing thing. "So long as the gods are good," she quips, her chestnut ringlets bobbing with every dip of the wooden vessel.

NARELLE

She clenches the thick slab of oak that is her desk with both hands, nails digging into the wood-grain. *I shouldn't guilt her*, Narelle thinks admonishingly. *She has a duty, and I have mine.* Removing a tan hand from the top of her desk, she pushes back a strand of chestnut hair.

Her eyes glance at the ticking clock on the lefthand side of her vanity, and Narelle knows that her next visitor will be coming soon. The boning of her corset is slightly digging into her sides, the pain dull and annoying and keeping her from a deeper level of concentration. *Ten minutes*, she hopes. *Just give me ten more minutes.*

The sound of birds chirping outside of her window draws her mind away from the letter and back to a simpler time, a time when it was just herself and Piper, the little urchin girl that she took in from the streets.

"But I don't want to go downstairs," Piper protests while sitting upon the yellow cushion of the window seat.

Narelle laughs. *"Well, you have to. Even if you don't want to be around Gissaira's daughter, even if she is the meanest, most inconsiderate person you know. Do you know why?"* the courtesan asks, long fingers tucking a piece of dark brown hair behind her child's ear.

Piper shakes her regal head back and forth, her delicate nose staring up at Narelle, patiently awaiting an answer.

"Because it is your duty, and sometimes duties are not things that we choose, but things that are chosen for us. And most of the time, when we do these things, we help to make the world a better place."

Narelle wakes from her trance, turning her large, hazel eyes back down to the blank paper. *I have a duty, too.* Pushing aside the custom stamp that the former Master Tasman had made for their secret correspondence, she dips her quill in a black ink and begins to write to the lost princess, to her lost daughter.

My dearest Piper,

Times are changing here on the mainland. The castle is teeming with guards, and I am watching my back constantly. I worry about you always. Your sister is sending hordes of guards around the city to do nightly watches, especially in the

*slums. A few have been known to stumble into our ladies'
bedrooms, and—*

A soft knock on the wooden door induces a tiny jump
from Narelle, who drops her quill on the oak desk.
Turning with a sigh, she straightens her shoulders and
presses her full lips together as she makes to open the
door.

One of her coworkers greets her with an arrogant
smile. "Your five o'clock is here," the courtesan points out.

"Send him in," Narelle nods, before quickly shutting
the door. She stuffs the half-written letter into the nearest
drawer, haphazardly brushing out the wrinkles in her
sapphire robe as she prepares for her guest, *and my other
duty*, she thinks with dismay. *A duty that was chosen for me.*

AIMELIE

Aimelie Larking kicks her giddy legs to and fro while she perches on the side of her bed. She clutches the silver post of her bed in angst, awaiting her only friend and lover. A quick knock on the door has her hands squeezing the bedpost, a wide smile blooming across her freckled cheeks.

Linden enters the youngest princess's royal bedchambers with a stack of papers in his hands and a bright smile about his face, his caramel eyes peering into her own big blue ones. *Eyes that have never been so happy to see,* Melie realizes as her Royal Mentor sets down his stack of parchment to extend his arms. Seizing the opportunity, Aimelie hops off her teal bed and leaps into his outstretched arms, giggling ecstatically as her honey-blonde curls cascade over his shoulders.

"I missed you," he murmurs into the blue fabric of her dress sleeve.

"Not nearly as much as I missed you," Melie quips, and she can feel the movement of laughter in his chest against her own. She pulls back to stare into his glowing brown eyes and runs a hand through his chestnut hair. "What does my Royal Mentor have in store for me this fine morning?"

Linden chuckles, a warm and compassionate sound. "I'm afraid it's just more of the same, my lady. Old parchment and cheap jokes."

Melie awards him with a hearty laugh. "I love your jokes. We need more joking around these dusty halls. Even the books have shown accelerated wear from Adrianna's reign."

Her paramour laughs, lowering his hands to her small waist. "Does my princess have anything new and exciting to share with her humble mentor?"

Melie's childish smile grows wider, her large doe eyes twinkling with an untamed sense of wild innocence. "I do. I have a plan to share with you," she says. "And you are going to be the star of it."

At this, Linden's eyes widen with something like shock and unease. "Of course, because who else would willingly partake in one of Aimelie Larking's incredible ideas?"

Playfully smacking one of his shoulders, she tugs her

mentor over to her bed where they sit side by side, the princess curled up on the soft teal blankets beside Linden.

Choosing to tell Linden about the fact that Annalise, her lost sister, is still alive was one of the most dangerous games that Melie had decided to play. *How do I know that I can fully trust him, especially being that he was sent into my life by Adrianna?* But despite the anxiety it had given her to take such a risk, the hope that Melie had within herself gave her the power to overcome her previous doubts. *And besides, Linden is trustworthy. I can see it in his eyes.*

Linden's eyes meet her own with a soft gaze, so full of unconditional happiness and affection that Aimelie practically bursts into flames. *What did I ever do to earn a love so precious?* she wonders, her heart melting like the butter on her morning toast.

The princess tilts her head to one side. "What is it?"

The chestnut-haired boy laughs, shaking his head slightly. "Nothing. I just can't seem to make sense of it all. How did I get here, with you? And why have I been able to stay with you, loving you under the cover of secrecy?"

"The gods must truly be good," she responds, stealing the opportunity to press a kiss to the side of his cheek.

His careful fingers gently lift the princess's chin upward, and Aimelie stares into the wholesome warmth reflecting from his light-brown eyes, waiting for his soft kiss. *A secret promise, a hidden alliance. A silent burden,* Aimelie realizes, as her stomach sinks every moment too soon. For as long as she continues to bask in the enjoyment of their carefree, pure love for one another, so too does she know the ease with which it can be taken away from them.

Every day is a constant struggle of hiding the remarkable, most amazing feelings of passion and joy from an ever-threatening world conditioned in right and wrong-doings. If the world knew that a princess had taken her mentor as her lover ... *People do not like to break old patterns, even if they are useless and make no sense. Hiding change is the only way to avoid conflict, at least for now.*

Melie smiles at Linden. *No matter the weight, I can bear it. My love for him is eternal. No force in this Universe can stop it—not even the gods.*

A shrill squeal from one of her room's open windows draws Melie's attention away from her paramour. A black raven pecks at the stray flecks of birdseed that she had left on the windowsill from the morning prior, and in a gust of merry excitement, Aimelie swirls away from the comfort of her bed, dragging Linden along by a hand.

"This is what I meant to show you," she says giddily, her blonde curls bouncing with every joyful step.

Linden eyes the raven cautiously. "A bird?"

"Linden, it's a *raven!*" Aimelie giggles. "I've been training them with the raven keeper, feeding them and sending them on errands ever since they were babies. They like to visit me at my windows almost every morning." She motions to the remnants of birdseed on her windowsill. "Most likely because they get more food than they should be having."

Linden watches its black wings flare into the afternoon sky. "You send them on errands?"

Melie nods, her youthful eyes serious. "This is where you come in."

His back stiffens. "Me? Melie, for the love of the gods, please do explain this plan that you have in that beautiful head of yours."

Aimelie smiles broadly, a pretty, happy thing. "I know where Annalise is. And I need to communicate with her." A pointed look toward the window. "But these ravens need to be trained to fly to her location first; they need a fresh flight pattern." She looks back to Linden. "When the time is right, I need you to visit the tower and inform Master Tasman on how to handle such things.

"I have a letter that contains all of the necessary information on how to care for the birds, when to expect them, how to properly tie a parchment roll to their ankle." The youngest princess turns her blue eyes to the open air of her chamber window. "I would have loved to have been able to see her face again, to talk to her and tell her that I always believed, that I just never had the freedom to search for her myself." A frown creeps upon her face, clashing with the joyfulness of her freckles. "If you could, I would ask that you deliver this letter on my behalf so that we can set up a form of communication between us," she finishes quietly.

Her lover stares back quietly for one moment, then two. "Melie, you do understand what this does to us?"

The princess toys with a golden curl nervously, eyes falling to the slate gray tiles of her floor.

"If anyone would find out ... If anyone would find out that we were working as double-agents ..." He runs a hand through his chestnut hair. "I wouldn't just lose my job—"

Aimelie bolts toward her love, taking his face in both of her hands. "Don't even think about that, please don't ever think such things again. I cannot bear even an *ounce* of that thought." She shakes her head, trying to clear it of the disturbing possibilities. *But he is right*, she knows. And what is worse, she could see it happening. *If Dria ever found out, it wouldn't just mean death for Linden ... it might very well mean death for myself, too.*

He draws a heavy sigh, pressing his forehead against her own. They stay like this for some time, the minutes pressing in on them almost as much as the insurmountable weight of their present burdens. *That are only getting heavier*, Aimelie thinks fearfully.

"Melie," Linden whispers quietly. "This world needs a new beginning. This world ... needs something that Adrianna can't give it and will never be able to." He brushes back a piece of honey-blonde hair from her face. "The only way to get to this new beginning is by taking risks. And now that we know Annalise is still alive ..." He shakes his head in exasperation. "The chance for this new beginning to become a reality is greater than ever before."

Aimelie ponders his caramel eyes carefully, awaiting his verdict.

"We have to do this. If not for ourselves, then most definitely for the world. Your people need a strong ruler, one who is fair and gracious, loyal and poised. I'm not saying that Annalise is any of those things—we have no idea how much she has changed. As far as we know, she's an elusive criminal."

The princess smirks, and Linden continues. "But if we don't do this, I feel like we would be failing those people who are deserving of the best."

Perhaps it is the sheer weight of his words, or the overwhelming realization of what they are about to do, but something prompts Aimelie to press the entirety of her body against Linden's own. She closes her eyes, cheek against his chest, gaining peace from the steady rhythm of his pure heart.

"I agree," she says. And with that, she straightens to once again peer into his brown eyes. Taking a final glance around the room, she drops her voice to an almost imperceivable whisper. "You will find them in the old watchtower."

NARELLE

She tried to forget it. Tried to forget the way he tasted, the way his sweet cologne sliced through every ounce of air, suffocating her in yet another way.

Nothing could prepare her for it again.

Narelle Lambric breathes in and out, tan hands shaking well past the end. The criminal stands now, bending a well-muscled back as he reaches down to the floor to collect his clothes. *And my own*, she notes.

"You've held up well, my lady," the man remarks. His cold blue eyes are expressionless, like that of a statue in frost.

Narelle knows not what to say. Her full lips part, but no words are able to slip through. Beside each hand, the sheets are crumpled into a bouquet of fabric. *He called me a lady*, she thinks humorously.

The man takes his time buttoning his pants as he turns to the courtesan, eyeing up every inch of her as she lay still on the bed. "It's been years since I first saw you, and I'd say that age rather suits you just fine."

She swallows. Her chestnut hair is undone and knotted, spilling down the edges of her shoulders.

He stalks toward the bed. With her sapphire robes still on the floor, the man perches beside her. "I hope I have not troubled you too much."

"What more can I do for you, sir?" Narelle clenches her teeth, her heart still racing.

A cool smile, one full of secrets and mystery as he reaches into his pant pocket. "Actually, there is one more thing. You can answer some of my questions," he says, removing a wrinkled letter adorned with an unofficial stamp—a stamp with the mark of Princess Annalise Larking.

VEGA

"Mind if I borrow that for a moment?"

The sailor spits. "Do ya really think I'd lend m' knife to some captive? A' might look stupid, but I'm not!"

Vega turns red, from embarrassment or fury she cannot tell. Her jet-black hair is nearing her shoulders now, and all she wants to do is cut it. Of course, such things as scissors or knives are hard for Vega to come by— not only because she has been stuck on a ship, but also because she has been Christa's hostage for the past three weeks.

Christa, her former friend. Christa, her closest and most trusted ally. Christa, Anzac's shadow pawn, who captured her and is taking her somewhere near Larkingsport.

It is hard to say that Vega has not been going a bit mad living off salt bread and fish, but truth be told, it hasn't been all that bad. Even the deckhands seem to be chipper. *All except for old Cragshead, I see.* The gods have blessed them with good weather, and they are more than halfway to Empeirus.

The master manipulator stalks the deck of *Our Lady's Crown* and sighs. A white gull glides through the air above her head, letting out its majestic voice. *I'm trying, Dimity. I'm moving as quickly as I can.* In the distance, a low rumble of thunder groans across the afternoon sky. The waves are starting to pick up, but not by much. *Perhaps our streak of good weather is at an end,* she wonders, eyeing the gray-blue color of the Javirian Gulf.

Kicking a rock across the deck, Elouthera watches the horizon rise and plummet. There is hardly anything to do at sea, save for counting the crests on each wave and trying to keep your lunch down when you sail over them. *Hardly anything to do at all, aside from hiding from Christa ...*

Anzac's shadow pawn had been more lenient this past week, and for what, Elouthera did not know. *Perhaps the ruse is taking too much energy for Anzac to pull off?* But the quiet female had known the God of Darkness and Decay for eons and had taken note of his power. *He takes stock in it, until you believe he is vulnerable ... and that's when he strikes.*

A bitter memory surfaces, one of white satin and lips warm as sunlight ... Elouthera jumps at Cragshead's tone.

"Are *you* gonna pull these ropes? Then get out of m' bloody way!"

Vega loses her footing when a rogue wave plunges through the Gulf. Catching herself on the floorboards, she takes in the briny scent of the watery world around her. *How long does it take for someone to get their sea legs?* The wooden deck is slicked with sand and mud, mottled by bits of rotting seaweed—with more to come from a pair of olive-green boots.

"Well, well, well," the familiar voice laughs. Its bubbly undertone makes it hard for Vega to bear. *Another traitor*, she thinks grimly. *Who can I trust?*

Vega picks herself up off the deck. "Can I help you, Christa?"

The shadow pawn smiles. Then smiles deeper. Her former best friend's eyes are no longer their vibrant blue hue, but an eerie gray instead. "Yes. You can stay belowdecks, so that I don't risk you jumping overboard." She walks closer. "What were you doing up here, anyway?"

An unsettling feeling rolls over the Goddess of Dreams and Mysteries. "I wanted to cut my hair."

A chuckle. "Why don't you just manipulate it to be shorter?"

"Because I want it to be permanently short." *And*

manipulating would require a constant output of energy to keep it that way, and I can't get my hands on enough metal to make scissors. But I can't let Anzac know that.

Another low grumble of thunder, this time rolling toward them over the waves. Maybe it is the sheer number of dull days spent at sea, or the simple fact that her closest friendship turned out to be some dark god's charade, but Elouthera has had enough. She could let Christa finish, but she isn't interested in another boring day where she is the only one being chastised. She moves closer, her black boots clicking with annoyance against the wood.

"Where are you, Anzac?" she whispers.

Christa's dark eyes widen almost imperceptibly. Her pink lips curl into an arc. "Where do you think I am, Elouthera?" she whispers back—though it is not Christa at all. Anzac's voice slithers through her mouth and into Vega's small ears.

Before she can respond, a boom of thunder explodes across the sky, shards of lightning chasing after it. The deckhands begin to yell.

"Secure the rope, ya blockhead! I'm not payin' ya to doddle 'round my ship!"

The storm is moving fast. *Too fast.* In fact, the sky had turned from its typical blue to a murky gray in mere minutes. *Weather must move quickly here.* She continues to maintain eye contact with Christa.

"Get everyone who isn't part of the crew belowdecks! This one's gonna be a big one, I can feel it!"

Christa narrows her gray eyes. "You heard them. Get belowdecks."

Vega makes to turn on a black heel when the sails above their heads suddenly turn quiet, the fabric standing still for one moment, then two. *Three.* Vega glances up at the mast. *Then—*

A gust of wind so strong that it rips three of the sails in half and knocks most on their behinds. Hats are whipped off heads, and while people scream and scramble to find purchase on the sandy deck, *Our Lady's Crown* begins to rock with the incoming waves.

"The storm! It's here!"

With another boom of thunder comes a skeletal hand of lightning, sending its electric energy crackling across the salty air and straight down the crow's nest of the ship. Fire lights the darkening sky, and if screams were flames, so too would they. *Gods almighty!*

"Fire!" the shipmates cry as the flames begin to lick their way down the wooden pole. *It won't be long until they make it to the deck.* She looks to Christa, who is looking tired and burdened, practically melting into the ship's bow. *Does Anzac realize that this could be it? That this whole journey to deliver me alive and well could be at its end? No, it's a trick,* Elouthera knows. *He wants me to believe that she can be taken down easily.*

But despite having the opportunity to rid herself of Christa, Vega must focus on the most important task at hand: starting with the realization that her ship is going down. The men line up in rows with buckets of water, waiting for the captain to shout his orders to extinguish the fire. Each gallon helps to keep the powerful flickering at bay, and one by one, the buckets are emptied until there are no more flames left.

The waves continue to grow, as one major swell sends most of the people sliding to the other side of the deck. *Oh gods, oh gods, no!* Another rogue wave, this time even larger than the last, comes tumbling toward them and slams into the hull, sending three men overboard while the others hang on for dear life. *Lazarus almighty! Please, have mercy on us!*

The enraged gulf slaps two more men overboard as the goddess grabs hold of the railing to keep herself from falling in, but the wind is gusting ever-faster, blowing her hair into her lime-green eyes. *My arms*, she thinks. *They can't keep holding on forever!* Vega's thin fingers were built for manipulating, not for strength. Sooner or later, they would lead to her demise.

The ship begins to tilt, stuck in an incessant rock to its starboard side. Below them, the dark waves promise an unwelcome surprise to those who must face its doom. She glances at Christa, who is clutching to the wheel of the ship as the deck begins to crest a vicious wave.

"Don't you *dare* let go," she snarls at Vega, her dark eyes pinning her to the wooden rail. "I can't afford to lose you again, Elouthera!"

The ship groans as the swell pushes it nearly vertical.

Actually, you can, Vega thinks, and she slips into the stormy waters of the Javirian Gulf when at last, her fingers finally give out.

EDEN

The scents of burnt caramel and licorice cling to the night air as though she is still performing. Eden Sharpkey draws in a rattling breath— well, what she has left of a breath—as she lies silently against the dark floor. The padded flooring of the training room serves her no comfort tonight, just as it hadn't the night previous or the one before that, despite her persistent prayers. She tilts her head to one side, watching a black beetle skitter across the cold cement as a tear rolls its way down her cheek.

His hands still press against her, even if nobody is present. The dank air surrounds her quivering lips, each inhale deeper than the last as she steadily recovers herself from his beastly touch. At last, using her bruised arms to prop herself up, she stands, moving her lithe body from the ramshackle tent to the center of the training room. Eden tiptoes over her eight other siblings, avoiding the oldest, and she soon finds herself pushing the striped canvas aside to enter the open arena.

The aerialist runs a muscled hand over the suspended ring, finally gathering enough strength to slip her silk sleeve back over her shoulder. There is no crowd at midnight, but Eden can still see the ghosts of guests past delighted by the sheer peculiarity of it all.

She often wonders what delight is.

The tightrope is high and glorious, the only highlight of her days as a well-adored performer. Longtime stars of the Iribus Circus, the Sharpkeys were three solid generations of highly sought-after entertainers, and very few could match their skills. Especially that of Eden and her twin brother, Edris. Both were bred for the arena, born wide-eyed and grinning at the sight of a golden lion cub, raised for more than just simple somersaults. *No*, Eden admits to herself. *We were groomed for more.*

The nineteen-year-old darts her eyes nervously around the open arena. *It is not safe here. He could be anywhere, especially in the dark.* But Eden remembers what her mother had taught her, that where fear can win, no courage can prevail, and it takes all the strength left in her sore arms to grab hold of the ladder rung before her.

Each grasping of her hand pulls her closer and closer to safety, high above the world, high above the floor that houses both her comforts and her nightmares. As she crests the top of the ladder, she can see it floating before her. Thin and strong, it slices through the night air like a knife through pudding, stopping only at the top of the opposing platform.

The girl adjusts her sleeve once more, fixing her custom shoes to ensure proper form. She breathes in, and she breathes out. The world fades away. There is no more worry, no more pain. There is only Eden Sharpkey and the rope, until at last, bound only by air and restraint, she walks.

She needs no balancing pole; no, those were not for Sharpkeys. The common performer would be expected to use them, but the most elite professional should have no use of that sort of crutch. In truth, however, Eden was never allowed to use one.

"*We are not meant to perform, Eden,*" her mother would tell her. "*We were meant to inspire. We were meant to evoke emotions so strong, that even queens would fear our skill.*"

Eden did not think her mother against the monarchy, but she understood her meaning. Remarkable skill. Inexplicable strength. Admirable determination. These were the qualities with which Eden was raised, and she prides herself on fulfilling them. Well, fulfilling them as best she can, considering her circus's recent change of regime.

She is halfway across the high rope now, toeing her way one foot in front of the other like she really can walk on air. Her dirty-blonde hair flows behind her head as she holds her chin steady, parallel to the ground. One step, another one ... *Just one more* ... And she makes landfall successfully, rocking back and forth on her strong feet and stretching out every inch of her body.

The victory is small, but she allows herself this moment to be proud anyway. Her mother would have been, before hers and her husband's untimely deaths two years ago. The cause of death was a tent fire, set alight by a candle's desire to caress a blanket, but Eden knows better. Regardless, what was written in their will was something that had changed Eden's life forever.

She turns her mismatched eyes from the candlelit chandelier down to the training room door, releasing a shudder. *All this*, Eden reflects. *All this, for him.* The horrifying thought is enough to have her realize the time, that it must be past curfew and that she will face consequences should she be seen wandering about the arena.

The girl turns on a shoed heel and begins descending the tall ladder, wincing at the pain inside and outside of her body, but she must hurry. Her feet hit the ground with a thud, but before she scurries back into the training room, Eden remembers again what her mother had said —that where fear wins, no courage can prevail—and she stills her body.

She opens her eyes, of two different colors, watching the stillness of the world at the hour. Absorbing the peace of the chill, Javirian air. A beacon of moonlight streams in through the high tent window, and for a moment, however brief, Eden wonders at the pure possibility of the world. At the freedom, at the opportunity to—

"Ah, I always knew you were a rule breaker at heart." His voice crawls across her skin like the spider he is.

She locks her jaw, pointing her blue eye back toward the window.

"Can't possibly think of anything witty to say? No? You never can." Her twin frowns, and before any words or squeals can make it out of her pretty mouth, he covers it with a brawny hand while locking the other around her wrist.

Her mother was right. Where fear wins, no courage can prevail. But even courage is subject to the laws of physics, and Edris is just too strong. She promises herself that it shouldn't last long tonight. *Our training was long today, he must be somewhat exhausted.* But nothing in this precious world is certain; only that when the last sight of the arena slips away from Eden's view, she is sure of one thing:

There is no crowd at midnight, but there is always a show.

Part IV

Fire

ADRIANNA
SIX YEARS EARLIER

Adrianna clenches her scraped palms as she makes her way down the dirt road. She never meant to fall off the stool she had used while listening through her parents' bedroom wall, and her delicate hands had been the cost of such clumsiness. *If anybody asks, I will just say that I fell down the Blue Hall stairs. Everyone knows that the Blue Hall stairs are uneven and dangerous.*

Dust plumes around her booted ankles with every strut she takes down the infamous path. The Iribus Trading Post has been known to have all sorts of rare oddities, ranging from the horned camels of Calleeit to the priceless lavender pearls of the Savek Coast, and everything in between.

Had her royal parents known she was headed here, she would have been locked up in her chambers. *But had they known I was spying earlier, they would have done the same. The key is to not get caught.* Which is why Dria had swapped her precious taffeta gown for peasant's attire and a worn cloak, courtesy of some cook's son she had befriended earlier. It had only cost her a kiss.

Disguised and diligent, the canopies of one thousand colors coming into view, thirteen-year-old Dria takes in the briny scent of the nearby Falvedrie Sea. Every summer, the Iribus gathers hundreds of vendors from across the world to sell their fine treasures at the Royal Harbor. They set up their tents half of a mile from the docks to make unloading their goods easier. Dria has never been to the Iribus Trading Post; would never have been allowed to, for her safety. *But there is a first time for everything,* she supposes. *Besides, this is the only place near home where I might find what I am looking for.*

The crowds of people are growing thicker now, obstructing Dria's view of the tents. With a healthy dose of determination, she pushes her way past the others and beholds the sight. Sturdy wooden beams uphold tapestries in a range of one hundred different colors. Burgundy, turquoise, goldenrod yellow, sunset orange, peacock teal, grass green, all morphed together into a patchwork quilt of a roof, shading its occupants from the warm summer sun. Rugs in similar hues have been placed out beneath the stands of each vendor, and behind each wooden counter are numerous merchants of a thousand tongues, surrounded by their exotic wares.

The princess gasps in disbelief. It is so much more incredible than the stories she has been told. *They likely played it down to prevent me from visiting*, she ventures.

"Luminescent beans," one man with a thick, rolling accent calls. "Grow plant flowers that glow in the dark."

"Come! See for yourself the magnificence of a *siphlor* ring and gain the ability to breathe underwater!" Another man shouts with incomparable enthusiasm.

Dria smiles under her hood at the tempting offers, but she is on the lookout for only one rarity: the Nevs. Of all the fortune-tellers and occultists in the land, the Nevs are the only group of psychics whose claim to fame has been unrivaled by centuries of uncanny accuracy. Long ago, the psychics formed a band that vowed to deliver spiritual wisdom to the world, and by traveling across land and sea, the Nevs have been doing so ever since.

The scent of smoke and spices whose names Dria cannot place waft across the cool shade of the tents. The light is dim, no doubt to keep hidden some items whose legality should be questioned, but she is not phased. Only children would cower from the unknown, and Dria is a child no longer.

"Care for a rose, love?" A young woman with eyes like glass pulls at Dria's sleeve. "For finding your one true love."

Dria yanks her arm back. "I don't need true love. I prefer the freedom of being alone."

Ignoring the woman's gaping mouth, the young princess marches through the dirt for what seems like ten minutes, until she reaches the other end of the Iribus. She has searched every table, every vendor counter, but there is no sign of the Nevs. Irritated and tired, Dria exits the tents via the colorful wall of draped fabrics.

I have wasted time and energy. And for what? Renai can only hold my cover for so long, and I still have no answers. Dria digs her nails into her already chaffed palms, clenching her teeth. All at once, the world begins to seem heavy. There is nothing for her here, nothing around that will help. A sudden need to free her rising anger has her picking up the nearest rock and hurling it off into the rushing waters surrounding the docks. She grunts as she chucks another stone, this one larger, into the Falvedrie Sea.

"Careful there, girl," a deep female voice drawls from behind a caravan. Her accent leads Dria to believe she is from the western lands, perhaps somewhere near Nesvla.

Adrianna turns to face the husky woman. She is probably around forty years, though no taller than young Dria, and she wears a long black cloak with a hood that shadows her features.

"And who might you be?" the young princess asks, fire glinting in her cold blue eyes.

The dark woman laughs. "Feisty one, aren't you? But who am I to judge?" The woman pulls out a silver necklace, its matching pendant a crescent moon encrusted with three circular amethysts in its center—the symbol of the Nevs. "I'm an oracle."

Dria's blue eyes widen under her peasant's hood. *Perhaps my lady-in-waiting's ruse will not be all for naught.*

"Care to have your fortune read?" the woman asks, a devious smile dancing across her half-hidden face.

Nodding cautiously, she turns to follow the woman's whipping black cloak over to her mysterious abode, a black and silver caravan. Dria's hood nearly blows off her head in a hurried gust from the nearby Falvedrie Sea, its powerful waves like greedy hands reaching for all the treasures of the Iribus. The woman stops at the door, unlocking it with a key that Dria cannot see. The Nev jiggles the rusty doorknob and throws it open with a small grunt, nearly toppling off the caravan's rickety steps, and tucks the silver and amethyst moon pendant back into her cloak.

Incense greets Dria's pointed nose when she enters into the flickering candlelight of the caravan. The Nev seats herself across from Adrianna at the small square table and removes her black hood at last, revealing a plump, round face that perhaps once would have been quite beautiful. Raven black ringlets fall alongside each cheek, and her pale skin is accented by a pair of citrine eyes that seem to peer deep into the soul.

Yet Dria does not balk. She places her youthful hands atop the wooden table, palms facing up. "Do you need to see my palms?"

The woman smiles. "No dear. I need to see your *eyes.*"

Dria swallows. *What if she recognizes me? How could I make it out of here, with all these merchants? If someone should kidnap me, take me to another territory* ... Dria shakes these thoughts from her mind. If she wants to know her destiny, how else is she going to find out about it? This might be her last and only chance to meet with an oracle of the infamous Nevs.

She takes a shallow breath and removes her borrowed cloak. Golden curls cascade over her thin shoulders, which she pushes back with the ferocity of any queen. Her pretty blue eyes look down her nose at the oracle, whose smile has grown serpentine.

"I take it Mother and Father don't know you are here," the oracle quips.

Dria's jaw tightens ever so slightly.

The oracle shrugs, selecting a polished bone from a collection of crystals and jewels nestled along the side of the table. Taking the bone in one hand, she grabs Dria's in the other, and closes her burnt orange eyes.

The princess hopes that the oracle cannot feel her hand begin to shake, or her palm start to sweat. She is nervous to know her fate, but without knowing, what could she do to right it if such measures need to be taken?

Abruptly, the oracle flashes open her eyes. "You've grown up in the shadows, my dear. Your soul is relentless, and you will do whatever you can to find what you seek."

Dria's eyes narrow. "And what is it that I seek?"

The oracle gently squeezes Dria's hand. "Glory. Power … But obviously, something—no, *someone*—stands in your way. I see a rock resting overtop of a planted seed. A pile of freshly-tilled dirt beside a deep hole in the ground. Jewels running through your fingers. A quilt with your name on it. A female's hand that pulls a single thread, unraveling it entirely."

Adrianna's face must show her confusion because the oracle laughs quietly. "There is no path to this fortune you seek unless extreme measures are taken. And by extreme, I mean that the path is a dark one." The oracle's face grows very serious.

Dria nods. She suspected as much. After all, everyone knows that Annalise is the first in line for the throne. But as much as she dislikes her perfect older sister, Dria is not about to go murder her because of it. *No, that would be a faulty plan.* But speaking of fault, perhaps there is another way to go about advancing her own reign.

The oracle's citrine eyes see the wheels turning in Dria's head. "Do not think that such measures will ever be excusable in the eyes of the gods, especially for your own personal gain. I would not believe even you to be capable of such horrors, even if your soul is a bit misshapen and jagged around the edges."

There is nothing for Dria to do but inwardly laugh at such a statement. *Just more validation that my soul really is black as night.* "Thank you for your reading. What do I owe you?" She makes to move for her coin purse.

"I do not take the usual currency." The oracle eyes the princess's honey-blonde curls. "I'll take a lock of your hair," she says with a poisonous smile.

Something like dread unfurls in Dria's small stomach. She opens her mouth to object, but thinks better of denying a Nev their payment, and hesitantly reaches up to grasp a discreet chunk of hair growing from just behind her neck. The oracle slides forward a pair of scissors, which look to be pure gold, and Dria lifts them to a honey-colored lock.

"Tell me one more thing," Adrianna demands just before she makes to squeeze the scissor blades together. "If I take no action at all, what will I become?"

The smile upon the oracle's round face softens into a

mask of stillness. Her citrine eyes droop with sorrow when she at last opens her mouth to reply:

"Forgotten," she whispers.

The word itself is enough to send Dria's hand squeezing with an electric jolt, and in the moment her golden lock falls to the wooden table, she knows that she will do anything in her power to prevent such a pitiful existence.

NARELLE

The tang of blood fills her head where any thoughts of hope had once lived. Below the muffles of their voices is the stinging, throbbing pain from his unspeakable punishments, some too cruel to be thought of ever again. She had been all too familiar with his traditional form of torture, but this was something else altogether.

"I told you not to be too harsh," the queen whispers to her spymaster.

He bows his head. His pale gray eyes narrow with self-disgust. "My apologies, my queen; —"

"No apologies needed, Calix. Just find a different means to pull the information from her living corpse."

She can see him almost fully now, his beady eyes staring heartlessly through her shattered body. Narelle flinches, her vision weaving in and out of consciousness as she tries to drown out the images of his deadly touch. She sits a few yards before them—if it can be called sitting—watching them with her bloodshot hazel eyes, gently swaying from left to right. Beside her chair and her bound limbs is the pile of vomit that she heaved up during Calix's previous round of interrogation. Just before she makes to add to it again, the queen lifts a slender hand.

"Calix, please give us a moment. Alone."

The quiet man bows deeply before turning on a booted heel, his silver queen's pin glimmering in the light of the dungeon as he leaves the bucket of ice water on the ground.

Beneath her cracked ribs, Narelle's heart softens at the thought of her oldest enemy giving her a reprieve at long last. The only sound in the room is that of Queen Adrianna's heels clicking softly as she closes the distance between them.

"I've heard very little about you," she begins.

The courtesan chuckles a broken laugh. "Then you're doing yourself a service. I'm a boring book to read."

A derisive snort from the queen. "So you say. But you are the keeper of information that no one else in the entire kingdom knows about, which makes you the most *interesting* book to me." Adrianna steps over the fresh pile of vomit and stands before Narelle, meeting her half-conscious gaze. "Do tell me," she says with a crimson-stained grin, "how does a well-groomed princess end up sharing beds with a common prostitute?"

Narelle spits at the queen's golden slippers.

"You filthy—"

From within the bucket to their right, a bubbling sound catches Narelle's attention. *What in the name of Lazarus ... the water, it wasn't hot before.*

Adrianna offers a seething smile, one that could curdle milk without so much as a glance in its direction. "Boiling water. On your head. If you don't tell me how you met my shit of a sister."

And just like that, the courtesan parts her sultry lips. "She came to me in the rain one night, said she was on the run from her abusive brother. I always wanted a child, so I asked permission from my madame and took her in as my own. She told me her name was Piper, so that's what I called her."

The Crimson Queen continues rounding Narelle's chair, her golden slippers clacking over the hard dirt floor. "And for how long has she been living with you, this 'Piper?'"

A swallow from the fallen woman. "For about six years."

The queen closes her icy blue eyes. She sighs, and Narelle can't help noticing that the boiling water in the bucket gets significantly cooler within seconds.

"And all this time, she has been hiding in a brothel, right beneath my nose. Lazarus almighty," Adrianna curses, her long blonde braid swinging with disgust. She rakes her manicured nails over her scalp. "Tell me one more thing. Where is she now?"

Maybe it is the sheer amount of head trauma, or the fact that the courtesan really did feel as though she played an essential part in raising the oldest princess, but Narelle Lambric cannot for a second stomach the tone of this twisted female. *You distasteful coward. I know who you really are. Did you actually think that I would fall for your games? I will do anything to protect my Annalise, my child, and the rightful heir to the throne.*

A fresh pain begins to bloom deep inside of her chest, not one from Calix's hand but rather from pure emotion. *My Annalise,* she cries internally. She remembers the feeling of happiness and elation upon taking her in so many years ago, the fulfilling responsibility of raising a daughter in a better way than she herself had been raised. The breaking of her heart sucks her into a peaceful thought, into the eye of the storm that is currently her own life. With every passing breath, Narelle can feel the weight of her own body pushing against her lungs.

Annalise, my only child. Annalise, my only future.

"Well?" the queen drills into her thoughts with a cold blue stare.

Annalise, the only future of this kingdom.

Her mind wanders, weighing the options one by one, shielding her emotions like a stream hidden beneath a layer of ice. On the other side of the running water, Narelle can see her raise a golden brow, waiting for her to spill the truth as Calix soon would her brains. The smell of her perfume so at odds with the stench of the dungeon, Adrianna crosses the golden fabric of her sleeves impatiently.

You like to play pretend? Well, guess what? I've been doing it for most of my life. For if there is one thing that Narelle's line of business has taught her, it is that people want to see what they want to see. *So, let's give them a show.*

"I don't know."

The queen narrows her gaze. "*What?*" she seethes. "I know you are lying to me, Narelle Lambric. I will give you one more chance before I turn things over to my less gentle business partner. *Where. Is. She.*"

The courtesan's bloodshot hazel eyes drift somewhere toward the floor, praying to the gods that she is doing right. "I don't know."

A snap of the queen's fingers has his footsteps returning, the sound of his tall figure sauntering over like the frigid Godrian wind.

Narelle braces. And the back of his hand smacks across the side of her beautiful tan face. The courtesan breathes heavily, attempting but failing to catch her breath while Calix continues making heavy blows to each side of her face.

"I know you have the answer, Narelle. All you need to do is tell us, and all of this will stop." Adrianna watches as her chief spy puts even more force into the movement.

I don't know how much more of this I can take, Narelle thinks. *It might be time to appease them.*

She screams when the spymaster grabs hold of her wrist, bending her thumb backward while the queen's face turns vicious.

"Where is she? *Where is she*, you whore?"

Narelle cannot take it, cannot stand the agonizing pain anymore. "Javir! She fled to Javir!"

Calix drops her arm, turning his clear eyes to Adrianna, who looks ever confused. The courtesan huffs her way back to her new sense of normalcy, swallowing tears as she moans from moving her right hand.

Amidst her hushed sobbing, Narelle gets an overwhelming feeling of relief and dread when she hears the queen mutter one last thing:

"Keep her alive."

EDEN

The rusty crimson hood is hardly long enough to conceal Eden's mismatched eyes from the lantern lights of Javir. It wasn't hard to sneak away from the Sharpkey's arena. *No,* she thinks with a hint of sadness, *it wasn't hard at all.* A waft of cinnamon and chai spices is carried on a brisk wind, blowing her hood up above her head.

"Gods!" Eden whispers to herself. The last thing she needs is somebody to figure out that Eden Sharpkey has attempted to escape her own circus. *Edris has friends in every corner of this town, and likely the next. I have to keep a close watch.*

To be fair, Eden has no idea of where she should be watching, since she hasn't exactly left the circus since the age of sixteen. Sure, there were times when her parents took them out to eat at an inexpensive restaurant, but other than that, the arena was her home. *And my demise.*

Eden thinks back to a time before the reign of her twin brother Edris, back to before things took a turn for the worst.

"Tell me what you see, Eden," her mother would ask.

A bubble of purple light would come about upon closing her blue and gold eyes. *"I see purple. I don't see much else ..."*

A mellifluous laugh. *"I see a child whose gift she needs practice to learn."*

Eden's mother was always her greatest inspiration. Prized legend of the Iribus Circus, international award-winning aerialist, Laraya Sharpkey was a woman of great talent. She made it a point to focus on giving Eden that talent, and her oldest daughter has maintained those wishes ever since. Which is why Eden was so confused upon hearing of her will's appointment of Edris as the Iribus leader following her death.

"Watch your step," a local vendor spits. His balding head is a pleasant view compared to his red eyes.

Eden pulls her crimson cape over herself more tightly, trying to remain calm as she counts her footfalls against the heavy, stone road. Before leaving, she had stolen five hundred copper stars from beneath Edris's pillow—*The only perk of being there too often*—but she isn't even sure it will be enough to buy her passage on a ship. Her end goal is to reach Empeirus, where perhaps she can find a new opportunity to start over.

Maybe not an aerialist, she thinks, since that would give her away. *But rather something more discreet, like a healer or a painter.*

In the midst of her pacing, Eden slows to a stop. She closes her mismatched eyes, and in the center of the blackness forms a cloud of bright green. Anxiety begins to take hold of her, but a feeling of comfort seems to give her reassurance.

"Hey dimwit, the infirmary's that way!"

Eden opens her gold and blue eyes, ignoring the sting of the woman's comment. It still hurts, but the nineteen-year-old continues sneaking through the alleys of Javir toward the harbor, avoiding stray black cats and the occasional nagging sales merchant. Her heart races as she traverses grounds that she can only know through memory, her brain searching the faraway corners of her mind from before her twin brother's rule. *The Salish Lad. Oh, yes! I do remember passing that by with Mama! I must be close to the harbor.* Eden pins her gold eye on the tavern sign as she passes around the corner.

A haughty whistle. "Well, well ..." a masculine voice drawls from the alley.

Eden Sharpkey trips over a cobblestone.

Another man chuckles, low and cold. "Just when I

thought it couldn't get any easier. What do you wanna do with her, Strag?"

The aerialist picks herself up off the ground and makes to turn around, only to bump into the first man behind her. *I'm damned. And after they have their way with me, they'll turn me over to Edris and he'll do the same.*

The black shadow looks Eden over. "Hmm. I'll hand her over to you. I had the last one."

The second man huffs a laugh, moving closer to Eden, who is ready to scream and claw her way through hell. *I may have been chained to a bed in my past life, but I won't let it happen again in this one.* She opens her mouth for a scream, and—

"Let her go," a female with an unfamiliar accent orders.

Eden pauses in confusion. *Who would ...*

A pair of lime-green eyes emerge from the dark, glinting in the dim tavern light. "I said, *let her go.*"

Eden can feel the night air as closely as a shroud, just as she can feel the two strangers exchange baffled glances. A belt of male laughter.

"Come a little closer, and maybe you can join the fun." The second man whips a rope at the mysterious female in an attempt to latch onto her arm, which he successfully does, until she wraps her other hand around the braided leather.

"And here I thought you would be better competition."

In a matter of moments, the rope transforms into a long, black snake, releasing her arm and slithering across the floor of the alley toward the man who threw it.

"Bloody hell! She's a witch!"

The man in front turns around to bolt, while the one behind Eden pushes her forward. "Take her, we don't care!"

Eden stumbles toward the strange witch, catching herself before she falls again. *Dear Lazarus!* The aerialist doesn't know whether to run or to thank her. *I'm already too close to get away now, and if she wanted me dead, why would she want to save me?*

"I ... I thank you," she finally manages in her Javirian accent.

"No need to thank me," the female replies. She moves forward, letting the lights of The Salish Lad expose her true form.

She is nothing like Eden had imagined her to look. No gaudy witch clothing, no loosely-draped fabric with big golden bracelets. No, just a petite girl, with short black hair and a small, pointed face, whose cat-like green eyes are even more pronounced in the alley's darkness.

Eden tugs her crimson hood farther over her own. "My mother never told me that the Nevs have those kinds of powers," Eden starts. "Only that they are seers, and—"

"I am not a Nev," the girl corrects quickly. "And I am not a witch either. My name is Vega, and I am not even from here."

"I can tell from your accent. I've ... I've never heard of yours before. You ..." She swallows. "You must not be from around here."

The girl smiles, a friendly but enigmatic grin. "I'm not. My ship crashed during the big storm yesterday. I need the first ship I can get on that's headed to Empeirus."

Eden balks. *Empeirus? The gods really are good! We could travel together! But what if she doesn't want to stay together, or what if she thinks me annoying? Or worse, a dimwit?*

"You wouldn't happen to know of any ship at the harbor?"

"Oh, yes! No. I, um, I am looking for a ship to Empeirus too. That's where I was headed right now, actually."

Vega's green eyes betray a hint of bewilderment. "I see. Well, which way is the harbor from here?"

Eden bites her lip. "I'm pretty sure it's that way, back where you came from, but over the hill."

Vega smiles. "Great." She turns, but then checks to make sure Eden is in tow. "What do you go by?"

Beneath her hood, Eden lets out a breath of relief. "Mara. You can call me Mara."

ADRIANNA

"I thought I'd find you here," Dria begins as she sails across the room in her golden slippers.

Incense plumes around his stoic silhouette, clouding the candles from view like a thick Javirian fog. Desmond opens an eye. "And I thought you'd make your way here," he quips. Quiet and concentrating, the queen's lover sits in the corner of her bedroom, silently pushing the methodically placed stones with the tip of a finger. "What can my dear Dria be interrupting my work for this time?"

It had been months. Months of his dedicated, laborious efforts to ensure the perfect arrangement of his shadows. *He was so close,* Dria thinks, *so close to having her brought directly to us.* The sparks of a flame dance over her skin as she clenches her hand into a fist. *And just like that ...*

She runs a hand over the silk of her corset, biting her lip at the embarrassment of disturbing his progress. "My apologies, Des. I've come to you with new information. I just had the most interesting conversation with Narelle Lambric."

The Captain of the Royal Guard furrows a black brow. "The prostitute?"

Adrianna snorts. "Yes, and the unfortunate second mother of my sister, Annalise."

A push of a stone, a deep sigh.

"I had the opportunity to speak with her this morning, and she told me that we were wrong. Annalise isn't in Empeirus at all. She's in Javir."

His silver eyes look up from his work. "Javir? Why would she be in Javir?"

"Your guess is as good as mine," Dria starts as she seats herself on the floor beside him. "But you do know what this means for our plans."

A devilish smirk forms beneath tired eyes as Anzac puts the pieces together.

While they had failed after losing Elouthera to the Javirian Sea, Anzac's shadow pawns had caught word of a likely female being spotted in a town along the Javirian coast. With the hope of it being a possible lead on Elouthera's new whereabouts, he already sent more of his shadows to explore the area. *And with Annalise potentially being in the same territory as well ...*

"With the two of them being in the same vicinity, we can focus most of our efforts on one place," Dria grins.

Desmond nods, happy but exhausted. "We could kill two birds with one stone. We still have no information on Dimity, but that should come in time. 'Vega' should be able to answer a few questions to that extent."

Vega, the queen recalls. *Such a fitting name for the Goddess of Dreams and Mysteries.* A flicker of jealousy has Jedda gritting her teeth.

"How close are you are to finding her?"

Beneath a halfhearted laugh, Anzac rubs a dark circle. Adrianna worries about him, hates to see him like this, but she knows it is a necessary evil in their plans to find the biggest threats to the throne.

"I've narrowed it down to somewhere in the fishing district. I'm going to plot an attack once I know her exact location, but based on hearsay of the locals—"

"*Hearsay?* You think that this is something we can trust *hearsay* for?"

"Dria," Desmond turns his entire muscled body toward hers. "I understand your impatience, but you must trust that I am trying my best."

"I'm sure you are," the queen spits before standing from the floor. "Just like you tried your best to keep her away after you fell in love with me!"

"Jedda!"

Anzac turns to grab her wrist, but it is too late. The memories have already begun to sputter back to life, and it is all Jedda can do but turn and walk away. They have plagued her many times before, and when they do, she must remove herself from him. It is painful, perhaps the most painful experience in her immortal life to be hurt by the one thing that gives her the most happiness. *He could have done better. Could have done better to push her away for his one true love.*

The Dark Goddess places herself on the edge of her golden bedcovers, toying with her matching braid. Anzac knows not to mess with her during these bursts of emotion, that the only thing that will help is time. And so, she waits. She drowns out the sound of Elouthera's polished voice, burns the memory of her hand in his, even if it was before he was her own. She incinerates the image of her lover sharing a poisonous kiss with some half-witted female.

And she stands from her bed. Brushing out the folds of her gown, she finds Anzac still working relentlessly on his shadow pawns and takes a few quiet steps in his direction. She knows it isn't his fault, that he can't change his past, even if it was with Elouthera. *Beautiful, mysterious, radiant Elouthera.* With every step she takes toward him, she releases another bit of anger.

At last, Jedda peers down at her soulmate and his

work before him. The tiny chess pieces are laid out strategically across a bowl of dark sand. Watching a bead of sweat slip down the scarred side of his face, she places a hand on his shoulder in apprehension.

One by one, he places his fingers on the pieces, until both of his hands are full. Anzac whispers to her, softly but forcefully.

"Everything has always been for you."

On a sharp inhale, he pushes the pieces toward an X drawn in the sand, the movement inciting a grunt. When he releases his trembling hands, the stone objects form a complete circle surrounding the letter.

"I will find them, Jedda," Anzac promises beneath his visible strain, "if only to prove to you how much I love you."

ANNALISE

SIX YEARS EARLIER

The night is still black when a fervent hand shakes Annalise from her deep sleep.

"Anna, wake up!" Adrianna whispers urgently.

She rubs her dark eyes, sitting up upon a spread of wrinkled sheets. "What time is it?"

"I think something is wrong," Dria adds, and the very fact that she has chosen to speak to Anna is, in and of itself, something wrong in its nature. It is this thought that has Annalise crawling out of bed and tugging on her emerald-green slippers.

"I heard a noise coming from Mother and Father's bedroom. It sounded like a high-pitched sound."

"It's probably just an animal crawling around in the castle walls," Anna ventures, but the night air seems to disagree, its uneasy atmosphere clinging to her nerves like ice on a windowpane. "Stay here," she orders Dria, who is paying more attention to her manicured nails.

Her stomach in knots, the eldest princess tiptoes her way down the corridor to her parents' room. A few torches are still lit near the few guards on duty in the hall, but she tries not to wake another soul at this late hour. Her parents' chambers are just around the corner from her sisters' and her rooms, so the trek isn't far.

She stops just before the large entrance, stealing herself before she opens the door, guards nodding at her presence before she steps foot in the grand chambers. The door closes behind her, and Annalise takes a few careful steps into the empty space, searching for a wall to grip in the darkness.

"Mother?" she calls into the night, but there is no answer. Anna bumps into a cedar chest, the one she knows her father uses to store correspondence. The noise should have been enough to rouse anyone after scratching its wooden legs against the hardwood floors, but there is still no sound from either of them. In fact, there seems to be no sound at all.

Perhaps they are out of their room, Anna thinks. She begins toeing across the bedroom floor to their bed, going mostly off memory rather than physical cues.

"Mother," the princess voices again, this time a bit stronger. Still no answer.

At last, she runs into her parents' bed, and she knows from unintentionally feeling the bumps under the covers that her parents must still be asleep. *How can they still be asleep after all the raucous I just made?* She turns to the adjacent wall and draws open a curtain. *At this point, I don't care if they are angry at me for waking them.* Ivory moonlight streams in through the glass windowpanes, bathing the bed in an eerie gray light. She steps closer to her parents, who lie like statues beneath their burgundy blankets.

"Mother?" Anna whispers, hesitantly moving closer to the bed. "Father?"

Her silk slippers slide over the carpet with the last bit of bravery that she has left in her. Alas, the king and queen make no response. Only their stone faces give any indication as to what has happened to them.

Her heart lurches into her throat while she reaches to cover her mouth, stifling a scream. Their bodies are stiff and swollen, and she knows with certainty that the notion she is trying so hard to displace is the one that is painfully true. Annalise grabs her mother by the shoul-ders and begins to shake her.

"*Mother. Mother, wake up! I need you!*" Tears well in her dark eyes as Anna runs around to the other side of the bed in a vain attempt to rouse her father. The king's matching brown eyes are closed, his palms resting upon his stomach as if still asleep, only his stomach is rising no longer.

"Gods, no. Gods, please *no!*" she cries, throwing their burgundy covers off the bed. No scars or wounds or marks of any kind. Bolting for the door, Annalise begins to scream hysterically. "Guards! *Guards!*"

Two guards throw open the door as she runs toward them. "They won't wake!" she screams, tears staining her red cheeks.

The soldiers dash over to the bed, checking their pulses before the leader blows a horn two long blows.

Annalise has only one thing in mind as the horn sounds: *My sisters. I have to find my sisters.* She bounds down the dimly lit hall and practically stumbles as she rounds the corner, but Anna manages to coordinate herself long enough to reach her bedroom, where she left Dria. *Dria!* She flips open the door with a forceful arm, but Adrianna is not there. *Where is she? Where could she be? How—*

"What's happening?" a small, worried voice asks Anna at her back. Aimelie stands in her white nightgown, blue doe eyes wide with fear.

Anna grabs her arm and pulls her close. "Melie, we need to find Dria. Do you know where she is?"

Aimelie crinkles her little nose in confusion. "Did you try her room?"

No, why did I not think to try her bloody room? She drags Melie along with her as they sprint to Dria's bedroom, the painted red door more reminiscent of blood than it should be. All around the girls, doors begin to lock, the sound of turning keys dropping Anna's stomach another ten levels. A dozen more guards are making their way down the hallway while Annalise turns the doorknob to Dria's room.

Adrianna sits stiffly on her bed, flipping through the pages of an old book. "I heard the horn, so I decided to hide myself in here."

And forget about little Melie? And me, who risked my life for your curiosity? Annalise hurriedly slams the crimson door shut and locks it behind them. She sits Melie down in a chair and rests herself upon its arm, brown eyes marred with eternal disbelief, fear, and determination.

"What's going on?" Dria asks with a casual grace.

A few moments of silence pass between them all, each of the sisters suspecting the same dire news that none wish to speak of.

Annalise decides to bear the burden with as much poise as she can muster. "Mother and Father have been found ... unresponsive in their bed," she says as gently as she can. Telling them that their parents are dead would make it true, and Anna isn't ready to come to terms with that yet; isn't ready to mull over what that might mean for her sisters, and especially for herself.

A vision of the courtroom fills her mind. She feels the

eyes of countless courtiers, the weight of a heavy crown, the bickering of one hundred councilors ...

Dria drops her book. Melie's eyes meet Anna's in circles round as saucers. And then those saucers fill with tears. Annalise drops down to the cushion beside Melie and embraces her youngest sister as plump tears soak the sleeve of her nightdress. Her jaw tightens in sorrow, tears pushing against the backs of her eyes like a dam ready to break, but she cannot let herself cry in front of others, especially her sisters. *Especially right now. I have to lead them to safety.*

Dria wipes rogue tears from her ruddy eyes and begins to pace around her bed, book still in hand. A forceful knock on the red door shatters the somber silence. The hair on Anna's arms stands on end.

"The rain on St. Ione's Day should be a short one," a brusque, familiar voice speaks the code words from the other side of the bedroom door.

Dria unlocks it, letting the Captain of the Guard step into her room. One look at Captain Ivo's face tells Annalise all she needs to know, confirming that her suspicions are indeed correct.

"The guards are doing a castle-wide search as of right now," his rumbling voice announces. "Residents are being moved into the main hall so that each room can be investigated from top to bottom. It is in our best interests to extend our search to each of your Highness' rooms as well. I hope it will not be of great trouble for you to join the others in the Great Hall?" The captain's voice is deep and sincere but laced with sadness. He had grown up with the king, becoming good friends with him over the years.

"Of course, it will not trouble us," Adrianna replies, drying the last of her tears. "Nothing could trouble us if it is for our own safety." She turns to make sure that Anna is taking care of Melie, and once satisfied, stalks away with a backbone of steel.

AIMELIE

She knew it wasn't the safest thing to do, but now was the best time to do it. Princess Aimelie steps over a puddle as she sneaks through the alleys of town, sniffling in the brisk fall air. Beneath her feet, dried leaves crunch with her every cautious step toward the forge.

He had taken up residency here as per the queen's orders shortly after Annalise's supposed death, and Melie had no need to bother him anytime thereafter. *Until now,* she swallows.

The man himself was never hostile, but he wasn't pleasant, either. He was from Godrus, a land of winter and storm, and his personality matched it, especially when Queen Adrianna cut him off from his line of work at the castle. *And he moved here, of all places.* Mel sighs. *What a pitiful change of events.*

She approaches the door to his workshop now, trying to ignore the persistent sound of hammering and the sharp scent of metal in the air. Lifting her slender hand to knock, Aimelie takes a deep breath. *This is dangerous*, she reflects. But if she doesn't go through with it now, she may never have the opportunity to in the future. Aimelie needs to have it ready before she sends Linden on his first journey to the watchtower. *I need to do it now.*

The wooden door opens under the third knock. Urayus Helva stands before her with a hammer in hand and sweat on his brow. He nods quickly, signaling for her to come inside.

The forge is hotter than a mid-summer's day, its fire basking the room in flickers of orange and yellow and red. The smell of sweat and metal mingles with her sweet perfume as the princess drops her hood, turning to face the former Royal Jeweler.

"It is hotter in here than it was the last time we met," Melie begins.

"Yes, yes. It is always hot in a forge. Were you followed?"

The princess shakes her golden curls.

"Good. Such would complicate things even more." Urayus checks to make sure the door is locked before setting down his hammer with a muscled arm. "I have what you asked for. I hope it is enough, being that it came from the hand of a common blacksmith."

Melie closes her blue doe eyes at the shame in his statement. "I am certain that it will be everything my father dreamed of."

"*Hmph!*" Urayus laughs. "And everything your sister the queen dreads." He moves to his desk, turning his gaze to a silver pin, its engraved falcon staring him in the eyes. "You're sure it was really her?" he asks, a glimmer of hope shining through his dour expression.

The youngest princess takes a step closer to the blacksmith, meeting his powerful gaze. "I saw her with my own eyes, and I have been tortured ever since. All I want is to ..." Aimelie gathers herself, blinking back tears. "All I want is to talk to her, to find out what happened to her in these past six years, but I only have what Captain Ivo and Master Tasman have to go by."

"Ivo and Tasman? Never thought I'd hear those names again. And I'm sure the queen doesn't either." Urayus blots the running sweat off his forehead, gesturing to the familiar plans on the workbench beside them. The parchment is faded from time and hand, but the ink of her father's handwriting still reads clear.

Aimelie's heart skips a beat when she watches Urayus remove the covered object from beneath the table, setting it gingerly atop the gnarled wood. He lifts his brown eyes to Melie's. "Perhaps in a different life, your father could have witnessed this moment."

Her jaw drops at the unveiling of his project. The silver spires and arches have been executed in a hundred delicate patterns that no common blacksmith could have forged. Embedded in the silver are tiny pieces of inlaid jet, the black stones forming a ring around the base of the crown. Every inch is gleaming, glistening in the forge's powerful glow, and above it all are the emeralds, perfectly cut into solid diamonds and aligned exactly in the fashion of King Tiberius's original drawings.

"*Lazarus almighty*," Melie curses. "Urayus … I think you may have exceeded my father's expectations!"

The former Royal Jeweler laughs, hard and weathered, like the laugh of a man broken from the loss of his family's legacy and passion. "We'll leave that up to your sister to decide." A break of silence, one of reflection on their current situation. "When will you give it to her?"

The princess swallows. "I am having my colleague establish secret communication between the watchtower and myself at the castle. Once the route is established, I will send him with it to be delivered to Annalise."

The blacksmith polishes an emerald for a moment in silence. "These are not the queen's colors, Princess. You do know to take care—"

"I do," she replies quickly. "I will be watching her every move, Urayus."

"Aye, but we both know that simply watching her every move may not be enough." He points a glance toward the silver falcon pin on his desk, to the sigil that he once worked for and is now banished because of.

Yes, but it is a risk I am willing to take. The princess nods, setting a bag of one hundred golden suns atop the table and looking shocked when it is pushed away.

"Spare me your pity, young princess. This job was in the making since before you were old enough to count to ten. Consider it my final repayment to your royal parents, Lazarus rest their souls." The blacksmith covers the crown back up in its cloth, carefully placing it into Aimelie's leather satchel with his brawny hands. "Take care, Your Highness. If you should need anything else, you know where to look."

Melie curtsies her thanks, making her way to the door when he calls to her again.

"Princess Aimelie," Urayus begins. "If you should live to see her again ... tell her that there are more of us than she knows who tire of the Crimson Queen's rule, and more still who are willing to rise against her to restore justice to the throne. Tell her that there stands an army already in her name."

The youngest princess lifts her blue hood before turning to meet his gaze. "If it is the last thing I do."

Annalise

"I can't believe Ivo let us come with you," Modgen says as they paddle their way to the shore by the hollow tree.

"Me neither," Annalise laughs. *Although he did put up a good fight.* She brushes a stray water droplet from her sleeve while she reflects on last night's exchange.

It had been three days since Annalise's declaration that she was going to leave the tower to pay a visit to Narelle. And it had taken all three of those days to convince Ivo that bringing Modgen and Oliver was a good idea.

"Like I said before, Captain, two men is better than one. I might need them both should I get into trouble—"

"They could be the ones getting you into trouble! You've

known them for little more than a week, how can we be sure they aren't Adrianna's pawns?"

While her captain was right to question, logic dictated that he look past his fears. *Why else would the queen have a warrant out for their heads if they weren't on her side? These men are wanted by the Crown, and their stories seem to match up with the truth that we know of. I've actually seen guards chasing them down when we were escaping from the hayloft!* Besides, Modgen was Annalise's childhood best friend. *I can tell when he is lying.*

The men continue their rowing until they make landfall on Guorden's Beach, toeing their way onto the sand before they help the princess out of the boat's wooden hull. Annalise Larking thanks them both before scampering over to the hollow tree. She peaks her head into the carved-out hole, dark tresses cascading over her shoulder. *No mail,* she thinks. *How odd? I expected a follow-up letter from Narelle by now.*

"Well, we made it to the mainland, at least. So ..." Modgen blinks. "How exactly are we going to make it to the Sapphire without getting caught?"

Oliver finishes tugging the rowboat behind the brush, taking extra measures to cover any tracks on the sandy shore. "Modgen, relax. I'm sure the princess knows this area, and the guard routes, like the back of her hand."

The lost princess hides a smile. "He's right, Modge. I

will lead you away from the main roads and avoid any areas where my sister's guards like to convene."

"And yet, we are headed to a brothel." Modgen palms his forehead. "All right; I trust you, Ann."

The group begins following the princess, the sound of woodland life luring them forward in silence. A frog ribbits on a fallen log, and somewhere in the distance a pelican cries overhead.

"So ..."

"Modgen, this process may entail you actually being quiet for just a few minutes." The princess chuckles as she closes her brown eyes. *Now, where are we?*

She brings up her mental map of the kingdom, recalling every known location from her stay in the slums and her royal life alike, remembering guard routes and street pubs and forges nearby. "The walk shouldn't be far," she announces. "We will have to cut through the thicket, so try not to trip over any loose roots."

The trek through the woods isn't terrible; the foliage of the densely wooded area helps to conceal their bodies better than they could have hoped for. As her footfalls land against the leaves and mud, Annalise reflects on the last few times she stepped foot in this forest, during her time spent at the Sapphire. *So young*, the princess laughs. *So young, and so naive.*

But despite the new sense of confidence that her goddess memories have given her, Annalise knows that she must do her best to keep this in check. *If someone finds out the truth ...* Anna isn't sure how any mortal would take to meeting Dimity incarnate.

Her mind wanders back to a few days ago when a certain green-eyed ex-Master of the High Council watched her freeze an orange at the dinner table. *If Oliver knows, he hasn't said anything.* But the thought alone is enough to turn her cheeks red.

A stick cracks beneath Modgen's foot, and the three outlaws freeze in their positions. Annalise raises her hand until she gauges the area with her superior knowledge of guard locations but hears nothing. "Clear," she tells them in a nearly inaudible whisper. *We are almost there anyway.*

A few more steps reveal the edge of the forest, and just through the clearing, the pale brick of the Sapphire. The sight and smell of town is as comforting as it is horrifying, but it brings a smile to Anna's face to see a horse for the first time in weeks, and to feel the breeze blowing off the South Bay against her skin. *I guess we don't realize what we miss when we are trapped inside a tower for too long.*

The back door of the Sapphire is lined in blue trim, and Anna scurries up for the hundredth time in her life after deeming the dirt path safe to cross. Her men in tow, the lost princess enters the basement, taking in the familiar sight of sapphire rugs and white linen curtains. "We can take these stairs to reach Narelle's room," she points.

The plush cobalt velvet makes little noise beneath their feet as the outlaws tiptoe their way up to the main level. *It's rather quiet for a Saturday*, Annalise thinks. In fact, all the doors are shut, and she sees not a soul in the main lobby. The princess scrunches her eyebrows together before padding toward Narelle's room.

She gives the wooden door a knock, but there is no answer. Anna glances at the boys, who are silently awaiting her orders. *I suppose I know this place better than they do.* Her hand presses down on the handle, the door opening to Annalise's horror. Every nook, every cranny, every object in her second home has been flipped over and thrown about in what looks to be a search conducted by Lazarus himself.

"*By the gods*," Modgen curses.

"By the gods indeed," says the cold-eyed man seated to their far right.

The princess racks her mind for who this man might be, if his shock of black ringlets looked familiar in the slightest, but wastes her time. He raises his hand to display the queen's silver pin, decorated with a crimson-red snake.

"Hello, Annalise Larking."

VEGA

Vega doesn't know what to think of the girl with the cloak. *Her quietness, her awkwardness ... I don't think she's made a peep in the past forty minutes.* Mara, as Vega soon discovered, is not accustomed to traveling with a partner. *Or at least not one with a voice.*

"How much farther are the docks?" Vega asks her mysterious companion.

The female stutters. "Um, I-I believe not much farther. Just past the Oronian Clocktower, then over the hill."

I do hope that Dimity is a bit more talkative than Mara. I'm beginning to get bored with my own thoughts. They continue trudging along the damp Javirian cobblestones as the sun attempts to crest the horizon, two strangers with nothing in common but a single ultimate goal: *to leave this gods-forsaken territory and flee to Empeirus.*

Empeirus. Elouthera hasn't another thought in her mind save for finding her one true ally. *Without Dimity, the war is practically won if Jedda and Anzac find their way together.* Vega doesn't want to think about what that kind of union would mean for the Earth, for their people. The only way to stop them from destroying it is for Dimity and Elouthera to join as a team, one that would be equal in power to their own.

Which brings Vega here, to the beautiful territory of Javir. *Of all the places, why did I have to wash up here? Couldn't I have been magically carried against the current to the golden spires of Nesvla, or better yet, just so happen to float on the shipwreck rubble to Empeirus?*

A former war zone, even Javir's inhabitants resemble the iron and steel the territory is so plentiful in providing, each bearing sharp personalities to match. *Except for Mara. Mara hardly has a personality at all.*

The silent traveler tugs her crimson hood over her eyes once again. Her body is hidden beneath the cloak, but Vega can at least glean a few bits of information from her strange partner. *Is that gold on her boots? And her black gloves, they are lined in gold trim. Her gait ... it is as if she is walking on water.*

"There," Mara points, and the first sign of the harbor is at last in view. "It is still far away, but—"

Vega stops. "Did you hear that?" she asks, turning her lime-green eyes down the cobblestone road from which they came.

The cloaked girl turns with Vega, her dirty-blonde hair peeking out from beneath her hood. "Wh-what is it?" she asks in her Javirian accent.

The manipulator examines her colleague once more while she continues to listen. *She is too well garbed for wanting to be discreet.* "You aren't being followed, are you?"

Mara stares through the crimson fabric of her hood. "Are you?"

Elouthera makes no reply. *Well played.* She turns back around when Mara makes a small grunting noise, one that escalates into a groan.

"What's wrong? Are you hurt? Talk to me, Mara."

Beneath her cloak hood, Mara clutches her forehead in agony. "I can see them ... they move like the clouds ..."

Before Elouthera can make sense of this, dark shadows begin to bleed from the alleys. *Anzac? No ... they are people ... and we are severely outnumbered.*

They emerge from the dawn air like a cloud of dust, dispersing throughout the caliginous Javirian roads.

"Why didn't you tell me you were being followed?" Vega whispers through grit teeth.

"I-I was sure no one saw me leave." Mara pinches the bridge of her nose.

All around them the men appear, one by one with grins of malice and shoulders brimming with muscle. *Dear gods, what have I gotten myself into? Where in the name of Lazarus did this girl come from?* Vega would have continued wondering that very question had not a strapping young male sauntered his way to the front of the party.

"Well done, Eden," he remarks in his gold-trimmed tunic.

Eden? Who is—

"I never thought you had it in you to say *no* for once, let alone to run away from the arena."

Arena? Vega opens her mouth, but a look from the male steels her lime-green gaze. *The gold accents on his pristine clothing, his perfect posture ...* She looks back at Mara, who she finds to be visibly shaking.

"I must say, you weren't the hardest needle in the haystack to find, but why should I have expected anything more from you?"

The man's eerie blue eyes give Vega a feeling of disgust, her stomach roiling at the tone he uses to address her colleague. Deep within the recesses of her mind, she recalls a time when someone else used to talk down to her in a similar way ... A stray puddle on the cobblestone morphs into liquid silver.

She turns to face her trembling friend. "Who is this guy? He sounds like a real prick."

Without a word, Mara lifts the front of her hood with those gold-trimmed gloves. The crimson fabric falls, revealing a head of wavy, dirty-blonde hair and a face that would have been almost average to look at if it weren't for a set of unsettling, mismatched eyes.

"He is my brother," the female finishes, before a shiver runs down Vega's spine.

There are three things that the manipulator can piece together at the time of this unfortunate interaction. The first is that this female is not who Vega thought she was. The second is that she does not have a good relationship with her brother. *And the third would be that we need to get the hell out of here.*

The strong man takes a step forward in his black and gold boots, ruffling a hand through his own dirty-blonde hair. "Come now, Eden. Don't make this harder than it has to be. We both know this isn't what Mother and Father would have wanted."

An exasperated sound from Eden. Her teeth are beginning to chatter, despite the balmy Javirian morning.

A smaller part of Vega nudges herself to get out of here, to leave the strange girl and hitch a ride on the nearest boat to Empeirus. After all, that is her ultimate mission. *But what good would I be if I let him get away with this? It is obvious that he is plotting something cruel against her, and I have had my own fair share of that business, however long ago. It isn't fair to her. And besides, what kind of goddess just abandons an innocent? Not a goddess that I would want to pray to.*

Elouthera steps a black boot forward. "She can't go back. It would ruin our agreement."

Sniffles of laughter from across the twenty-or-so men. One of them spits at the ground. She eyes them all, her jet-black hair whipping in the wind.

"Your *agreement*," Eden's brother repeats, until two familiar faces draw his attention.

"Edris, it's her!" says the first, pointing at Vega.

The other nods enthusiastically, "Aye, the witch from the alley!"

Of course, the men from the alley that I scared away from Mara, or ... Eden. Were they working for this 'Edris' the entire time?

A look of realization falls upon Edris' brutal face, one that has Vega more confused than unsettled.

"Look, we had a deal. Now just let us be on our merry way."

Faster than the strike of a cobra, the stealthy male lets a throwing knife loose straight toward Vega's face. She has all of half a second to throw out an arm, melting it into a puddle of liquid silver. Her heart skips a beat as she watches the men gawk with terror or awe, she cannot tell.

Only Edris smirks. "Ho, ho," he exclaims. "How lucky can a man be, to find the only two women in the world he wants most?"

What in the... The girls exchange glances, eyes narrowing in confusion.

"You see," the male begins as he inches a foot closer, "a little bird told me that he once lost someone near and dear to his own heart ... someone with certain gifts. He promised that should I return this precious female to him, he would reward me heavily—and I am never a man to pass up an opportunity for pleasure." He waves his finger in a circular motion to signal his men.

Eden's gaze finds its way to Vega, who is teeming with rage. *Anzac. So, he was at least partially behind this whole charade.*

The men move in behind them now, and Elouthera knows that despite having master-level manipulator skills, her odds against twenty-something men would be slim. Bitterness courses through her as they seize them both at once, taking care to secure the ropes far enough above her hands so that she cannot manipulate them into individual fibers.

"Where is he? *Where is Anzac?*" Vega screams, her frustration getting the best of her as they push her and Eden to their knees.

"Relax, darling," Edris admonishes with a golden smile. "You will be reunited with your love in no time."

ANNALISE

SIX YEARS EARLIER

The Great Hall is filled with the castle's patrons from all departments and backgrounds: cooks, stablemen, knights, maids, members of the High Council, even children torn from their nightly rest all mesh together in the airy space of the royal gathering hall.

Annalise Larking stands with a hand on Melie's shoulder, daring glances at faces in the mob. *Could one of them have done it? Did they think it wise to kill the very beings whose presence ensured the existence of their jobs, to rob a family of the parents that held it together?*

Anna stops her storming thoughts with a breath. Dwelling too much on the subject would break the concentration she is trying so hard to use to mask her uneasiness. Even if she does not feel confident, she must look the part. *There are too many faces, too many critical eyes.*

Dria is seated in a plush chair to Anna's right; the three princesses have been surrounded by guards and awaiting answers for the better half of an hour now. Dawn is near approaching, judging by the look of the sky as seen through the overbearing arched windows.

Annalise taps a finger repeatedly on Melie's tiny shoulder, keeping rhythm like the second hand of the nearby clock. The noises of the mob seem to be growing louder with restlessness, like a swarm of bees doubling in number and volume, and Anna swears that they are all trying to get a peek at her. *They wonder what will become of them if I am to sit the throne. They wonder how I will compare to my parents. Will I be just? Will I fill their coffers again? How will the queen's face look at her coronation, knowing that she is only inheriting the crown after the murder of her royal parents? Will she herself be the next victim of the royal bloodline?*

"Can you please stop that?" Aimelie grasps Anna's drumming finger with a gentle hand.

It takes her a moment to fully come back into reality. "Sorry, Melie," she apologizes quietly.

In the midst of her embarrassment, Anna catches a flash of red hair making its way through the crowd. "Modgen!" she calls to her friend between the backs of two guards, attempting to distract herself from the agitation of her troubled mind.

He rushes up to meet her, only to have a guard stop him with the palm of a black-leathered hand. "No farther than here," the burly man warns him.

Nodding, Modgen looks at Annalise through the crack between two castle guards. "How are you doing?"

"As all right as we can be for the time being," she answers, the knot in her stomach tightening with every passing second. "How are you?"

Modgen smiles and shrugs. "I would be better if Clarice hadn't turned me down this morning."

She manages a small laugh, eternally grateful for her best friend's ability to add humor to even the most dire of situations. "Would a round of *halsen* make it up to you?"

"Only if you're ready to lose."

"That's not what happened last time," the princess replies with a devilish grin.

With a clatter, a group of castle guards led by Captain Ivo himself bursts through the Great Hall doors. He posts his guards in front of them and walks straight toward the ring of princesses and their protectors. Modgen disappears back into the crowd, whose buzzing quiets to a mumble.

Adrianna pushes her way to the captain. "Tell me you have news," she pleads.

Ivo swallows, pinning his gray-blue eyes on Annalise.

"Your Highness, we've found something of question in your room."

There are no words to describe the unfettered shock she feels at this statement, but she cannot let her mask crumble. "What have you found?"

The captain opens his mouth to reply but closes it. Reaching into his pocket, he discreetly reveals to the princess an unfamiliar wooden jewelry box. He lifts its small lid to display jeweled bracelets, and beneath those, a small black bottle of liquid. Written on the tan label is *Egvivius fasayra,* commonly referred to as Widow's Breath, for its historical use in making widows out of those who mixed the odorless poison into their husband's evening tea.

Bile burns the back of Anna's throat and her hands begin to tremble. *That is not my box. Those aren't even my bracelets!* She didn't do it, could never in a million years even think of doing something so abhorrent, but she cannot find the words to speak.

"What is that?" Aimelie asks innocently.

"*That* is why our oldest sister is going to rot in the dungeons," Adrianna tells her with eyes like chips of ice.

A pang of betrayal splinters her heart when she watches Dria pull a crying Aimelie to her chest. *Leave Aimelie out of this. She is too young for this, this ... whatever this is!*

"Was it too long to wait for the throne, sister? Did

impatience get the best of you?" Annalise swears that Dria's fury could set the earth aflame.

"I love them Dria, I love them with all my heart. I cannot begin to describe the disgust I feel upon even *remotely* thinking of such an act," Annalise speaks, a tear making its way out of her eye. "How could you even *wonder* if I could do such a thing?" It is becoming harder and harder to talk without crying now.

The captain interrupts. "Your Highness, I cannot believe it with mine own heart, but we must treat this like any other case in our kingdom. I will personally oversee your cell—which will be temporary, I am sure of it—and make sure you have all the comforts you have tradition-ally known until the day of your trial." Ivo's eyes are tired but determined, and reality grips Anna like an omnipo-tent hand.

They believe me to be a murderer. They actually believe that I killed my own parents. She looks around at the crowd, attempting to think through what is likely to happen to her. *What could possibly prove my innocence in this case? A bottle of poison in my bedroom ...* A hopeless sob escapes Annalise's lips, and she knows that when they take her, she will never see the light of day again. The only evidence for the trial will be a black bottle of *Egvivius fasayra*, silently dooming her for the rest of her outnum-bered days. *How can I ever be proven innocent?* She glances at her sisters for help.

Aimelie's face is hidden in the folds of Adrianna's dress, but Adrianna herself is gazing at Anna's head like a target. Ire swirls in those blue eyes, so fierce it could melt metal.

"Dria, I—"

"Seize her, the traitor!" she cries to the guards, who make to grab Anna's arms.

Like a doe startled in a meadow, Annalise turns on a heel and bolts around an open corner, leaving the Great Hall behind.

The dining room is large and airy. Most people wouldn't suspect it to be a place of secrecy, but Annalise had familiarized herself with the entire castle as a child, exploring every crack and crevice it had to offer. *Please, gods, let it still be here*, she prays. The pounding footsteps of twenty-or-so guards chase her into the room before she lifts a hanging tapestry, disappearing on the other side.

This should at least slow them. The two-foot-wide passageway is pitch black, and Anna finds her small feet stumbling over the misshapen steps. Every jagged brick is an obstacle to walk on itself, let alone in the dark. Her heart beats so hard against her chest that she thinks it might explode. *And what if it does? It would be better than the doom I would face if taken to the dungeons and tried.* A brief light illuminates the passage as three guards lift the tapestry and enter, trailing just a few yards behind.

Palms sweating, she runs her hands along the crooked

old stones, listening to the grunts and panting of the guards behind her. Her feet continue struggling to find purchase as she makes her blind ascent. *If I am having trouble, no doubt that fully grown men will have some as well.*

The princess has no idea where this particular tunnel leads; it is one of four that are connected to the dining hall, and she could never keep them straight. *Wherever it goes, though, I have no choice now but to follow.* Far below her, one of the guards suffers a misstep and falls down the black abyss with the sound of a yelp and clashing armor. *One down, two to go,* Anna thinks uselessly.

Her hands continue to hurry her farther up the stone stairs, nails digging into the crooks between bricks as she wills her arms to move faster. Behind her, the two remaining guards sound nearer than before, and Annalise can feel her strength dwindling with every fervent step she takes.

On a sharp inhale, the princess's foot slips on the next step, sending her knees cracking into the sharp stone. *Ione's grace, that hurts,* she curses, but not before a greedy hand wraps around her shoulder.

"Hold still, your High—"

She has only a second of time to elbow the guard in his groin and wriggle free, scampering up the stairs now on her hand and knees. *Good lord Lazarus, whose strength I draw from thee—*

"Did you get her, Lenus?"

A curse sounds from a few steps below, the voice fading as Anna climbs for her life, for her freedom. She doesn't dare think of what that freedom might mean for her, or for her sisters. *Just a little bit farther ...*

The steps of the narrow passage transform into a stretch of flatness, and Anna's knees buckle with relief. *There is more room here though; the guards will be able to move faster now.* It is all she can do but to keep sprinting until at last her hands slam against another wall, this one directly in her line of escape. Panic begins to seize her at the sound of rushing footsteps and nearing bellows, the princess throwing her hands against the black wall. *They have reached the flat ground*, she realizes with terror.

Something warm swirls with the ounce of hope she has left in the pit of her stomach, its tingling sensations beginning to pulse through her arms. There is no time to explore the oddness of the feeling, so she allows herself one quick, deep breath and hurls her body against the wall with all her might, the action shattering the darkness of the passageway with muted sunlight. Warm spring air permeates the opening as Annalise leaps over the heap of wooden rubble, struggling to find her breath.

Dear gods, that just happened.

One look at the flower-adorned field tells Anna all she needs to know: *The castle courtyard.* Gray storm clouds overlook the stone walls towering at ten feet high, running along the perimeter of the yard behind the castle.

Within the walls, there are only three exits: two doors on the sides, which are frequently used, and a third, directly in the middle of the two others. *Which everyone knows to avoid.*

The guards emerge mere footsteps behind her as the princess wills her thin body to move faster. *If I turn to run for any side door, the guards will likely catch me before I can make it another foot.* The only way out of their hold is the center path, whose rocky cliff face descends into the churning waters of the Falvedrie Sea. *My odds are looking more and more grim.*

The courtyard is running out of grass, and the center door looms closer and closer. *The gods have given me a choice, and now I must choose.* Annalise makes a beeline for the fern-covered outcropping, preparing for what lies ahead. She passes beneath the arched doorway, the sea air twining its fingers through her earthy hair, her legs burning from running for so long.

Her body is ready to give out, but she knows she has only one more move to make.

"Princess, *no!*" A guard's voice calls out in terror, just before she clears the edge of the cliff.

Her shrill scream pierces the dawn air. Arms flailing, her white nightdress billows about her knees as Annalise Larking plummets into the dark, swirling depths of the Falvedrie Sea.

ANNALISE

It wasn't long before the queen's guards flanked them at Narelle's doorway that the three discovered the Sapphire was being held by castle forces. *A trick*, Anna realized. *They must have held it in hopes that I would return after not hearing from Narelle. But how did they know that she was even one of my contacts? Was it Robbin who snitched out of spite for stealing his clothes? What evidence could they have that would rule Narelle guilty?*

Annalise stops. The empty tree, the lack of mail recently ... *The stamp. Perhaps there was some correspondence they might have found?*

The guests of the Throne Room titter with interest as the three outlaws are brought in, each of them being dragged by golden-armored guards before the queen's marble dais. *So, we meet again, sister.* The former Master of the High Council and Royal Treasurer are a bit less humored by this unfortunate affair. Oliver seems more vigilant than worried, but Modgen looks as though he could shed a tear.

While their dire situation would have eaten her alive only weeks ago, the realization of her powers and being Dimity have grossly dampened Annalise's anxieties. Adrianna might be a queen, but what power could a mortal hold over a goddess? *I have nothing to fear, even if my hands are tied and bound.*

Queen Adrianna Larking sits atop her ornate throne, her sultry lips in mid-conversation with her lady-in-waiting Renai. *Renai? By the gods, I haven't seen her in a while. She looks about the same though, conniving and fox-like.* Annalise and her accomplices catch every eye on their journey to the dais, all except for the queen's, as she continues to share such intense gossip that it prevents her from noticing the three wanted criminals standing in her white marble Throne Room.

"Your Majesty," Annalise's guard interrupts. "My apologies. I have brought you some good news, I hope."

Her blonde braid shifts below her waist when she leans forward in unsettling glee. "Well," Adrianna begins with her wolfish smile. "Lazarus really is good."

Ignoring the chafing of her wrists, Annalise pits her

brown eyes against her sister's icy blue ones, at last letting her get a complete look at her face. The Crimson Queen rises from her throne, golden heels clicking against the marble as she surveys her captors, taking in what Annalise thinks must be every weakness of theirs she can peg.

"You have no idea how long I've waited for this moment," says Dria. "I'll admit, you did rather well at usurping my guards all this time."

A shuffle from the left of the dais. Aimelie Larking, their youngest sister, darts her blue doe eyes nervously above a crimson blush.

"Tell me," the queen continues, "how many more traitors like you must I endure for the rest of my reign?"

Annalise lifts her chin. "Judging by the current political climate, I'd say we're one of the last."

The Throne Room air shifts, hovering with whispers.

Modgen murmurs to his left. "Splendid job, Anna—you're really helping our cause!"

The queen huffs a laugh and steps down the dais. "I always knew I'd see your wretched face again. Murdering our beloved parents and then escaping your destiny of drowning in the Falvedrie. And all this time, hiding beneath our noses for years in some *brothel*."

How long did they torture you, Narelle, before they gleaned that information? A flicker of flame lights in the pit of Anna's stomach. "You are as good a queen as you are a liar."

"Oh! Yes, you are doing such a *fantastic* job!" Modgen bursts at the second insult.

Her icy eyes narrow, and then, a smirk. "I forgot how close the two of you were growing up."

"Then it's a wonder why he wasn't even put on trial, for being the best friend of a supposed murderer. You would think that after the murder of our own parents you might expand your search, even if there was evidence planted on myself. A just daughter would go to all lengths to ensure the treason was not to be found so long as she lived."

The flame grows a little brighter as she shakes her brown waves in disgust. "*Egvivius fasayra*? Dropped in a jewelry box with belongings that weren't even mine, somehow placed in my chambers, which only the Royal Family had the means to enter. So how did it even get there, Dria?"

"My queen—" Captain Desmond Jrehart begins, but she raises her hand. Her breathing is heavier now, her chest rising and falling above the top of her crimson corset, feasting on the prevalence of her sister's anger.

"The maids who cleaned my chambers that night could have attested to the fact that it wouldn't have been placed in my room until past our bedtime. I would have been asleep, only for you to wake me—"

"*Enough!*" Adrianna exclaims. "I've had enough of you, Annalise. I thought I'd been rid of the traitor who murdered our parents years ago. I should never have stopped until they brought me your body." She glances at her captain. "My mistake."

Aimelie Larking covers her mouth in horror as tears begin to threaten her composure. *Melie,* Anna inwardly calls. One look at her blue eyes tells her everything she needs to know. *I can't let her take me.* Annalise glances to her sides, to the other wanted criminals in the kingdom, to her brand-new allies and right now, her accomplices. *No, I can't let them take us. Because as long as Dria sits the throne, chaos will reign.* And the only fighting chance Annalise has lies in the hands of these two men beside her.

Beads of sweat dampen the front of Anna's tunic while she awaits her sister's call. She can feel the flames reaching higher now, burning down the length of her arms as if they are glowing. *My powers. If I use them now, in front of everyone …*

"Your Majesty—" Modgen cuts in.

"I should have had you all *gagged* before you came in here. Desmond," the queen finishes. "You know what to do."

Annalise's stomach tightens, the flames of her godly powers mixing fully with her blood. Desmond and his guards bolt toward the queen's captors, but the fire runs straight through her fingertips, sailing across their bindings and scorching them to ash.

The Throne Room squeals.

In the two seconds it takes the guards to realize what has happened, the heat within her body morphs into cold, and the lost princess flashes a wall of ice between the guards and her own faction.

"*No*," Desmond whispers, his silver eyes wide with an ethereal curiosity. "It can't be."

Annalise pauses to catch her breath, watching her comrades staring at their wrists, and finds the queen staring at her. *She looks ... like she isn't intimidated. Like she is more content than scared.*

Above the screams and bellows of the Throne Room, their queen stands tall and strong, the rubies of her crown glimmering in her refined sense of rage. The ground begins to rattle, the precious relics of their parents' past shaking in their glass cases, but it is not from Anna. A mysterious smirk blooms across Dria's face before she parts her ruby lips.

"And just when I thought I couldn't hate you more."

A bolt of ice shoots out from Adrianna's hand, slicing through the air toward Anna's head. The princess dodges, watching the arrow travel behind her and straight into a courtier's chest. His pitiful moan is the only thing Annalise can process before turning to find the queen readying herself for another attack. *By the gods! Dria ... how can she have powers, too?*

And then it clicks. Their childhood, Adrianna's despicable, fiery personality, the terrors that she enjoyed bestowing upon any watchful eye. *And the murder, the murder of our own parents.* Annalise Larking is Dimity incarnated. *But Adrianna Larking, my royal sister...*

"*Jedda?*" Annalise whispers across the electric air.

The goddess pauses, pinning her heartless eyes on her sister. "*Dimity.*"

Her slender hands come together in a sharp movement that has the water from the nearby glasses launching from their vessels, freezing in mid-air as they fly from all directions at the three traitors. Annalise releases the fire she has been holding on to by letting it explode into a protective arc around them, the entire Throne Room witnessing the ice melt above their heads. *We need to get out of here.*

"Go!" Anna tells her comrades. "I can hold her off if you can make it through the door!" Right now, even the guards are cowering at the sight of two goddesses wielding powers on planet Earth.

Without a word, Oliver and Modgen bolt toward the nearest exit, and Dimity turns her attention again to her sister as she begins inching backward down the aisle way. In half a second, Jedda casts a channeled beam of ice toward Dimity, who decides to melt it with a fire shield.

I'm not sure how much longer we can keep this up, the goddess thinks, since she hasn't exactly had much time to practice using her powers.

"It's not too late to change your vote, Dimity. Admit it," Jedda spills over lips turning blue from the cold. "The Earthlings aren't what you expected."

Another bead of sweat drips down the side of Dimity's forehead, her body struggling to maintain the balance. *If only I had Elouthera.* "I'll fight to the death for my vote. I will be Earth's champion no matter what."

The Dark Goddess laughs above the cacophony of the racing crowd. "What makes you think that you will be any such thing?"

"What makes you think that I won't?"

Jedda smiles, cold and twisted. "Because you are outnumbered."

It takes all of one heartbeat for Dimity to see the black shadows sweeping across the marble tile. Beneath the mass hysteria of the courtiers, she can feel the temperature drop a few noticeable degrees. And in the corner of the room stands Desmond, his hands splayed before him, silver eyes concentrating on the darkness before Dimity. *No. No, no, no, no, no!*

Dimity's hold on her sister's ice beam weakens with her fleeting concentration, the ice beginning to overpower her flame. The shadows begin to dance on the floor, their compositions morphing into what looks like the beginnings of an overgrown serpent. *Anzac. Jedda has been with bloody Anzac this entire time!* Dimity focuses on her sister, who is beginning to look a bit too much like death. *I imagine must I look a similar way. We don't know how to control our powers yet.*

The idea has Dimity wasting no time. Before Anzac makes to morph his shadow monster into something larger, Dimity inhales sharply, drawing in just enough energy to push her flames around the outside of Jedda's ice beam. *I am too well matched for the ice to melt, but ...* With a grunt someone from the slum district would be proud of, the Goddess of Wisdom and Justice thrusts the combined power of their magic sideways—directly into Anzac and his shadow monster.

"*Anzac!*" her sister screams, but there is not enough strength left in either of the goddesses even to stand.

Dimity watches the glass case shatter atop the Captain of the Royal Guard, the queen's ruby dress collapsing in a heap atop the marble dais with Dimity falling shortly behind.

Her head rests upon what should be cool white marble, but even the ground is scorching from the use of her magic. *I need to get up*, the lost princess thinks. *I need ... I need ...*

Sturdy hands haul her body upwards, throwing her over a shoulder to carry her out of the Throne Room. Her brown eyes are too dazed to see who it is, but she swears she can smell something like pine or cedar. *Who would touch me after seeing what I truly am? I'm ... not human ...*

Annalise's dark eyes roll in her head, glancing up at the Throne Room ceiling just in time to catch an engraving of a hawk soaring over the ocean. *Water,* Annalise dwells uselessly. *I need ... water ...*

And with that thought, she passes out.

VEGA

She moves her wrists downward once more. A bead of sweat trickles down the side of her pointed face, remoistening a lock of matted black hair. Vega's hands don't have to be touching an object to manipulate it, but they need to be close. *Perhaps just a few inches above the surface is all I need, but I'd be lucky to get my wrists a hair closer than they are now.*

The contraption that the men rigged is anything but tasteful—iron pikes and pieces of log and bits of fabric scraps—but nonetheless, it does the job. Sitting on her knees, the mechanism holds Vega's arms straight out before her, ensuring that her hands cannot grab hold of any portion of it, eliminating any chance of escape by manipulation.

As for Eden, her means of captivity were much

simpler with some rope tied to a bedpost. *And could perhaps be simpler still, since the gag really isn't necessary.*

All at once, the room shakes with the clang of a thunderous bell, its murmur so deep it is a wonder not every brick in the tower has been rocked out of place. The rumbling of the Oronian Clocktower as it chimes on the hour leaves the captives' heads swimming, but it is all they can do to close their eyes and breathe through it.

They hadn't spoken for at least two hours since they were dragged into the brick room, but Vega has a multitude of questions. *Too many questions, but too little trust. Who is this girl? Why did her brother want to take her hostage? Is she somehow valuable?*

The manipulator doubts that Mara—or Eden, as her brother so kindly pointed out—would be much help speaking up against their captors, but perhaps there is something hidden beyond the surface that Vega knows nothing about. Curiosity gets the better of her as she searches for anything to take her mind off the endless throb of her bindings.

"So," Vega begins. "Who is he?"

The damp cold of the brick room offers no comfort, save for the shabby bed which Eden is tied at the foot of. Her bottom on the floor, she shifts her wrists against the wooden bedpost.

"I told you already. He is my brother."

"I know he is your brother, but who *is* he? Why does he want you back?"

"Why does he want *you*?"

Elouthera bites a lip. *At least she is speaking. This might be the most I've heard her talk.* "If I told you, you wouldn't believe me." Her lime-green eyes trail the outline of a brick beneath her knee. "The thing you said before they saw us in the street, when your head hurt ... what was that about?"

Before the female can answer, a gaoler opens the door with a kick, the wood creaking on its hinges. "Food for the captives. 'pparently they want you two alive."

The burly man unties Eden's ropes but drops a chunk of bread in Vega's bound hands. "Don't drop it," he warns her on a heel, before stepping back to keep an eye on Eden. Craning her head forward, Vega consumes the stale bread with disgust.

They eat in silence, neither saying a word until Eden's bindings are retied and the gaoler leaves with enough confidence that they will not be breaking free anytime soon. *This better not go on for too much longer; how do they expect us to relieve ourselves?*

The Goddess of Dreams and Mysteries peers back up at the stranger's eyes, one blue and one gold. *So odd, so uncommon ...* "All right. If you won't do the talking, then I will. My name is Vega. I am from Wembleton."

Silence.

"I was on my way to Empeirus when my ship crashed during a mad storm just off the coast. That's how I made it here."

A quick glance at the door. "Y-You are a witch," Eden starts. Her gold-trimmed gloves lay scattered on the brick floor beside her.

Vega smiles. "That's one thing to call me." She thinks back to her schooling, to her studying, to her accomplishments that will be wasted now that she is trapped in a brick box. "But I'm really a nobody."

Mismatched eyes blink at her with surprise. "I'm not sure that ... Edris wouldn't want a nobody ... he is too hungry for power."

The manipulator huffs a laugh. "He seems like it." She pauses. "I can't believe he found me."

"He has men on every corner of this town."

"No," Vega shakes her head. "I was talking about Anzac."

Eden stares. "Anzac," she repeats in her Javirian accent. "Anzac ... the god?"

Do I dare explain? She could tell her brother, but I guess it wouldn't matter anyway, since his knowing is the reason I'm in this mess. "Yes," Vega replies as another bead of sweat drips from her sharp nose. "Anzac the god."

Those mismatched eyes dart back and forth. She nods.

Vega scoffs, chastising herself for even bringing it up.

Some things are best left unsaid, especially when they make you sound crazy.

"I believe you."

Her heart stops, green eyes widening at the sudden declaration that only an insane person would admit. "You what?"

A shrug of her muscular shoulders. "My mother always told me that one day the gods would return to Earth. It ... it doesn't seem improbable, considering that they created the world as we know it. She said for us to stay away from the dark gods, but that never stopped Edris."

The manipulator blinks. *Is she spiritually mature or just out of her bloody mind?* Desperate to change the subject, Elouthera thinks of something, anything, to ask her new acquaintance. "Were you close to your mother?"

"Yes," Eden smiles shyly, leaning her head against the bedpost. "I always looked up to her. Of course, any young girl with Laraya as her mother would want to be just like her."

Wait, what—

The door kicks open once again, only this time it is under the boot of none other than Eden's brother, Edris.

Laraya, as in ...

She takes in the sight of those gold-trimmed gloves, the black leather boots gleaming such that one could see their reflection in them if they so wanted, the girl's fit and well-muscled physique.

"Well, well. How are my fair ladies enjoying these fine quarters?"

"When were you going to tell me that your mother was Laraya Sharpkey?" Vega snaps at Eden.

"I ..."

The pain is like none other. It begins as a dull throb before escalating into a pointed, stabbing headache behind Elouthera's eyes, moving then to the rest of her head. Behind the ringing in her ears, the rest of the world fades away until all she can hear is Dimity's clear voice on the other side of the bond.

"Go!" she tells the two men beside her. *"I can hold her off if you can make it through the door!"*

Dozens of guards in golden armor cower before Dimity and who is presumably the queen, her crimson gown pooling at the floor as does the blood of her enemies. Her fingers are splayed before her as she forces an ice beam against Dimity, who returns the favor with a shield of fire.

"It's not too late to change your vote, Dimity," the queen says. *"Admit it, the Earthlings aren't what you expected."*

The marble room rattles with each pulse of the females' undeniable powers.

"I'll fight to the death for my vote. I will be Earth's champion no matter what."

Vega chokes on water, blinking her green cat-eyes awake in the grim room of the Oronian Clocktower, only to find Edris Sharpkey staring coldly back at her.

"I know who you are, *Elouthera*. Now, it's time you tell me everything."

ADRIANNA

Desmond! Adrianna cries without speaking. Her mind is still frozen from the use of her ice magic, but it is quick to thaw when she finds her soulmate unresponsive on the opposite side of the dais. She needs to get to him, move to him; needs to pull him from the rubble and into the safety of her arms to make sure he is okay. *Because if he is not, this world shall never see the light of day again. Because if he is not, it shall be my undoing.*

If only her body were as willing as her mind. The use of her untrained power has left her entire being ravaged after her encounter with her sister in blood and bond, Annalise Larking. *Annalise, who we now know is Dimity. My father must think himself hilarious for setting up such a fitting incarnation.*

A groan from Anzac has her attention shifting back to the most important matter at hand. *I need to go to him, and if I can't walk, then I will crawl.* Jedda forces every muscle of her body to twist herself onto her hands and knees, her frostbitten extremities peeling from the spot where she collapsed after her battle with Annalise. Her golden-suited guards continue to tremble in fear, but it is no matter; Jedda doesn't need their help. Even though there is no energy, no ounce of her magic left to burn, she can always turn to the one thing that has never failed her.

She lets the rage consume her, lets it lace her blood like venom. Lets herself reflect on the unsettling strength of her sister, lets herself process the uncanny arrangement of their earthly incarnations, lets the way that Dimity marred her only true love fuel her body one inch at a time until it is all she can do to collapse beside Anzac on a pile of broken glass. She releases a moan of pain, her body finally defrosting from some movement, and turns to face her lover.

"*Jedda,*" Anzac whispers hoarsely. "*She is—*"

"I know," Jedda responds, glancing at the broken shelf pinning him down across his back. "I know who she is."

Minutes pass, the two of them staring at the destruction of the empty Throne Room from the floor of the dais. They silently exchange glances with every broken chair and table, every empty water chalice, every scorched area around which Dimity was standing. *She won,* Jedda thinks, wiping a drop of blood from her swollen lip. *She was outmatched, and she won.*

For a time, all that can be heard is the sound of their ragged breathing, at their bodies' only way of voicing what suffering their mouths cannot. She replays the entire scene through her mind once more, watching her sister murmur to her accomplices.

"*Go!*" she had said, before her arms were aglow with blazing fire and she managed to crash a bookcase on top of Anzac. Jedda knows that she and Anzac are a force to be reckoned with, even against three gods. But being outsmarted by one … The Dark Goddess can make as many excuses as she wants, but she still winds up with the same unsettling conclusion: *Anzac and I are going to need to train hard, and plot harder.*

The smell of burning hair brings Dria back to her senses, only to realize that the bitch had singed the tip of her braid. She bites her lip hard enough to draw more blood, a fitting match for the bitter disdain she feels toward her goddess sister. Sitting in silence, she continues to pull off tiny pieces of burned hair until the sound of footsteps has her turning up her bloodshot blue eyes.

Desmond peers up from the dust, a few pieces of glass raining down from his night-black hair. The footfalls echo about the Great Hall as Dria claws her way to a half-sitting position, ignoring the tiny shards of glass piercing the flesh of her palms.

"I see the townsfolk tell no lies," the woman begins, her purple and black robes grazing the Throne Room floor. Her jet-black hair glistens in the dull light as she takes in the aftermath of the scene. Smiling at each of the cowering guards, her booted feet continue padding toward the god and goddess. "I must say, I am shocked to know my own queen and the captain of her guard as some of the very gods we mortals pray to."

Adrianna pauses. Ashes dance in the milky afternoon sunlight, but a glint of light on metal catches her cold gaze. The stranger's citrine eyes do little to distract from the silver and amethyst moon hanging about her neck while she toes her way toward the bottom of the dais.

"And to think that I had offered my services to not just any little mortal, but to a *goddess*."

Her full figure, her sharp little nose ... And nestled deep within the pleats of her robes seems to be a vial, one filled of sand and what looks to be a beautifully maintained lock of honey-blonde hair.

"*You*," Dria whispers, her broken blue lips trembling.

"Allow me to formally introduce myself at last," the Nev replies. "My name is Cyndeya Kutchrik. It has been a while, Your Majesty—or should I say, your godliness?"

"Who the hell are you, and what do you want from us?" Desmond growls from his pile of glass, no guards daring to come close enough to remove the wooden rubble across his back.

Cyndeya Kutchrik offers a smile, one full of enough mystery to make even a goddess a bit uneasy. *Who does she think she is?* Dria wonders. *A goddess herself?*

"What could a shit fortune teller like you have to offer a pair of deities?"

"I suppose for a god and a goddess, there is not much that I can offer that you would not already have. But what I can grant you is knowledge. Gossip. A tactic small but mighty, even for a god." The oracle steps a foot closer. "We Nevs take pride in sharing our gifts with the world. I have connections all over the continent, many of which reside in a certain *ore-deposited* territory."

Dear Lazarus, is she actually referring to Javir? How the bloody hell can she know about that? Adrianna swallows the blood from her bitten tongue. "All of this ... you are offering all of this ... and for what?"

"My queen is right," Desmond adds. "You want something from us. What is it?"

Cyndeya toys with a ringlet of her curly, jet-black hair. Her citrine eyes take in the high ceilings of the Throne Room, the dais before her, the throne upholstered in the finest crimson velvet. She shrugs. "Power. Glory. In all honesty, I want all that I have lost."

"You want a dowry," Desmond finishes.

"No," the Nev corrects. She smooths the pleats of her

black and purple robes. "I want back my estate on the coast of Nesvla. I want a proper divorce from my husband and lifelong protection against him. And when I have helped you win this war against your sister ... I want you to help me get my daughter back."

An unsettling feeling of mistrust coats her tongue, but Adrianna knows that having allies in a time of war is almost necessary. She finds herself staring at the lock of honey-blonde hair dangling from Cyndeya's pale neck. *My hair*, she reflects as her stomach roils beneath her cold skin. *My hair from when I gave it to her during my reading so many years ago. She still has it, and she wears it around her neck. Did she know who I really was during that reading? Not that I was a princess, but that I was actually a goddess? Regardless, if we worked with her, we would already have the upper hand.*

Growing up as Annalise, Dimity would have the fewest connections to help her cause, but already having a kingdom's worth of resources, and building a network of spies across the kingdom ... *That's what I'd call being ahead of the game.*

"Deal."

Anzac's silver eyes meet hers with surprise. *Are you sure you want this?* He asks her through the bond. *Her services will not come without a cost. We would be indebted to her.*

Jedda's blue eyes soften. *You worry too much, Anzac. We*

are gods! If she gets out of hand, we could take her down like squishing an ant beneath our boot.

"Well then," Cyndeya smiles like a hyena beneath orange eyes. "I am looking forward to working with some of my creators. Where shall I focus my energies?"

Adrianna trails her gaze off to the window in the back of the Throne Room, to the one that Annalise jumped out of the day that her guard Mig drug her into court wearing ropes. She peers at the mahogany door, left ajar by the fleeing patrons of today's session when she again appeared, only this time leaving by someone else's grace.

Where will she go? she wonders. *She will surely have to rest and recover. If her old hideout has not yet been found, I doubt she would try hiding someplace new.* A memory surfaces of a courtesan with bloodied hazel eyes, one of a secret spilling from her lips after one last strike ...

Desmond's moan has her attention in a heartbeat, and she moves to cradle his wounded cheek before stroking the hair out of his eyes. A blistering sense of fury begins in the pit of her stomach when she remembers who did this to her love, to her life. She tosses her braid to one side, pinning her icy blue eyes on the Nev.

"I want all your eyes on the major roads leading out of Empeirus, and most importantly, on Javir. Do I make myself clear?"

"Crystal," the Nev responds in an instant. "I will notify my colleagues of Annalise's looks and her potential whereabouts on the morrow." With that, Cyndeya bows before sweeping her robes around. She makes it all of halfway before Desmond's voice calls out:

"You aren't just looking for Annalise," he manages. "There is another ... goddess." He winces. "My own sources have her trapped in Javir, somewhere near Tryflin. She goes by the name of Vega."

The Nev stops. Slowly, her citrine eyes peer over the robes of her left shoulder. "I shall inform them," is all she says, before disappearing outside of the smoking mahogany doors.

AIMELIE

Aimelie Larking clutches the fistful of orange fabric against her chest like it is the only means to revive her sanity. Head against the pale castle brick, her large blue eyes take in the chaos of the kingdom from the view of a commoner. It wasn't enough to escape from the Great Hall to the temporary safety of her royal chambers, not after what she had witnessed at court. *What most of the kingdom had witnessed at court.*

Amid the rushing courtiers and frantic castle guards, Melie fled with the rest, never daring to look back at the immortals she dared to believe were her sisters. And after blending footsteps with the mob down the castle stairs, her ivory slippers had led her here, scrounging at her heart and gasping for air against the exterior of the palace she used to call home.

"Melie—"

She screams, tripping over her skirts and toppling onto the cobblestones before Linden takes her head gently in his hands.

"*Gods*, Linden. You scared the almighty hell out of me!"

"I'm appalled a princess would say such a thing, especially in public," he quips. "Melie, we need to talk. You're in shock."

"And you aren't?" Aimelie blinks her baby blues at her Royal Mentor. "Though I suppose it must come as more of a shock to me considering that my own sisters have *supernatural powers* and seem to be *goddesses in mortal form!*"

"Don't forget the captain, too—"

Melie screams again, covering her freckled face and shaking her full head of golden curls as if she can rattle the memories right out of her mind. *They even called each other by the names of gods. Dria called Anna Dimity, and Anna ... if Dria is Jedda ...*

It is all she can do to focus on her breathing, to take stock in the one thing that is constant and certain in this world. *First suffering over the loss of my beloved sister, then elation at the news of her existence, and now this. I wasn't even over the tragedy of Sven but a few measly days until the gods shook my life upside down again!* How she can manage to get through this ruse is beyond her, and perhaps even beyond the gods. *The gods, who might be my sisters!*

"I don't know what to do with myself, Linden," Melie breathes. "I don't even know who I am anymore." The youngest princess shakes her head. "All this time, I prayed to the gods each and every day to send my Annalise back to me, both for selfish and political reasons. I groveled to Dria because I knew it was the only thing to do until that time. And then," she chokes on her tears, "and then Anna came back. There was hope for the world. Even if it was just a rumor, people were beginning to believe those who had seen her firsthand in court that day. *I* believed, Linden. *I believed.*"

Linden takes a seat beside Aimelie on the pale cobblestones, ignoring the never-ending stream of commoners rushing from the castle's vicinity. He places an arm around her orange-covered shoulders. "Then why are you stopping?"

She lifts her blue gaze to meet his own. "What do you mean?"

"Aimelie." Linden gently wipes a tear from her soft cheek. "This is insane. I mean, this is absolutely ludicrous."

The young princess chuckles.

"But," he continues, "if your sisters are actually Jedda and Dimity, and Desmond is Anzac ..." A shiver from them both. "Maybe what we were believing in before isn't so different from what we should be believing in now. Annalise has always been kind and wise, with a keen eye for justice. Isn't that Dimity? And Adrianna is as much of a witch as it gets; she has always embodied the personality of Jedda. The same can be said of Desmond—or Anzac."

"I suppose." Aimelie moves her hand from her heart to her lap.

Linden's warm caramel eyes stare into the entirety of her soul. "Do you see it? Your sisters and Desmond have always been who they truly are. Annalise might be Dimity, but she will still stand for everything that Annalise always has."

"How do you know that?" Melie questions. "What if having powers or being a goddess has changed her from who she was before?"

"Because she said it herself, Melie. She told Dria in front of hundreds of people that she would be Earth's champion no matter what."

And there is another mind game. What the hell is she talking about, being 'Earth's champion?' Why does Earth need a champion? Is there something we need protecting against? The last stragglers of the castle can be seen taking to the streets, their shoes clacking against the stone roads. Aimelie looks up again at Linden. "You are suggesting that we continue to support Annalise, even if she is Dimity in her mortal form." *And not the sister I thought she was.*

Her paramour swallows, then nods. "Whatever Jedda and Anzac are up to, it was obvious that Dimity wants to put a stop to it. Why else would she have fought so hard against them, or told Master McHenry and Lord Sprightly to run?"

She blinks back to the faces of her sister and her two accomplices, to the former High Council members that Dria wanted dead for marring her lover. She recalls the way Anna told them to run, the concern in her expression when she realized that her friends were in danger. *The fire, the beads of sweat from her determination to ward off Dria and Desmond ...* Aimelie had never seen anything like it. *No one had ever seen anything like it; one second, we were holding court and the next there were humans wielding supernatural powers!*

"You're right," Melie begins. "I believe that Anna ... *Dimity* still has our best interests in mind. Even if she can shoot fire from her palms."

Linden huffs a laugh. "Well then there is only one thing left to do; you need to find her."

Aimelie's innocent face whips toward her lover at the implication of such a statement. "You want *me* to go find her?" the princess repeats with fear in her large eyes.

"Melie, I—"

"I can't leave you, Linden, especially not when the world is going to hell and I can't even trust my own *family*."

"Then go to the people who you do trust." He runs his hands carefully through her honey-blonde locks. "Go to

Tasman and Ivo. Find them at the watchtower, as long as they are still there. With any luck, Annalise will be too, and if not then they might be able to help you find her. Melie, you need to get away from the castle. So long as the queen has you, she has leverage over Annalise, and I wouldn't put it past her to treat you as she does her other pets."

Aimelie knows what that means. *Now that she has exposed herself as a goddess, I will mean nothing to her as a sister. Dria will no longer need to pretend like she cares about me. She will use me as a pawn, throw me in the castle dungeons with no way of escape, and no means for Annalise to save me. I would be the next Sven.* The realization has her fighting back tears of a different kind as she moves her body closer to Linden's. "And where will you go?" she dares to ask the light of her life.

His forehead presses against her own. "I will stay here," he whispers.

"Lin—"

"Someone needs to be on the inside, and who better to do it than a servant? My excuse will be that I have nowhere else to go. I will fake my allegiance and continue to send word by raven—that is, as long as you take up residence at the watchtower."

At this point, the princess cannot hold back her tears. They well up in her blue doe eyes before tumbling down her cheeks, some of them running away onto the orange silk of her skirts. *My Linden,* she thinks. *The only man I have ever loved.* Now she is leaving him in the hands of the gods. *And not just any gods, but two of the darkest.* "You should come with me. We could run away together, never look back at this mess!"

"But what a disservice that would be to the world, Melie. Isn't that what we are here for? Isn't that our dream, to help change this world for the better?" He leans in to plant a kiss on her cheek before standing on his feet.

Melie's heart flutters. "No, Linden, *please!*"

"Aimelie, we have to do this. If not for us, then for the people, remember?" He takes her gentle hands and hauls her onto her cream-colored slippers, walking her in the direction of the Royal Harbor.

"Please," she sputters, the last of her hope fleeting as quickly as the sun in the sky. Raindrops begin to mingle with the tears on her freckles. The docks just ahead are empty, the guards nowhere to be seen. The only thing waiting there is a small wooden dinghy, staring at her patiently.

Her paramour stops.

With trembling fingers, Linden reaches into his shirt and removes a golden necklace, one with a small sphere pendant. He hooks it around the back of her neck, letting it sink just below the neckline of her corset. "Go to Tasman and Ivo. Find Annalise."

Her blue eyes see, but do not believe. She shakes her head again in vain.

"I almost forgot," he murmurs as he removes the satchel from his body. "You will need this, too. I swiped it from your chambers before I went to find you."

The familiar shape of the crown presses firmly against her side, her arms clutching the leather bag like it is the death of her. It hits her that this may be the last time that she will ever see this man again, this man who has been to her what words cannot define.

Without preface, he grabs her, pressing his lips against her own in a kiss so passionate that on any other occasion, on any other day, it would have made the princess collapse with ecstasy. Today, she nearly collapses with dread.

Linden pulls away, taking one last peer into his princess' eyes. "I love you, Aimelie."

She chokes, an exasperated sound. "I love you too, Linden."

When his hand slips out of her own, it takes every muscle in her body not to walk away with him. Her legs ache to run, her arms yearn to grasp what they cannot hold, but it is not her destiny. *I must go.* For floating on the Falvedrie Sea is a world worth saving, its hull bobbing stubbornly against the chaos of incoming waves.

ANNALISE

"... **S**hould have seen it! ... Have to believe me—"

"Shh! I don't care if she could move moun-tains with her hands. Now Adrianna knows you three are teaming up together."

Annalise Larking can make out their muffled whispers above the ringing in her ears. *Where am I? How did I get here?* But after fully opening her eyes, the lost princess realizes that she has been relocated to the cozy quarters of her tower bedroom.

Their voices carry on a level or two below.

"*I'm telling you, I've never seen anything like it!*"

"*I don't believe in hearsay. Focus on keeping her safe.*"

The princess painfully rises to a seated position upon her makeshift bed, only to gasp.

"Please," Oliver McHenry puts his hands up after

closing a book. "I mean no harm. I was only up here to monitor your recovery."

Annalise squints. *Why would they trust you to do it?* A strange feeling of realization falls over her. *Perhaps now they trust me even less.*

The green-eyed man reaches over to her desk. "I brought you some water. You must be dehydrated. You've been asleep for over a day."

The princess doesn't move. Her arms are too limp to raise them higher than her heart, which is weary in and of itself at the thought of scaring off the only people that she loves. "They are afraid," she asks, though it comes out as more of a statement.

Oliver lowers his head. "They are startled. Wouldn't you be?"

At this, the princess has to smile. She imagines how she would feel if she were a human who suddenly witnessed other humans shooting ice from their palms. "I suppose so. But you should be down there with them. You saw what happened yesterday, why aren't you just as intimidated?"

He sets the glass down on the floor, seating himself a few feet from her bed. "Because contrary to popular belief, I don't believe you're a monster."

Anna huffs a laugh. "I feel like one. Even if I *was* fighting for justice, even if I *was* trying to protect Earth's people, I was still putting them at risk by escalating the situation. I should have—"

"You couldn't have done anything differently. If you did less than what you had, Adrianna and Desmond would have destroyed you and everyone else." The former Master of the High Council pauses. "I'm not exactly sure of the politics between gods and goddesses, but in the grand scheme of things, it sounds like more of the same."

Her brown eyes grow wide. "More of the same. Gods and goddesses in mortal form, battling in Larking Castle is just 'more of the same.'"

A glimmer of humor in Oliver's pine-green eyes makes Anna just the slightest bit more comfortable, despite the circumstances. "Not exactly. But it sounds to me like each of you still wants the throne and will do anything you can to protect it."

The Goddess of Wisdom and Justice lowers her gaze in thought. *He's right. Without the throne, we lose the power we need to ensure the well-being of Earth's people—or in Jedda's case, the malnourishment of them. And with myself on the throne, I could help restore the peace and justice Jedda needs to change her mind. Because if she doesn't switch her vote, Earth will never be accepted into the Alliance, and this planet will never make it.* Dimity doubts that her father would waste more time convincing himself that Earth is worth keeping. *Our precious creation will be gone—and so will everyone on it.*

"Maybe you're right. We've been pitted against each

other since childhood for different reasons, but our missions do remain the same."

A nod.

The two of them share a moment of quiet, Anna reflecting on yesterday's happenings. She thinks back to the screams of the courtiers, to the utter shock on Aimelie's face when she witnessed both of her royal sisters wielding godly powers, to the way the smooth white marble felt on her cheek before some brave soul collected her from it. She shifts her sore muscles to get a better look at her sister's former master.

"It was you, wasn't it? You were the one who carried me out of the Throne Room."

His emerald eyes are sincere. "It's not in my nature to leave injured friends unattended."

The comment catches Annalise by surprise. *Friends. I suppose we are … friends.* She doesn't know why the concept feels so foreign to her. Perhaps it is the fact that for years, her only true friend had been Narelle during her life in the slums. *Before that, I had Modgen, but …* Anna had never felt comfortable opening up to other people, especially given her background. *Being shy is one thing, but hiding eternally from the wrath of your queen sister? That is quite another.*

"Thank you," she tells him genuinely.

"I do what I can to make this world a better place, too." The former master retrieves her glass from the stone floor. "But before we persist in making it better, you need to regain your strength, starting with drinking some water."

The goddess stifles a cry as she lifts her hand to receive the water glass. "I need to train, to make it better."

"Healing comes first, Your Highness. Training comes after you are whole again."

The princess takes a sip. Then another. She finishes the glass, handing it back to Oliver with a wince. "Thank you. And please, spare me the formalities. I dare say you've earned it."

A flash of a reserved smile, one which the princess finds to be just a bit too captivating.

"Well." She pushes up her sleeves with unease. "I suppose we need to meet with the others."

"Annalise, I don't think—"

But the goddess is as stubborn as she is injured. She rises with a grunt from her blankets, nearly falling to the ground before catching Oliver's arm. The princess bites her lip, the pain spreading everywhere in her body where the warmth of her magic was. *Mortal bodies must not be meant for wielding magic, especially not the magic of the gods.*

"Are you sure you can walk?"

A tear slips down one of her porcelain cheeks. "Of course, I can. But," she flushes with embarrassment, "I might need your help."

The walk down the tower stairs is perhaps the most

awkward thing Annalise has ever managed, mostly because she does not like asking for help, but also because her despised sister's former master is the one helping her. *Of course, I certainly couldn't do it without him.* Every footstep is agonizing; her arms, legs, and abdomen all throbbing with varying levels of pain. *Especially where the magic was most prominent, like in my fingers.*

After two flights, they finally reach the bottom floor where Modgen, Ivo, and Tasman have taken seats at the kitchen table. The three are dead quiet as Oliver helps Anna seat herself in a wooden chair. *Perhaps I should have just stayed in my room.* She turns to face the others.

"Modgen. Tasman. Captain Ivo."

"You going to name McHenry, too while you're at it?" Ivo pins his gray-blue eyes square on Anna's brown ones. "Your Highness. Sprightly here tells me wild fairytales of the happenings at the castle yesterday afternoon. I'm not even going to ask you about them; all I want to know is what you plan on doing next."

In the midst of thinking up an answer, the goddess glances at Master Tasman, who strokes his white beard in silence while tapping his cane on the ground.

"Can you show us?"

Ivo practically bursts. "*What?*"

But Tasman simply watches, waiting for a magic trick that may never come. "Can you show us, if it is true?"

She doesn't know why, but Anna turns to Oliver, who

gives her a nod. With a little concentration, she summons a flicker of fire through her index finger, using it to light the tallow candle before them.

Their stares are intrigued, all except for Ivo's.

"Looks like a simple parlor trick, to me."

She closes her brown eyes, changing her focus to the thin layer of moisture surrounding the candle, then freezes it. The flame goes out as the wax splits from the cold, and the former captain's face turns three shades paler.

"Well," Tasman begins. "That's that. Now that we can be sure at least of your powers, perhaps you can tell us more about your ... divine matters?"

Modgen fidgets in his chair.

"Where to begin ..." Annalise clears her throat, ignoring the fresh pain in her extremities. She explains the entire issue of Earth not passing to join the Alliance, that if they fail, all hope will be lost. She goes on in detail about the bargain struck between the gods to let Dimity and Jedda incarnate with their protectors, that it could change their minds to help them reach an agreement, that Adrianna is Jedda and that Desmond is Anzac incarnate. And she finishes by adding that while Jedda and Anzac are already together, she and Elouthera are still far apart.

"I need to find her. Without Elouthera, I am powerless against them. I could hardly stand my ground in the Throne Room."

Her master strokes his long beard in thought. "Have you any idea where Elouthera has incarnated?"

Annalise looks inward for a moment. *Elouthera, where are you?* She sighs, shaking her head as she follows the thread that links them straight into a black wall. *I suppose if it hasn't worked before, then it won't work now.*

Suddenly—a flash of gray brick, an image of a clock. *I recognize that building. It's one of the most famous monuments in the kingdom!* "She's in Javir. Somewhere near the coast. I saw the Oronian Clocktower and heard the water nearby. I have to go look for her!"

"You will do *no* such thing, Princess," Ivo cuts her off. "A goddess you may be, but you are in no condition to do anything of the sort."

"Then how will I ever find her? How can I be united with her?"

The outlaws ponder, thinking through everything that has just been said.

Modgen leans forward on the table. "Perhaps ... perhaps I could go in your stead."

All eyes fall to the former Royal Treasurer.

"If you can't go, then I can. What do I have to lose? Mom is gone, and the only one I have left is you, Ann. Oliver and I were planning on doing some traveling before we met you, anyway. A few new sights could do me some good, even if it is ...*Javir*," the redhead shutters.

"Modgen, I can't possibly—"

"No, no," he begins. "Listen, Anna. I want to do whatever I can to help you and your cause. Especially if it means, somehow in a way that is *very* confusing to a common bloke like me, to save the world. Annalise, *Dimity*, whatever your name is, you are my best friend and I would be beside myself if I sat on the sidelines and did nothing to help you. So, if that means finding *Elouthera*, then that is just what I will do."

Her brown eyes brim with tears of gratitude. "Modgen, you are too kind." But the mention of motherhood leaves Anna with a hole where her heart should be. "Narelle," she begins, tears threatening her composure. "I need to get her back from Dria's hands."

Ivo turns to face his princess. "Your Highness, as much as we want to help Narelle, right now might not be the best time. Right now, Dria's forces hold most of the power. She has far more alliances and far more resources. If you mean to take Narelle back, you will need to have eyes on the inside of the castle." The captain turns to Tasman. "Leave that to us. But trust me, Princess, she can't do much harm to her. She will need her alive and well to use her for leverage against you."

Anna sighs mournfully. *Alive and well. Gods, I hope he is right.* Her stomach roils at the thought of losing the closest thing she has had to a mother since childhood. *Her kindness; so thoughtful and always so loving.*

Modgen gives her a semi-cheerful smile. "And what will you do?"

The princess opens her mouth to speak, but Tasman beats her to it. "Annalise. Please trust me when I say that I do not think this place is safe for you anymore. You need to go. Let Modgen find ... *Elouthera,* wherever, *whomever,* she may be. But you should not stay here in Empeirus, not when your sister and her captain know that you are still in the area and that you are teaming up with her two outlawed council members. You need to leave the territory and prepare."

Annalise is shocked. "You want me to just *flee* and hide under a rock? Like I've been doing for half my life?"

"I am advising you to take refuge somewhere safe, somewhere your godly friends won't go searching for you. While you are there, you will recover."

"And train," Oliver adds. "She mentioned that she needs to train herself to better use her powers."

Tasman nods. "In the meantime, Ivo and I will tend to matters of the homeland and cultivate alliances." He turns his wrinkled blue eyes toward the captain. "I have an idea of where to start."

Annalise furrows her brows. "You and Ivo would stay here, while Modgen would search for Elouthera in Javir." She turns to Oliver in confusion.

"I was hoping that the former Master McHenry would be willing to help you on your journey. He has proven himself thus far to be a trustworthy ally during all of this, just as Modgen has."

Good. Great. A journey with a man I hardly know! She takes a deep breath. *Why does my life have a habit of completely changing at the drop of a hat?* "Very well. Since you suggested it, perhaps you would have an idea of a discreet, safe place where I may lie low and take stock, *Tas?*"

Her old master looks to his colleagues. Ivo leans back to cross his arms, but Modgen and Oliver exchange glances.

"We had previously settled on fleeing to Nesvla," Modgen chimes. "But seeing as you want somewhere discreet ..."

Anna twiddles her thumbs. Tasman's cane continues to tap the floor.

The sound of Oliver's sigh is quiet but audible. "I ... might have a place."

Ivo shoots him a look. "You either have a safe place or you don't, McHenry. There is no room for error in this instance."

He nods. "The town is safe. It would be the last place they would look."

"We can't keep her in Empeirus, Mr. McHenry—"

"It's not in Empeirus. It's a town along the shoreline of the Savek Coast."

Anna looks to her colleague and finds him toying with a silver ring beneath the table.

Tasman leans back, nodding. "The Savek Coast, yes. They would definitely not suspect one to flee there. Most people from that corner of the map are quiet folk who lead quiet lives." He raises a finger. "There is, of course, the issue of traveling by ship. We would have to conceal her identity fully. It would be risky."

"I know a great deal of sailors, Master. It wouldn't be hard for them to find me a ship with limited passengers, and I am sure that Modgen could come up with a decent backstory."

The princess intervenes. "And where will we stay in the Savek Coast? Do you have an idea for lodgings?"

Oliver swallows. "I ... we can stay at my family's old house by the sea. It's outside of a small town, about a mile's walk from the local market. There are secluded areas along the beach you can use for training purposes."

Annalise raises her chin to speak, then bites her lip. *Another adventure, another world ...* Her stomach drops at the sheer uncertainty of it all, at the idea that if their plan fails in any regard, Dimity's mission will be all but burned. *I need to train hard. I need to master my powers to protect this planet and to defeat Jedda and Anzac if they cannot be swayed to support Earth. I need to do this—for Aimelie, for Modgen, for Narelle, for the* world.

With a straightening of her shoulders, the princess whispers to the bond with hope:

Elouthera, I am coming for you.

"Then it's settled. Unless there are any objections, of course?" Tasman looks at the captain, Modgen, Oliver, and finally, to Annalise.

The princess shakes her head.

"Well then, Lazarus guide us. We will act on the morrow."

EPILOGUE

The cold draft from the Great Hall window stirs beneath her orange taffeta skirts.

"Your Grace, still no word from the Fetlanders. Whether you want us to continue pushing for the new trade agreement is of course, up to you, but—"

"I'm not interested in the old way, Lord Manik. Without this change, they are simply of no use to us, and we need every penny we can muster. After all, what is Nesvla without its coin?"

The bearded man bows. "Yes, Your Grace. I shall report this to the ambassador at once."

The queen nods, dipping her bronze crown toward the velvet-adorned stairs of her dais. Outside, she can hear the leaves of her courtyard rustling in the golden sun, the breeze playing with a strand of her black hair.

She breathes in, then out, savoring the sound of nothing else as she sits in her empty courtroom. *No bickering courtiers, no squabbling lords. Just the sweet sound of the autumn Nesvlan air.*

It is refreshing, really, especially after countless days spent going over trade agreements, council positions, and everything in between. *I'm shocked I've caught myself a break, be it however small.* Still, while such time to relax is time well valued, it is a queen's duty to rule her domain. *And to rule it well.*

The Queen of Nesvla rises, brushing out tiny pleats in the fabric of her burnt-orange corset. The sound of footsteps meshes with her own in the echoing of the cavernous, golden Great Hall.

"Queen Minerva," the Nesvlan courier bows. "A letter from the east. I feel as though it may catch your interest. It comes from the Empeirian throne."

The queen startles. *Empeirus? We haven't had the honor of correspondence with the Empeirian throne since ...*

She recovers herself. "Thank you, Henred. I shall read it at once."

Henred retreats from the Great Hall, leaving the queen with no one but the tenfold golden knights watching her as she unfolds the heavy parchment. Her heart flutters when she breaks the red wax seal. *I remember when it was burgundy, once. But that was a long time ago.* Her cool blue eyes peruse the first few lines:

"Queen Minerva of Nesvla ... writing on behalf of ... comes to my greatest and most sincere pleasure to announce ..."

"Mother, I've been looking all over for you."

She raises a black brow. "You know I hold court at this time at least three times a week. What is it, Darren?"

Her son stands before her like a reflection in the mirror. While the Crown Prince of Nesvla had inherited his father's face and chin, Darren Eldric's black hair and blue eyes were of his mother's doing.

He toys lazily with a button on his lapel. "Briar has caught a cold. I suppose we can't expect her to attend the candle lighting ceremony tomorrow. She will have to find another way to honor the fallen."

Minerva's lips part in shock. *"Impossible,"* she whispers.

"I know. I thought the same thing, too."

The queen lays a trembling hand atop her stomach. "She's *dead.*" She shakes her head. "Supposed to be ... *dead.*"

The Nesvlan Prince presses his own black brows together in deep concern. "Mother? Mother, *please*; talk to me."

"This letter is for you." The Queen of Nesvla swallows. "Darren ... Annalise Larking is alive."

Acknowledgments

I never thought that what started as a poolside hobby would one day evolve into a full-blown novel! It took me a total of four years to write *Daughter of Lazarus* from start to finish while I juggled my studies, multiple jobs, and almost every other life event under the sun. Words cannot fully express how grateful I am for those who were involved in the making of this book, but I can start by saying thank you.

To all my fabulous beta readers, I offer my sincerest thank you for taking the time to read my first novel. I am so appreciative of your valuable feedback and much needed support! I honestly couldn't have done this without you.

To my outstanding editor, Lucia Ferrara, thank you for your incredible eye for detail and heartening commentary. It was such a pleasure working with you! Please know that you have helped me in achieving my wildest dreams.

To my fantastic cover artist and designer, Agata Broncel, thank you for harnessing the power to take my most abstract concepts and transform them into something beautiful that can be shared with the world!

To my map illustrator, David Steindl, thank you for your dedicated and skilled hand in creating such a magnificent representation of my mythical world.

To my beloved family, whose encouragement and kindness I can never repay. Thank you to my mother and father, who taught me that perseverance is always the way, and that no dream is unattainable. I'd also like to thank all my precious dogs for their reliable charity and unmatched ability to make me laugh.

I want to write a special thank you to Eric, the love of my life and my best friend. You have been there for me during high and low, and your endless compassion has helped me to conquer so many obstacles that otherwise seemed too daunting. Thank you for being there for me during this incredible journey and every other one.

Last but certainly not least, I'd like to thank you, reader! I can write as many pages as I want, but without you, my words are meaningless. Thank you for helping me be of service to this world.

PROLOGUE

The flames dance in a million different directions, the reflection of their persimmon embers bouncing off her baby-blue eyes. Her fingers graze the smooth pendant of Linden's necklace for the hundredth time today, the golden metal warm from the heat of the fire and her trembling touch. Sitting on a heap of rags, Princess Aimelie Larking watches the former Royal Jeweler put away the last of his remaining belongings, his graying brow furrowed seriously as he turns to face her yet again.

"Your Highness," Urayus Helva begins. "I know it is not my place to say, but delaying the inevitable will not eliminate it."

The youngest princess is as silent as she had been

yesterday when her slippered feet carried her away from the harbor to the temporary safety of her friend's forge. Her golden curls are tangled from running, and her head aches from the misery of losing both of her sisters and the love of her life. *Should I have known? Should I have been able to predict something this improbable after knowing Annalise and Adrianna for most of their lives? And Linden ...*

Aimelie dips her forehead down to the dirt floor of the blacksmith's forge. Her heart has not yet been able to comprehend the events of yesterday afternoon. It seems like a lifetime ago that Melie's royal mentor had deemed it necessary for her to find Annalise while he stayed behind at Larking Castle. *I can only imagine the hell my love will face with Dria now.* For as much torture as Linden experienced working as a servant for Queen Adrianna before, there will surely be more of it working for the Dark Goddess, Jedda. What that will mean for Linden's safety and well-being ... Aimelie tries not to let herself think about that much.

Urayus closes the last of his satchels, his horse's neigh audible from outside the wooden door. Sighing, the burly blacksmith seats himself on the chair beside Aimelie's place on the floor.

"I don't know what to think of it either," he admits. "But there are many times in life when we don't know what to think, just yet."

The crackle of the fire is his only response. Aimelie's doe eyes drift from the flames to meet his gaze.

The blacksmith leans forward to rest his elbows on his knees. "The day the Crimson Queen stripped me of my title as Royal Jeweler, I exploded." Urayus swallows. "I knew I was skilled. I knew I was admired. My work was of the finest in the kingdom. I knew why she did it, but I couldn't fathom *how* she could.

"One night, I drank myself into oblivion and woke up face down in a pile of what I wanted to believe was mud." He shakes his head, fighting a faint smile. "It was enough to make me realize that I had let her win. That same day, I went into town and found myself a new home, one where I could start anew. Not a year later, I fashioned myself this business and a new life of my own." Urayus gestures to the forge around them.

"And now you're leaving," Aimelie points out.

Her friend chuckles. "This is exactly my point, Princess. What the gods grant us is only part of what determines our fate. The rest is what we make of it. We must adapt." Urayus stands with a groan. "It is my time to leave this city, Your Highness. Whatever these gods have in store, I want to be with my family in Godrus to face it."

The princess works a thread loose from the orange fabric of her skirts. "I don't know if I have it in me to face those gods again," she whispers. Her mind churns at the reflection of a marble Throne Room, of Adrianna and Annalise trading fire and ice like it is something humans are supposed to do.

The light of the glowing fire shifts against Urayus's face. "You do," he states simply, tossing a bag over his muscled shoulder. "You have your mother's heart."

She doesn't know how, but hearing the declaration warms Melie's broken heart, if even just a little. Maybe it is the fraction of her soul that still clings to the hope of a brighter future, but something urges her to stand from her throne of rags. "I suppose this is goodbye, then." Aimelie smooths out the pleats of her dress.

"I suppose so," Urayus replies. His tired eyes fall on the leather satchel pressing against Melie's waist, the one that holds the crown he forged for the true heir of Empeirus, Princess Annalise Larking. He reaches into his bag to pull out a gray cloak, handing it to Aimelie with a sort of gentleness few are likely to see from him. "It's starting to get cold out this time of year."

Aimelie nods, trying not to let her emotions get the best of her. *I might never see him again*, she realizes. *Just like I might never see Linden again, either.* "Thank you for all your help. And thank you for your advice. I shall never forget it."

Urayus offers a weathered grin. "Take care of yourself, Princess. If you need me, I'll be in Godrus." He opens the wooden door of his forge for the last time. "The gods be with you—and on your side."

Aimelie watches the door close, listening to the sounds of a horse ready to pull its cart. Before her, only the empty forge stands witness to her rumination, the weight of the blacksmith's words sinking in at last. "We must adapt," Aimelie repeats to herself out loud, her eyes darting between her new gray cloak and the orange silk of her gown.

She sets down the cloak and the satchel before beginning to undo the laces of her bodice, then her skirt, until all that remains is her simple white underdress. *Better for blending in,* the princess notes. The satchel finds its way to her hip once again, and Melie fastens the enormous cloak over her shoulders. Gathering up her previous dress, she takes a shallow breath, willing her arms to thrust them into the open hearth.

Aimelie watches as the orange fabric is devoured by the matching flames until they are nothing but ash, her hand clutching the golden necklace beneath her cloak. When the fire has been satiated, Aimelie lets herself out of Urayus Helva's former home and back into the world that had similarly scorched her fragile heart.

The town is bustling with horses and people, most of whom seem to be headed away from the capital. *Fleeing,* Aimelie corrects. *And I'm going to be one of them.* The only difference between the princess and the townsfolk is that, instead of running away from gods and goddesses, Melie is running in pursuit of one.

So many people, she thinks. *How many will stay to endure what Adrianna and Desmond have to offer? And, while the individual territories of the kingdom maintain some of their own rights, the Empeirian throne still rules above them all. Wherever they go, they will still be subject to Adrianna's—or Jedda's—schemes, as long as they are still within the king-dom.* Aimelie swallows. *But even outside of it, in Calleeit ...* She reflects on the supernatural powers both of her sisters put to use at the castle yesterday. *A god's reach may extend beyond any border.*

All around the castle, the cobblestone streets are barren and deserted, with only a few guards standing watch in their traditional spots. Aimelie averts her eyes to keep from being identified, pulling Urayus's cloak down over her forehead as she approaches the docks once again. There isn't a soul to be seen where Linden had said his goodbyes yesterday afternoon, and, by the luck of some gods, the wooden dinghy still waits for her exactly where it had before.

Carefully lowering herself into the boat, Melie unties its ropes and begins to paddle. The Falvedrie Sea is calm today, its usual swirling gray waters lapping at the hull of her vessel with a languid sort of energy. Had Aimelie been accustomed to rowing boats regularly, such a voyage may have been easier for her, but the adrenaline in her veins keeps her arms pumping.

The marshes are to her right now, and from looking at the map a hundred times since she sent Captain Ivo and Master Tasman there years ago, she knows exactly where to turn. After ramming the hull of the dinghy into the muddy banks, Aimelie makes landfall in her ivory slippers, watching them turn brown from the earth. She waits for a moment to ensure she has not been followed and continues to push her way through the dense vegetation and mud.

Just ahead, beyond the tree line, the watchtower climbs into the sky, its base surrounded by a light fog. Aimelie's heartbeat quickens, her body suddenly aware of the weight of the satchel on her shoulder. *She could be in there*, the youngest princess hopes and frets at the same time. She turns her freckled face to the skies, watching a black crow fly overhead before moving another footstep closer to the tower.

The feeling of a blade pressed against her neck would have her spewing a vicious scream if it wasn't muffled by someone's rough hand.

"Who are you, and what the hell are you doing here?" the familiar voice asks from behind her ear.

Aimelie's chest rises and falls faster than ever before. For a moment, she believes she might pass out, until an elderly man hobbles his way into her field of view.

"For the gods' sakes, Ivo, let her go! It's the princess," Master Tasman whispers to the former Captain of the Royal Guard.

Ivo immediately drops his hand and blade, apologizing profusely in hushed tones.

Aimelie nearly collapses, taking some time to collect herself. "You are forgiven, Ivo," the princess finally musters. *Why aren't they taking refuge inside of the watchtower?*

"You shouldn't be here, Your Highness," Tasman warns her. "You should be leaving Empeirus, too. We were just on our way out."

"Your way out?" Aimelie glances around in search of her sister, but no one else is in sight.

Ivo sheathes his dagger. "Unless you have someplace to be, I suggest you come with us."

"I shall, but ..." she swallows. "I've come for Annalise."

The former master taps his cane. "Then, I'm afraid you're too late. They left at sunrise this morning."

The youngest princess furrows a brow. "*They?*"

Tasman adjusts the strap of the small bag on his shoulder. "She and the former Master of the High Council, Oliver McHenry," he clarifies, taking another step. "The rest of the gods willing, they should be on their way to the Savek Coast by now."

Master McHenry? The Savek Coast? Why would she have fled Empeirus with a man who was once part of Adrianna's inner circle? Aimelie hikes up her skirts to catch up with her two colleagues. "So, we're meeting them there, then?"

"Gods, no." Ivo spits.

Aimelie's head spins. "Then where are we going?"

Tasman pauses his hobbling to remove a letter from his robes, his wrinkled eyes gleaming with delight as he hands her the parchment. "To meet an old friend."

DON'T MISS THE LATEST NEWS ON **ARDEN'S EPIC SERIES** ...

BOOK THREE COMING SOON!

Sign up for her newsletter at

WWW.JUNIPERARDEN.COM/CONTACT

Follow Juniper on social media!

@JUNIPERARDEN

ABOUT THE AUTHOR

Seasoned traveler, dog-lover, and drinker of fine teas, Juniper Arden spends each day dreaming up her next ambitious idea like she has since she was a child. When she isn't putting pen to paper, you can find her braving mountains and meadows, cuddling with her fur babies, or whipping up a batch of her famous chocolate cupcakes. *Daughter of Lazarus* is her debut novel and will be the first of a series.

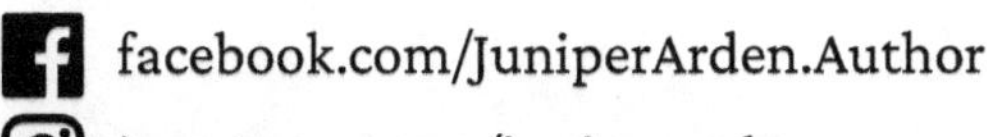

www.ingramcontent.com/pod-product-compliance
Lightning Source LLC
Chambersburg PA
CBHW022015300726
48970CB00003B/904